RENNO—One of America's great heroes, he has served as warrior, as spy, as pathfinder, for the father of the nation, George Washington. Now he is called upon to sacrifice once more, for the feisty second American president, Thomas Jefferson . . . and to face a terrifying opponent with supernatural powers who knows how to rend the soul as well as destroy the heart.

RENNA—Inheritor of her father's indomitable will and her mother's beauty, she is approaching womanhood too quickly to be wary of life's pitfalls: a violent tragedy, an island of lush charm and lewd acts, and a chance to let the world hear the war cry of a Seneca maiden fighting for all she loves.

LITTLE HAWK—Son of Renno, a young man torn between his mother's world and his father's, he is determined to prove his worth. But his desires lead him into a bed of sin where his will can be crushed and his body can become the bait in a trap set by a witch and a killer.

OTHON HUGUES—Twisted villain of foul passions and satanic lusts, he is well trained in the oily black arts and in the smooth ways of the diplomat. Power is his goal, murder his pleasure, Renna the woman he wants to enjoy with kisses and caresses . . . before he destroys her.

MELISANDE—Her alluring dark eyes will entrance any young man who listens to her promises and feels the heat of her desire—and blind him to the ugly crone beneath the voluptuous woman, a creature of the netherworld who makes her partnership with evil and bone-chilling terror.

The White Indian Series
Ask your bookseller for the books you have missed

The White Indian Series
Book XXI

SACHEM'S DAUGHTER

Donald Clayton Porter

Created by the producers of
The Holts: An American Dynasty,
The First Americans, and **The Australians.**

Book Creations Inc., Canaan, NY • *Lyle Kenyon Engel, Founder*

BANTAM BOOKS
NEW YORK • TORONTO • LONDON • SYDNEY • AUCKLAND

SACHEM'S DAUGHTER

*A Bantam Domain Book / published by arrangement with
Book Creations, Inc.*

Bantam edition / June 1991

*Produced by Book Creations, Inc.
Lyle Kenyon Engel, Founder*

ISBN 0-553-29028-2

Published simultaneously in the United States and Canada

*Bantam Books are published by Bantam Books, a division of Ban-
tam Doubleday Dell Publishing Group, Inc. Its trademark, consisting of the words "Bantam Books" and the portrayal of a rooster, is
Registered in U.S. Patent and Trademark Office and in other
countries. Marca Registrada. Bantam Books, 666 Fifth Avenue,
New York, New York 10103.*

PRINTED IN THE UNITED STATES OF AMERICA

OPM   0 9 8 7 6 5 4 3 2 1

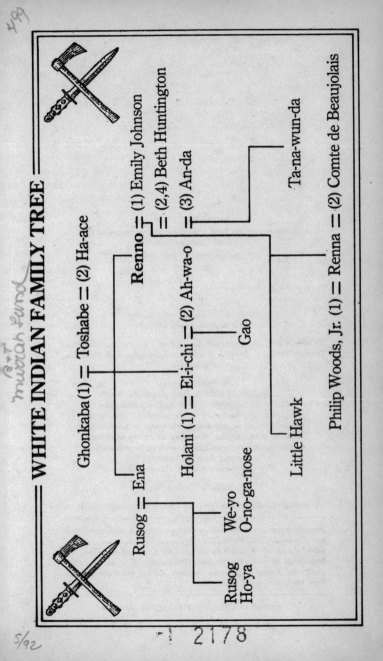

WHITE INDIAN FAMILY TREE

Ghonkaba (1) = Toshabe = (2) Ha-ace

Rusog = Ena

Rusog
Ho-ya

We-yo
O-no-ga-nose

Holani (1) = El-i-chi = (2) Ah-wa-o

Gao

Renno = (1) Emily Johnson
= (2,4) Beth Huntington
= (3) An-da

Little Hawk

Ta-na-wun-da

Philip Woods, Jr. (1) = Renna = (2) Comte de Beaujolais

SACHEM'S
DAUGHTER

Prologue

Othon Hugues, envoy of the ruling body of Revolutionary France, rode through a dense forest of firs, pines, and birches toward a pretty little town lying under the slopes of Segovia's Pico de Peñalara. There, in the comely resort of San Ildefonso, seven miles southeast of the city of Segovia, France had once before dictated terms to Charles IV of Spain.

Although it was midday and although Hugues was surrounded by an honor guard consisting of twelve brightly uniformed French dragoons, he was sensitive to the gloom cast by the overlapping branches of the trees. The impenetrable shadows reminded him of the darknesses of the woodlands near his home and sent him moodily seeking into his past, to a time when, to escape the gibes, laughter, and cruelty of his half brothers, he sought sanctuary in the forest.

Hugues wore the plain, black garb of the Revolution. His hat, not at all stylish, was pulled low over his brow to protect his unusually pale eyes from the occasional dazzling rays of the October sun, which penetrated the canopy of the trees. They were the color of light reflecting off ice, his eyes, and men who were seeing him for the first time were often mistakenly led to believe that the irises' lack of pigment connoted weakness. His face was deeply marked by the same pox that had killed his mother when he was eight years old. His shoulders were broad and his torso long, making him half a head taller in the saddle than any of the soldiers who rode on the jangling, leather-creaking escort.

San Ildefonso, where Spanish kings had summered since before the reign of Philip V, boasted gardens designed by the famous Frenchman E. Boutelou, with twenty-six fountains by R. Fremin and J. Thierri. Philip V and his wife, Isabella Farnese, were buried in the palace chapel.

The loveliness of the town was lost on Othon Hugues, a man who, as chief executioner of Paris, had risen to sanguine prominence during the early stage of the Revolution and, it was whispered, now had the ear of Napoleon himself. Only a certain kind of beauty moved him; to him true loveliness was the spurt of blood from the severed necks of men and women like those who had lorded over him in his early life. The elegant neck of Marie Antoinette herself had provided him with one of the more satisfying moments of his life. He had stood for long, long minutes, his hand on the trip cord of the guillotine, savoring the thrill before letting the heavy blade fall.

It was true that Hugues had the ear of the first consul, the man who had restored France to glory. Before his stint as executioner, he had earned a reputation as a soldier in many battles early in the Revolution, then as a representative of the Directory with the general during the Egyptian campaign. Hugues had made himself useful while proving that his loyalties lay with Napoleon Bonaparte, not with the political fools back in Paris. He would balk at nothing in carrying out his general's requests, so no one had been surprised when the first consul chose Hugues to journey to the little Spanish resort. He would represent the consulate in the continuation of Napoleon's plan to seize new colonies abroad to provide food for the French armies during the struggle for dominance in Europe.

* * *

Hugues's dark, pitted face was expressionless as his host, the king of Spain, accompanied by his top advisers, took him on a tour of the royal apartments. There the envoy saw Flemish tapestries from the era when Spain had been a power in Europe, cartoons by Goya, and a grotesque golden statuette from Peru.

"Shamefully," King Charles said, "many such works of art were melted down and have long since been dispersed as coin around the world. For a time, my friend, the gold of Spain enriched all of Europe."

Hugues made no comment. His predetermined opinion of the king of Spain had not been altered by the man's polite hospitality or by his garrulous comments on the riches displayed in the royal apartments. It was well-known that the power in Spain was in the soft hands of Maria Luisa of Palma, the queen, and her lover Manuel de Godoy, a government minister who had been appointed by Charles himself. And certainly it was Charles who had allowed Spain to become a vassal of the French, forced into France's wars as nothing more than a satellite, a poor relation.

Hugues remained silent until the tour of the apartments had ended. He declined a glass of wine, waited for the king to seat himself, and, standing, delivered the message from Napoleon. Othon Hugues was not a diplomat. He was a soldier. The only softness in him was hidden deeply, in the form of his attachment to a woman years his senior—an odd, unearthly creature whom he had first met when he was an unhappy ten-year-old hiding in the dark shadows of the dense Pyrenean forest. Melisande . . . no matter how often circumstances forced him to leave her, he never ceased to be surprised by the intensity of his longing for her.

Even as he stood delivering Napoleon's message in a low, roughened voice, his thoughts were never far from Melisande's little house in the forest near the chateau where he had been born. Hugues was the bastard son of a milkmaid and the master of the estate, a man who boasted endlessly of his noble blood. Finally Othon, as an adult, returned to the place where he had been exposed daily to the arrogant cruelty of his rich, spoiled half brothers. On that day his father made no boasts. Instead, the man who had never acknowledged Othon as his son screamed in agony. The master's noble blood flowed down the sharp blade of Othon's sword.

And the half brothers? They had no laughter, no harsh words, no orders for him—only frightened pleas for mercy and screams of fading mortality as Othon killed them slowly, one by one, as Othon's revolutionary allies looked on.

Now, as he stood uncomfortably in the presence of the Spanish aristocrat, moments from the past flowed back to him. He lost patience with diplomatic talk.

"The first consul thinks that the time has come to rectify the mistakes of 1763," Othon said in his deep, gravelly voice.

"I must confess," said Charles, "that I sometimes have difficulty remembering dates."

"Sire," said an adviser, speaking in Spanish, "I think the ambassador is referring to the time when France turned over to Spain her holdings in the New World, specifically the areas west of the Mississippi River."

"Ah," Charles said, his face clouding.

"The first consul is prepared, of course, to return value for value," Hugues said. "Even though he doubts Spain's ability to maintain herself in her American possessions for any length of time."

"See here, sir—" said an adviser, rising to the insult.

Charles waved the adviser into silence. "Has the first consul noted my request that my son-in-law be given the throne of Tuscany?" Charles asked.

"He has," Othon replied.

Charles turned to his advisers. "There is no gold in Louisiana. For Tuscany we exchange deserts and wilderness inhabited by wild Indians. You will draw up the agreement immediately."

Never had a decision that would affect the lives of so many been concluded more quickly. Othon Hugues departed San Ildefonso on the day of his arrival. To the chagrin of his escort, he rode hard and long, making camp only after darkness had fallen. Now that he had concluded his business for Napoleon, his only desire was to be at home, with *her*.

He dismissed his honor guard after crossing through the Basque provinces in northern Spain. The young officer in charge had served with Othon in Egypt and could be trusted not to open the sealed pouch that contained the Agreement of San Ildefonso. As Napoleon had instructed, the negotiations with Charles of Spain would be kept secret—at least while the agreement was in the care of Othon Hugues or his men. What would happen once the agreement reached Paris was not Othon's responsibility. Knowing Paris and the consulate as he did, Othon believed there was little likelihood of any secret being kept for long.

Soon he was galloping through country that he knew well. As he rode he could see Melisande's face, could hear the sound of her voice. Was the awareness of her that hovered over and around him a manifestation of her odd powers? Had she sensed his nearness? He had long since ceased trying to answer such questions.

When he had first met her, she was twenty years old. He had given in to her blandishments and placed his ten-year-old cheek against her prim bosom. He reveled in the tenderness of her touch, the musky-warm smell of her, the delightful taste of her. She was living in a hut that, in winter, admitted the frigid winds from the mountains. Over the years he had improved her dwelling place: rooms had been added, a fire sizzled in the stone fireplace, and the house hidden away in the shadows of the forest became snug and warm.

Before his horse had come to a full stop in the tiny clearing by her door, Othon leaped from his saddle and hurried inside. She was expecting him. She had dressed in a lacy, frilly black gown. Through the cut lace he could see the pale glow of her skin. The flickering fire cast moving shadows on her cheek. She had matured over the years into a creature of lush and splendid softness. The full, round breasts of her youth were still enticing mounds. He never tired of her beauty.

"I saw," she told him, as he stood just inside the door. "You have done well."

"Yes," he said.

She smiled as she loosened her hair. It cascaded in an ebony mass over her shoulders. He could anticipate its clean fragrance, the pleasant tickling sensation even before he moved to press his face into it and inhale deeply. The goodness of her in his arms caused him to shiver uncontrollably.

"I know, I know," she whispered. She took his hand and led him to a wide down cushion, sat, pulled him to her, and opened her loose garment with one hand while pulling his head into the softness of her breasts with the other. As his lips closed over one swollen nipple, she inhaled through her teeth in quick ecstasy.

Her teeth were bizarre. They were sound and strong, but they were dark, an iridescent black. It was as if the arcane and ancient quality of her talents gleamed there, hidden except when she smiled. But her breath had the freshness of a forest fern, and her lips were full and soft.

The warm flow of her milk into his mouth soothed away the tiredness of his body and obliterated all concern from his mind. He felt like a child again, and the nourishing, pungent stream strengthened him. He did not question the perpetual abundance. He accepted it now as he had of old until, sated with the rich warmth of it, he let his hands search down and away from the fullness of her breasts. As she removed his clothing, he let himself drift into lazy sensuality.

He had seen many naked women, but he had never seen a woman who was as soft, as smooth, as beautiful as his Melisande. She prepared him and, with deep-throated croonings, mounted him. She rode him with passion, and he quickly spent himself.

Long after she had drained him of all desire, he lingered with her, touching, clinging, sipping her substance from her fecund breasts.

It was she who broke the comfortable silence. "You will travel far," she whispered.

"I must go to Paris."

"No . . . beyond Paris, beyond France."

He pulled away and sat with his strongly muscled legs folded under him. "Tell me what you perceive."

"The sea. A far land of moist heat and a polyglot people."

"America?" he asked.

She nodded. Her eyes, tilted in exotic loveliness, were as black as the night, sparkling ebony orbs flirting from behind long lashes.

"Then you must leave this house and the forest, for I will not go without you."

"Yes," she assented, and from that he knew that her prediction was true, for she had never consented to leave her home before, not even when he had gone with Napoleon to Egypt.

"And what else do you see?" he asked.

"An opportunity to serve the master."

He felt his pulse increase. "Tell me," he said hoarsely.

"In the American wilderness you will be your own law," she whispered. "There you will have the pleasure of serving him. You will praise his greatness with the blood of many."

He was breathing rapidly, and the thought of such opportunity had sexually aroused him. "Many?"

"The red Indians of the wilderness," she confirmed. "And those who oppose the will of the general."

"You know the content of the Agreement of San Ildefonso?" he asked. "You know what I accomplished in Spain?"

"Yes," she said, nodding, showing her dark teeth. "Those who resent the return of France to the North American continent will speak out against her, and it will be your *duty*"—she put a certain amount of irony into the word—"to educate them."

"More slowly this time," he whispered, reaching for her.

And this time, imagining rivers of blood and remembering past displays of pleasurable agony, he was the aggressor.

Chapter One

To the residents of the Cherokee and Seneca villages it seemed as if Flame Hair, wife of the Seneca sachem Renno, was always entertaining company. Citizens of the new state of Tennessee came from Knoxville and Nashville to see the house that had become known as one of the man-made wonders of the Southwest Territory. Roy Johnson, the sachem's father-by-marriage, had once jokingly called it "Huntington Castle." Solemn Indians traveled from the western reaches of the Cherokee Nation, from Chickasaw Bluffs on the distant Mississippi River and from Creek and Choctaw lands to the south, to see the Lodge As Big As a Hill.

Not everyone who appeared before the whitewashed gate of Huntington Castle came merely to see the house. Some came partly to see the house and partly to see Beth herself. The Englishwoman's beauty was as much a topic of conversation in some quarters as was the house.

Beth Huntington Harper, whose Seneca name was

chosen because of the autumn-leaf tint of her hair, genuinely liked people and possessed considerable political astuteness. Thus, she made everyone welcome. Even before the house was finished, Beth had realized that the future of both her husband's small tribe of Seneca and the great Cherokee Nation depended upon the friendship of men who wielded power in the states adjoining the Indian lands. On behalf of her adopted people she had appointed herself goodwill ambassador for the new state of Tennessee. She was less in evidence when the visitors were chiefs or senior warriors from the various tribes of the Southwest Territory. In those instances she left the greetings and talk to her husband, who had signed his name Renno Harper on the marriage certificate at St. Philip's Church in Wilmington, North Carolina.

All visitors, Indian and white, were offered sustenance that included produce from the gardens of the Cherokee women and from the plantings of the Seneca women, whose allegiance was to Beth's husband, the sachem Renno.

Beth called her home "The House." Once or twice she had tried to explain that the residence was not nearly as grand as the name that Roy Johnson had thrust upon it. To Beth, accustomed to the great manorial halls of old England, hers was just a T-shaped two-story frame house with a colonnaded veranda rising in front to the full height of the roof. From front to back the main wing was two spacious rooms deep and extended north-south for just over one hundred twenty-five feet. The rear of the house greeted the morning sun. Each room of the main wing had either a western or an eastern exposure, planned to catch the breezes of summer and escape the icy northern blasts of winter. A dog-trot extension from the dining room, at the center back of the house, led to the kitchen and servants' quarters. That wing formed the base of the T.

The furnishings of The House—or Huntington Castle, as some visitors preferred to call it—were still arriving by wagon from Knoxville, some items having made the long Atlantic crossing on one of Beth's merchant ships. Each arrival was the cause of intense celebration for the flame-haired, mature mistress of the house and her petite, shapely stepdaughter, whose name, Renna, was a variation of her father's.

Roy Johnson might grumble, "Where in tarnation is she *putting* all of it?" and Renno might shake his head in bemusement, but Beth ignored their teasing. She simply directed the black servants in trying each new item in as many as half-a-dozen rooms and dozens of individual locations until Renna and she were satisfied—at least temporarily.

The servants—like the furniture, the linens, the sets of fine English china, and the racks of ringing crystal goblets—had arrived by wagon from Knoxville. They had been purchased just as the furniture and goods had been purchased, and their arrival had sparked a disagreement between Renno and his wife.

"I do not keep slaves," Renno said quietly. The glint in his blue eyes told Beth that no discussion would be allowed. "My wife does not keep slaves."

Beth solved the matter by drawing up papers of manumission for the servants while continuing to treat them as they expected to be treated, as valued workers who received remuneration in the form of ample food, adequate clothing, and a place to call home. Once the former slaves viewed their cozy quarters, they chose to remain in Flame Hair's employ.

Huntington Castle had another name, also. To many, especially the Cherokee and Seneca warriors, it was "Renno's House." Such men knew the white Indian as a great sachem, a stalwart warrior, and a leader dedicated to the welfare of the Cherokee Nation as well as to his smaller group of displaced Seneca. It did not matter to them that payment for building materials, workmen, artisans, and furniture came out of Beth Huntington's cache of gold. In the Indian society, men had their place and women theirs.

Perhaps the most inquisitive Seneca wondered why their friend and sachem seemed attracted to women of the whiteface, but they did not voice such questions. Renno was Renno, and it was his business that he had married the daughter of the settlers Nora and Roy Johnson, to give her two children, a boy and girl. To Renno's credit, after the death of his first wife he had married a Seneca maiden. Together they had one son. But the sachem lost her, too, before bringing the flame-haired Englishwoman to the land of the Cherokee for her second time.

The Cherokee Nation was at the very center of a titanic collision between cultures. Violence, blood, and death were its products since shortly after the white man's arrival on the shores of the North American continent. For three years, however, Renno's family had enjoyed peace and togetherness. For the boy called Os-sweh-ga-da-ga-ah Ne-wa-ah, or Little Hawk, there was sometimes entirely too much togetherness. On evenings when his stepmother read aloud or tinkled odd, minor melodies on the harpsichord that had come all the way from England, Little Hawk longed for the freedom to go "torching" possums in the woods—spotting the reflecting eyes of the taciturn little beasts by the light of a blazing brand.

Unfortunately, Flame Hair did not cook possum. When Little Hawk did manage to sneak away from all that family cohesion into the nighttime forest, he took his catch to his grandmother Toshabe, probably the finest baker of possum east or west of the Mississippi. Toshabe knew from her own experience of raising two sons the appetite of a growing boy.

On balmy afternoons, when other lads of his own age were splashing and playing chase in the swimming creek beyond the village, Little Hawk was imprisoned in the classroom. There, with his sister, Renna; his half brother, Ta-na; his cousin Gao, son of his uncle El-i-chi and Ah-wa-o the Rose; and his aunt Ena's twins, Rusog Ho-ya and We-yo, Little Hawk was exposed to the writings of men with names like Plato and Josephus, to the mystery of numbers, and to the oddities of the spelling of the English language. Little Hawk, who had inherited his father's sense of responsibility, understood that his education in the lore of the white man fulfilled a promise made by his father to Little Hawk's dead mother. But there were times when he longed for the old days, before he became a junior warrior, when he could spend a whole day in the woods without attracting the attention of an adult.

On this evening in May, when the breezes were cool and the moon was due to come up full, Little Hawk felt no desire to sneak away into the woods, for Beth's visitors included his rangy, ruggedly handsome grandfather Roy Johnson and a gaunt, leonine man who had greeted Renno by name and with a firm handshake.

Andrew Jackson was thirty-three years old, four years younger than Renno. With Roy Johnson as his guide, Jackson had ridden out from Knoxville on a handsome stallion to confer with the white Indian.

Renno and Jackson had first met when Jackson, along with Roy, was a member of the convention drafting a constitution for the new state of Tennessee. Renno had been in Nashville to present the views of the Cherokee and the Seneca. The last time Andrew Jackson and Renno had seen each other was in Philadelphia, during the last days of George Washington's presidency. Jackson, a member of the House of Representatives at the time, had been elected to the Senate shortly afterward, only to resign in 1798, swearing that he was finished with public life. He was currently serving as judge of the Tennessee Superior Court. Upon his arrival Jackson greeted the sachem in Cherokee and was answered in the accents of the British upper class, an affectation that Renno reserved for certain types of white men. He was not fond of Jackson, for the politician-judge had never been a friend to the Indian.

Jackson then turned to the son of the house and held out his hand. "And you, Hawk?" he asked.

"I am fine, sir," Little Hawk said, taking Jackson's hand.

Jackson's eyes crinkled with amusement. "I hear, young man, that you left Philadelphia in a hurry."

Little Hawk squirmed uneasily. His hasty departure from the nation's capital, where he had been a Senate page, was still a touchy subject in The House. "I think one could safely say, sir, that I did not tarry for too many good-byes," he said in an accent much like his father's.

Jackson laughed. "Well, every now and then we have to show those dag-blamed easterners what's what, don't we?"

It was a small dinner party for The House, only the family, which consisted of Renno, Beth, Renna and Little Hawk, and the two guests from Knoxville. Jackson was dressed for dinner in fashionable black evening wear, slightly the worse from having been carried in his saddlebag. In spite of the wrinkles in his trousers and coat, the white of his collar and a touch of lace at his throat gave him a dapper appearance. He seemed genuinely interested in Beth's reaction to life on the frontier.

"Although," he said with a chuckle and a wave of one graceful hand, "one can hardly think of this excellent house as being an isolated oasis of civilization three days' ride from anywhere."

"But, Mr. Jackson," Beth said with her best smile, "we're only a stone's throw from two well-populated towns."

"Yes," Jackson responded. "I see." He obviously did not believe that an Indian village qualified as being somewhere.

Beth, having landed her little barb, changed the subject. "Speaking of civilization, Mr. Jackson, I am surprised that you did not take to life in the nation's capital."

Jackson snorted. "My dear, I did not like being separated from my family. Moreover, the hypocrisy of national politics makes my stomach queasy."

"You'd never know it by your actions, Andy," Roy remarked. "You were one of the very few who had the guts to tell George Washington that he was wrong to support the Jay Treaty."

"Yes, that," Jackson mused. "Well, the general *was* wrong. Only twelve of us out of the whole House of Representatives spoke out. All the others voted to reply cordially to his Farewell Address. I still say that the Jay Treaty gave too much to Great Britain, and mark my words, we'll pay for it in the end. We haven't heard the last of 'good' King George the Third. We keep flip-flopping on what some folks in Philadelphia call our foreign policy. One minute we're scared out of our wits by Napoleon's France and the next we're talking turkey with him. But our main enemy is still the nation with whom we share a common language—England."

"Mr. Jackson," Renno said, "I pray that you are wrong, but I fear that you are not."

"In a year, two years, perhaps five, we will begin to see our recent allies showing their true colors again," Jackson predicted.

When the meal was finished and topped off by an excellent after-dinner sherry, the men retired to the front veranda. Jackson puffed life into a battered corncob pipe. It soon became apparent that Jackson was slowly leading up to the purpose for his visit to the Seneca sachem. He spoke of hunting and horses and the vast, undeveloped lands of the frontier. At last he turned the conversation to the unrest in the Indiana Territory.

"I have heard of your contributions at Fallen Timbers," Jackson told Renno.

"If you heard of them from a certain ex–father-by-marriage of mine, you might have to pick and choose to find the truth," Renno remarked with a chuckle.

"All I told him was that you not only scouted the field but drew up and directed Anthony Wayne's battle plan," Roy protested. "Now if that isn't the truth—"

"I suppose," Jackson said, also chuckling, "that I'll have to accept it as fact, Roy, since General Wayne, rest his soul, isn't around to deny it." As he turned to face Renno, his eyes gleamed in the glow of moonlight. "Let me say only that I've known Roy Johnson for a very long time. The slaughter at the fallen timbers was a sad affair, my friend, but there are those among the Indians who are not content to confine such tragedies to the past. Even in these times of peace, isolated instances of violence are erupting all along the frontier. And up north there's a chief who is showing every sign of trying to follow in Little Turtle's footsteps."

"If you're referring to the Shawnee Tecumseh," Renno said, "oddly enough, he is not a chief."

"So I have been told," Jackson responded. "Nevertheless, he has sworn to unite all the Indian tribes for one final campaign against white penetration of Indian lands.

Now it's none of my affair—not yet, at least, although I do have connections with the Tennessee militia—but I'd be curious to know if the sachem of the southern Seneca still believes that the future of the Indian rests with the United States."

"So I have stated," Renno confirmed.

"And the Cherokee?" Jackson asked.

"I speak only for myself," Renno replied, "but I know my brother-by-marriage, Chief Rusog, and his people. The Cherokee have stood at the side of their white neighbors in the past. They will do so again should the need arise."

"I have been told that you are wise," Jackson said, nodding in satisfaction. "Now I believe that is true. Interesting times are on the horizon. Interesting times, indeed." He rose, as if his business was finished. "Now, if you don't mind, gentlemen, I'd appreciate being pointed in the general direction of a bed."

Jackson left Renno's home after a one-night stay. The sachem, who had suspected from the first that Jackson's visit had not been dictated by mere curiosity about The House and its sunset-haired mistress, asked Roy to give his opinion of Jackson's motives in asking questions about the loyalty of the Seneca and the Cherokee.

"Well, Renno," Roy said, "just open one of Little Hawk's schoolbooks and look at a map of the United States. Here we are"—he drew the map in the air—"a little band of states along the Atlantic Ocean. To the west are two thousand miles of almost unknown land peopled by an uncounted but intimidating number of Indian warriors. You have the Spanish along the Mississippi, to the south in New Orleans, and in the Floridas. Those British that Andy was grousing about are up north in Canada. Now rumors are circulating that France might be moving back into Louisiana. I expect old Andy had his feelers out for potential allies, just in case."

"I suspected the same thing myself," Renno said.

The white Indian, however, was too content to give the matter much thought. He was in the prime of life. He

had a beautiful wife, two fine, white-skinned children, and
one red-skinned little one who looked like his dead Seneca
mother. Renno didn't want to think about possible wars or
the seemingly endless problems that confronted the United
States. Instead he suggested to Roy that The House could
use a supply of fresh meat.

Johnson heartily agreed, as did Little Hawk. With
alacrity the three of them packed their few necessities and
left the village to range wide and pass up generous deer
sign while seeing what was beyond more than one hill.
And, on the return trip, they killed two young buck deer
within easy carry of The House.

On a June day when the sun ruled a cloudless sky,
there was no breeze, and half the population of both
villages splashed and swam in the creek, two warriors
arrived at the lodge of Rusog, principal chief of the Cherokee. One wore a deceptively mild visage and seemed to
be not of this world. The other was a handsome man,
long of face, strong of eye and nose. It was he who spoke
first.

"You are the honorable chief Rusog?"

Rusog nodded.

"I am called by some the Chief of the Beautiful River,"
the stranger said. "I prefer Tecumseh, the name given to
me by my mother."

"Your name is well-known to me," Rusog said.

"This is my brother Tenskwatawa, the shaman, He
Who Has Opened the Door."

"And you, Prophet," Rusog said, "your fame travels
before you as well. Please come in and share our meal."

Tenskwatawa inclined his head in acceptance.

Ena, sister of the white Indian and wife of Rusog,
heated meat and served it on fried cornbread. The two
travelers ate hungrily.

"You have traveled far today?" Rusog asked.

"Today, yesterday, and all the days of the world, or so
it seems," replied the dreamy-eyed one.

"You are welcome to rest here for as long as it pleases
you, brothers," Rusog invited.

"It is true, Brother Rusog," Tecumseh said, "that we are all of one blood."

The Cherokee chieftain was not ignorant of Tecumseh's avowed goal of uniting all Indian nations against the encroachment of the white hordes from the east. He did not, however, acknowledge the Shawnee's obviously leading statement.

"My brother Tecumseh asks a boon of his brother the great chief of the Cherokee," said the Prophet.

"If it is within my power," Rusog agreed.

"We ask only to be allowed to speak to a gathering of your warriors—your chiefs and shamans and wise men," Tecumseh said.

"It will be so," Rusog said with a brisk nod.

"There is among you a band of Seneca," Tecumseh began.

"I speak only for my own," Rusog told him. "The sachem Renno must answer you regarding his people."

"I have long wanted to stand face-to-face with this Seneca warrior," Tecumseh said. "More than once I have seen him from a distance. The last time was when he fought at the side of the white chief Anthony Wayne."

Rusog glanced at his wife. Ena's face showed no emotion, but he knew her well enough to recognize that the woman's anger was growing. This was not the same fiery, hot-tempered girl he had married. That Ena would have spoken out with harsh disapproval. Even though the words of the Shawnee would be a call to war, she kept her peace and, with only a quick, dark glance at her man, offered the travelers melon, which they accepted with eagerness.

Renno was wearing the regalia of a Seneca sachem when he stepped from his longhouse in the village to greet Tecumseh and his brother. Rusog stood beside them. On Renno's head was the *gus-to-weh* headdress, a skullcap made of a circled ash splint, covered with buckskin and decorated with beadwork strung by his daughter. One hawk feather extended upward from the headdress. His chest was bare except for the paint that marked him as a war leader. Around his neck he wore a ceremonial necklace of claws, the *o-ji-e-ra*. Over his buckskin trousers was the *o-fa-sa*, the warrior's kilt, buckskin with fringe and beadwork. When he offered the arm clasp of friendship, he felt the strength in Tecumseh's arm; when he repeated the clasp with the Prophet, he looked into eyes that seemed filled with drifting stars.

"I pray that you are rested from your journey," he said.

"Yes. We are grateful for the hospitality of the Cherokee," Tecumseh replied.

"And I," Renno said, "bid you welcome to my own house."

"My brother is kind," Tecumseh said. "I pray that he does not take it amiss when I ask of which house he speaks—the longhouse of a Seneca or the white-man's house of his wife?"

"In either house you are welcome," Renno said. He stepped aside, then motioned the two Shawnee and his brother-by-marriage into the longhouse, which was situated opposite his mother's home.

Tecumseh stepped inside and waited for his eyes to adjust to the change in light. He sat on hides, with his brother at his side. He appeared somewhat surprised to find that he faced only Renno and Rusog.

"I am not unaware of your purpose here," Renno began.

"It pleases me that my efforts are taken seriously enough to be spoken of so far from my homelands beside the beautiful river."

"The name of Tecumseh is known from the lands of the Creek to the land of snows in the North," Renno said, "and throughout the United States."

Tecumseh bowed his head in acknowledgment of the compliment.

"I saw you, Sachem," said Tenskwatawa, "that time our blades did not clash."

Renno raised one eyebrow.

"My brother speaks of the battle at the fallen timbers," Tecumseh explained.

"I saw you, Sachem," the Prophet continued, "fighting at the side of the enemies of all our people."

"So," Renno said without expression.

"When the time for battle comes again, will Renno be a Seneca or a whiteface?" the Prophet demanded. His eyes had taken on a new life, a sparkle of challenge.

"Enough, Brother," Tecumseh said. "Forgive Tenskwatawa, Sachem."

It was said that Tenskwatawa spoke directly with the Master of Life, but Renno was himself no stranger to the manitous. "I will answer Tenskwatawa's question," he said, his own cold, blue eyes matching the challenge. "My belief is well-known to my people, to my Cherokee brothers, and to the great white chiefs in Philadelphia. My father cast his lot with the United States, and some of my people chose to follow him. Nothing that has happened since has proved that my father was wrong."

Tecumseh opened his mouth, but Renno held up one hand to silence him.

"Perhaps I can state your argument for you," Renno offered. "You will point out that the promises of the white men melt like the icicles of winter. Next you will cite the inequities that were written into the Treaty of Greenville, which took much of the territory of the tribes of the Ohio. And then you will point out that in addition to the lands taken by treaty, lands are continually being demanded by the governor of the Indiana Territory, your sworn enemy William Henry Harrison. All this I know. Moreover, I know that the fragile peace we enjoy on this southwestern frontier can be broken by the greed of a few white men who hunger for land." He spread his hands. "Perhaps, as some say, I fight a losing battle in my belief that peace and cooperation will work to the advantage of the Indian as well as the white man. But I know this from the events of the past: negotiation with the United States will be a continuing necessity for all tribes along a frontier that will be constantly moving westward. And it is far better to negotiate from the strength of peace than to sit at the conference table as a people defeated in war."

"Whatever the circumstance of the talks with the whitefaces, the results are always the same," Tecumseh pointed out.

"Yet it is necessary to talk," Renno said. "I see only one other choice."

"And that is?" the Prophet asked.

"Extermination," Renno said flatly. "As at the fallen timbers, where a generation of young warriors was destroyed while following the advice of war leaders."

"We lost because we were not united," Tenskwatawa protested.

"Nor will *we* ever be," Renno said, "not if you expect all tribes to join you. Your tongue may be plated with gold, Tecumseh, but will it convince the Creek, who already have their own battle with the state of Georgia? Has it convinced the Choctaw, who have chosen the way of peace and accepted the white man's way of life? Will it lure the Choctaw farmers away from their fields? Will it convince the rich Choctaw—who own black slaves and enjoy the good things of life that can be purchased with the white man's money—to leave home, don war paint, and engage in yet another futile struggle?"

"It will not be futile," the Prophet retorted.

"When next you speak to the Master of Life," Renno said, a touch of impatience in his voice, "ask him to inform you of the outcome of the great white man's war. Ask him to show you how the men of the United States put vast armies in the field, from the swamps of Georgia and South Carolina to the hills of New York and Canada, to defeat one of the most powerful nations of the world. Ask him how the Indian warriors who ran in panic before the long knives of the American Legion at the fallen timbers or any force that your brother musters will match the trained armies of the United States."

"Do you question my courage?" Tenskwatawa bristled.

Renno would not let the open challenge pass. "Perhaps one day I will be forced to test not your courage, of which there is no doubt, but the strength of your arm." He let his icy eyes bore into the Prophet's until Tenskwatawa looked away.

"I pray that will not come to pass," Tecumseh said fervently. "But should we face one another on opposite sides, Sachem, it will not be my brother's blade that opposes you."

"So," Renno said, accepting that possibility as well.

"My brothers," Rusog interrupted in a conciliatory tone, "I will remind you that we sit in council." He looked at Renno. "I have said that we—my people and I—will listen to the words of Tecumseh."

"He deserves nothing less after making his long journey," Renno agreed. "The Seneca, too, will listen."

Tecumseh nodded. "That is all that I ask at the moment."

"So," Renno said. "I have asked my mother to prepare food. My Shawnee brothers will be our honored guests."

Toshabe had enlisted the aid of other women, and the feast was held in the central clearing of the Seneca village. Since it was the time of fruitfulness, the gardens of the Seneca and Cherokee women had produced an abundance of squash, beans, and corn. Poke sprouts cooked with eggs, a delicacy introduced to the tribe by the ever-inquisitive Cherokee scholar Se-quo-i, who had started keeping chickens, caused Tecumseh and the Prophet to compete in finding words of praise for the cooks. There were box-turtle soup, venison stew with corn and forest seasonings, melons, nuts . . . so much that the two travelers begged for mercy as the women tried to serve them more.

A soft breeze came from the northwest with the dusk, a harbinger of a change in the balmy weather. Far off, heat lightning flickered on the horizon. At sunset a whippoorwill began to call, and a hush fell over the gathering. Little Hawk and other young lads added wood to the fire that burned at the center of the village square and then vied for places in the circle that was formed.

"I have asked our visitors to tell us of their travels," Toshabe announced.

If any generality about Indians was true, it was the fact that they all loved a good tale. An atmosphere of pleasant anticipation prevailed as the Prophet, Tenskwatawa, took his place at the center of the group. The low-burning fire flickered, making dark, shadowy patterns on his face and reflecting from his wide, unfocused eyes.

"It is true that we have traveled far," he began in a voice so low that Renna, sitting with Beth, Toshabe, and Ena, had to lean forward to hear. Renna had made herself comfortable on her blanket. Beth sat beside her on a low stool. "My brother and I have traveled from the Great Lakes to the land of the Cherokee. Next we will trek to the Gulf of Mexico and the rivers beyond the Father of Waters. We have seen many peoples. We have found that when cut, all bleed alike, and when they make love, their women bear children. We have learned that the Indian, whatever his tribe, has the red blood of his ancient fathers."

The Prophet paused. He took in the upturned faces of the young, who crowded around the fire. "Each tribe, each family, each clan, each individual, is unique, but while each tribe has its own legends, many legends have elements in common, for we are all descended from the same fathers. The Cherokee tell tales of the marriage of the North and the South. The Seneca relate the story of the woman who fell from the sky. And I have yet to know anyone who does not speak, in one way or the other, of the Master of Life."

Little Hawk, sitting cross-legged next to Se-quo-i, smiled contentedly at the learned Cherokee, whose leg, broken years before in an accident, was stretched out before him on the ground.

"Yes," Tenskwatawa went on, "my brother and I have spoken with many, with the tribes of the Ohio and Canada, with the tribes of the Iroquois, Chickasaw, and Choctaw, the Creek, Quapaw, and Santee, and with the Yankton, Sioux, and others from beyond the Father of Waters. Once, we walked with a far traveler who described snow-covered mountains of rugged crags, forests that reached to the sky, and far waters that lie in the lands where the sun comes to rest. He called himself a Cheyenne, and he said that he had received a vision. In his dreams a man had come to him to say: 'Brother, your time, too, will come.'

"The Cheyenne knew not the meaning of the dream. He knew only that he was led by the spirit of the wind to seek the morning sun. It is of this far traveler that I will speak to you this night. When my brother addresses the gathering of your chiefs and your brave warriors, he will tell the tale of the Cheyenne's long journey and his reactions upon seeing his first whiteface. I will tell you a story now that was told to my brother and me in the light of a lonely campfire in a land far to the north, where there is no peace. The Cheyenne told us this:

"On a plain below the high, snowy mountains lived a man, his wife, and two children. Because they were alone, each morning, for his wife's protection, the warrior painted her body with sacred patterns before he left for the hunt. As it happened, there came a time when, upon his return, the man found that the magic paint was gone. He asked what had happened. And his wife explained that she had bathed in the lake, and her paint had washed off.

"On a morning not long thereafter, the warrior pretended to leave for the hunt after painting his wife's body, only to return and follow her to the lake. There he saw a large, brightly colored snake rise out of the water. 'Come to me,' the snake said to the woman, 'for I am waiting for you as I wait for you each morning.' The woman said, 'Yes, I come.' She took off her clothing and waded into the lake, and the snake enfolded her and ejaculated into her."

A gasp of shock and horror sounded from a group of young Seneca and Cherokee maidens.

Renna looked at Beth and said, "Ugh."

Beth made a face and laughed.

"And so," Tenskwatawa continued, "the warrior jumped onto the snake and cut it to pieces with his blade. Then he caught his unfaithful wife and cut her up—"

There were more gasps.

"—and took her meat home, cooked it, and fed it to his children."

Renna took Beth's hand and squeezed it, and her face showed her distaste.

"The children knew not that they had eaten their mother," the Prophet explained. "Their father said, 'When your mother comes home, tell her that I have gone hunting.' And he left them. The two children waited for their mother to come home, and when she did not, the younger said, 'It is hateful of our mother to stay away.' The older said, 'Do not speak ill of our mother.' They were frightened and lonely until one day the severed head of their mother—"

A young girl made a frightened, strangling sound.

"—came rolling up to them and said, 'You are my children, and yet you have eaten me.' The children ran away, but the head rolled after them until they could run no more. The older girl dug a trench so deep in the earth that the head could not roll across it. The younger was crying from hunger when a deer came walking by. The child said, 'Sister, that deer would be very good to eat.' And so the older girl looked at the deer, and it fell down dead as if shot with an arrow. The sisters ate of it."

"Ah," Little Hawk said, for he loved all tales of magic.

"With her magic the older girl built a comfortable lodge, which was guarded by two large panthers and two black bears. Inside were all sorts of good things to eat. But it came to pass that a camp of Cheyenne were starving. There were no buffalo, nor any other game. Hearing that the two children had food of all kinds, the people went to the sisters' lodge and were invited in. And so at last the girls once again had a family and were cared for. When their father came back, the older girl said, 'You killed our mother, and you tricked us into eating her. But in her love she has given us magic,' and the girl told the two panthers to jump onto her father and kill him."

There was silence around the fire. Thunder rumbled in the distance, and the far flashes of lightning were more vivid. The whippoorwill had ceased his lonely calling. Renna moved closer to Beth, who put a comforting arm around her stepdaughter's shoulders.

Tenskwatawa's voice rose. "And now, my brothers, who can guess the true identity of the brightly colored snake? Could it be, brothers, that the snake of the dream of the Cheyenne warrior is the white man, who seduces

not our wives but our brothers, who pits Indian against
Indian, for his own purposes? And is the magic child in
the tale a symbol of he who would unite us, driving out
only those who turn against their own?"

Renno rose and strode into the firelight. "We accept
your story with interest and gratitude, Tenskwatawa. Your
preachings, however, will be best saved for the gathering
of warriors, as you suggested."

"So be it," Tenskwatawa agreed, and there was a
smile on his face. He had obviously made a strong impression on many of the warriors who had heard him.

So it was that Tecumseh spoke to the congregated
Cherokee, many of whom had arrived after several days'
travel. He spoke eloquently and for a long time. The
Prophet sat behind him, eyes widening into an odd, blank
stare, and when Tecumseh had finished, words belonging
to the Master of Life issued forth from the lips of
Tenskwatawa, exhorting, "Hear, hear, O my brothers.
Hear the wisdom of Tecumseh."

Fiery enthusiasm filled many of the younger warriors.
They leaped to their feet and chanted as Tenskwatawa
continued to utter the words of the Master of Life until
Rusog stood and in silent dignity reminded the young
ones that they were in a place of council.

"You know who I am," Rusog said after order had
been restored. "Do I have to remind our younger members that I have taken my scalps, that I have faced my
enemy with arrow, blade, and musket?"

"No," came a chorus of voices.

"We have heard our brother Tecumseh call us to
another war against the whitefaces," Rusog continued.
"And you have often heard our brother Renno of the
Seneca advise us that the time to fight is past—it makes no
difference if we battle other Indian nations or whether we
fight the men of the United States. I will state now that
although Tecumseh speaks well and although he speaks
many truths, I and those who follow me will keep my
treaty with the United States. To challenge the soldiers of
the United States would result in the destruction of our

homes. Our children would be left fatherless. Our women
would subsist on the berries of the wilderness and wear
rags."

Rusog looked around. He caught one glance of Ena,
his warrior wife. Her eyes glistened with pride. He raised
his chin. "I cannot forbid our young men from answering
Tecumseh's call to battle. But I can say this: once, we
were great, we Cherokee. Once, we ruled much land and
protected our hunting grounds from even the excellent
warriors of our cousin tribes among the Iroquois. Once,
we battled against the white settlers who followed their
long hunters over the mountains that smoke, and we were
powerful and great. But many Cherokee died, and lands
that were once ours have been cleared and used as fields
of corn for the whitefaces. And yet there is still much land
and good hunting. I agree with my brother Renno, who
has warned us that change will come and that we can
affect the degree of change only if we are alive—not dead
and decaying on some field of battle."

There was a hiss of disagreement. Rusog straightened
his shoulders, threw out his chest, balled a fist, and lifted
it. "Let the man who derides me speak openly!"

Renno rose and clasped Rusog's arm. "He who would
hiss at such words of wisdom is not worthy of meeting you
in combat, my brother. You have spoken well—so well
that I have nothing to add save that as for me and mine,
we will be at peace."

Tecumseh and Tenskwatawa had a guard of honor
from village to village as they made their way southward
to the great bend of the Tennessee River and entered the
lands of the Creek. The young ones who had sworn allegiance to Tecumseh took leave of him there, for the war
that was Tecumseh's goal would begin in the North, not in
the warm and humid southern climes. And as the young
warriors returned to their villages, only a handful of hot-
tempered Cherokee prepared to journey northward to join
those who would, according to Tecumseh, drive William
Henry Harrison and all whitefaces out of the lands of the
beautiful river.

Once again peace prevailed in the adjoining villages of Rusog and Renno. The lazy heat of summer made life pleasant. Tennesseeans continued to come to view The House, and now and then, in the early morning, one could look out a window and see Indians, alone or in small groups, gazing upward at the height of the Lodge As Big As a Hill.

The last load of linens and dry goods arrived, wrapped in canvas as protection against the vagrant weather while making the trip in a covered wagon, and Beth and Renna busied themselves in sewing curtains for the upstairs bedrooms.

The political revolution of 1800 had come and gone, to be read about by Renno and Roy Johnson after the fact as eastern newspapers made their way beyond the Smoky Mountains. The presidential election had, it was being said, put an effective end to the Federalist party. In the popular vote Thomas Jefferson and Aaron Burr easily bested President John Adams and Charles Pinckney, the man who had been so ineffective as Adams's minister to France during the X,Y,Z Affair.

Jefferson and Burr had tied in the electoral college, and thirty-five ballots were required in the House of Representatives before the tall, auburn-haired Virginia aristocrat was elected third president of the United States with Burr as vice-president.

Before the end of the year rumors of the Agreement of San Ildefonso had drifted out of Europe and across the Atlantic. Spain was reported to be ceding all of Louisiana to France. Those who believed the rumor experienced both fear and anger. As the unconfirmed news made its way beyond the mountains, westerners reacted strongly against the threat of having mighty France take the place of the weak and tired Spanish Empire on North American shores.

Thomas Jefferson, more sensitive than most politicians to the voices of westerners, a man who had already conceived a singular vision regarding the future of the United States, stated: "There is on the globe one single spot, the possessor of which is our natural and habitual enemy. It is New Orleans, through which the produce of three-eighths of our territory must pass to market. The day that France takes possession of New Orleans we must marry ourselves to the British fleet and nation. We must turn our attention to a maritime force."

These words were prophetic for both the United States and for a man who had often been called upon to serve the nation that was not his own—Renno, the white Indian.

Chapter Two

Lieutenant Philip Woods, Jr., observed his eighteenth birthday without ceremony during his journey through Kentucky and Tennessee to Fort Wilkinson, on the border of the Cherokee Nation. More trading post and Indian agency than military installation, Fort Wilkinson was better known as Tellico Bloc House to residents of the frontier.

Philip Woods had matured into a strong, handsome young man in the nearly five years since Renna and he had skated on a frozen pond in Philadelphia. His uniform had been tailored to fit his well-muscled thighs and calves, and his tunic showed a good width of shoulder. His hair, grown rather long during his journey, was dark and curly and clung closely to his head. His eyes were a penetrating black.

None of the small contingent of fat and happy army personnel at the Bloc House was pleased to see a dewy-faced new lieutenant make his appearance. The detachment had been under the command of Sergeant Major Samuel J.—for Julius—Lemon, who had been with Anthony Wayne's forces along the Maumee River. Sergeant

Sam Lemon, content to spend his last few years of active
service in a quiet, pleasant spot without too much army
hassle, was no more pleased to see Lieutenant Philip
Woods than were his baker's dozen men; but he felt better
when the young officer explained that he was in transit to
a newly established fort on the Mississippi, south of
Chickasaw Bluffs.

"Sergeant," Philip said politely, "I'd be obliged if
you'd let me bunk here for a few days. Then I'll be on my
way." He was tired. He'd ridden hard that day to reach
Tellico Bloc House.

"Yes, sir," Sam Lemon said. "Glad to have you, sir.
The 'commodations ain't as fancy as Philadelphia's, but we
manage to keep the blankets clean and the varmints in 'em
more or less under control."

Philip followed a corporal to his assigned quarters and
didn't take time to undress fully before falling onto his
cot. . . .

When he was awakened by a knock on the door, the
room was light. He'd slept over fourteen hours.

"The sergeant thought you might want breakfast, sir,"
said a haphazardly dressed private. It was apparent that
Sergeant Major Samuel Julius Lemon didn't enforce a
uniform code at the Bloc House, but Philip decided that
that wasn't his affair.

He splashed his face with lukewarm water from an
enameled basin, swished out his mouth with more of the
same, and followed the private to a mud-chinked log lean-to
from which savory aromas emanated. He made no protest
when the men seated at tables made of hand-hewn planks
showed no intention of standing or snapping to attention.

Sam Lemon, wearing only uniform trousers and long
johns, waved Philip to a seat next to him at the table. A
chubby little woman in a black woolen dress, which reeked
of cooking grease and sweat, piled pork chops, fried eggs,
fresh green onions, and fried bread onto his plate, then
slopped hot tea into a battered pewter mug.

"Dig in, Lieutenant," Lemon invited. "One thing
about the frontier—we eat well out here."

Philip, who had been living on trail rations for several

days, ate hungrily. Eating was a serious business to the men at the rough tables, so there was very little talk until, plates emptied for the second time, Philip and the sergeant, sated, looked at each other and grinned.

"Well," Lemon said as the little woman in black poured more hot tea, "I reckon I'll live if we have an early dinner." He leaned back and gave a huge, satisfying belch. "Think you'll be here for dinner, Lieutenant?"

Philip, still smiling, realized that the sergeant was asking him just how long he planned to hang around and let his shiny new lieutenant's bars disturb the peace and tranquillity of the post. "I'm going to visit friends while I'm here, Sergeant," he answered. "In fact, my orders are nonspecific as to an exact date for reporting to my new post."

"That's right convenient, sir," Lemon said.

"It might have something to do with the fact that the man who drew up the orders was my father," Philip said with a laugh.

Lemon slapped his leg. "I thought I knew that name! Philip Woods. Your father wouldn't be Colonel Philip Woods, fought with the legion at the fallen timbers?"

"General Woods now," Philip said.

"Well, I'll be hanged!" Lemon shouted, reaching for Philip's hand and pumping it energetically. "Best officer I've ever served under, your father. You make half the man your father was and—" He stopped, waved a hand. " 'Scuse me, sir. Got a little full of myself."

"No problem," Philip said.

"Well, sir," Lemon said, "any son of Colonel Philip Woods is welcome here, even if it does complicate the paperwork a bit, what with drawing supplies and rations for an extra, unauthorized man."

"I'll try not to create any problems for you, Sergeant," Philip responded. "In fact, I'm quite eager to be off to see my friends. Unfortunately, I don't know how to find them. The person—" He paused, and his shy grin made him look younger than his years. "Well, the *girl* I want to see is the daughter of a Seneca chief called Renno, and they live somewhere near here in Cherokee country."

"Yes, sir," Lemon said, nodding. "I can help you there, sir. I know the Seneca village. It's right next to the town of the principal Cherokee chief—fellow named Rusog. I haven't had the pleasure of meeting the sachem, but I can take you to him myself." He was looking at Philip from a new perspective, wondering why a son of Philip Woods would want to go calling on an Injun squaw.

"If you'd lend me a fresh horse and point out the way, Sergeant, I'll get out of your hair so that you can"—he paused, smiled—"get on with your, uh, duties?"

" 'Preciate that, sir," Lemon said. "But with the lieutenant's permission, I'll ride along and show you the way. It gets a little wearin', if you know what I mean, staying here in the Bloc House all the time with no one to talk to 'cept the agent and his wife and fat Bessie and a few knucklehead soldiers."

"Glad to have your company, Sergeant," Philip agreed.

They were under way an hour later. The horse that Lemon had chosen for Philip was a good mount, strong and well trained. They rode through a virgin wilderness, sometimes along game trails, and often had to pick their way through brush under a dense canopy of branches. The early-summer heat plastered Philip's seat and thighs to the saddle with his own sweat. A dark patch formed between his shoulder blades on his best tunic. He was not thinking of the heat or his discomfort, however. He was thinking of a little girl. That's how he remembered Renna, as a child of ten who had shown a thirteen-year-old boy a hint of the woman she would be someday.

Renna. Her face had haunted him for almost five years, and she was a girl with Indian blood, a girl without a surname. What would she have become? She would be going on fifteen. He had seen Indian girls who, at fifteen, had babies strapped to their backs. They seemed no longer young. Aged before their time, they had flabby, much-suckled breasts, a protruding stomach, and fat buttocks. On the frontier even girls of European descent were judged to be women early. Indian females became women at the onset of puberty.

Several times during the trip to the Seneca village he almost turned back, for if he found Renna—and even that was not a certainty—only to see her fat and married and burdened with child, something precious would go out of his life. He would lose a pleasant dream, a poetic ideal, the last vestige of his youthful romanticism. He was not ready for that to happen, because the memory of the girl with whom he had skated in Philadelphia had come to mean much to him.

On the other hand, he was not capable of eliminating the risk by turning back when there was even a small chance that Renna was there, only a couple days' ride away, and that she would remember him with fondness. He had told her that he would find her when he reached the age of sixteen. He was running two years late. He had been involved in other business at the age of sixteen—his education, his entry into the army.

He fervently prayed that she would be as beautiful as she had been in Philadelphia, that she would be as slim and graceful as he remembered, and, above all, that she had not forgotten him.

Renna Harper—for she had acquired a surname, the name taken by her father from the family of the original white Indian—was a splendidly contradictory young lady. Wearing the buckskin skirts of a Seneca maiden, she rode as well as her older brother. Under the secret tutelage of her aunt Ena, once a warrior-maiden who had taken her share of scalps, counted coup over her enemies, and braved the wilderness and the British army as a scout for George Washington, Renna was learning the care and the use of weapons. She had shown unusual aptitude for the throwing knife. Her right arm did not have the strength of Ena's, but what she lacked in power she made up for in accuracy. With bow and arrow she was merely adequate. With the musket or a brace of pistols that had been given to Ena by her brother the shaman El-i-chi, Renna was better than average. With the tomahawk she was worse than acceptable, mainly because hacking and chopping at someone's head and face were not ideas that she could

stomach. Abhorring the weapon as she did, it was no
surprise that she did not become skilled in its use.

The other aspect of Renna showed itself in The House,
when she dressed in one of the splendid gowns purchased
or designed and made for her by her stepmother. The
lithe grace of a natural athlete transformed itself into a
regal elegance when she wore the frills and skirts of an
English gentlewoman.

Renna was pale haired like her late mother, Emily
Johnson. Piled atop her head in august array, her hair had
the silvery sheen of the bark of a cottonwood tree in
winter, sparked through with hints of gold. She had taken
her eyes from her paternal ancestors. They were large,
wide set, and the blue of a sky swept clean by a winter
storm. Her face combined Emily's gentle beauty with the
strongly chiseled features of her father. Her years with
Beth, whom she had come to love, had added sophisticated poise to her charming personality.

In speech, she had patterned her English after Beth's
aristocratic accent, but she could imitate the growingly
unique argot of the frontiersman of the Southwest. She
had learned frontier French from her grandmother Toshabe.
From Beth and Renno she was accumulating an impressive command of Spanish. She spoke Seneca, of course,
and Cherokee. She could get along in other Iroquoian
dialects, in addition to Chickasaw and Choctaw and a bit
of Creek. Renna had taken well to Beth's efforts to educate her stepchildren in the ways of her own people,
without forgetting her Seneca heritage.

There were times when even the urbane and well-
traveled Beth was surprised by her stepdaughter's ability
to move back and forth between two alien worlds. During
the time of the new beginning, Renna, having come of age
by Indian standards, had been initiated into the world of
the Seneca woman. Although her coloring was fair and her
blood only one-quarter Indian, she had looked and acted
the part of a Seneca maiden so perfectly that Beth had felt
concerned. Would the girl choose a mate and settle down
immediately? Beth wondered. She hoped not, prayed not.
She herself was the wife of a Seneca, but Renno was not

an ordinary Seneca—he was the white Indian. Renno was a man who had dined with, dealt with, and fought for, with, and against men of wealth, education, and power.

Beth's worries had been eased to a great extent, however, during the traditional courting time for new women; Renna offered no insult to the young men of the tribe, but neither had she shown any encouragement.

Once or twice Beth had tried to talk to Renno about his daughter. Renno, always the doting father, indulgent in the fashion of the Seneca, was apparently unaware that Renna was turning into a mature and stunning young woman before his eyes. Being a man, he was more aware of his older son's progress, for with Little Hawk he could measure the journey toward manhood by the strength of the boy's arm and his height, which had, in the past year, matched Renno's own.

"With girls," he asked Beth when she brought up the subject, "how does one tell?"

She laughed. "My dear husband, your eye is sharp enough to spot the movement made by a mouse hundreds of feet away and yet you are blind to that?" She pointed.

Renna was seated in the summerhouse across the lawn from the veranda, where Beth and Renno were enjoying the afternoon air. She was arrayed gracefully on a chaise longue, ankles crossed demurely, a book held before her face.

"That is my little Renna," Renno said.

"That is, indeed," Beth said. "And one fine day, Sachem, a young man is going to come along and see what you apparently cannot. And then he will stand before you and say, 'Mr. Harper, may I have the honor of asking for your daughter's hand in marriage?' "

"I see no problem there," Renno said softly. "I shall simply scalp him on the spot."

Beth laughed, then became serious. "Or perhaps he will be Seneca," she suggested.

Renno did not answer, for he was trying to imagine Renna in a Seneca longhouse, her silver-pale hair in braids. He envisioned her wearing the buckskins of a Seneca wife, cooking in a blackened pot over an open fire. He was

Seneca, and yet the images gave him discomfort. He reminded himself that Renna's mother, Emily, had been a good Seneca wife, happily doing exactly those things. He was reassuring himself as much as to answer Beth when he said, "I think that there is time before we must concern ourselves with such problems."

"My dear," Beth said, "I think it would behoove you to take a closer look. At least prepare yourself for the inevitable."

"No," Renno said, rising and taking her hand. "For at the moment I have other plans."

"You, sir, are indecent," she whispered, seeing the look in his eyes. "It is broad daylight."

"In fact, a rather lazy afternoon," Renno agreed. "An ideal time, wouldn't you say, for a nap?"

She squeezed his hand. "I would say so, indeed," she said throatily.

Although Renna had no desire to rush into adulthood, she had, of course, thought about marriage. From an early age boys had tried to put their claim on her in the precourtship ways of the Seneca. Shy messages delivered by mutual friends of hers and the besotted boys, meaningful looks exchanged—both rituals introduced Renna to an awareness of the wonderful differences between the sexes. She had never selected a favorite lad, nor had she committed herself to anyone. Instead she had radiated friendship to all with a pleasant smile and a willingness to talk.

During her initiation period at the time of the new beginning, while her brother Little Hawk was busy with his False Face Society, she had received several offers of marriage. Her refusal to choose a suitor had caused talk in some longhouses in the Seneca village. It was said that the daughter of the sachem had become more white than Indian, that she considered herself to be above accepting the attentions of a Seneca. Needless to say, such talk did not reach the ears of any member of her family.

She knew that she was young. Unlike her Seneca girlfriends, Renna did not consider herself to be a woman simply because nature had matured her body. She had

seen more, done more, and traveled more than any of the
Seneca girls; yet at times she felt very much younger than
her friends who had already taken a mate. Already several
of them walked proudly with distended bellies.

At other times, Renna felt much older than her con-
temporaries. Without being snobbish, she was astute enough
to know that her background, her education, and her very
way of life with Beth and her father in The House made
her different.

Feeling unlike and set apart from the only other
adolescents within miles often worsened into an ache, a
loneliness that made her moody, weepy, and sent her to
her books to seek solace. As she lost herself in the senti-
mental love poetry of the English, she wondered if she
might not be happier if she, like her friends, had chosen a
strong, handsome young warrior at the time of the new
beginning. She tried to look into the future, but she did
not have her uncle El-i-chi's gift of clairvoyance, so she
could only speculate. Would she be an old maid, living
with her father and Beth, serving as their caretaker in
their old age? Or would a handsome prince come riding
down the road from Knoxville, sweep her into his arms,
and tell her that he had been looking for her all his life?

That last dream was not so farfetched, for a few years
before not one but three French princes—Louis Philippe
and his two brothers—had ridden into the village. The
youngest nobleman, the one whom she had called Beau,
had paid court to her and flattered her shamelessly.

Ah, well. Memories of that heady time and half-
expressed hopes that something similar would recur were
only the dreams of a young girl caught between two worlds.
She told herself that there would not be another prince.
The odds of a man like Beau riding up to the whitewashed
gate of The House were minuscule. And in her heart she
knew that there would be, for her, no Seneca or Cherokee
warrior. Who then? What of her life? How long would she
be alone?

Chapter Three

When Lieutenant Philip Woods turned his horse into a lane bordered on either side by young pecan trees, he whistled in surprise. The lane was arrow straight for at least a quarter mile, and at its end was a brown-painted two-story house bigger than anything he'd seen since leaving the governmental complex in Philadelphia.

"Not yer typical Seneca longhouse, eh, Lieutenant?" asked Sam Lemon.

Cows grazed placidly in the fields on either side of the lane. Behind a rough-hewn, whitewashed fence, a mare and colt raced past, kicking up their heels in sheer exuberance. A young black boy ran out to meet the two riders at the gate that provided entrance to the grounds. Philip dismounted and gave over his reins to the boy.

"Is the master of the house at home?" Philip inquired.

"Naw, suh, he sho' ain't," the boy replied.

"The mistress?"

"No, suh, she ain't home, neither."

"Do you know when they will return?"

"Naw, suh, I sho' don't."

"Thank you."

Philip looked up in frustration at Lemon, who was still mounted. "You go on ahead, sir," the sergeant suggested. "I'll see to it that this boy takes good care of the horses."

Philip closed the gate behind him. From the east side of the long, attractive house came shrieks as one might imagine would accompany a full-fledged Indian massacre. Curious, he walked up the graveled path between rows of rosebushes. Late bloomers perfumed the air. The windows of the house were open. He mounted the steps and knocked on the ornate front door, waited, then knocked again. Silence.

He went to the end of the porch, leaped down, walked around the corner of the house to see a gaggle of Indian youngsters in the process, it seemed, of dismembering one another. As he approached, the roiling mass of young humanity surged toward him.

The grassy expanse beside the east wing of Huntington Castle had been scythed and raked into a lawnlike field devoted to a game played with a leather ball, carefully fashioned sticks, and an abandon just short of mayhem. The game had rules, but when the youngest descendants of Ghonkaba gathered with their friends in fierce competition, the rules were often ignored or, at best, stretched just short of the breaking point.

One of the players most respected by her opponents was We-yo O-no-ga-nose, Good Water, daughter of Ena and Rusog. At twelve, We-yo was a darker, slimmer version of her mother. She had Ena's long, lithe legs and small waist. She had inherited healthy stamina from both parents, stubbornness from her father, and the fierce will to win from her mother. She had been the first player chosen by Renna, who was the team captain of the Hawks. We-yo's twin brother, Rusog Ho-Ya, Fruit of Rusog, was captain of the opposing side, the Bears.

Renna's half brother, Ta-na-wun-da, was a member of the Bears, along with his cousin Gao, nine-year-old son of

El-i-chi and Ah-wa-o. The cousins considered themselves
brothers, never to be separated and never to be pitted against
each other except of their own choosing. Then the matter was
resolved with a colossal but bloodless wrestling match, which
almost always ended in mutual exhaustion and no clear victor.

Renna and We-yo had been playing well. Renna, the
eldest of Toshabe's granddaughters, was skillful in passing
the ball. We-yo's forte was her willingness to hurl her
twelve-year-old body recklessly into a mass of opposing
players and find a way to push the leather ball into the
woven basket for a goal. The Hawks were in the lead,
although the Bears loudly protested that Renna had mis-
calculated the number of goals.

Renna wore a short, faded buckskin skirt, the *a-kia-
ta-wi*, over boy's leggings. Her hair was plaited and wound
tightly around her head, then secured by a scarf lest flying
braids give her opponents something to grab. Because the
afternoon was hot and the game strenuous, her face was
covered with sweat, blood, and the paint that she had
applied in preparation for the game. The blood, fortunately for her, was that of an opponent whose nose had
collided forcefully with Renna's forehead during a scram-
ble for the ball.

The Hawks had come into possession, and with a
flying wedge of young boys leading the way, Renna and
We-yo were moving the heavy leather sphere toward the
Bears' goal. Ho-ya, who would have faced the evil ones
themselves in defense of his twin sister, was fiercely com-
petitive against her on the playing field. For two weeks
now the Hawks had consistently beaten the Bears, in spite
of Ho-ya's efforts to make the best choice of players in the
initial choosing of sides. He barked out orders to his team.
His younger cousins, Ta-na and Gao, with complete disre-
gard for bumps, abrasions, bruises, grass burns, and other
painful but temporary results of collision, threw themselves against the point of the flying wedge.

Gao "accidentally" laid his stick alongside the ear of
the thirteen-year-old Seneca boy leading the wedge. The
opponent went down, and other players tumbled over
him. This left the way clear for Ho-ya to dart through and

intercept a hurried pass from Renna to We-yo. Ho-ya's stick first contacted the ball and then his sister's shin.

We-yo yelped and rolled onto the grass. She leaped to her feet quickly and gave limping chase as her brother started for the Hawks' goal, but the blow to her shin had slowed her. It was left to Renna to save the score.

Renna immediately moved after Ho-ya. Her stick was poised as she closed the distance between herself and the sturdy, stocky boy. Renna caught him just as he lifted his stick to toss the ball into the goal basket. She threw herself between her cousin and the goal, and she and Ho-ya tumbled and rolled. Ho-ya's elbow jammed into her stomach, knocking the air from her lungs. Renna ended up on top, gasping for breath.

Her considerable efforts had been in vain, for Ho-ya's goal was good. We-yo limped over and called time out. Renna untangled herself from the laughing Ho-ya, took a shuddering, deep breath, felt her ribs to see if any were broken, and looked up into a pair of piercing black eyes set in a face that had been buried in her memories for years.

"I am looking for the sachem Renno," Philip said, obviously not recognizing the wide-eyed, dirty-faced urchin standing before him. The shouts of the others faded as they became aware of the presence of a stranger. "I understand that this is his house."

Renna, thanking the manitous that Philip had no idea who she was, experienced an unfamiliar fluttering in her stomach. For a fleeting moment she feared she had been injured in the collision with Ho-ya, but then she realized that the feeling was not pain but something else. She opened her mouth. No sound came.

It was Ho-ya who spoke. Son of Ena, who was one-quarter white, one-quarter Seneca, and one-half Cherokee, the heir of Rusog, as much a Cherokee as a man could be, Ho-ya did not care to acknowledge that he had one-quarter white blood. He had resisted all efforts to teach him proper English and said that a man's native language was sufficient. Renna was one of the few who knew that Ena's instruction had been more effective than

Ho-ya pretended; when the occasion warranted, Ho-ya spoke not perfect but fairly good English.

"Renno's house," Ho-ya confirmed.

"I knocked on the door," Philip said. "There was no answer."

"No," Ho-ya said.

Renna wanted to laugh. Ho-ya was being deliberately uncommunicative, playing the inscrutable Cherokee.

"Well, I say," Philip said uneasily, "could you tell me where I might find either Chief Renno or the mistress of the house?"

"No," Ho-ya said, rising, dumping Renna off his back. She landed on her rump and bounced once, then returned her gaze to the face from her memories, stunned by Philip Woods the man, whose masculine beauty eclipsed the memory of Philip Woods the boy and left her with a curious and breathless anticipation.

"Well, thank you anyhow," Philip said, turning away.

"Bears' ball!" shouted Ta-na, streaking in to steal the ball from the goal. A swarm of brown-skinned players surged after the eight-year-old.

As Renna looked after Philip, she saw that his back was broad, straight. He had a proud walk that reminded Renna of the grace with which her father moved when he was dressed as a white man. She punched Ho-ya in the side with her elbow. "Tell him to wait on the front porch."

"You tell him," Ho-ya protested.

It was said among the younger members of the family that when Renna's eyes widened with displeasure and showed the color of a winter sky after a storm, it was best to keep one's distance. The blue eyes opened wide now, and her voice was level but forceful. "Tell him. Now."

Ho-ya shrugged. "White soldier," he called out.

Philip halted and turned.

"You will wait on the porch."

"I beg your pardon?"

"Wait there," Ho-ya said.

"Tell him you will fetch the mistress," Renna whispered behind her hand.

"I get mistress," Ho-ya said, sounding as if each word had been pulled out of him.

"Thank you," Philip said.

Renna waited until Philip had disappeared around the corner.

"What was all that about?" Ho-ya asked as she jumped to her feet.

"That's the man I'm going to marry," she told him.

"So," said Ho-ya, sounding very much like his uncle Renno as he hid his surprise behind an impassive face.

Beth and Renno had been strolling along the banks of the creek behind The House. Renno, always more comfortable in Indian dress, wore a dark blue decorated breech-clout over buckskin leggings tied off just below the knee with beaded sashes. He had let his hair grow long of late. It was pulled back and tied at the nape of his neck. Beth wore an at-home dress, but she had surrendered to the summer heat by wearing only a minimum of underthings, so the flowing material molded to her elegant form in a way that kept Renno's interest.

Beth had been talking about having a small dam thrown up across the creek to form a pool for swimming and for the importation of a few domestic ducks.

"While I would welcome a well-cooked duckling," Renno said, "I think that we would be in a constant race with the owls, the eagles, the wolves, and perhaps a stray bobcat to see who enjoyed the meal. I fear that we will have to content ourselves with wild duck taken in season. As for building a dam . . ." He shrugged. "It would seem to be much work for the doubtful advantage of enjoying a swim or two before the spring floods washed away your dam completely."

"Oh, you are always so bloody practical," Beth said with a laugh.

"So," Renno grunted.

She hit him in the belly, and the blow made a slapping sound on his bare skin.

"Zounds!" he teased, bending over. "I am slain. I am to expire in terrible agony with a mashed gizzard."

"I am immune to your suffering," Beth said haughtily. She squealed as Renno lunged for her and gathered her into his arms. Her struggles ceased as his lips found hers.

"Wild Indian ravish innocent white lady?" she whispered.

"All right," Renno said.

There was a mossy bower just across the creek. Renno lifted her, walked with her in his arms to the water, and was about to step in when he heard the sound of running feet. He set Beth down, then turned.

"Why do children always have such perfect timing?" Beth demanded, rolling her eyes in only half-pretended exasperation.

"Beth!" Renna panted, pulling to halt. "Quickly, please."

"Who's hurt?" Beth could not bring herself to watch that terrible so-called game that the young ones played. Every time the clan and their friends gathered on the field, she expected broken heads, punctured eyeballs, and jagged bones protruding from ravaged flesh.

"Hurt?" Renna asked, momentarily confused. "Oh, no. I need you to talk to him while I—"

"Talk to whom?" Renno asked.

"He's on the front porch," Renna said hurriedly. "I'll need at least a half hour to bathe and dress. Please hurry, Beth."

"Who is on the front porch?" Renno insisted.

"Philip," Renna said. "Are you coming, Beth?"

Beth looked at Renno with a little smile. "I do believe, Sachem, that we are caught up in an emergency situation. You recall, I hope, our conversation from . . . five days ago, was it? About Renna's—"

"So," Renno grunted.

Beth was smiling more broadly now. "I think it would be best if I accompany this child."

"But who is Philip?" Renno roared as Renna turned and dashed toward The House.

"The boy I skated with," Renna called back over her shoulder. "Philadelphia. Remember?"

It was coming back to him now: the conversations with Beth, her warnings that Renna was no longer a child. He remembered clearly how this Philip Woods, as a slim and graceful boy of thirteen, had skated with Renna on a frozen pond, his arm around her waist. And he recalled vividly the look on her face as the young couple swept past him. Now that boy—become a man—sat on the front porch and waited to pay court to his daughter. His emotions protested that Renna was only a child. His reason told him that he was wrong.

Philip sat stiffly in a hard chair between a steely-eyed, bare-chested man in leggings and breechclout and a shapely Englishwoman whose flowing summer dress and lack of petticoats revealed rather more of the shape of feminine leg and thigh than he was accustomed to seeing.

"So, Lieutenant Woods," Beth was saying, "you have come from Philadelphia. Did you have a good trip?"

"I would say so, madam," Philip answered. He caught Renno's steady gaze for a few moments, then looked away. The man had said only a half-dozen words. He'd been far more cordial in Philadelphia. Perhaps in the wilderness the sachem reverted to his Indian nature, Philip mused.

"We're pleased that you took the time to visit us," Beth said. "I'm sure that Renna will be happy to see you."

"Well," Philip said, "I hope so." He was remembering the disgruntled look he'd received from Renno when he asked about Renna.

"And your father?" Renno asked gruffly.

"He's well, sir," Philip said, brightening. "I told him that I might take you up on your invitation to visit your village."

"I don't recall extending such an invitation," Renno said.

"Renno," Beth chided with a little laugh.

"I suppose it was Renna who invited me, then," Philip allowed uneasily.

"If I neglected to issue such an invitation," Renno said stiffly, "I remedy that breach of hospitality now. Is your horse being tended?"

"Yes, Sergeant Lemon is with the black boy who met us when we arrived."

"Good, good."

"My father sends his greetings and good wishes," Philip said.

Renno nodded, then he turned toward the sight of a man walking up from the stables.

"That's the sergeant now," Philip said. "I'd better meet him at the gate."

"I believe you *would* scalp him," Beth whispered with a mischievous grin after Philip's retreat.

Renno made an elaborate charade of reaching for the Spanish stiletto at his waist.

"Lieutenant," Beth called, "bring the sergeant inside, if you please. I'm sure you're both hungry after your ride."

"I'd be much obliged, ma'am," Lemon said, approaching the veranda.

"I'll wait here," Philip offered. "She—Renna is coming, is she not, ma'am?"

"Oh, yes," Beth said. She turned to Lemon. "Sergeant, if you'll walk directly through the house, you'll find yourself at the dogtrot leading to the kitchen. The women there will feed you."

Lemon disappeared, and Philip took his seat nervously between the father and stepmother of the girl he hadn't seen in several years. Renno was toying with a jewel-hilted, deadly-looking stiletto. Philip cleared his throat, searched unsuccessfully for small talk. "I guess you do a lot of hunting," he ventured.

"Yes," Renno said.

"When are you to report to your new station?" Beth asked, having difficulty in hiding her amusement at Renno's open belligerence toward the first serious candidate for his daughter's affections.

"Well, ma'am, there's no real hurry. My orders are not dated, you see. I'd hoped . . . uh, to get—reacquainted with Renna and . . ." He trailed off weakly.

Beth breathed a sigh when she heard quick footsteps on the stairs inside. She knew that Philip was relieved, too. Renno glowered and turned his head as the footsteps slowed and paused just inside the door.

He was standing when she opened the door and stepped out. He was so tall, so slim, so handsome in his uniform. His black eyes widened when he saw her, a petite girl in pale pink satin trimmed in gleaming white lace. On her honey-tone cheeks were twin streaks of red and black paint, the Seneca markings of celebration. She saw first gladness, then wonder in his face. She smiled. The Seneca paint had been an afterthought, added just before she had floated down the stairs on dreams and memories. The paint was to tell him, "You saw me before, on the field, but you didn't recognize me. I am who I am, Renna of the Seneca." As she looked past Philip and to her father, she saw that pride misted his eyes in reaction to her gesture. The paint said blatantly, "Look, at least a part of me is Seneca."

For long moments the two young ones stood facing each other. She watched Philip's eyes as they swept down to take in the graceful flow of skirt, then went back to her face. His eyes crinkled at the corners. She was momentarily confused when he burst into laughter.

"So it *was* you out there," he said, pointing toward the east end of the house.

"Yes," she confessed.

"I should have known," he said. "Those eyes. The way you looked at me. Forgive me."

"If you saw her playing that dreadful game," Beth said, "it is a miracle that you did recognize her."

"I told you that I'd come to find you," Philip said quietly.

"You said you'd come when you reached sixteen," she whispered accusingly.

"I'm here now," he said.

Her heart was full with him. She extended her hand. He took it. "Come," she said. "We'll walk down to the creek."

"With your permission," Philip said, giving Renno and his stiletto a slight bow.

"I think, sir, that it would be best if you comply," Beth said, smiling at her husband.

Renno nodded, but neither of the young ones noticed, for winter-sky eyes were lost in black orbs, and ebony eyes were falling deeply into blue depths.

"Husband," Beth said when Renna and Philip had disappeared around the west corner of The House, "you must do one of two things: you must sharpen your scalping knife or make this young man your friend."

"He comes of good family," Renno admitted reluctantly.

"It's odd, really," Beth said. "She has spoken of him only once or twice, but did you see the way she melted when he looked at her?"

Renno scowled and refused to answer, for he had seen.

"Tell me about his family."

"Pennsylvania people," Renno responded. "The senior Philip Woods is now a general, probably nearing retirement age. The Woods family owns considerable land in southern Pennsylvania, in one of the most beautiful areas of rolling hills and rich farmlands that I've ever seen."

"Wealthy people, then?" Beth asked.

"Moderately so, I would guess," Renno answered.

"He has charming manners." Beth was silent for a moment. On the east meadow the ball game reached new peaks of pandemonium. When she spoke, there was a note of pleading in her voice. "Couldn't she do much, much worse, Renno?"

From the second they set eyes on each other, the young couple accepted the inevitable. Renna knew, for example, that when Philip talked of journeying onward to the fort on the Mississippi in Chickasaw country, she wanted nothing more than to live there with him. Not for one second did she doubt his ability to care for her and protect her.

The top of her head came to his nose. She had only to tilt her head slightly to look into his eyes, and reflected there she saw herself and his love for her, and she was no longer aware of the distant shouts of the ball players.

As they strolled along the creek, they talked easily together. No, he had not gotten in much skating since they had glided side by side on a bone-chilling winter day in Philadelphia.

"I've never skated with another girl," he said. "Isn't that odd?"

"No. It makes me feel glad."

"I've danced with other girls," he confessed.

"Oh, well, that's all right."

"Renna . . ."

She looked up at him expectantly.

"Nothing," he said.

A mockingbird made a dive at their heads as they walked beside the mossy banks and past the nest tree. Then it flew back to its perch to warble in satisfaction at having protected its young.

"I didn't expect all this," he said, waving his hand toward The House.

"Beth does not do things by halves."

"She's a very beautiful woman."

"Yes, isn't she."

"And not the only one in that house."

She smiled up at him. "And how would you know?"

"When the proof is before my eyes, I know."

"Philip . . ."

"Yes?"

"Nothing."

They walked on in silence. Water gurgled over smoothed stones. Behind them the din of play became muted. A bend in the creek put a stand of willows and cottonwoods between them and the house.

"Renna . . ."

"Yes, and if you say 'nothing,' I'm going to—"

"How can I ask you to leave all this for a log cabin on the frontier?" he asked in a light, teasing tone.

She stopped, turned to face him, and answered him in kind. "Are you asking?"

His voice became serious. "My reason tells me that I have no right. My best judgment tells me to wait, to come to you after I have served my years along the Mississippi, when I have earned a promotion and have more control over my army career."

He saw disappointment darken her blue eyes.

"My heart tells me that I am not man enough to ride away and leave you without having asked."

She sighed.

"So I suppose that I'll just have to spirit you away before your father goes after my hair with that jeweled knife of his."

"Don't worry about the knife." She laughed. "If he were going to scalp you, he'd use his tomahawk first."

"Then I shall be alert if I see him so armed."

The tone of their conversation stayed a mixture of the serious and the bantering. Their what-ifs were voiced as if in fun but were effectively binding.

"I suppose," he said as he stopped by the creek and turned to face Renna, "that I'll have to build you a mud-chinked lean-to. You'll have to cook over an open fire until I can have a stove shipped down the river from Ohio."

"I can manage that, but I don't chop wood."

"All right, slave master, after a long, hard day of soldiering I'll come home and chop the wood. But I will not change the nappies on your brats."

"On the contrary, a good father must learn that skill, too." She faced him. "And where do you get the idea that they'd be *my* brats, sir? I would hope that I will not be expected to produce them without your participation."

Her innuendo caused him to blush. "And to think that I have never allowed myself to appreciate the joys of being an unmarried man. All these years I've been concentrating solely on you—on the memory of your eyes, your face, your smile. I fell in love with a child when *I* was not much more than a child, and—"

Now that his tone had become serious, she knew that he was going to kiss her. She lifted her full lips and closed her eyes. The kiss was experimental at first, but they learned quickly.

The usual friction existed between red and white on the long frontiers of the United States, and people continued to die in isolated incidents and raids. Overall, however, things were so peaceful that Roy Johnson, a general of the Tennessee Militia, was free to spend more time at

Huntington Castle than in Knoxville. He was afraid to stay away for too long, lest his grandchildren, Renna and Little Hawk, become fully adult and unrecognizable. It seemed to Roy that Renna had become a woman overnight. The compensation for the loss of the child, however, was the appearance of a charming young lady so much like his dead daughter that at times tears came to his eyes when Renna appeared.

Roy always put on pounds when he visited his former son-by-marriage and the grandchildren, if the gardens of the Seneca women were in full production. Since he chose to sleep in Renno's longhouse across the village common from the longhouse of Toshabe, he joined his old friends to partake of that woman's excellent Seneca cooking. He'd palaver with Rusog and Ena and senior warriors from both tribes when the occasion was ceremonial. As the widow of the great sachem Ghonkaba and the respected tribal pine tree and senior warrior the Panther, Ha-ace, and as the senior matron of the Bear Clan, Toshabe was never bored or idle. If there was no tribal business for her to attend to, she could be found in her longhouse, preparing meals. Often one or both of her sons joined Little Hawk at Toshabe's table, for the treats from her cooking pots.

On his latest visit Roy had encountered his grandson on the outskirts of the village. Little Hawk told his grandfather that Renna was being courted by an army lieutenant who had arrived at The House several days before. Roy, wanting to hear all about the young man and the family's reaction to him, peppered Little Hawk with rapid-fire questions. The sachem's son, laughing, suggested that Roy partake of the midday meal at Toshabe's place and ask the family personally before going on to The House. Roy agreed with alacrity.

Lunch was served to a large gathering. El-i-chi and Ah-wa-o were there. Their son Gao and Renno's son by An-da, Ta-na, were spending the day with Rusog and Ena's twins. The adults spoke highly to Roy of Philip Woods, then enjoyed some good talk and warm memories as Roy and El-i-chi looked back on war and travel. Little Hawk, with a couple of questions, prompted his grandmother to reminisce about the old days in New York State, before Ghonkaba had led his Seneca south. It was, all in all, a very pleasant afternoon.

Roy spoke Seneca almost as well as those who had been born to the language. Most white men found Indian dialects to be difficult because the way of thinking that had formed Indian tongues was so alien to the European mind. Roy figured he must have Indian blood in his veins from somewhere, because he had no trouble at all with words that totally changed meaning with the addition of one syllable.

"Toshabe," he said, "you have led me into sin once more, the sin of gluttony."

"The Master of Life recognizes no such sin," El-i-chi pointed out. "When food is plentiful, the bear eats so that he may survive when food is scarce."

"Indeed," Roy said. "And if I stayed here for any length of time to eat Toshabe's excellent cooking, I'd be as big as a bear." He yawned, stretched, and turned toward Little Hawk. "Son, I wonder if you and I couldn't just help each other across the common and fall into bed for a nap in Renno's longhouse."

Little Hawk grinned and rubbed his stomach. "My grandfather is wise."

"Are they not expecting you at the grand house of my new daughter-by-marriage?" Toshabe asked.

Roy grinned and winked at El-i-chi. Renno and Beth had been remarried for two years now, but to Toshabe, Beth Huntington would be the "new" daughter-by-marriage as long as Toshabe lived.

"No," Roy said. "I didn't let them know I was coming."

"I'll go there with you after you rest," Little Hawk offered. He spoke English with the affected accent of the British upper class. "It's veddy, veddy formal and proper there this evening, don't you know."

"What's up?" Roy asked.

"Beth's having a family dinner in honor of Renna's suitor," Little Hawk answered.

"Then I'll want to get washed up and changed out of my travel duds," Roy said. The time would soon come, he realized with a quick lurch in his heart, when he would be saying good-bye to his lovely granddaughter.

Early that evening Renno greeted Roy with genuine pleasure, giving him the warrior's forearm clasp and then a more emotional bear hug. "I thank thee that thou are well," he said in traditional Seneca greeting. "Time rests kindly upon the grandfather of my children."

"Healthful living," Roy said in English. "A slug of good moon whiskey now and again, a good pipe of 'baccy, and a plate of your mother's cooking every chance I get." He took Beth's hand, bent over it in an exaggerated pose, then stuck out his tongue and licked her knuckles. She squealed and jerked her hand away, laughing. "Jest cain't seem to git the hang of this English folderol," Roy said, chuckling.

"You are a delightfully wicked old man," Beth said, "and we all love you."

Roy looked around the veranda. "I hear my granddaughter has a visitor."

"I'll wager you did hear," Beth said. "I declare, I thought that no one could match the tendency to gossip of servants in an English manor house, but I do believe the women of an Indian village best them."

"Young feller is the son of General Philip Woods, eh, Renno?" Roy asked.

"Yes," Renno confirmed.

"Renno has not yet decided whether to pat him on the back and call him son or to scalp him," Beth confided.

"Know how you feel," Roy said. "Felt the same way when you were courting my Emily."

An icy sadness stunned Renno for a moment. The truth of Roy's statement was profound. He felt even closer to his father-by-marriage and better understood his own ambivalence toward this young man who was so obviously in love with Renna.

"The lovebirds are walking," Beth said, "but they should be back soon to dress for dinner. Shall we go in or sit out here in the evening air? It's rather pleasant outside."

They sat on the porch. Roy settled in a bent-willow rocker made by a frontier craftsman. "Serious, is it?" he asked, looking at Beth.

"I fear so."

"But he hasn't spoken for her."

"Not yet," Beth replied. "But I think we can expect it at any minute." She rose, motioning Roy to keep his seat. "You men stay here and natter a bit; I'll check on the dinner."

They sat in comfortable silence for a while. At last Roy said, "Renno, it's eating at your guts, isn't it?"

"I feel as if I had swallowed a porcupine," Renno admitted.

"I reckon we have more reasons than usual to love that child," Roy said, "what with Emily's dying after giving her to us. But that doesn't change things a'tall. Little girls become women. We put in a lot of years loving them and caring for them and protecting them, and it just doesn't seem fair that some young buck can come along, and all of a sudden that little darlin' who never loved anyone but her daddy becomes almost a stranger, and Daddy is replaced in her heart with something so much bigger and so much more, well . . . fundamental—"

Renno stirred uneasily.

"Renna's not one to go off half-cocked," Roy remarked.

"She is a girl of uncommon good sense," Renno agreed.

"Maybe she'll just tell this young man that she's a mite young yet."

Renno nodded, for Roy had voiced his own secret hope.

"But it'll happen," Roy concluded. "If not now, then soon. When it does, Renno, you'll have to let her go. The United States frowns on having its army lieutenants scalped."

At dinner Beth and Renna were radiant in finery that had made the long trek from the shops in the East. Renno wore an evening suit in dignified gray. Roy had donned his one good suit and was glad he had thought to bring it along. The other guests—the family—were in their own finery, the dress of the Seneca and the Cherokee.

The children were being fed in the kitchen. Rusog Ho-ya had chosen to be classed as a child, although his twin sister, We-yo, was at the adults' table, next to her mother.

Renna, feeling responsible for Philip's comfort, kept an eye on him. She could tell by his subtle reactions that he had never experienced a family dinner quite like this one. Chief Rusog of the Cherokee made no pretense of observing what he called "artificial white man's manners." He employed his hands when it was more efficient than using knife and fork. The others—El-i-chi, Ena, Ah-wa-o, and Toshabe—were familiar with English table customs and observed them or not, as it pleased them.

Renna decided that it was the nature of the conversation that amazed Philip most. Here he was, on the back end of nowhere, about to plunge into virgin wilderness and travel to the far Mississippi. And yet a pigtailed Indian woman named Ena was discussing the finer points of the French Revolution and its aftereffects, and old, gray-haired Toshabe offered her commentary in flawless French. Then, encouraged by Renna and Little Hawk, El-i-chi told of travel to the Far West and of Spanish gold in a mountain filled with ghosts. This fablelike tale was followed by a discussion of the current problems of transatlantic trade, which included speculation about the impact the new administration's policy might have on Beth's shipping business. A bronze-skinned man in elegant formal wear who wore a knife at his sash under his jacket spoke with unpretentious familiarity of such men as George Washington, John Adams, and the intellectual Virginian Thomas Jefferson, who was now president in the new capital of the United States.

Renna was proud of her family without being arrogant about it. Her father had always been an extraordinary man; he had a remarkable background. For as long as she could remember he had been consulted by and had served well the president of the United States. In her young mind it was difficult to comprehend that there could be presidents other than George Washington. Her uncle El-i-chi knew a shaman's magic and spoke with the manitous, as did her father, and to her that was a natural state of affairs, as commonplace as Beth's elegant sophistication had become to her. She loved all of them totally and uncritically, even gruff, fierce Uncle Rusog. And so it was that she wanted to share her moment of happiness with them.

Before speaking, she waited until the serving girl had made her rounds with a splendid pudding made with summer blackberries. The way she began, the tone of her voice, the tense way she sat in her chair alerted all of them.

"Father, Beth, family, there is something I'd like to say," she began, causing Renno's face to freeze into his impassive, Indian look, and Beth's cheeks to flush. "I'm sure you are not unaware that Philip and I have been seeing a lot of each other."

"Indeed we are not," Beth said. She cast a quick, sympathetic glance at Renno while, at the same time, she clearly wanted to make this moment easier for Renna.

"I know that you might say we've known each other only for a short while," Renna said. "Actually we met nearly five years ago in Philadelphia. Both of us were much affected during that time—so much so that when Philip arrived here . . ." She paused and looked up with wide, stricken eyes toward Philip, who had suddenly pushed back his chair to stand and face Renno.

"I apologize to everyone here," Philip said, "but especially to you, uh, sir, ah, Sachem Renno. I told Renna that I wanted to speak with you alone, man to man, to ask you for your daughter's hand in marriage."

Toshabe was smiling as tears ran down her cheeks. Ena caught Renna's eyes and winked. Everyone was looking back and forth from the strained faces of the young couple to the impassive face of Renno.

"Father," Renna said softly, "I do love Philip so much. I pray that you will give us your blessings."

"And if I do not?" Renno asked.

"Please don't force that decision upon me," Renna said, her eyes grown large. "Please."

"May I have some time?" Renno asked.

"Yes, sir," Philip said, obviously relieved that Renno's reaction had been so nonviolent. "Take all the time you like, sir."

*   *   *

Beth was not surprised to awaken during the night to find Renno's side of the bed empty. The house was quiet. To confirm her guess as to his whereabouts she checked the wardrobe in which he stored his weapons. He had taken musket, ball pouch and powder horn, plus the English longbow and his tomahawk.

She walked to an open window that looked toward the western wilderness. An owl hooted his contentment with life from a tall cottonwood on the bank of the creek. The moon was a crescent, a shimmering galleon sailing seas of rippled clouds. The virgin forest stretched far and away toward the Mississippi, and her man was out there somewhere, moving in the night as quietly as a surefooted wildcat.

Beth shivered and pulled her nightdress closer around her throat. This was not the first time he'd left her alone to seek in the depths of the forest that which she could never give him. Her logical mind accepted the fact. Her emotions, her fears, however, called that compliance a lie. She would not and could not try to keep him from his solitary, days-long communions with whatever spirits haunted the forests; but she could resent the spirits and pray to her own God to keep Renno safe and, above all, to bring him back to her . . . for in her deepest fears, reinforced by a recurring nightmare, the forests and the manitous of the Seneca had assumed a single image: the misty, partially formed figure of a woman, a woman with pale hair and demon eyes. And in Beth's most terrible dreams, she of the pale hair took Renno away forever.

It was as if they had been waiting for him. Never had he been afforded such easy access to the spirits of his ancestors. Renno had traveled slowly by night, moving toward the southwest, away from the Cherokee towns. He had run with the morning sun on his back, first at the warrior's pace and then with the wind until his lungs strained for air and his leg muscles burned like fire. By nightfall he had put the traces of man behind him. He made his camp on a stone outcrop beside a little stream and spread his blanket on a carpet of thick moss overgrowing the sandstone. The crescent moon came late to find him cross-legged beside a dying fire, his eyes seeking substance in the glowing embers.

At first the manitous seemed not to be aware of his presence. It was as if a tableau were being staged for his benefit, with the actors so engrossed as to ignore the solitary man who sat with a blanket around his shoulders to ward off the late-night coolness. He saw the beautiful Ah-wen-ga, wife of his grandfather, Ja-gonh . . . Ah-wen-ga, of Seneca and Biloxi blood, too comely, some said, for her own good.

"Grandmother," he said, but his words did not penetrate into that world that existed before his eyes. Ah-wen-ga was dressed in the beautifully antique fashion of pre-Revolutionary France, her dark hair piled high, her face lightened with powder and rouge. In one hand she held an ornate fan. The other hand was extended, and over it bent a slim man in silks and satins, his hair white with powder, his face lost to Renno's ken. The white Indian knew that the spirit of his grandmother was speaking French, but he could not discern her words; the message was unclear. Ah-wen-ga had been abducted and carried off to France, but what was the meaning of the reminder that she had seen that far country? Slowly the vision changed. The man who had been bending over Ah-wen-ga's hand straightened. His silks and satins shredded and became decaying rags on his back, and when he turned to face Renno, his face was a noseless, eyeless skeletal mask.

"Grandmother," Renno called, "Grandmother, tell me. Speak to me. For whom does death come?"

The manitou was weeping as she faded, her beautiful face the last thing to be seen, and then only her red-rimmed eyes.

His heart leaped as his beloved, lost Emily appeared. She was dressed in a fancy white gown for a special occasion, and a rose adorned her pale hair. His eyes could not get enough of her face. How much she looked like Renna! She was humming happily as she looked not at

Renno but through him. Her obvious gladness pleased him.

"Will you, too, remain silent?" Renno asked. "Love of my youth," he whispered, "are you happy for me?"

"For you," the manitou replied. "For our daughter."

"Then she is to marry this one?"

"So it is ordained," the manitou said. "Be glad for her, Husband. Make her day a day to remember."

"I hear," Renno whispered, holding out his arms to her.

But the vision faded. He let his shoulders slump. The ethereal stage before his eyes was empty when his ears were assailed by a piercing scream. A face appeared in the flurry of odd light, the mouth open, the eyes wide and terrified. The scream came again, tearing into him, but the vision was too dim for him to see anything but the gaping, screaming mouth, wide, blue eyes, and pale hair. These were screams of agony, of hopelessness; yet he could do nothing but chant his prayers to the manitous and search for meaning as he waited and waited. He got nothing in reply. The morning sun seemed too bright for his eyes. And was it his imagination, or was there truly a faint echo of that scream that had filled him with helpless horror? Was a voice calling faintly "Renno, Renno, Renno . . . ?"

He chanted. He protested. He questioned. He sought answers throughout the day and until the sun of another morning came. When at last he started back toward The House, he knew no more than he'd known immediately after the visitation from the manitous. The spirit of his grandmother had wept in sorrow for death, perhaps for the death of a man. And pale-haired Emily had screamed in terror, had called out to him for help.

The white Indian had never made a crucial decision without first seeking wisdom from the manitous, and most often the manitous had answered him not with clear-cut advice but with hints, glimpses of the future, which prepared him, perhaps only subconsciously, to meet crises. But never had he been more puzzled by the messages of the spirits than he was now. Only one thing was clear: the

spirit of the wife of his youth, of the mother of Little
Hawk and Renna, had said that the girl would marry
Philip Woods. As for the rest, he would have to wait and
pray that when the call for help came, he would be ready.

He came running lightly into the mossy bower that
he had considered to be Beth's and his private place. He
found Renna there in Philip's arms, clinging tightly, her
mouth to his. Renno halted, as his anger flared, only to
fade with the echo of the manitou's words. *So it is ordained.*

Philip leaped back when he saw the painted face of
the sachem. Renna blushed furiously and opened her mouth
to speak but was silenced by Renno's raised hand.

"I have given your request much thought," Renno
said. He put his hand on his tomahawk. "I said to Beth—
jokingly, or so I felt at the time—that when a man came to
take my daughter from me, I would simply scalp him."

He lifted the weapon. Its blade was good, of steel
fashioned on the forge by the Cherokee Se-quo-i, and it
was sharp enough to split a hair.

Philip fell back a couple of steps, his face going white.
Renna gasped, not believing what she had seen and heard.

Renno continued, "Beth told me on the day you first
appeared, Philip Woods, that I would have to sharpen my
scalping knife or make you my friend." He grinned widely,
put his tomahawk back into his sash, and extended his
hand. "I would hope that the man who is to be my
son-by-marriage would also be my friend."

Philip stepped forward quickly and grasped the extended hand. "With great pleasure, sir!" he said.

"Thus do warriors of the clans of the Bear and the
Hawk greet each other after separation," Renno said, demonstrating the warrior's clasp.

Renna laughed happily and came to put one arm
around each of the two men she loved most in life.

Chapter Four

Sergeant Sam Lemon, who had spent only one night in the Seneca village, was long gone. Philip had been assigned a room in the guest wing, at the opposite end of the dwelling from the family quarters. He had fallen into the routine of the house. Breakfast was served shortly after sunrise, the midday meal when the sun was at the zenith, and dinner at that time of day when oil lamps had to be lit to dispel the growing darkness in the dining room. Now and then Beth observed the British custom of high tea, but she had long since ceased making it a ritual.

Before the tense scene at dinner when the entire family heard Philip plead his suit for Renna, the two young sweethearts had been free to take leisurely walks or to sit in the summerhouse and exchange likes and dislikes, inquire about and reveal that multiplicity of minute, often mundane feelings and reactions to episodes that make up an individual personality. They were experiencing the importance of getting fully acquainted, and since they had grown up under drastically different conditions, there was much to learn for each of them. Nothing about Renna's life as a Seneca was too dull to escape Philip's interest. On her part, Renna could not hear enough about Philip's early life on the farm in Pennsylvania and about his days in Philadelphia.

It was a comfortable, leisurely period of total happiness for Renna, but she was not discontent when it ended with an abruptness that left Philip abandoned. Beth, filled with the urgencies and instincts of a woman planning a wedding, swooped down upon the young lovers.

"Do run along, Philip," Beth said more than once during the first couple of days after Renno's return from his solitary stay in the forest. "Renna and I have much to do."

Beth was a woman who planned for the future. She had not been thinking specifically of Renna's wedding when she had bolts of cloth shipped to The House from points east by way of the general store in Knoxville, but now that there was a need, she had at hand the means of putting together not only a wedding gown but a trousseau. Although one of the former slave women had been trained as a seamstress, Beth sent for the young wife of a settler on the border of the Cherokee lands to help out with the sewing—the sheer volume of work was too much for one woman. The household servants were set busy doing spring housecleaning all over again.

Roy Johnson extended his visit to watch Beth in action. He was pressed into service, traveling to Knoxville and Nashville and hand-delivering invitations. On his return trip, he brought in extra provisions.

Roy asked Philip if he'd like to go along to see the country. Philip thanked him politely but declined; he did not want to be separated from Renna, even though Beth was keeping her so busy that Philip and she had very little time together.

Renno, who had always been capable of handling any situation, felt oddly ill at ease in the young man's company.

"Do something with Philip," Beth suggested. "Go hunting or fishing or something, for heaven's sake."

Renno allowed that taking his future son-by-marriage

hunting might be a good way to get better acquainted. He went looking for Philip, only to be told that the lieutenant had gone off with Little Hawk. Renno reluctantly admitted to himself that he was relieved.

In his middle teens Little Hawk was a throwback to the original Renno. He had grown as tall as his father and had developed the smooth, long muscles of a natural athlete. His waist and hips were slim. His chest was that of a runner, and his shoulders were wide and powerful. He kept his blond hair cropped short. His blue eyes were his father's eyes and could be as cold upon occasion. Like Renno he preferred the buckskins of a Seneca warrior to white man's clothes, and he often wore the warrior's kilt over leggings with or without the *a-kia-kara* shirt. Standing side by side with Philip Woods, Little Hawk was the taller.

The sachem's son had been cordial with Philip since his arrival at The House, but he had not engaged his future brother-by-marriage in serious conversation. He made no attempt to do so now as he took Philip to the swimming creek.

At the water's edge, Little Hawk stripped out of his clothing and dived in. He looked back. Philip was standing on the bank and looking doubtful.

"The water is very cooling," Little Hawk called out, splashing water in Philip's direction. "Are you just going to stand there?"

Philip, modest, went behind a bush and pulled off his clothing. He made a dash for the water and tumbled in. Aside from a V of sun-browned skin at his neck, his body was very white. He swam not gracefully but powerfully. The water was refreshing.

After their swim the youths talked, and then Little Hawk demonstrated the art of throwing a well-balanced tomahawk. He allowed Philip to give it a try. Next came instruction in the use of a Seneca bow. It was during this activity that El-i-chi sauntered down from the village to sit on a stump and watch as Philip tried unsuccessfully to hit a tree from a distance of about thirty feet.

"I think, Lieutenant," El-i-chi said, "that I would stick to muskets and pistols if I were you."

"I have decided to do exactly that," Philip agreed good-naturedly as he handed the bow back to Little Hawk.

"Did you know that my uncle El-i-chi held the rank of lieutenant in the American army?" Little Hawk asked.

"Very briefly," El-i-chi explained. "It was during the time when it was feared that we would have to meet a French invasion on the eastern beaches."

"You scouted for Anthony Wayne as well, didn't you?" Philip asked. "My father has spoken of you and your brother and Roy Johnson."

El-i-chi nodded. "So, during this time of woman's things you are asked to stay out of the house?"

"That's about it," Philip replied. "Makes a man feel damned useless."

"And so we are at such a time," El-i-chi commented. "Perhaps we could hunt."

"I would like that," Philip said.

"And you, Nephew?" El-i-chi asked. "Do you think that we could teach our brother-to-be how to track down the elusive mileormore bird?"

Little Hawk nodded, watching Philip closely, and was forced to hide a smile when Philip earnestly responded, "I don't think I'm familiar with that sort of bird. What was it again?"

"The mileormore bird," El-i-chi said. "Small bird. So big." He held his hands about ten inches apart. "With a bill about this long." He held his hands five inches apart. "Good eating, but devilishly hard to catch because when you go into the woods after them, they send warning signals to others of their kind."

"Millmore?" Philip asked.

"Mile-or-more," El-i-chi enunciated.

"Odd name. Why are they called that?"

"Because," El-i-chi said, "when you go to hunt them, the first bird that sees you flies into the air, then dives to drive his long bill into the ground. He spins around on his bill so fast that the other birds can hear the wind whistling through his asshole for a mile or more and—"

Little Hawk smothered laughter. Philip's face went red, and then he, too, began to laugh.

"—thus he warns all his fellows that . . ."

There was no need to go on.

"Got you, didn't he?" Little Hawk asked.

"Fair and truly," Philip conceded.

"A man who laughs at himself cannot be all bad," El-i-chi said. "Perhaps my niece is getting a man, after all."

"*I* think so," Philip said.

"So," El-i-chi agreed. He pulled a knife from his sash and cleaned dirt from under his thumbnail, then looked up at the summer sky, which was afloat with white-fluffed clouds. To the Indian—and especially to a shaman—clouds were always worthy of observation. A man with the abilities of a shaman of worth, such as El-i-chi, could find much meaning in the sky. These cottony clouds of summer were auguries of good, of pleasure and family togetherness and peace.

El-i-chi yawned and said, "I suppose, Nephew, that since my brother seems to be otherwise occupied, it is up to us to see if this young man is capable of providing for a Seneca girl when he is not near a general store."

"I know a little bit about living off the country," Philip said, "but I'm sure that I can learn much from you."

"Yes, I do like a truly modest man," El-i-chi said. "Tonight, then. I will come for you just after dark. Just the three of us, Nephew."

Little Hawk nodded.

"What are we going to hunt at night?" Philip asked. "Possums?"

"Snipe," El-i-chi answered. "It's a little bird about this big." He grinned. "About the size of a mileormore bird."

Philip laughed. "Oh, no. I think I'll find something else to do."

"But unlike either the mileormore bird or the kee bird—"

"Uh-oh," Philip said.

"—the snipe is a real bird and quite tasty."

"All right." Philip rolled his eyes. "Let's take them one at a time. What's a kee bird?"

"Little bird about this big," El-i-chi said. "Lives far to the north in the land of eternal snows. Walks around on the ice saying, *'Keeeeee, keeeee, keeeerist, it's cold.'* "

"I'm afraid to ask about the snipe."

"Real bird. No fooling," El-i-chi said. "Be ready at dark. Nephew, you get the bag."

"Bag?" Philip inquired.

"Be ready," El-i-chi asked, turning away.

"Bag?" Philip said, turning to Little Hawk.

"I'll take care of it," said the sachem's son.

"All right."

"It might be a good idea not to mention to the women that we're going snipe hunting," Little Hawk said. "They worry, you know."

At dinner Beth and Renna were full of details about their preparations. Renno listened with interest and managed to ask Philip a stilted few questions. "How was your day, Lieutenant? And what is your assessment of the tomahawk as a weapon?"

Philip had hoped to have a few moments with Renna, but the seamstresses were just finishing a gown, and she was needed immediately after the evening meal for a fitting. He went to his room, dressed for the hunting trip, and found Little Hawk awaiting him on the veranda. Philip was handed a sackcloth bag. El-i-chi arrived just before dusk became darkness and led the way south from The House, over the creek and into the woods.

The moon was nearly full. Silver light filtered down through the mass of branches. Now and then the moon ducked behind a cloud, and in the intense darkness Philip relied on Little Hawk, directly in front of him, to find the way. It seemed to Philip that El-i-chi was making a lot of twists and turns, but he did not comment. He kept his eye on the pole star, thus orienting himself with each change of direction.

He estimated that they'd walked two to three miles before El-i-chi halted and beckoned his two companions close. "This is a very good place," he whispered. "We will post you here, Philip."

He pulled Philip down into a shallow erosion gully. After heavy rains the little gully would run with water, but now it was dry, and dead leaves from the past autumn had formed a soft mulch.

"Just kneel here in the gully," El-i-chi instructed. "Hold the sack open on the ground. Little Hawk and I will make a large circle and drive the snipe toward you. They like to move about in protected gullies like this one. If you'll be very quiet, they will run down the gully directly into your sack."

"I understand," Philip said. "How long should I wait?"

"Be patient," El-i-chi advised. "Some nights we get results immediately. At other times it takes, oh, an hour for the beaters to find birds to drive into the sack."

"All right," Philip said, kneeling and opening the mouth of the sack.

"Be quiet, be patient," El-i-chi whispered, and then, with Little Hawk at his side, he faded into the darkness.

Philip remained still until the slight sounds of movement had ceased. He stood carefully, folded the sack, and checked the position of the pole star. Next he laid a false trail to the south, then circled away from the direction taken by El-i-chi and Little Hawk.

As he had suspected, the erosion gully was only about a mile from the creek behind The House. He didn't move as silently as an Indian, and when the moon went behind a cloud, he had to feel his way, but he made it to the creek quite quickly, moving directly north. Lights glowed in several windows of The House. He entered through the kitchen, tiptoed to his room, and changed from his hunting clothes into his uniform. He went to the library, lit a lamp, chose a book, and settled in for the long wait.

El-i-chi and Little Hawk sat in a mossy glade munching on Cherokee honey-and-nut balls. More than an hour had passed. Little Hawk, envisioning Philip kneeling on the dead leaves in the gully and holding the sack, chuckled. "Think we've left him there long enough, Uncle?"

When the snipe-hunting trick was played on an Indian boy too young to know better, the custom was to leave the boy in the woods to find his own way home. But Philip Woods was not an Indian, and, Little Hawk thought, the path created as they had walked away from The House had been extremely confusing. The sachem's son wasn't sure that Philip was capable of finding his way home.

"If you like, you can check to see if he's being quiet and patient," El-i-chi said.

Little Hawk nodded, then moved away with the silence of a hunting cat. He unerringly found his way to the spot where Philip had been left. But Philip was not there. Little Hawk scouted around, and a hundred feet toward the south, in a direction leading directly away from The House, he found the abandoned sack. He hurried back to El-i-chi to tell him that their victim was moving in exactly the right direction to become seriously lost.

"He was not very patient," El-i-chi grumbled.

The two Seneca went in search of their lost companion. It was impossible, however, to track Philip's movements in the dark. Just to the south of the point where Little Hawk had found the bag, the shaman noticed there was a freshly broken branch.

"He moved this way," El-i-chi said.

Little Hawk laughed. "Got him, didn't we?"

"Perhaps too well," El-i-chi remarked.

They searched for three hours. They broke the silence of the forest in a very un-Indian like way, calling out Philip's name.

"It's no use," El-i-chi said when the moon was beginning to make its plunge down the western sky and there was still no sign of Philip. "We will go to The House and wait for light, and then we can track him."

"Renna will kill me," Little Hawk groaned.

"She need not know."

Renno moved silently to the library door and looked inside, where, in the circle of light from a lamp, Philip was reading, his feet propped up on a hassock. Renno smiled. He had noted the covert preparations, had watched his son carry out a small bundle of sackcloth that could only have been a bag. He nodded, pleased to know that his future son had turned the tables on the pranksters, although he did not condemn activity that was a part of Indian lore. He went to the front porch and sat there, musing, until Beth and Renna came out, finished with the day's preparations.

"Have you seen Philip?" Renna asked. "He isn't in his room."

"Is it proper for an unmarried girl to go seeking a boy in his room?" Renno asked.

"Oh, Father," Renna said.

"He went hunting with El-i-chi and Little Hawk," Renno said.

"Hunting?" Renna's eyes blazed. "What could they be hunting at night?" Then she remembered. "They didn't! They wouldn't!" She was sputtering with anger. "Which way did they go? I'll—I'll—"

"Don't you think that the man you are going to marry can find his way home from a mile deep in the woods?" Renno asked.

"Yes. No. Oh, I don't know," Renna said. "Father, he's not—"

"Like us?"

"Well, he hasn't grown up in the woods."

"Still, he is a soldier, and a soldier should be able to find his way around the forest, even at night." If El-i-chi and Little Hawk were to learn a lesson about their future relative, perhaps it would be good if Renna, too, learned to have more faith in the man she planned to marry.

Renna stood and reached for Renno's hand. "Come," she implored. "We must go after him."

Renno laughed. "And in which direction shall we begin this search?"

Fuming, Renna stood, hands on hips, looking out into the darkness. Fireflies spotted the velvet night with points of light.

"I think it's time to choose up sides and go to

bed," Renno said. "I choose you, woman." He took Beth's hand.

"Hadn't we—" Beth began, anxiety in her voice.

"No," Renno said, pulling her along. He turned at the door. "You should get some sleep, Renna."

"In a little while," Renna replied.

"She won't go to bed," Beth pointed out as Renno and she climbed the stairs. "Not until he returns."

"So," Renno said.

"It's natural for her to be worried about him."

"Yes."

"Renno," she said plaintively as he opened the door to their bedroom. "Were you in on this? Did you plot with El-i-chi and Little Hawk to play this trick on Philip?"

"They did not ask me," he said with a chuckle. "I suppose they think that I'm getting too old and dignified for such fun."

"You're terrible, all of you," Beth muttered, moving toward the door. "I'm going down to wait with Renna."

"You said that you have a long day tomorrow."

"I do."

"Then let's go to bed."

"And leave that child to fret all by herself?"

"As you please," Renno said.

For three hours Renna and Beth waited on the porch. Midnight passed. A chill breeze blew with a strong smell of rain. Lightning flashed to the southwest, coming nearer. Renna paced, Renna fumed, Renna seethed. Beth soothed, Beth ached for the girl, Beth worried.

"He'll be caught in the storm," Renna moaned.

"He'll be all right."

"I'm going to kill them for leaving him alone out there!"

"Would you like another cup of tea, dear?"

"No."

After Beth had gone to join Renna, Renno crept downstairs to the library. Philip leaped to his feet on seeing him.

"Sit," Renno said quietly, his eyes glittering. "I take it you have hunted snipes before."

"No, as a matter of fact," Philip replied with a wide grin. "It's just that I don't like being left in the woods alone to hold the bag on a dark night. Whether or not there is such a bird as the snipe doesn't matter."

"So," Renno said, smiling. "There is such a bird. He's also called the woodcock."

"But he is not hunted in darkness with an opened bag."

"No."

Philip chuckled. "Your brother should not have told me the joke about the mileormore bird first."

"Come," Renno said. "It is time we both went to bed."

"I think I should wait."

"You will have a long wait. Best that you sleep."

"As you wish," Philip agreed, for there was a feeling of being at ease with Renno that he had not experienced before.

Two figures came trotting across the expanse of the front garden. Renna ran to the stairs, then halted when she saw that El-i-chi and Little Hawk were alone.

"Where is he?" she demanded. The line of thunderstorms was moving closer. Thunder rumbled in the distance.

"Don't worry, Sister," Little Hawk said, although he sounded concerned.

"You've left him out there alone," Renna accused. She moved to put her hands on Little Hawk's chest. "No, don't go inside. Go back and find him."

"We can't track him in the dark," Little Hawk protested.

"He's lost!" Renna cried. "Oh, by the manitous, what have you done?"

"We will find him," El-i-chi promised. "When it is light."

"You're not going to leave him out there all night," Renna said, bursting into tears. "You can't. Beth, please go get my father. Tell him—"

"There's no need to disturb our father," Little Hawk said. He sighed and glanced briefly at El-i-chi. "Look, Renna, I'll go back. I'll find him. Will that please you?"

"It would have pleased me if you had not played your childish tricks in the first place," she retorted. "Are you going, or do I have to call my father and tell him that you've lost my—my—" She didn't know exactly what to call him.

"I'm going," Little Hawk said with resignation.

"I will come with you," El-i-chi offered. "Better to brave the thunderstorm than the tears of a woman."

And so it was that the shaman of the Seneca, with his junior-warrior nephew, spent the remainder of the night in the woods in a torrential thunderstorm. Lightning struck several times at the height of the storm, once not more than a quarter of a mile from them. Thunder rolled continuously as the rain sheeted down. Hail mixed with the rain at times, and the temperature dropped so precipitously that the bare-chested warriors were chilled and thoroughly uncomfortable.

Renna and Beth had fallen asleep in chairs in the parlor. They were still sleeping when Renno knocked on Philip's door. The two men were at breakfast when Renna entered the dining room, rubbing sleep from her eyes, her silvery hair mussed, her dress wrinkled.

"Oh, Philip!" she cried, rushing to kneel beside his chair and putting her arms around him.

"If I am to be greeted with such fervor each morning after we're married—"

"You're back!" she cried. "How?" She pulled away. "You're not wet."

"No. My mother taught me to come in out of the rain whenever possible," Philip said mildly.

Renna rose to her feet. "Who found you? Where are El-i-chi and Little Hawk?"

"The lieutenant had no need of being found," Renno said after swallowing a bite of buttered biscuit with honey. "But we might have to send a rescue party after your brother and your uncle." He caught Philip's eye and winked.

Philip winked back.

"You knew?" Renna sputtered.

"The lad is modest," Renno said with a chuckle. "I found him relaxing in the library quite early last night."

Renna's eyes flared. "You knew he was safe, but you let me worry all night?"

"My daughter," Renno said, "it was not I who let you worry. You made that choice yourself. It was not I who feared that Philip could not find his way home."

Renna's face relaxed into a rueful smile. "I think, Sachem, that I have just been given another lesson." She turned to Philip. "Forgive me for having so little faith in you."

"Of course," Philip said.

There was only one more point left for Renno to make. When Beth came in, looking as bedraggled as Renna, the white Indian smiled up at her. "Good morning," he said brightly. "I trust you slept well."

Beth soon realized that she was being teased. Renno was not a man to be so blatant as to say "I told you so," but he was making his point, for there was Philip, looking chipper and rested.

"*I* slept well. Didn't you, Philip?" Renno asked.

"Oh, quite well, thank you, sir," Philip replied.

"I think, Beth, that the sachem is trying to tell us something," Renna said.

"I think he has already done so," Beth said. She turned to her husband and bowed low, her flame-colored hair falling in a cascade. "I hear and understand your message, good sir. You did indeed advise me to join you in having that good night of sleep. I have only this to say to you, sir: may the fleas of a thousand camels inhabit your breechclout."

Rain had washed away all traces of Philip's passage home, but even if it had not, El-i-chi and Little Hawk were not searching near Renno's abode. Instead, they covered approximately five square miles of forest before returning to The House to get help to continue the search. When they rounded the corner coming up from the south, they saw a family grouping around a lunch table in the summerhouse. Philip Woods sat to Renno's right, engaged in conversation with the sachem. Little Hawk halted in midstride. "By the manitous," he breathed, "he is back."

Little Hawk watched as Renno nudged Philip and pointed toward the bedraggled pair.

"Gentlemen," Philip called out merrily, "you're back just in time for lunch. Did you have a good hunt?"

El-i-chi shrugged and grinned. He took Little Hawk's arm and led him to the steps of the summerhouse, then bowed from the waist toward Philip.

"He got you, eh?" Renno asked.

"Fair and truly," El-i-chi surrendered with a rueful smile.

Thus a barrier between a father and the suitor of his daughter had been breached. For the next few days no men were underfoot as Beth and Renna completed their preparations, for the prospective father-by-marriage and his son-to-be were out and away, over a line of ridges, eating rabbit roasted over an open fire, exchanging bits of knowledge, and seeing what was over the next hill.

The guests invited by Renno were the first to arrive. They did not expect to be put up in The House, nor would they have wanted to be. They slept in the longhouses of the Seneca village or made their camps on the outskirts of Rusog's village. Guests would still be arriving on the day of the ceremony, for runners had gone out to distant towns and villages telling of the time of joy for the family of the sachem Renno, which included his brother the principal Cherokee chief, Rusog.

Beth was not the only female relative who was kept busy. Toshabe called on the aid of other matrons of the Seneca to make welcome the numerous and lesser village chiefs of the Cherokee, many of whom had fought with Renno and Rusog against the Chickasaw so long before. Special welcomes were given to those few Seneca who had moved farther west to live among the Cherokee.

At night the fires flickered in the villages, and young and old gathered round for the dancing, singing, oratory, and story telling. Drums enlivened the darkness, frightening away the usual whippoorwills and owls to whom nighttime serenading was customarily left.

Toshabe appeared at The House—a rare occurrence—for her own fitting for the gown she made for Renna. The garment was a bleached deerskin dress decorated with fringes and beadwork. To be worn with the dress was a tiaralike *a-te-non-wa-ran-hak-ta,* beaded with traditional Seneca designs. Because Toshabe was not to be denied the right to see her granddaughter's union blessed by Seneca custom and by the tribe's shaman, there was to be more than one wedding ceremony.

Among those who would occupy the guest accommodations in The House, eventually to drive Philip out of his room to sleep with Little Hawk in Renno's longhouse in the village, was the governor of Tennessee, John Sevier. An old Indian fighter and the most successful politician to be produced to that date in the Southwest, he arrived a day early, asking Renno to arrange a meeting with Chief Rusog.

Renno had known John Sevier for years, and he respected Sevier as a fighting man. But he did not admire Sevier's attitude toward the Indian. "Governor," he said, "may I ask, sir, why you want to make council with my brother Rusog?"

"That's business between Chief Rusog and the state of Tennessee, Sachem," Sevier responded.

"Then that business can only be another demand against Cherokee lands," Renno said grimly. "I once heard a Tennessee politician say that whenever the state wanted more land, it merely called upon the Indian to write a new treaty. I think, sir, that we have had treaties enough, and I ask that you not intrude upon the joy of this occasion by asking my Cherokee brothers to give up any more."

For a moment Sevier bloomed red with anger, then he laughed. "By God," he said, "I have been told that you speak your mind, Renno. Now I believe." He raised his hand placatingly. "I think the politician to whom

you refer was our mutual friend William Blount, God rest
his soul."

"Yes," Renno said. "But I had not heard of his death."

"Died in March," Sevier said. "Well, I see your point,
Sachem. No treaty talk. But since you're not going to let
me discuss business, you'd better have some good sippin'
whiskey on hand."

Renno just happened to have some, supplied by an
authority on the subject, Roy Johnson.

Andrew Jackson arrived, and talk buzzed among the
other citizens of Tennessee because he had brought his
Rachel with him. Mrs. Jackson rarely appeared in public.
Beth went to her immediately and made her welcome.

Stiffly uniformed army officers came from the United
States Army headquarters in Tennessee. Sergeant Samuel
Lemon came from Tellico Bloc House and quickly joined
the egalitarian governor and the judge of the Superior
Court in sampling the sipping whiskey.

To Roy's immense pleasure, Renno had asked him to
assist in giving the bride away. Roy had gone all out,
buying a new evening suit at the general store in Knoxville. He looked younger than his almost sixty years as he
stood beside Renno and, on cue, said his one line in the
performance that would be the talk of the territory and the
state for months to come.

"And who gives this woman?" intoned the Baptist
minister who had been brought out from Knoxville.

"We do," said Renno and Roy together. They then
took one step backward, the symbolic step that removed
Renno as the prime male figure in his daughter's life in
favor of the slim young man who was so handsome in his
dress uniform.

It was, the guests marveled among themselves, the
"gad-damnedest, rootin'-tootinest, fancified peach of a wedding" that had ever been seen in North America, since the
one putting on the show was a "British Her Ladyship," no
less.

Half the political wheelhorses from Nashville dressed
up like popinjays, and their ladies were so prettified, they
were not even recognized by their dearest friends. The

men enjoyed a couple of barrels of the best sipping whiskey they had ever tasted, while the women eyed the Indians in native dress—or half dress—and gawked at the "dag-blamedest barn" of a house and gardens they ever saw.

And that wasn't the half of it. The guests couldn't stop talking about "that purty little girl all dressed in white, standing beside a boy in army uniform, looking so con-sarned sweet together, it made you wanta bawl your eyes out."

The guests were also impressed by Beth, "that there English Her Ladyship, *whoooooeee*. Great Gawd A-mighty, she was dressed like a queen and cryin' as that purty little girl said 'I do' jest as if Renna was her'n and not jest her stepdaughter."

After the ceremony, dinner was set out on a dozen tables on the side meadow. As the sun dipped in the west, drums began to sound, and Cherokee and Seneca warriors in full regalia and ceremonial paint performed ritual dances and chants. Renna, now dressed in the traditional snow-white deerskin outfit and feathered headdress that Toshabe had made, emerged from The House to be united with Philip according to the customs of the Seneca. The bride-groom looked a bit dazed from all the singing and dancing. El-i-chi led the chanting.

To the awe of the assemblage gathered beneath the clear, dark blue sky with the full moon just overhead, a bolt of lightning hit a pine tree at the edge of the village just as the shaman put his hands on the heads of the boy and girl and joined them.

Doubly married, Renna and Philip were given the privacy of a suite of rooms in the south wing of The House. With the morning they appeared, looking just a trifle sheepish, for a huge breakfast on the grounds. After the morning's repast, the Tennessee guests began to leave in small groups. Throughout the day Renno, Rusog, and El-i-chi were exchanging flowery farewells with the visiting village chiefs.

During that busy, festive time only Toshabe was uneasy about the strike of lightning at the closing of the Seneca marriage ceremony. She interpreted the freakish event as an omen of death, and she prayed to her own personal manitous that the ominous sign did not apply to the young newlyweds.

"If it must come, spirits," she prayed, "let it come to me, for I would not be averse to joining those who have gone before me to the Place across the River."

Chapter Five

Mrs. Philip Woods shed no tears when she and her husband left the village of her grandmother and the home of her father and stepmother. The new bride was too much in love with her husband to have room in her heart for anything hinting of melancholy. She was not ignorant of the meaning of distances. She knew that Philip's post on the Mississippi would separate her from all that was familiar to her by weeks of difficult travel, but she was the daughter of a man who did not view distances as obstacles. Many pioneer families who left, for example, eastern Virginia or a New England state for the Northwest Territory or Kentucky considered their act of separation as final as if they were traveling to China. Renna, on the other hand, fully expected to see her loved ones again. Her father and her uncle El-i-chi had made treks much more intimidating than the trip from the eastern Cherokee Nation to the Father of Waters.

In fact, Renna came from a family of travelers. Beth had done her share of exploration of the huge North

American continent, trekking with Renno to the Far West
and from Canada to New York; and Little Hawk had made
the trip from the Cherokee Nation to the North Carolina
coast and back in the company of his father. Alone, he had
journeyed from Philadelphia to the Seneca village following his difficulties in the former capital.

So, given the tendencies of the people Renna loved
most, she fully expected to see all of them—not often,
perhaps, but often enough to maintain her family contacts.

Beth's emotions were a bittersweet mixture of joy for
Renna and selfish sadness at the thought of the girl's leaving.
She had come to love her stepdaughter very much over the
years, and although she knew that a trip to visit the newlyweds was not impossible, she could feel in her heart the
vast expanse of empty wilderness that would separate them.

A Seneca junior warrior could not weep, nor did
Little Hawk have the inclination to; even though his sister
was leaving home, life does go on.

A father could weep inside and feel new doubts at
giving over his lifelong, paternal protection to a callow
youngster from the East. But Renno did not show his
emotion. He embraced Renna and gave her one last, hard
squeeze, and then he had no choice but to watch her ride
away with Philip and a small escort of men headed by
Sergeant Lemon.

And now, to Renno and Beth, The House seemed far
too large.

Summer heat combined with moisture from the south
to make sleep difficult. Renno spread a towel on his side of
the bed so as not to soak the bed linens with sweat, and he
longed to be outside, in the freshness of the open air,
where, at least, he would be able to enjoy a night breeze.
He knew, however, that Beth was missing Renna, so the
time was not right for him to seek solitude in the wilderness.

It took a wise woman, of course, to divert the sachem
and his red-haired wife from their melancholy. Toshabe
knew much about loss, having buried two husbands and
having sent her sons and her daughter off to distant and
dangerous places. Toshabe's plan was to escape the sod-

den heat of summer, and she mobilized the entire family and a few selected friends into a frenzy of packing and preparation and child gathering. The destination of the dozen or so Cherokee and Seneca families was a jewellike mountain lake with water so pure and so cool that to drink it or to swim in it was to experience instant refreshment.

Beth was, at first, unenthusiastic about going, but when she considered the alternative—sitting around the house and watching Renno perspire—she changed her mind.

Once under way toward the east with a noisy mob led by charging, gamboling, whooping young ones, Beth began to look forward to climbing the cool, wooded heights of the mountains that looked like blue smoke.

In the sweet little valley that enclosed the beautiful lake, El-i-chi, Renno, Rusog, Little Hawk, and the other men and young boys put up temporary shelters, huts with pine-branch roofing and airy, pole-supported walls. Ena's twins and the cousins Gao and Ta-na caught frisky trout that, when cooked over an open fire with a bit of traditional herb seasonings, were food fit for the manitous themselves.

Renno and Beth climbed intimidating rock faces with the youngsters, hiked the mountain trails to seek out new vistas, swam and splashed in the invigorating waters of the lake. After having matched the young ones' expenditures of seemingly inexhaustible energy, they fell into their bed each night ready to, as Beth said, "sleep the sleep of the just and pure at heart."

Renno responded wryly, "I think it is simply the sleep of those who have been led around by the nose all day by a merciless gang of young rapscallions."

Other Cherokee and a few Seneca came and went, for the lake was a popular retreat during the broiling days of July and August. Renno and Rusog, who were responsible for the welfare of others, kept in touch with conditions back at the villages by messenger and by reports from people coming and going. All was well.

* * *

For the newlyweds, the journey from The House to the Chickasaw Nation was a timeless interlude of enchantment. It was sometimes amusing—but more often slightly irritating—to Sam Lemon to see that love did indeed conquer all. Renna and Philip were totally immune to the discomforts of spending days in the saddle and nights sleeping on the ground.

Sam himself was having mixed emotions. He had been selected by the area commander to accompany Lieutenant Woods, to become part of the permanent garrison on the Mississippi. In addition to the sergeant there were four troopers, a strong enough force to give warning to isolated hunting parties of hostile Creek who might be penetrating into Cherokee and Chickasaw lands desirous of counting coup and building reputation.

Philip left the management of the travel party to Sam. Lost in the sheer luxury of fulfilled love, Philip had to reassure himself often by a touch that this wondrous, marvelous miracle of sheer femaleness was truly his.

During the day's travel Renna and Philip rode together, usually sandwiched between Sam and one or two men at the fore and the others at the rear. At night Philip would select a secluded camping spot for his bride and himself. At first Sam had objected to this, telling Philip, "Look, sir, if you and the missus sleep over there on the other side of the creek, you'll be out of my sight and almost out of earshot. If a war party comes by, they could scalp you, and I'd not even know it."

"We'll be very alert," Philip promised.

For a short time the troopers had cast sidelong glances in the direction of Renna and Philip's camping site and made ribald comments. Lemon let the behavior run its course for two or three nights, and then he said, "That's it, Trooper. That's all. We won't hear any more of such talk. Hell, two of you got wives yourselves. Now I don't care what the lieutenant and his missus are doing over there; it's their business, and I expect you to have the decency to leave it that way."

Actually, because of an innate modesty on the part of both Renna and Philip, all that the lieutenant and his missus were doing over there was hungering for each other with a frenzy of appetite that would take weeks to reduce from conflagration to a normal, youthful bonfire when they arrived at their new home. They did allow themselves the indulgence of a few torrid kisses and a quick caress, but even though they were separated from the soldiers by a hundred or more feet, they were held in check by the lack of privacy. Only once did their mutual desire overcome their reluctance to make what seemed to them to be a public display of their love, and both had dissolved into spasms of guilty giggling after swift, mutual completion.

After a week of travel, Philip began to take a greater part in planning the day, often taking the fore with Sam, leaving Renna to ride alone at the midpoint of the column. Philip was learning wilderness lore from both his wife and from Sam. Of the two, he was more impressed by Renna. When everyone first felt a yen for fresh meat, it was she who spotted a game trail crossing their line of march and led Philip to a vantage point where he potted a young buck deer. It was Renna alone who noticed the traces of passage of a small group of Indian warriors wearing moccasins. As a result, Philip and Lemon moved the group with extra caution for a time. When nothing came of the observation, it was concluded that the tracks must have belonged to a Chickasaw hunting party.

Lemon led the travelers south of Chickasaw Bluffs and explained, "No need for us to get tangled up with them Indians. They'd steal us blind while filling us up with things to eat and drink. It'd just be a waste of time."

Finally Renna laid eyes on the place that was to be her home for an unknown period of time. She was not, to say the least, thrilled. Fort Jefferson was a log palisade encircling a few mud-chinked log buildings. Clustered around the fort in motley disorder were huts and lean-tos occupied mostly by Chickasaw, Choctaw, and a few Indians from the tribes across the wide river that flowed below the high bank on which the fort sat.

The log cabin assigned to the newest officer at Fort Jefferson had for some months sat unoccupied except by spiders, wasps, flies, and a particularly belligerent rat, which lost a dispute with Philip over squatter's rights and was unceremoniously tossed into the river after being promptly dispatched with the butt of a musket.

While Renna applied herself to the sizable effort of making the cabin livable, Philip reported to his superior.

Captain Derral Talbert was a grayed, sun-dried man pushing sixty. The captain was juiceless in appearance but congenial in temperament.

"Well, you're young enough," Talbert said after Philip crisply saluted. "And just married, eh?"

"Yes, sir."

"Looking forward to meeting your wife. Understand she's Indian."

"Partly, sir."

"Mrs. Talbert will contact you, to tell you when to bring your missus to dinner." It was not an invitation; it was an order, an observance of army tradition. The new officer was always invited to dine with his commanding officer. If the commander and the officer were the only commissioned personnel on the post, the tradition was still to be served.

Fran Talbert proved to be as thin as her husband but was more lively. She twinkled with goodwill, took Renna under her motherly wing, and gave Philip strict orders regarding the care and keeping of such a pretty wife.

"What we're here for," Captain Talbert explained to both Renna and Philip at dinner, "is primarily to show the flag. As you may know, the situation downriver is uncertain, what with the rumors that Spain is giving the whole kit and kaboodle of Louisiana back to the Frenchies. Second, we're here to make this an official Indian agency, although right at the moment we ain't got no Indian agent." He grinned. "Don't really need one, I reckon. All an Indian agent is good for is to hand out government food, and the Chickasaw and Choctaw are capable of feeding themselves. We can feel grateful for that, since we have enough trouble getting rations just for the garrison. I guess the most important part of our duty is that if this feller Napoleon takes over from the Spaniards and marches up the Mississippi Valley to take Tennessee, Kentucky, and the Ohio country like he took most of Europe, we'll be here to stop him."

Talbert chuckled with satisfaction and patted Philip on the back. "Yep, son, I'll put you, Sergeant Lemon, and six men in rifle pits 'bout a mile downriver, and you can hold off ole Napoleon whilst I organize the damnedest strategic withdrawal you've ever seen."

"Derral," Mrs. Talbert reminded gently, "these nice young people don't know you well enough yet to realize that you're just joshing."

"Who's joshing?" Talbert asked disgustedly. "All I have are two officers and exactly a score of men, counting old Sam Lemon and the troopers he brought with him from Tellico Bloc House. And with twenty men and two officers I'm suppose to stop a French or Spanish attack? I couldn't even turn back a Creek attack if ole King McGillivray decides he wants to beat the French or the Spaniards to it."

"You're going to frighten this young lady," Mrs. Talbert scolded.

"No, it's all right," Renna said quietly.

"Heard this feller Tecumseh went downriver to talk to McGillivray and other chiefs," Talbert continued. "So not only are we here to stop Napoleon, we're expected to stop a full-scale alliance of all the tribes that Tecumseh can talk into following him."

"I don't think, Captain Talbert, that Tecumseh will be successful in forging a new Indian federation," Renna said. "The Indian is too independent, too much the individualist to be a good follower."

"Is that what your father thinks?" Talbert asked.

"Yes," Renna replied.

"Renna heard Tecumseh speak, you know," Philip remarked proudly. "And his brother, the one they call the Prophet."

"Is that so?" Talbert asked.

"He came to counsel with my father and my uncle Rusog of the Cherokee," Renna explained.

"And he wasn't able to talk your father and this Rusog into joining him? I understand he is quite a persuader, quite an orator, and that his brother has big medicine."

Renna laughed. "Every Indian, given the opportunity, can be a spellbinder, Captain. My father has heard some great orators, from George Washington through Little Turtle and Joseph Brant. Although my father sympathizes with Tecumseh's desire to prevent further seizure of Indian lands, he will not fight with Tecumseh. And as for the Prophet's magic, I'd match my uncle El-i-chi against him any day."

"I'm relieved to hear all that," Talbert said sincerely. "I'd like to meet your kin someday." He stood, indicating that that particular subject was closed. "Well, it's nice having you young folks here. Since there are only half-a-dozen white women here, Mrs. Woods, we've lowered the formal barriers between the enlisted ranks and officer ranks a bit. Mrs. Talbert will introduce you to the wives of the sergeants, I'm sure—"

"Of course," Mrs. Talbert said.

"—and you, Lieutenant, will work closely with Sergeant Lemon. He's the best frontier hand we have. He will know what I expect."

The captain expected a patrol to leave Fort Jefferson now and then to ride a few miles downriver, then a few miles inland, to make sure that a French or Creek army had not moved in during the dead of night.

The Indians seemed friendly—at times too friendly for Philip's taste. The progress of the patrols was often slowed as the soldiers fraternized shamelessly with Indian women. Philip consulted Sergeant Lemon about this behavior; Philip had learned a lot from his father about army life and the proper way to conduct and advance one's career, but of all the things that General Woods had told his son, one basic fact had been clear: sergeants ran the day-to-day affairs of the army, and a good sergeant was worth his weight in lieutenant's insignia.

"I'd go easy on that subject if I were you, sir," Sam Lemon advised. "We're a long way from home out here, and the men have little to divert them. Besides, we're expected to stay away from the fort for a few days."

So while Philip waited for his men to divert themselves with their Indian paramours, he had opportunity to talk to the Chickasaw elders and learn the ways of the tribe. He rationalized ignoring the fraternization as a program for future peace.

Patrolling was an occasional thing, and after a couple of months Sam Lemon was able to cut the number of patrols so that Philip had to leave the fort no more than once every fortnight.

The work load inside the fort was quite low, and Philip had a lot of time to spend with Renna. They swam in the muddy river, fought its slow but powerful current in canoes, fished and cooked and ate the boneless but delicious flesh of the ugly catfish, and explored the environs of the fort on the three landward sides. They exchanged dinners with not only the captain and his wife but with the sergeants who were married. Only three children lived in the fort, and, coincidentally, all were under six years old. One, a delightful, smiling little charmer of four years, won Renna's heart immediately and learned to tease Philip into playing horsey with her. Philip was the steed, prancing around on the rough plank floor of the log cabin with little Tess on his back.

Philip and Renna had talked of many things, having children among them. They had decided that it would be best if the Good Lord waited to give them a family. As the months passed and their love grew ever stronger, it appeared that He was cooperating with their wishes. Little Tess satisfied Renna's motherly instincts, so the desire to have her own children came to her very seldom. She was too content with her love for Philip, too pleased to be the center of his attention and the pivotal point of his life, to be desirous of any change. She felt that she would be happy to live for an eternity with Philip in the little log cabin at Fort Jefferson.

John Adams's Federalist party had called their rival Thomas Jefferson an atheistic infidel who would gladly toss the Bible into a bonfire. If Jefferson were elected to the presidency, warned the Federalists, the Democratic-Republican party would revert to mob rule and destroy the government. But now John Adams, who had wanted the office of the presidency to be given the adulation reserved for kings, was gone.

Back on 4 March 1801, Thomas Jefferson, who had been defeated four years before by John Adams and forced to spend those years in the thankless office of the vice-presidency, became the third president of the United States. Now Jefferson was starting a new administration in the new capital of the United States, a town carved out of swamp and wilderness, still not complete on Inauguration Day.

The mud in the streets of Washington was axle deep. A morass separated the new executive mansion from the unfinished Capitol Building. To show the nation that he was a man of the people, Jefferson, unlike both Washington and Adams before him, walked to the Capitol instead of riding in a coach. He grew impatient with all the inaugural pomp.

In spite of the fact that his speaking voice was thought by many to be poor, with not even a fraction of the power of conviction contained in his pen, he spoke to the Congress. He tried to soothe the wounds of the bitter campaign by offering conciliation to the defeated Federalists. He said that his main objective was to have a wise and frugal government, which gave equal and exact justice to all men. His administration would make no further attempts to interfere with the rights of the individual states of the Union. He would, he promised, seek peace, commerce, and honest friendship with all nations, but entangling alliances with none.

When he was finished, he bowed his head for a moment. He had not always seen eye to eye with his fellow Virginian George Washington, but in that solemn moment, when he had completed his first speech as president, his thoughts were with Washington. *General, I am here, as you told me I would be, and now that I am here, I understand you better. Help me to do the things that are right for our country, and I pray that the Good Lord will above all, give me the wisdom to keep this nation at peace.*

Washington had been dead since 14 December 1799, and although Thomas Jefferson may have been the only man directing what was almost a prayer to the general on that day, he was not the only one who, on occasion, sensed Washington's presence.

Thomas Jefferson began to realize that he had actually been fortunate in not being elected the nation's second president. George Washington had been larger than life, and John Adams suffered in comparison, as would have any successor. Now that the United States had seen four years of John Adams and the Federalists, the country was ready for a change and would be receptive to the Jeffersonian belief in states' rights and the separation of state and federal powers.

George Washington had had Alexander Hamilton and Jefferson as his chief advisers. Jefferson had James Madison, another Virginian, as his secretary of state and Albert Gallatin, a Swiss-born gentleman of good family who had joined Jefferson's party in the 1790s, as his secretary of the treasury.

Madison had helped Jefferson found the Democratic-Republican party. His background was impressive: he had served in the first Virginia state legislature and in the Continental Congress. He was instrumental in defeating the Virginians who opposed the state's ratification of the Constitution—men such as Patrick Henry, George Mason, James Monroe, and John Tyler. He had served in Congress from 1789 to 1797, when he retired to become a member, once more, of the Virginia legislature.

It was evident from the beginning that the two Virginians, Jefferson and Madison, would make a formidable team in determining the nation's foreign policy, but neither man expected so quick a test of the national fiber. Fewer than ninety days after taking office, President Jefferson had a war with Tripoli on his hands.

For centuries the North African states of Morocco, Tunis, Algiers, and Tripoli had spawned pirates who, with the blessings and cooperation of their rulers, preyed on shipping in the Mediterranean. Cervantes, the author of *Don Quixote*, had been a prisoner of the Barbary pirates before the first English colony was settled on the North American continent. Daniel Defoe's fictional hero Robinson Crusoe was captured by Moroccan pirates. Before attaining their independence, the American colonies, sheltered by the might of the British navy, were little affected by the North African marauders. But once the protection of the Royal Navy was lifted, ship after American ship was seized. The cargo of the vessels was sold, the crews held for ransom.

An agreement with Morocco was negotiated in 1787, but pirates of the other states, especially Algiers, continued to prey on American ships. Agreements during the Adams administration with Algiers, Tripoli, and Tunis resulted in the payment of the outrageous sum of over two million dollars in tribute before Jefferson's inaugural in 1801.

James Madison came to the executive mansion to tell the president that the pasha of Tripoli had stated that America's annual tribute of eight thousand dollars was not enough and had declared war not only on all American shipping but on the United States as a nation.

"I hardly think we can dignify this camel herder's status by honoring his declaration of war," Madison said, "but I do feel that something must be done."

"I feel," said President Thomas Jefferson, "as if I am a character in a comic opera."

Jefferson was experiencing a feeling of déjà vu. As secretary of state under Washington, he had urged that the dens of the pirates be eradicated under a crushing naval attack.

"James," Jefferson said, "only a few weeks ago, I made a promise before the assembled members of the Congress of the United States that my administration would be a force for peace. Even if I wanted to break that promise, I, as president, could not, under the Constitution, consider the United States to be at war, even though the pasha says that he is." He was silent for a while, musing.

Madison also remained quiet, respectful of his president's moments of meditation.

"However, Mr. Secretary," Jefferson said with a cold, tight smile, "I don't think it would be taken amiss if an American ship of the line should return fire when attacked. Now take the *Enterprise*. . . . Suppose she should choose to exercise her right of passage in international waters to cruise in the sea off the coast of Tripoli—"

"Yes, sir, I agree," Madison said, understanding Jefferson's intentions and also smiling. "It is my opinion that the *Enterprise* is in need of an extended cruise in Mediterranean waters for the purpose of training her crew. Would you like me to pass along your orders, Mr. President?"

"If you would be so kind, James." Jefferson sighed, looking at the mass of paperwork on his desk.

"There is another thing, Mr. President," Madison added. "As you instructed, we are keeping open all channels of information that we may have with the French republic, especially in regard to the rumored cession of Louisiana by Spain."

"And?" Jefferson asked quickly.

Madison spread his hands. "Once again, and from a different source—the ambassador of Russia in Paris—we have heard that such an agreement does indeed exist."

Jefferson sighed again.

"There is this to remember," Madison said. "There has been trouble among the Negroes in Haiti. Napoleon sent his own brother-in-law Victor Leclerc to bring the unrest under control."

"Do you feel this has some bearing on Louisiana?" Jefferson asked.

"If the continued troubles in Haiti are severe—" Madison shrugged. "Napoleon would need Haiti to safeguard his sea-lanes to Louisiana. Without ships of war stationed in the ports of St. Domingo to protect his shipping against the Royal Navy, his sea-lanes to New Orleans would be virtually useless should hostilities erupt again."

"Yes, I see," Jefferson said. "Well, I find myself in the odd position of crying for peace, while at the same time wishing for a lack of peace in an island not far from our shores."

After Madison had left, Jefferson sat alone, resting his chin on his hand. He had promised governmental economy —the United States was still in debt from the War for Independence. He had often stated his opposition to war and entanglements with foreign governments. He felt very disturbed that so early in his administration events were demanding expenditures for building the tools of war— specifically for warships to protect American trade in the Mediterranean. And if France moved into Louisiana, a new and powerful army would be needed to guard the borders with Florida and Louisiana and to ensure that the Mississippi remained open to American trade.

Ah, well, the world was wide and the oceans deep. There was still time before anything needed to be done. In spite of the pasha of Tripoli's declaration of war, not much had changed along the Barbary Coast. Even with the payment of tribute, American ships had been at risk before, and they were still at risk. Jefferson decided to keep a close eye on the political situation in the French colony in Haiti. Any large-scale movement of French warships into the Western Hemisphere could not take place without some warning. He had time to concentrate on his domestic policies in consultation with the secretary of the treasury, Albert Gallatin.

In accordance with the president's decision, the *Enterprise* was sent to cruise off the coast of Tripoli, with orders to return fire when attacked.

And when *Enterprise* allowed the Tripolitan ship of war *Tripoli* to come near enough to mount an attack on what the pirates guessed wrongly was an unarmed merchant ship, *Enterprise* proceeded—much to the satisfaction of President Thomas Jefferson when the news finally made its slow way back to Washington—to outsail, outshoot, and outfight the *Tripoli* until the pirate ship was a smoking ruin running up the white flag of surrender. Then, because the United States did not consider itself to be at war with a camel-herding despot of the North African desert, the surprising Americans told the battered *Tripoli* to go forth and sin no more, freeing her and her blooded crew.

In a small and cozy room on the south side of The House, Renno and Beth sat before a blazing fire—old folks at home, just the two of them. Beth was snug in woolens, and Renno had a colorful blanket around his shoulders. Little Hawk, his father's son, was away and gone over the nearest ridge, hunting alone. Letters from Renna arrived at regular intervals via military messenger. Soon it would be time for the main Seneca festival at the time of the new beginning.

Another year of peace and contentment for Renno had passed. The corn crop had been very good. Game was plentiful. For a change the state of Tennessee was not agitating for a new Indian treaty, meaning that at least temporarily, no demands were being made for more Cherokee lands.

Renno's youngest son, Ta-na, and his cousin Gao were showing signs of intelligence, taking to Beth's teaching with less and less opposition. The family enjoyed good health. The winter fevers had, so far, spared the entire village.

Because it was so easy and so gratifying to live with a woman he loved and who loved him without demands or questions, Renno hadn't been on a long hunt since the previous winter.

"That is as it should be," Toshabe had told him when he had laughingly claimed to be acting more white than Indian. "Let the younger ones caper about in the snow and rain."

Beth, like Renno, was content. She missed William, her brother, and her sister-in-law, Estrela. She wondered how much her brother and sister-in-law's brood had grown, for William and Estrela seemed intent on making sure that England had no shortage of Huntingtons for the next few generations. Now and then she received communications from England and from North Carolina, often in the form of bank statements showing that her shipping enterprise was being well managed by Adan Bartolome and Moses Tarpley.

Beth had recently purchased a herd of beef cattle, and this, too, had shown a profit, even with having traded several head to the Seneca and Cherokee in exchange for corn and other produce. Men came from all over the area to pit their fastest horses against Beth's imported English thoroughbreds, and several times a considerable amount of gold had been placed in Beth's hand in exchange for a colt or a filly.

One small cloud lurked in Beth's skies. It was a tiny cloud, insignificant at most times, but on winter evenings when she and Renno sat, having finished a last cup of tea but not quite ready for bed, it was a cloud nonetheless. Beth was thirty-five years old, coming to the end of normal childbearing years, and she had not given Renno a child. When the house was empty except for the two of them and the servants, she wondered how it would be to hear tiny feet running, to have a sweet, childish voice calling her Mother. She was not barren for lack of opportunity to conceive, so the fact that parenthood apparently was not to be made her sad.

She was indulging in her one form of self-pity on that cold, January evening after dinner when large, not tiny, feet made sounds in the hallway outside, and after a knock, Roy Johnson entered the room. His hat and coat had a dusting of snow. He brushed it off on the wide, pine floor planks, stomped his boots, stepped onto the area rug, and put his backside to the fire with a sigh of anticipation.

"Too late for supper," he said. "Just in time for bed."

"Good timing, Roy," Renno said, rising to clasp the man's hands. He was pleased as always to see his ex-father-by-marriage.

"Well, it's your fault I've been riding in a snowstorm since six o'clock this morning," Roy accused.

Renno grinned. "I don't recall standing behind you with a gun saying, 'All right, Roy, you have to ride out in a snowstorm.' "

"No, but this did," Roy said, pulling a much-handled

envelope from his inside coat pocket. "If you didn't get letters from presidents of the United States, I might be able to keep my rheumatism under control by staying in my cabin in front of a fire, like some folks I know seem to do."

Renno took the letter and bent to the light of an oil lamp.

"What is it?" Beth asked impatiently.

"It's from Thomas Jefferson," Roy said.

"Renno . . ." Beth wailed in curiosity.

"It concerns Little Hawk," Renno said. He read on in silence for a time, then explained: "An academy to train officers for the United States Army is being established. Mr. Jefferson states that he wants to make the first class at the academy representative of the population of the country, and that includes Indians. Therefore he would like the Seneca boy Hawk Harper, called Little Hawk, to be his appointee to this academy."

"Well, I'll be hanged," Roy said. "Quite an honor, Renno! Quite an honor, indeed."

"He goes on to say that he personally investigated the incident that caused Little Hawk's departure from his position as Senate page in Philadelphia. He found witnesses who had seen Little Hawk pushed into the street in front of the coal wagon by the boy whom he later attacked."

"Er, never told you about that," Roy apologized. "I figured it was up to my grandson to explain what had happened."

"I will not question my son regarding the affair," Renno said.

"Quit trying to outdo each other in loyalty to Little Hawk and tell me what else the president has to say," Beth demanded.

"There is more," Renno admitted. He handed the letter to Beth. She bent toward the lamp, squinting.

"Well?" Roy asked after a few seconds.

"Be patient," Beth said.

Renno looked at Roy and shook his head. Roy said under his breath, "Uh-oh."

. Beth finished reading and looked up. Her eyes were misty.

"Beth?" Roy asked.

"Mr. Jefferson states that he agrees with what George Washington told him about Renno, that Renno believes in the ideals expressed in the Constitution of the United States. He writes that it would be of great benefit to all peoples—the people of the United States, the Seneca, and the Cherokee—to have the interests of the tribes intertwined with the interests of the larger nation."

"Sounds to me as if he's working up to something," Roy said.

"He is," Beth confirmed. "Listen. He writes: 'I am sure, Sachem, that you must have heard the rumors of a cession of Louisiana from Spain to France. And, I daresay, you have read my public statements giving my objections to such a cession. I fear greatly having the lifeline of the western part of our nation, the Mississippi, under the control of a government given to excesses—to wit, Revolutionary France. It would be of the utmost importance to the interests and security of the United States and, indeed, to those Indian nations near or fronting the Mississippi, to have early knowledge of any move by France to invest the Louisiana and Florida territories.'"

Beth looked up. "He goes on to say that he has men in Europe trying to ascertain the truth of the rumors, but he would like to have someone he can trust go to New Orleans to report any unusual activity at the mouth of the Mississippi. I quote: 'A man is needed who can blend into the American water traffic going down the Mississippi, a frontiersman who can first make his way without undue notice into the city and, once there, be able to alter his appearance and to speak the languages one encounters in Louisiana, namely French and Spanish.'"

Once again she looked up at Roy, deliberately keeping her eyes off Renno's face lest she weep. "Of course, he can think of no man more qualified than Renno."

"Well, neither can I," Roy said.

Renno walked to the window and pulled back the heavy draperies. It had stopped snowing. A full moon lighted the white-coated world into a silver, shimmering flatness studded with rounded nodules of beauty.

"Well," Roy said, "I think I'll take a look in the kitchen. If there's still a fire in the cookstove, I'll bet that I can find some food to warm up."

"There's a pot of beans," Beth said. "And cold roasted beef in the window box."

"Sounds good," Roy said. "Now you two go on about your rat killing. I'll bunk out in that room next to Little Hawk's when I get my belly full."

"If you need another blanket, take one from the blanket chest in Hawk's room," Beth said.

When Roy's footsteps had faded down the hallway, Beth walked to put her arms around Renno and press herself against his back. "When will you go?" she asked.

"Not soon," he said. "I will observe the feast of the new beginning with my people."

"Good. We'll wait until it's warm. I hate traveling when it's cold."

He turned in her arms, looked down into her face, and pecked a little kiss onto her nose. "Now wouldn't you blend in splendidly with a mob of trappers and farmers on a flatboat floating down the Mississippi?"

"I'll wear ugly men's clothing and cut off my hair," she said.

"By the manitous, Beth, I do not want to leave you," he said.

"Then don't. Take me with you."

He leaned back and looked into her eyes. In the dimness of lamplight she was so beautiful that it caused a catch in his heart. "Ah, Beth . . ." he whispered.

"I know," she said, clasping herself to him fiercely. "I know. You must feel as I feel. I can't help but be proud of you, that you are needed by the president himself. I know that what you do for the United States is important, that it's more than just your commitment to good relations between their country and ours."

It was the first time that he'd heard her even hint that she might consider herself to be a Seneca. He smiled.

"So I'm very proud of you," she added, "but I still hate the president for taking you away from me."

It was Roy who spread the word that Renno had once again been called upon by a president of the United States. Roy had always liked talking almost as well as going off on a long hunt or getting involved in small wars, so it was predictable that he would mention Thomas Jefferson's letter while enjoying one of Toshabe's meals.

El-i-chi and Ah-wa-o were the other guests, along with their boys, cousins Gao and Ta-na-wun-da. El-i-chi made no comment when Roy revealed that Renno might be leaving soon after the festival of the new beginning, but Ah-wa-o noticed that her husband stopped chewing for a moment. She knew him well and perceived that the news upset him. She touched his arm covertly and, when he looked at her, smiled. He patted her hand.

Later, when they were alone, Ah-wa-o said, "I believe, Husband, that you are entertaining thoughts of going with your brother."

"He has not yet asked me to go with him," El-i-chi responded.

The second son of Ghonkaba and Toshabe was in his midthirties, a man in his prime. Of a height to his brother, he was more wiry than Renno. Renno's strong legs and well-developed chest were the result of his love of running. El-i-chi could keep up with Renno on a forced march for a time, but on the third or fourth day of traveling at the warrior's pace, he would begin to feel the strain. It was simply a difference in muscular development. Renno, over his lifetime, had formed the chest and muscles of a runner. El-i-chi had trained his own body to respond to stimuli quickly and with burning bursts of power and activity. In a fight this quality made him a warrior much to be prized.

He was fair complected but bronzed by the sun and of late had taken to wearing his hair in the ancient Seneca manner. A sun-bleached ruff ran from forehead to nape, with his scalp shaved and tanned on either side. Never as willing to don white man's clothing as Renno, El-i-chi observed the Seneca dress customs and was, according to his mother, as set on observing the ancient ways as any doddering matron.

Having been heir to the secrets of the shaman Casno, and through Casno's teachings to the arcane knowledge of generations of Seneca shamans, El-i-chi held an important place in the life of the southern Seneca. There were those who still resented the fact that he had defied a tribal taboo and the will of the matrons to marry the girl who was his sister-by-marriage, but his willing service to the tribe, his wisdom, and his knowledge of healing and other magic arts had largely erased that one blot from his record. He was a model husband and father. He could always be depended upon to come in time of trouble, and when nursing of the sick was needed, Ah-wa-o was always willing to help.

Unlike her husband, Ah-wa-o, the Rose, was a full-blood Seneca. Her once girlish slimness had matured into womanhood with her almost thirty years, and that ripening had enhanced her beauty. She, like El-i-chi, rigidly observed the traditions of Seneca dress. She was an accomplished seamstress, even though she often worked with that most difficult of materials, deerskin. She complained that softening the hides in the old manner, by chewing them, was wearing away her teeth, but that did not stop her from keeping her family supplied with new clothing for every change of season. For warm weather she departed from Seneca traditions to the extent of condescending to use the manufactured cloth of the white man to make skirts, trousers, and shirts.

El-i-chi's family had four members: there was Gao, three-quarters Seneca, active, all boy, inseparable from Ta-na-wun-da, the son of Renno and An-da, who lived with him as a brother. El-i-chi and Ah-wa-o's boys were not as old or as large as Ena and Rusog's twins but made up for it by being twice as loud and half again as active.

As for Renno's son, there was no confusion at all in Ta-na-wun-da's mind about his place in the scheme of things. Once he told El-i-chi, "I am lucky to have two fathers. Gao has only one father and an uncle in the sachem and in Rusog. I have an uncle in Rusog, but I also have my father El-i-chi and my father Renno."

It had been an eminently successful arrangement, having the son of the dead An-da live with his cousin. The boys had been born less than one year apart. At the time of An-da's death at the hands of the evil shaman Hodano, Renno had not been in a position to care for a babe in arms, and there had been room in Ah-wa-o's heart and at her breast for the motherless little one. Now that the boys were almost nine and ten years of age, the Rose had to admit that there did not always seem to be room in the longhouse for everyone, but she loved her sons equally and fiercely. She joined with all the other relatives in being typically Indian—in short, she allowed Gao and Ta-na to do just about what they pleased.

Ah-wa-o wanted other children. It was a gift of the manitous to try to create a baby with the aid of the man she adored. Aside from that fact, she felt that it was her duty to bear another Seneca. Ah-wa-o worried, with other matrons, about the southern Seneca being slowly absorbed into the larger Cherokee tribe. But try as she might— much to El-i-chi's satisfaction—she had remained unfruitful since the birth of Gao.

"It is the curse of the Indian," Toshabe said when Ah-wa-o discussed her inability to conceive a new child. "The most frail, sickly-looking wife of a white settler pops out children as easily as a squirrel spits out burrs from a pinecone, but Indian women bear one, two, seldom more than three children."

Ah-wa-o, however, did not live with regret. Life was too good to waste time dwelling on unhappy things. She delighted in watching the antics of her sons, loved talking with Ena's blossoming daughter, We-yo, got along splendidly with Toshabe, admired Renno second only to El-i-chi himself, and was polite and friendly with Beth Huntington Harper, although she was not quite able, ever, to bridge the gap between Beth's absolute whiteness and her own identity as a Seneca.

The Rose's one fear was that like Toshabe, who had outlived two husbands, she would be left alone someday as the result of accident or war. Thus, when El-i-chi obeyed the call of the wilderness and disappeared for days on a long hunt or simply on a jaunt into the forest to consult with the manitous, a behavior he shared with Renno, she worried.

And when she heard Roy Johnson say that Renno would be going on a long trip, down the Father of Waters all the way to New Orleans, her heart fluttered and sank.

Now, alone with El-i-chi, she heard the flat, neutral tone of his voice and reached out to him. "He has only recently received the letter," she soothed. "You know that Renno will not make a major decision without consulting you."

In that, Ah-wa-o was proved right. . . .

On a chill morning Renno, dressed for the hunt, entered his brother's longhouse. Gao and Ta-na leaped to greet him, and he lifted both boys in his arms, exclaiming at their weight. "Soon you two will be so tall," he said, "you will have to stoop as you go in and out the doorway."

"Before that," Ah-wa-o said, "they will probably have made a new door through the very wall."

"You're going hunting," Ta-na said. "May Gao and I go with you?"

"This is a hunt for men," Renno replied, lowering the boys to the floor. "For brothers who need to talk with each other while supplying fresh meat for three households."

"Uncle, you always say that *this* is for men, that *that* is for men," Gao protested. "Look at us."

Renno looked: their heads came almost to his shoulders.

"Soon we will be as tall as you and my father El-i-chi," Ta-na said.

"When you are," Renno told him, "then we will talk of your joining the hunt."

El-i-chi dressed warmly, took down his musket, and checked the powder horn and shot bag. Renno, with his longbow on his shoulder and his musket leaning against the wall beside the door, was traveling light, too. El-i-chi spoke soft words to Ah-wa-o, tousled the hair of his boys, and followed Renno into the bright, frigid morning.

Renno set the warrior's pace, that ground-covering lope that was more than a walk but less than running. Soon his blood was pumping, so he removed his outer coat of deerskin and tied it around his waist. He slowed to a walk when El-i-chi and he had left the villages behind.

Toward day's end the brothers stopped. El-i-chi took the opportunity to bag a wild turkey, cleanly removing its head with one shot. He waited while the bird flopped out reflexive life, then he cleaned it and put the meat to cooking over a fire built in the shelter of a rock overhang. Meanwhile Renno set about making the place comfortable for the night.

Soon each of them was gnawing on a juicy turkey leg and corn cakes that had been carried in their pouches. The sun had gone into hiding behind a rising bank of clouds to the west. A fitful wind stirred the fire and whined through the piled branches that made the shelter under the overhang cozy.

"Our mother said yesterday," El-i-chi remarked, "that her bones ached, that it would snow."

"Our mother and her old bones are not always right," Renno said.

"This time she is."

"This is the judgment of the shaman, that it will snow?"

"It is my judgment."

"From your bones?"

El-i-chi grunted.

Idle talk . . . a good feeling. They had traveled far together. They had stood side by side and back-to-back in battle. They shared the responsibility of the welfare of the southern Seneca as sachem and shaman. They were more than brothers; they were friends.

"If it is to snow," Renno said, "I have little desire to spend the night here."

"Is my brother getting old?"

"Only two years older than his brother."

"And yet—a little snow would send my brother home to his fireside?"

Renno laughed. "As a matter of fact, we could talk

just as well over a cup of hot cider in front of a fire-place."

But neither moved. They tossed the bare bones of the turkey legs out of the cozy little shelter. Renno added wood to the fire and pulled his deerskin robe close about him.

"It is said that you have been called once more by the president," El-i-chi said.

Renno nodded.

El-i-chi lay back, covered himself, and luxuriated in the warmth of the fire. Long minutes passed before Renno spoke. In the meantime the wind had died, and the day had become darker as lowering blue clouds moved east-ward. A single snowflake drifted down, down, and fell to the ground just outside the makeshift shelter.

"There is no other man that I would rather have at my side," Renno said.

"So," El-i-chi grunted.

"And yet," Renno said, "we have left our people too many times in the past."

"Somehow," El-i-chi said, "they survived."

"I ask you to stay this time," Renno said. "I ask you, perhaps, to ease my conscience, but I do ask."

"Then the matter is settled," El-i-chi said. "I will do the sachem's bidding."

Renno put his hand on El-i-chi's shoulder and squeezed.

After a long silence the shaman said, "When you return from this pleasure trip, perhaps I will take Ah-wa-o to bathe in the hot springs of the Quapaw. We might stay a year, two—"

Renno laughed. "And without complaint I will accept the punishment of having my brother gone from me."

"By the manitous, Renno," El-i-chi said, "I would like to go with you."

"I know."

"We've had some interesting travels, haven't we?"

"Indeed. And, the spirits willing, there will be more."

"There are times," El-i-chi said, "when I wish that I had not been chosen by old Casno to succeed him. To be free of responsibility must be a comfortable feeling."

"One of which you would soon tire," Renno pointed out, "especially if you had to take the advice of another man who was shaman, or if you did not have a sympathetic sachem who understood you."

"Ha!" El-i-chi retorted. "My sachem is so sympathetic that he leaves me to do his work, to see to his responsibilities while he goes on a boat ride down the Mississippi." He sat up and looked into Renno's eyes. "Be careful, Brother."

"I will have the young hawk to watch my back trail," Renno said.

"He has become a warrior capable of trust."

"So," Renno said, touched by his brother's praise for his son.

"As will our other sons," El-i-chi said. "They would fight to the death against anyone who threatens one or the other. Yet they compete so fiercely between themselves that if will and effort count for anything, they will become great warriors."

"I pray that the manitous will be kind to them."

The snow had begun to drift down. The wind had died away, and the air seemed warmer. The two brothers gathered enough firewood to last until morning, ate the breast of the wild turkey, and talked of many things into the night. By word and memory they traveled back in time to the snowy winters of their youth in the Lake Region, the place of their birth, and traveled through time with their grandfather, blue-eyed Ja-gonh, and with their father, Ghonkaba, son of white Ja-gonh and the beautiful half-Seneca, half-Biloxi Ah-wen-ga.

Their lives had been eventful, full of war and danger with times of family togetherness and periods of separation, interludes of love, and episodes of tragedy—the murder of Ghonkaba, their father, and Ha-ace, their stepfather; the death of Renno's wives, Emily and An-da; the loss of El-i-chi's first love, the wild Chickasaw maiden Holani. But in spite of the sadness, shining moments stood out in their reminiscing. They spoke of Emily and how she had worried when Little Hawk, her firstborn, was exposed to the life-giving waters in the dead of winter. They remembered moments of laughter and pride, joy and anguish. They had always stood together, brothers against all challenges.

When, at last, they slept, with the fire banked and deerskin robes pulled up to their noses, the snow continued to fall, isolating them in the little nook under the rocky overhang.

Once, Renno awoke to the mournful howl of a wolf. "Eat well," he whispered to the animal, "and then find a place of warmth with your mate."

He was startled when El-i-chi said, "Had I the sense of that wolf, I would be in a place of warmth with my mate."

"You heard him, too?"

"He has killed," El-i-chi said. "And now he calls the pack to share his meat."

"So," Renno said. He was not expressing doubt, for his brother had an uncanny knowledge of the lives and habits of the creatures of the forest. "It is good to share. May we always share the love and respect that has been ours."

"By the manitous, I swear that we will," El-i-chi vowed. Then, after Renno had rearranged his skins and had closed his eyes, El-i-chi added, "Even if my brother does leave me behind when he goes off on his pleasure trips."

Chapter Six

It was as if the city of La Nouvelle Orléans had been made for Melisande. After spending a few weeks in Louisiana she told Othon Hugues that Jean Baptiste le Moyne must have had her in mind when he founded the city in 1718. Whereas Othon deplored the ocean-moist, enervating, subtropical heat, Melisande found it intoxicating. Othon scorned the noisy, often odorous subpopulation group made up of black-skinned slaves and ex-slaves; he had even less regard for the slaves' mixed-blood descendants, be they the Creole half-French or the high yellows whose blood flowed with only a hint of black. Melisande, on the other hand, found the Negroes to be creatures of charming simplicity, possessed of a naïveté that made them easily impressionable and, thus, potentially useful to a woman of her talents and inclinations. Furthermore, she admired the beauty of certain of the Creole women and marked them in her memory for possible future use.

Melisande, the self-named Witch of the Pyrenean Woods, liked the New Orleans climate for other reasons, which she had told no one, not even the man to whom she regularly transferred her own strength through the warm milk of her breasts. She had been born cold. She had been ejected unwanted and fatherless from the womb of a squatting, consumptive peasant girl onto half-frozen, dung-tainted straw in a horse stall in the stables of a wealthy farmer. This was not far from the country estate where Othon Hugues had been given the same worldly standing, bastardy. There in the cold, rough, filthy straw, drenched with the fluids of birthing, she had been left to die.

Although Mélisande could envision the events of that long-ago night in January, she knew that she could not possibly remember her birth. She had, however, been cold ever since . . . until a French ship sailed into the tropics south of the Florida peninsula into the balmy Gulf of Mexico, then north to the Isle of Orleans and the old city.

At the time of Melisande and Othon's arrival in the New World, French people were in the minority in New Orleans. That did not displease Melisande, for as much as she disliked being cold, she hated France much more. That country had produced the conditions that left her teenage mother to squat and strain all alone in a stable to be rid of what she, in her childish unconcern, considered to be nothing more than a momentary nuisance. Melisande did not hate all French people—just all the Frenchwomen she'd ever seen and every Frenchman seen or unseen, with the exception of Othon Hugues.

A Frenchwoman had left her to die in a stable. The Frenchman who had picked her up from the cold straw of that stable, wiped her off with a cloth used for rubbing down the horses, and carried her home to his vicious, ignorant wife had saved her life for two reasons, neither of them humanitarian in nature. First, the Frenchman, whose wife's own womb had always been barren, wanted a young girl upon whom to vent his perverted sexuality with impunity—and without the necessity of having to murder the victim and witness to his perversion, as he had done more than once in the past. Second, since he was giving

the bastard child a home, clothing of a sort, and perfectly
good food that could just as well have been enjoyed by his
hunting hounds, the girl could do a bit of helping around
the house . . . when he was not helping himself to her.
Melisande found no ally in the man's wife. The Frenchwoman
who had reared her to the age of ten had beaten her with
regularity, needing only the excuse that the girl had allowed herself to come within reach.

Melisande could never forget the horror of her childhood. She remembered having prayed fervently and often. The man who styled himself publicly as her father
paid allegiance to God with Sunday visits to the church
and nightly readings from the Bible. She had started praying
to that same God when she was quite young. She had not
known exactly how to pray then, so she directed questions
toward the invisible but omnipotent God of the French.
Although she had no way of knowing that the fate of every
girl was not as horrendous as her own, she nevertheless
had questions about life and suffering. She had nothing to
which to compare her life of unending work, undeserved
beatings, and the almost nightly slaverings and pawings
and probings of her "father," but somehow they did not
seem right—her drudgery, pain, and humiliation.

So she prayed questions to God on High, but her
answer came from Earth below, from her father. Ah, how
she had screamed, with only a cuff of his big hand as a
reward for her effort, when he forced her into womanhood
with pain such as she had never experienced in the worst
beatings. That pain was God's answer. She cursed Him,
that merciless God. She turned her eyes down and away
from the heaven in which, no doubt, her pious father
would be rewarded with dozens of little girls, since heaven
seemed to be a place where a good Christian would have
his fondest desires fulfilled.

She knew that there was another being, one who had
been cast from heaven into the abysmal depths to rule
over the most miserable of failed humanity. Could anyone
be more wretched than she? Perhaps one who knew rejec-
tion as she knew it, one who was the whipping boy of the
All-Powerful, would feel sympathy for her.

The voice of the entity she would ultimately claim as her own was a faint, frail voice, and at first she received no more satisfaction than when she'd prayed to the God above. But as she approached ten years of age and was performing the nighttime wifely duties for the man she was forced to call father, as the beatings became ever more brutal and the sexual demands ever more demeaning, she finally heard the call of her master and heard his instructions.

On a cold night in winter when icicles hung from the eaves, she was instructed by the voice to place her mouth on the neck of her father. She did as she was told, even though she feared that the gesture would waken him and be misinterpreted as invitation on her part.

Bite. Bite. The word repeated in her mind and echoed throughout her consciousness. Although she was frightened, she opened her lips and, inside her mouth, felt the pounding of her father's heartbeat in the large vein on the side of his neck. She positioned her teeth.

Bite. Bite. Bite.

He tried to jerk away. The woman who had never asked to be called mother was a sound sleeper and would not intervene. But Melisande feared that her tormentor would free himself, for she could not bite through his salty-tasting, tough skin.

You are a predator of the forest. Your teeth are as sharp as knives.

She ground her teeth together and felt a gush of something warm and sticky. She heard a hoarse scream and scrambled away as he thrashed on the bed and leaped to his feet. Moonlight reflecting off the snow outside illuminated the dark fluid pumping from his neck. He managed to open the door. He fell as blood continued to pump weakly from his neck.

Now you must leave this place.

She gathered her few items of clothing; she had nothing else to call her own. She took food from the pantry and carefully wrapped matches in oiled paper, then canvas so that wherever she went she could have fire. The blankets on her own bed were wet with her father's blood, so she stole the coverings from his mattress. From the shed outside she selected an ax. A bit of food, the ax, a few ragged items of clothing, two blankets, were all she could carry.

She knew that she would have to be far away by morning, so although she was cold and would have preferred finding shelter, she walked the road that led to the mountains. Clouds covered the rising sun, and snow came to obliterate her footprints.

I have prepared this place for you.

It was a woodman's hut far back in the dense forest. Winds mourned over the rotting roof and whistled through chinks in the rudely built walls. A fire in the rock fireplace gave her only a semblance of warmth.

Melisande had been in the hut for several days and had eaten all the food she'd stolen before she found the broken shard of mirror. She saw in it a young girl with sunken eyes, dark, tangled hair, and skin made red by the cold.

"My, aren't you the pretty one," she said, her voice sounding oddly loud in the small, chill room.

My pretty one.

She giggled nervously, certain that she was going crazy, hearing voices. She smiled, then screamed, for her teeth showed not white but iridescent black. She dropped the shard of mirror, but it didn't break. In a moment she gathered the courage to pick it up and show her teeth, not in a smile but in a grimace. They gleamed at her as black as coal but with a polished surface that reflected the light coming in the window.

"Why?" she asked aloud.

To show that you are mine.

"Who are you?"

You already know.

"Yes," she admitted. "If I am yours and if the burning fires await me for what I have done, then I ask more than this from you, more than being cold and hungry."

Be patient. Remain alert.

She heard a noise from outside and ran to look. A pig was walking gingerly toward the hut, its hooves breaking through the crust on the snow. She picked up her ax and ran outside to kill the pig. Soon she had meat to be cooked over the coals in the fireplace.

On the outskirts of the forest, the voice revealed, was a farm. She could sneak into the barn and fill a pail with milk from an uncomplaining cow without waking the farmer. In this way she survived. Often hungry, always cold, she lived through the winter.

With the coming of spring she was shown a source of income. She sold her sexual favors to the occasional traveler, usually a man of the mountains, rough, vigorous in his need, and poor. Her pay was meager. But always she was drawing closer to her master, learning from his small voice. Her master gave her a gift: no man could look into her dark eyes and retain his own will when she wanted to rule his thoughts.

Before the end of that first summer, she no longer had to satisfy the animal desires of the men who passed by her hut. When they looked into her dark eyes, she opened the doorway to their will, and the men believed that what had not happened had happened, and with an intensity that they would proudly remember for years. Untouched, she would extend her hand and be given more money than originally agreed upon.

Other supernatural gifts became hers, and the people who lived in the isolated cottages of the mountains and the foothills came to Melisande to hear her predictions. She saw all, but no one wanted to pay good money to be told that death or catastrophe awaited him. She learned quickly to relate only those things that people wanted to hear.

She saw the future only for others, never for herself. This led her to believe that her master was doing for her what she did for her clients—shielding her from the knowledge of something not at all pleasant that would come to her.

Patience, he urged when she complained that her lot was hard. It was still cold in the mountain hut, and even though her soul probably wasn't worth much, it was the only soul she had and surely worth more than what had been given her.

Tomorrow, he said at last, and on the morrow she found ten-year-old Othon Hugues in the forest. She was

twenty and had been known as Melisande, Witch of the
Woods, for a decade. She had never experienced love or
sexual desire.

Here is your future, she was told when she was led to
the weeping boy.

She knelt beside the boy, bared her breasts, and
pressed his face against her warmth. Tempestuous emotions left her feeling faint as a breathtaking need burned in
her. The voice said, *This boy is your future.* Maternal love
momentarily submerged her fiery passion as her breasts
miraculously filled. The boy's pathetic sobbing ceased as
he greedily drank her substance.

The master, looking on with prurient pleasure, laughed
aloud, but only Melisande heard. She smiled, for his
sardonic vision became clear to her: with the boy suckling
at her breasts as she sat on the floor of the forest, a
misshapen halo surrounded the pair; they had become a
caricature of Madonna and Son.

He drank long and eagerly from her bosom.

"Love me," he begged.

"Yes."

She took his virginity with a mixture of near-violent
sensuality and desire that stunned her, for she had never
experienced such emotions.

"God has answered my prayers," he said, resting his
face on her full and rounded breasts.

She hit him in the face with her hand. "The God of
the French had nothing to do with it," she told him
in a fierce, hissing voice. "I will help you to know our
master."

When Othon first came into her life, the Witch of the
Woods was a gaunt scarecrow of a woman. In the summer-
time she bathed, but not too often, in the stream near her
hut. Dirt was encrusted under her nails and in the folds of
her skinny neck. Her black hair was sticky with perspiration and body oils and stiff with filth. Until her breasts had
magically filled when she bared them to press them against
Othon's face, they were small and hard.

Neither her looks nor her pungent odor bothered

Othon. As the days and weeks passed, he received from her the love that he had lost with the death of his mother. His perception of Melisande was influenced by her wish to appear comely to him, and he thought her to be the most beautiful young woman in the world. He saw his mother. He saw all the world's wondrous, vibrant, fertile femininity, and he knew that this alluring creature would satisfy all his only half-understood, boyish, erotic longings.

It took only a little time for the master to bring new richness into Othon's life. He knew glorious moments of joy and vengeance when he led a rabble of revolutionaries to a series of victories. And then he came home for that last visit with his father and half brothers.

Melisande, fleshed out, beautiful in the eyes of all men now, and made sexually adept by the teachings of her master, was waiting for him. "I have been patient," she told her master, "but I want to leave these woods."

A *bit longer*, she was told, for Othon still had to go to Paris to claim a job that would give him great pleasure, and then to Egypt and to Spain. Then and only then was the Witch of the Woods free to leave the hut where she had lived from childhood. Then and only then did she set sail with the man who was a decade her junior but looked older.

It had been she who chose their house in New Orleans, but she was guided by her master. Around her lived people who had brought dark religions with them from old Africa. These neighbors' parents had been slaves in the French and Spanish islands of the Caribbean where, especially in the rugged mountains of Haiti, the old religions had been distilled into one black, unholy belief, voodoo.

There, among the dark people who worshiped the old gods of perversity, Melisande's dominance was to undergo a surge of growth. With her irresistible hypnotic powers she quickly was acclaimed a high priestess. Othon, lover of blood, became wielder of the sacrificial knife. At first the blade found the blood of goats and chickens, and then the sacrifice did not bleat or cackle but cried with the intensity of a terrified child. This forever assured the loyalty of all those voodoo worshipers who had been led to follow the witch.

"Yes," Melisande told Othon, "this city was made for us. Here we have endless opportunity to please the master."

Melisande's following grew, and life was good for her. Her reputation as a diviner of the future penetrated into the French and Spanish upper classes, and money flowed into her possession.

Othon had found paradise on earth. The master was pleased by agony, by terror, by blood. Othon was glad to have the opportunity to please himself while satisfying the master. When Melisande lifted her congregation into readiness with arcane chants and a sensual dance that led to orgiastic frenzy, Othon, prince of darkness incarnate, sacrificed to the voodoo gods the life of one of the beautiful Creole girls marked for such a purpose by the witch. It was not, of course, accomplished quickly, nor were the youthful charms of the sacrifice sent to the gods unused. Othon saw to that.

Only one flaw marred the crimson rituals that were Othon's world. The one mis-stitched aberration from perfection took the form of Othon's superior, also appointed by Napoleon. This Frenchman was a dandy, the type whom Othon hated ardently. While Othon was the chief executioner of Paris, he had separated many dandies like his superior in New Orleans from their heads. He promised himself that one day he would do the same for the man to whom he'd been ordered to report upon his arrival.

Before leaving France Othon had spoken with Napoleon himself. "But, sir," he had asked the general, "why must I take orders from one who belongs to the old nobility?"

"Because, my friend," Napoleon had replied, "we must keep our possession of Louisiana a secret for just a little while longer. This man whom you protest knows how to deal with the fops who control the Spanish lands in America."

So it was that although Othon Hugues was a personal emissary of the first consul, in the eyes of New Orleans society he was inferior to the comte de Beaujolais, the official French representative in the city.

"I am here for a better reason than to regale Spanish gentry with tales of the Revolution," Othon coldly told the comte one night after Beaujolais has insisted that Othon accompany him to a stilted dinner party. "I will leave it to you to entertain the Spaniards. I will begin my mission."

Othon's orders included making a survey of Spanish forts on the Mississippi. Although he was sanguinely happy with the life-style that Melisande had established for them in New Orleans, he felt that it was time he remembered his duties . . . even though he could not swim and the idea of water travel unnerved him.

"You intend traveling up the Mississippi, then?" the comte asked.

"I do."

"Since I have wanted to see that mighty river," the comte said, "I will go with you."

"That will not be necessary," Othon said.

"Perhaps I might even be of some use," the count pointed out. "Some years ago I traveled in the midcontinent, in the Cherokee Nation."

Othon quickly reconsidered his negative reaction to the count's suggestion, but not because of the offer to share knowledge of the country. The Mississippi was large and long; the wilderness was wild and deep. Yes, the comte de Beaujolais was welcome to travel with him. They would leave New Orleans together, but Othon Hugues would return alone.

"You are welcome," he said, his pocked cheeks crinkling in a smile. "I shall be grateful for your company."

The comte de Beaujolais asked his subordinate about time and distances. Would the survey trip up the Father of Waters carry them as far as the relatively new state of Tennessee? He smiled and shared with Othon the warm memory of a young girl whom he had met in an odd, unexpected place—an Indian village. The comte admitted that her face, her smile, her slightly husky, totally feminine voice, and her surprising sophistication had stayed with him over the years and the thousands of miles of his travels. She had been called Renna. She would be a young woman now.

Renna smoothed her thin, lawn nightgown over her stomach. She smiled, for even as she lay on her back, there was a small, rounded bulge under the soft material where, until now, there had always been a trim, athletic flatness. She turned her head to look into Philip's eyes as his hand pressed atop hers and then caressed her stomach.

"It will be a boy," she said to her husband. "I wonder if he will have dark and curly hair like yours, or fair like mine."

"I would like it to be a girl," Philip said, "who looks exactly like you."

She turned on her side to face him. It was Sunday afternoon. Fort Jefferson was observing the Sabbath with rest and quiet. Philip and she had made love in a lazy haze of sensuality. Their passion had not cooled during the months of residence behind the log palisade of the fort.

"My love," Philip whispered, brushing his lips against her cheek and causing her to shiver, "do you ever regret coming with me across the miles of wilderness, leaving your home and your family?"

"This is my home. You are my family."

He kissed her. "But not forever." He added quickly, "Not your *home* forever, I mean. We'll go back to Pennsylvania when my tour of duty is finished. You'll like it there."

"Where you are, I will like," she said.

"You spoil me," he teased. "Your shameless flattery will swell my head and make me insufferable."

"Then I will beat you about the head and ears with a skillet until your head has deflated."

"I like your practicality," he said with a laugh, "but let's not carry it too far."

"Philip?" she asked.

"Umm?"

"Is there a pond on your farm in Pennsylvania?"

"Yes, more than one."

"And does the water freeze in the winter?"

"Yes."

"Then that is where you will teach our *son* how to skate, as we skated in Philadelphia."

"And that is where I'll skate with you, as we did in Philadelphia," he said, holding her close. "And when our *daughter* is old enough, I'll put my arm around her waist as I once did with you, and we'll go sweeping into the wind." He paused, lost in memory, and kissed Renna with passion.

"You are a hopeless glutton," she whispered as his intentions became clear.

"Shall I take that as a complaint?" he asked.

"Not if you know what's good for you," she replied, rolling to throw one long and graceful leg across him.

On Monday morning Philip was awakened by a pounding on the door just as the sun pinked the eastern sky. He moaned, staggered across the cabin, and opened the door. "Yes, I'm awake."

"Yes, sir, thank you, sir," said a young enlisted man.

"And Sergeant Lemon?"

"Up and around, sir. Breakfast in half an hour, sir."

Behind Philip, Renna got out of bed and lighted a candle. She was beginning to dress when he turned. She had donned a deerskin skirt and was pulling a Seneca shirt over her head.

"I'm sorry that we awakened you," he said.

"I was already awake. It's a beautiful morning."

"A beautiful morning to stay abed," he said, reaching for her. She skipped out of his grasp.

"Breakfast in half an hour," she said, "and I'm hungry."

"Am I to have the pleasure of your company at breakfast, then?"

"Not only at breakfast."

"Oh?"

"I've decided, since the weather is so lovely, that I'll go with you."

"Just like that?"

She looked at him, eyes wide. "I'm sorry. Must I ask the lieutenant's permission?"

"When the lieutenant is about to set off on a five- or six-day patrol, I think it might behoove the lieutenant's wife to ask if she may accompany him. Yes."

"Sir," she said, stiffening, "Mrs. Lieutenant Woods requests permission to accompany Lieutenant Woods on his patrol, sir."

He grinned, for when she stood at exaggerated attention, her youthful breasts and slightly rounded stomach made her look very, very unmilitary. "Since you ask so nicely, Mrs. Lieutenant Woods, permission is granted."

"Thank you, sir," she said briskly. "You are so kind to me, sir." She tossed her hip at him, pouted her lips, and went about preparing for the trip.

Sergeant Samuel Lemon and the four other men who would accompany Philip on the routine swing to the south were already seated when Philip and Renna entered the mess.

"As you were," Philip said quickly as Lemon started to rise to call the men to attention.

A chorus of greetings came for Mrs. Woods, and she spoke to each man in turn, using his name.

She ate like a wolf breaking a fortnight's fast. Sam Lemon took it on himself to see that her coffee cup was full and that the scrambled-egg platter was passed when she finished her first helping.

"Thank you, Sam," she said. "You know I'm eating for two these days."

"It's pretty hard not to notice, Miz Woods," Sam said.

"You want a boy or a girl, Miz Woods?" asked one of the men.

"A boy," she said.

"Heck, you'd think they's enough boys in the world," said a young man who had been at Fort Jefferson since his fifteenth birthday. The word was that he had never kissed a white girl, and he obviously thought that Renna Woods was the most beautiful woman he'd ever seen.

* * *

The patrol left the fort two hours after sunrise. Fran Talbert, wife of the commanding officer, waved and smiled at Renna as the patrol rode out. It was not the first time that Renna had accompanied Philip into the northern extent of the Choctaw Nation. Philip had, in fact, told Fran's husband that Renna was a definite asset in talking with the Indians, since she had quickly picked up the Chickasaw and Choctaw tongues and now spoke them fluently.

No one objected to Renna's going out with the patrol. The duty was not considered dangerous. Things had been very peaceful in both the Chickasaw and Choctaw nations for years. Of course, the woman was about four months pregnant, but she was extraordinarily healthy, having been reared as an Indian. Indian women went about their business up to the day of giving birth, popped out their newborns into the hands of an Indian midwife, cleaned themselves, and went back to their work. Renna would be all right, and she'd be happy being with her husband. It did Fran Talbert's heart good to see that young couple together. She hadn't seen two people so much in love since Derral Talbert had come a-courting back in Virginia a lot of years before.

"Bye, good-bye," she called out as Renna turned to wave. "See you in a few days."

A summer fever and a large escort had interfered with Othon's plans for the blue-blooded comte de Beaujolais. The upriver expedition—which, in addition to the two Frenchmen, consisted of a small contingent of Spanish soldiers who were veterans of Mississippi travel and a larger group of Creek boatmen—had reached the mouth of the Arkansas River after weeks of hard travel. During those weeks, Othon never caught the comte alone, out of earshot of the others. Then, three days prior to landing on the east bank just north of the confluence of the two streams, Beaujolais had been listless. So weak was he that at times he had to have the assistance of the Spanish soldiers to get in and out of the canoe. The next morning he was tossing and twisting on his blankets and drenched in sweat, and his skin was burning with fever.

Othon's patience had been worn thin by weeks of having to listen to the prattle of the aristocrat. He was also irritable because he had not counted on being surrounded by a large Spanish escort. The young officer in charge of the Spanish and Creek forces, Juan Servera, was a boot-licker of the first class, always at the side of the count. Othon's chance to rid himself of the nobleman had not come, and now, to his chagrin, it seemed as if the ill humors of the lowlands along the river would deprive him of the pleasure of hearing Beaujolais beg for death in preference to the pain that the former executioner longed to administer.

"We will leave the count here, with a few of the Creek to look after him," Othon told the Spanish officer, for he was eager to complete his journey and return to Melisande. When he was away from her for any length of time, he experienced such a longing that only her touch could cure him of it, and he dreamed nightly of the rich, sweet, fecund softness of her breasts.

"My instructions, Frenchman, are to accompany the comte," said Lieutenant Juan Servera. "My orders say nothing about abandoning him to the doubtful mercies of savages and accompanying you."

"Stay then," Othon urged, pleased to be rid of all of them.

He chose six Creek who spoke Creole French and began his preparations to continue his journey up the river. The dominant Creek warrior in Othon's escort was called Bloody Tooth, for his habit of stringing the freshly removed teeth of his fallen enemies and wearing them around his neck.

At the last minute the Spanish officer came to Othon. "I will accompany you," he said, "with one man. The others will stay to care for the comte until we return."

Othon decided not to argue the matter. If he so chose, he could leave the moldering bodies of the officer and his man at some distant point to the north. The stoic

Creek would not concern themselves with the loss of two Spaniards.

The upriver journey continued at a heightened pace; with the travel group reduced, the burdens were lessened. Equipment and supplies were left in the camp where the comte burned with fever and muttered in delirium. Soon, when camp was made at night on the riverbank, it was in the land of the Choctaw. Chickasaw Bluffs lay only a few days' travel away, and beyond that principal town of the Chickasaw Nation was Othon's destination—the last Spanish fort on the Mississippi north of New Orleans.

In spite of the evening's muggy heat, Othon was in good spirits when he spread his blanket. Lightning flickered on the western horizon far beyond the river. Fireflies blinked as they flew among the voracious mosquitoes that bedeviled any exposed portion of a man's body. Lieutenant Servera assigned sentinel duty to selected Creek. Othon, however, knew that as soon as the lieutenant's eyes were closed, the Creek pickets would find their own beds. . . .

Bloody Tooth was awakened by a modest, feminine giggle. He rose silently from his blanket and glided toward the unabated sound. On a soft bed of detritus he found a young American soldier making love to a stocky Choctaw maiden. The American died swiftly under the blade of Bloody Tooth's tomahawk.

Within seconds Othon was up and taking one quick look at the dead man in the light of the rekindled fire. Then he turned his attention to the girl. Bloody Tooth, speaking in a language that Othon did not understand, was asking the girl questions, while the Spanish officer looked on. Othon put his hand on Bloody Tooth's arm. He was told by the Creek warrior that the girl was being asked about the dead soldier's companions and the location of their camp.

The young Spanish officer was concerned. "We did not come here to foment war with the United States," he said.

"Tell that one," Bloody Tooth growled to Othon, "to

hold his tongue unless he cares to have his own scalp dangling from my sash along with that of this long-knife soldier."

"I think," Othon said, after explaining to Servera, "that if I were you, I'd keep my mouth shut."

In spite of some uninspired but brutally administered pain, the Choctaw girl would not talk. Othon, restless with watching and feeling the need to seek his own satisfaction with the stubborn girl, pushed Bloody Tooth aside.

"There is this about administering pain," he explained to the sullen warrior. "Anyone with a strong heart can be brave as long as he or she can logically expect an end to the pain. I have seen both men and women die without giving information, simply because they did not believe that anyone could continue doing such barbarous things to them. Let me show you."

He inserted a forefinger into the wide nostril of the girl and with one swift jerk tore open her nasal cavity. A startled scream rewarded him. Blood flowed down the girl's chin and neck to wet her shirt.

"Now ask her what you want to know," Othon invited.

Still the girl was mute.

"But she is beginning to believe," Othon said. Using his heavy, razor-sharp frontier blade, he chopped off one of the girl's fingers at the first joint. "Now she knows. Something that will not heal has been done to her. She will talk."

The amputation of two more fingers was required before the girl spoke in a wild torrent of words, telling Bloody Tooth that the camp of the long-knife soldiers was not far, on the outskirts of a Choctaw village, and that in addition to the whiteface officer and his wife, only four other men lived there.

"A white woman?" Othon asked, his imagination soaring.

"We must hide this American's body immediately," said the Spanish officer.

"I did not come to these lands merely for your Spanish gold," Bloody Tooth snarled. Around him the other Creek were fingering their weapons.

"I order you to bury this man," Servera said. "I order you not to commence hostilities with soldiers of the United States."

"Come," Othon Hugues said to the eager Creek as he checked the priming of his musket. "I, too, came for something other than Spanish gold."

Philip and Renna awakened with the sun. Around them the camp was quiet. Renna dressed quickly, kindled a fire from the embers of the night, and started coffee in a blackened pot. Sergeant Samuel Lemon came up the riverbank, brushing back his hair, which was wet from a morning's splashing wash.

Philip looked around and saw only one man in his blankets. "Sergeant," he said, "it would be mighty nice if we could convince our stalwart soldiers that it is time to move on."

"I think they should be ready to listen to reason," Sam agreed.

The small patrol had been camped near the Choctaw village for two nights. The men, Philip was thinking, should be sated—or at least ready for variety, which would be available in an inland village. The Americans would pass that settlement as they swung eastward, away from the river, preparatory to turning northward for home in a couple of days.

"If you'd be so kind as to round them up, Sergeant?" Philip said.

It happened with a suddenness that froze the young man's heart. There was the zinging passage of an arrow near his head, and then he heard a startled, gasping cry. He looked to see Sam Lemon raising his hands to the arrow shaft that had entered his neck at the indentation below his Adam's apple. Another arrow killed the soldier sleeping in his blanket.

"Renna! Look out!" Philip screamed, and saw her leap for her bedroll.

Philip watched the sergeant fall and heard the zing of arrows passing close as he dived, scrambling for his musket. He shot a Creek warrior in the belly even as he was charged by three men. He met the other two with a tomahawk, to which he'd been introduced by El-i-chi. A Creek whooped with the joy of battle and ran directly into Philip's blade, forehead first, as Philip danced aside, amazed.

But another warrior was coming up from behind and slightly to the side. Philip watched as Renna's hand closed on her knife. As she circled into position, her arm came back and lashed forward. The blade buried itself in the spine of the Creek closing on Philip from the rear. The Indian dropped his tomahawk and made clawing efforts to reach the knife in his back. Philip's eyes met Renna's for an instant, then Renna was back to her bedroll, searching for another weapon.

A musket sounded from the shelter of the trees. Philip felt the jolt from the lead, and he was propelled forward before his legs began to crumple. He could not move, but he saw his wife seize a blazing limb from the campfire. As a Creek warrior leaped to seize Philip's hair, Renna thrust the brand into the assailant's face. The Creek screamed in agony and, blinded, staggered around in a circle.

Renna fell to her knees beside Philip and raised his head to her lap. Her probing fingers told him that the musket ball had taken him in the lower portion of his skull. Blood oozed down his neck. Even as Renna cradled his head in her lap, his eyelids flickered once, twice, and his heels began to drum a death dance on the ground.

"No, Philip, no!" she moaned.

Othon Hugues, having loaded his musket after shooting the white officer, caught the sightless Creek by the arm and demanded, "Control yourself."

"Give me the one who has killed me," the Creek begged. "Put his neck into my hands."

Othon looked closely at the man's face. The flames had seared his eyeballs and had burned away his lashes and brows. "As you say," Othon replied quietly, "you are killed."

He finished the job with a slash of his knife.

* * *

Renna looked up into the pockmarked face and color-less eyes and felt a shiver of dread. Four Creek warriors lay dead in the clearing, but dead also were Sergeant Samuel Julius Lemon, Lieutenant Philip Woods, and a seventeen-year-old soldier. She did not speak. Instead she held the colorless eyes with her own as her hand slowly, slowly, sought out Philip's fallen tomahawk. When her fingers closed on the haft, she leaped to her feet and hurled the weapon in one motion.

Othon, having seen her hand seeking the tomahawk, dodged easily. Then he laughed and bowed. *"Bonjour, mademoiselle. Comment allez-vous?"* he asked pleasantly.

Renna tore her eyes away from his and searched frantically for another weapon.

"Celui, il est allé," he said. This one, he has gone.

The French words brought realization to her numbed mind. Philip was gone. Philip was dead.

"I think it is best that you come with me," Othon said. "Do you speak French?"

"Je resterai jusqu'à ce qu'il revienne," she said. I will stay until he comes back. Her voice seemed to echo the inane words as if she were in a vast cavern. She felt the blood rushing from her head.

"But he will not be coming back," Othon said. "Come, little American girl." He held out his hand.

Renna lunged toward him, her hands formed into claws.

He chopped her to the ground with the butt of his musket. "If all you want is to die, little one," he said, "Othon will grant your wish."

It was Ta-na-wun-da's idea to become as rich as trap-pers. Miss Beth, who was a lovely person most of the time outside the classroom where she imprisoned Ta-na and Gao for endless hours almost every day, had assigned some reading to them. Ta-na had found the reading inter-esting for a change, because it told stories about the earliest French trappers who had ventured into the lands along the Mississippi.

"The pelts of animals are worth money," Ta-na said in an amazed tone of voice to Gao.

"But the book says that the Frenchmen trapped beavers," Gao said. "There are few beavers in this area."

"True, but the pelts of other animals are worth money," Ta-na insisted. "Coonskins are valuable."

"I don't see why. There are so many available," Gao said. "Not denying the fact, of course, that the skins are valuable to the coons themselves."

"Do you doubt my word?" Ta-na asked belligerently, rising, poising for action.

"No," Gao said, "I do not doubt your precious word. If I wanted to call you a liar I would say, 'Ta-na, you are a liar.'"

"If you called me a liar, I would teach you a lesson you'd never forget."

"You? Ha!"

"Shall I show you?" Ta-na challenged.

"You're sure you are big enough?"

Ta-na launched his attack, but it had been anticipated. The boys locked arms and swayed, straining for an advantage until Gao managed to get his foot behind Ta-na's leg. Together they pitched to the floor of the longhouse and rolled. Gao had a momentary advantage, and then Ta-na rolled atop Gao. They crashed against a pole that supported the roof. Dust showered down.

Ah-wa-o came running into the longhouse. She sighed in resignation when she saw that the shaking of the roof was caused only by her boys, who were at it again.

"Off with you," she said in a soft voice, thumping her moccasined toe against first one active boyish rump and then the other as they rolled past her. "Go before you bring the house down around our heads."

Once the boys were outside, they brushed off their trousers, straightened their shirts, and started off side by side for the outskirts of the village.

"And skunk hides are bought by the traders in Knoxville," Ta-na continued.

"Gaaaa," Gao moaned.

"There is a method of skinning a skunk that prevents becoming affected by the scent," Ta-na said.

"Good, I will let you show me how. That is, if you must skin a skunk."

"You still doubt my knowledge," Ta-na said.

"A little."

"Come, Gao, we will go to The House and ask Miss Beth. Then you'll see."

They found Beth with Roy Johnson in the kitchen of the house. Roy was in the process of showing Beth why he had become what was, most probably, the best biscuit baker west of the Smoky Mountains. He was covered with flour from his eyebrows to the bottom of his canvas apron as he kneaded dough on a breadboard.

"Well, lookee who's here," Roy said. "Didn't expect you two until I had these biscuits in the oven and the aroma started drifting out. But since you're here, run out and fetch me a load of stove wood."

"Yes, sir," Ta-na said. "May we ask you something first?"

"Shoot," Roy said. "If I don't know the answer, I'll lie a little just so's I won't disillusion you two about grandfathers knowing everything."

Gao grinned at Ta-na and winked.

"I see I have a doubting Thomas," Roy said. "Now you tell me this, little Chief Winking Eye. If grandfathers don't know everything, who does?"

"My father," Ta-na replied.

"Which one?" Gao asked.

"Maybe both of them," Ta-na said.

"You two gonna talk all day or ask me what you came to ask?" Roy demanded.

"Gao doesn't believe that the traders in Knoxville will pay white man's gold for the pelts of coons and skunks."

"Well, Gao, I hate to go against you, but Ta-na is right. Really. Last time I heard it was six bits for a good coonskin and half a dollar for skunk hides. Now don't ask me why coon hides are worth more than skunk hides. If I was about to set out to skin me a varmint and I had any choice in the matter at all, I'd take skinning a coon over a skunk any old day."

"Grandfather, how much are six bits?" Ta-na asked.

"Seventy-five cents," Roy answered. "You two warriors contemplating going into the trapping business?"

"How many dollars would it take to buy a new musket?" Gao asked.

"Oh, that depends on what kind of musket. A good one will cost you 'round twenty dollars, I'd say."

"Twenty dollars," Ta-na said quietly, counting on his fingers.

"That'd figure out to be forty skunks," Beth said. "Or twenty-six raccoons. I think you'd just about wipe out the local raccoon and skunk populations for one musket."

"On the other hand," Roy said, "a good bearskin'll bring you around twenty dollars."

"Now, Roy . . ." Beth said warningly.

"'Course," Roy said, "if you killed a bear, your pappy would tan your hides."

"I know," Gao said with reverence. "The bear is the totem of our clan."

"My father Renno talks to bears," Ta-na said.

"So does my father," Gao added.

"Well, my father Renno must have taught him how," Ta-na boasted.

"Did not."

"Did too."

"Business partners have got to work together," Roy said. "Now trapping is not a bad way to make a dollar, but it's infernal hard work."

"I guess we'd need some steel traps," Ta-na remarked.

"Naw, steel traps are pretty cruel," Roy objected. "If you boys are really interested, I'll show you how to trap 'em alive."

"Would you, please, Grandfather?" Gao asked.

Roy spent a few hours with the boys out in the barn. Beth could hear sawing and pounding. She made a pot of hot tea and carried a tray to the outbuilding, to find Roy demonstrating the trip-cord mechanism of a box trap.

Work was stopped for tea and some of Roy's warm

biscuits, stuffed with fresh butter and blackberry jam. When the snack was decimated, Gao, who had become as enthusiastic as Ta-na about the new project, ran out of the barn, box trap in hand, closely followed by Ta-na, who had thought to save half a biscuit for bait.

"Aren't raccoons rather strong little animals?" Beth worriedly asked Roy.

"Boar coon's a match for one hound dog any day," Roy confirmed.

"Will the boys really catch an animal in that trap?"

"Oh, sure, if they put it in the right place and if they don't leave too much human scent on it." He laughed heartily. "Don't worry. If they do get an old boar coon in that box, the only danger they'll be in when they open it is being trampled by that old coon trying to get away."

"Well . . ." Beth said doubtfully.

After a long and interesting discussion that ended in a tumbling, gasping, grunting wrestling match, it was decided that the best place for the box trap was on the bank of the swimming creek about a half mile from the outskirts of the village. The trap was baited—after Gao sneaked one more bite of the cold biscuit—and cocked. Then the two trappers lay silently in the brush nearby, waiting for their unsuspecting quarry to come along. Being so still allowed the cold to creep into the boys' bones, so they decided to go back to The House to see if there were any more of those hot biscuits with butter and blackberry jam. There were. And then it was night and time for the evening meal.

"We're going to be trappers," Gao announced to his mother and father.

"A worthy ambition," El-i-chi said. He waited for more information.

"Grandfather Roy helped us make a box trap," Ta-na said. "We've got it set down by the creek."

"And what do you hope to catch?" Ah-wa-o asked.

"Maybe a coon."

"They are such beautiful animals," Ah-wa-o said, sighing.

"Mother," Gao said, "we hope to save our father the

expense of buying weapons for us when we are older.
Besides, you eat coon when Grandmother Toshabe cooks
it."

"I would not care to eat enough coon for their skins to
pay for two new muskets," El-i-chi said. He looked at
Ah-wa-o with a little smile. "However, one young and
tender coon, baked with sweet potatoes and corn, would
be tasty. Make certain, if you should catch one in this trap
of yours, that you keep the meat clean and fresh for use as
food, for I do not approve of killing an animal merely to
steal his warm fur coat."

"We hear," Ta-na said. "And we will advise Grandmother Toshabe that we will be furnishing the meat for a
meal."

For several days the two boys kept the path to the
swimming creek well used, making as many as a half-
dozen trips a day to check on their trap. They had tried
various baits. The original piece of biscuit had dried up.
Corn drew birds too small to trip the trap. It was only
when, on the third day, Gao sacrificed his own sweet
treat, a Cherokee nut ball mixed with honey, that their
efforts produced results. On that day Gao spotted fresh
raccoon tracks along the bank of the creek.

It happened just after sunup. The boys had awakened
with the dawn, grabbed a handful of corn to ease their
hunger pangs, and rushed out of the longhouse into a
glorious morning that seemed filled with promise for both
of them. They heard the chirring call of an angry raccoon
even before they could see the box trap. Breathlessly they
ran forward to see that the trap had been sprung. Indeed,
as they approached, the animal inside the box lunged
about in panic, almost overturning the trap.

"Quick," Ta-na urged, "or we will lose him."

Gao, being in the lead, threw his weight onto the
box. The animal inside chirred in fear and fury.

Ta-na was nocking an arrow to his boy-sized bow.
"When I give you the word, lift the box," he instructed.

"What if you miss?"

"I will not miss."

"Wait," Gao said. "Let me ready my tomahawk." He pulled the weapon from his sash. It was a battered, often-honed blade that had belonged to Ha-ace the Panther. "If your arrow misses or merely wounds him, I will finish him off."

"That is good. I am ready," Ta-na said.

The raccoon growled deep in its throat, and then chirred intimidatingly.

Ta-na swallowed hard. "Now," he said, his voice cracking.

Gao removed his weight from the trap, put one hand gingerly under an edge, and lifted. At that moment the adult raccoon, a big male, chose to make one more attempt at escape, throwing his weight upward against the roof of the box. Gao, off balance and just a bit apprehensive, lifted his tomahawk as the box flew up into his face.

Ta-na loosed his arrow at a gray blur of motion. Gao swung the tomahawk and yelled a warning. The blow missed the frightened animal but nearly amputated Ta-na's small toe on his left foot. Ta-na cried out in pain and surprise. The raccoon growled and started to climb the nearest object, which happened to be Gao's body, and the startled boy found himself looking into the wide, frightened eyes and the toothy mouth of a full-sized raccoon. Boy and raccoon fell together. Boy yelped as he was trampled and scratched by the fleeing raccoon.

"I am wounded severely," Ta-na announced, bravely keeping back tears. His small toe was bleeding profusely, and it hurt badly.

As Gao picked himself up, his hand came away bloody from his face. "He bit me," he said in a strained voice.

"He merely scratched you," Ta-na protested. "You, on the other hand, have almost cut off my foot."

Gao, who had not noticed the blood, now looked down and went pale. "Manitous!" he breathed. He turned to run. "I'll go for help."

"No, you won't," Ta-na said. "You will support me so that I can walk."

"I think I'd better go for help."

"Let me lean on your shoulder."

"No, I know best. I can run like the wind and bring our father, who will know what to do," Gao said.

"By the time you return, I will have bled to death." Ta-na reached out and caught Gao's arm. "Now let me lean on you, and we will return to the village."

"Let me go," Gao insisted.

"Will not!" Ta-na said, wrapping his arms around Gao. The boys, losing their footing, crashed to the ground for a wrestling match, which resulted in Ta-na's toe spreading blood over both of them. It was finally decided that it would be best, after all, for Gao to assist Ta-na to the village.

Ah-wa-o went faint upon seeing them. There was so much blood that she asked her sons if they had encountered a black bear.

The cut on Ta-na's toe, clogged with sand from the walk, had stopped bleeding. He suffered stoically, with only a few pained grimaces, as Ah-wa-o cleaned the wound, announced that it was not fatal, and treated it with one of El-i-chi's medications.

"Gao released the coon before I was ready," Ta-na complained.

"He missed an easy shot cleanly," Gao said.

"Did not," Ta-na said.

"Did too!" Gao said.

"Perhaps you had best find another way to earn money," Ah-wa-o suggested.

"Next time I will be ready with my tomahawk," Gao declared. "He can lift the trap."

"At least I won't panic and let the coon out before you're ready," Ta-na defended.

"If you are not wounded," Gao said darkly.

"I will not be wounded forever," Ta-na said.

"If I thought it would bring peace for a while," Ah-wa-o said, "I would take your father's blade and cut a toe off each of you."

The boys looked at each other in amazement. Even that hint of criticism from their mother was unusual.

"Forgive us," Gao said.

"We do not mean to cause you concern," Ta-na added.

She smiled, then hugged them one at a time. "My only concern is for you," she said. "Couldn't you lure less energetic game to your trap?"

"We could go after possum," Gao said, "but their hides only sell for twenty-five cents."

"But aren't there more possums than raccoons around?" Ah-wa-o asked.

The boys exchanged glances. "Our mother is wise," Ta-na said. He did not voice the thought that possums were a lot more docile than coons.

Chapter Seven

~~~~~~

Renna first became aware of a lancing pain in her head. Angry voices, mixing with the pain, faded in and out. She opened her eyes with great effort to see odd, double-edged figures in a tableau of confrontation. She closed her eyes and tried to make sense of the voices. She couldn't move her arms, and this puzzled her until she realized that she was seated on the ground with her arms tied behind her, then secured to a tree.

Men were arguing in a mixture of Spanish and French. She forced herself to concentrate on what was being said. When she again opened her eyes, her double vision had cleared. She saw the man with the pockmarked face. Two Creek warriors with fresh, bloody scalps at their sashes stood behind the white man. She voiced a silent scream of total despair when she recognized the black, tightly curled hair of her husband hanging from the waist of the larger

Creek, but she controlled outward evidence of her agony of loss.

The morning had begun so peacefully. She had been looking forward to spending another day with Philip, to seeing new country. It had begun as a day created by the Divinity—like her brother, Little Hawk, she often had to make a conscious choice when addressing the Creator, sometimes thinking of Him as the Master Of Life, sometimes as God. It had begun as another day of sweetness and goodness and love for Philip and wonder at the miracle of life that was growing inside her.

So quickly had her entire life changed. The fight had begun and ended within a space of three or four minutes. In so short a time had she been deprived of what she had come to think of as her main reason for living, her love for her husband.

As she struggled to clear her head, which pounded frightfully, she began to understand that the argument between the pockmarked man and a young Spaniard in uniform concerned a Choctaw girl whose face was covered with blood. The girl, who seemed barely conscious, was tied to a tree across the small clearing from Renna. With a shock Renna saw that the leaves on which the girl sat were soaked with blood.

"We are not barbarians," the Spanish officer was saying. "I make no apologies when it is necessary to kill an Indian, for they are essentially savages. But I will not allow you or anyone else in my command, be he white or Indian, to lower the name of Spain to the level of the savages by torturing captives. You will release this Choctaw girl."

"You're a fool, Servera," the Frenchman growled. "Would you have the entire Choctaw Nation down on us?" He took three quick steps, bent to slash the bonds that held the girl, and lifted her. When he let go, she collapsed in a heap.

Renna felt quick panic, for now she could see that several of the girl's fingers had been amputated.

"There is but one fate left for this one," the Frenchman continued, lifting his musket and aiming it at the girl's head.

"If you do that, Othon, I shall kill you," Servera said, raising his own musket.

Othon brought up his weapon and pointed it toward the sky, then squinted with his colorless eyes at the Spaniard. "I will respect your humanitarian instincts, then," he said. "Do as you will with the girl. In fact, you are free to do as you will totally, for I will not stay here and be called upon to explain the girl's disfigurement to her male relatives. I will leave that to you."

He turned his back and strode toward the tree where Renna was tied. She closed her eyes and feigned unconsciousness.

"What do you think you are doing?" Servera asked as Othon bent to her bonds.

Othon's voice was soft. "You do not have the appearance of a greedy man, Lieutenant. I have given you the Choctaw girl. Would you begrudge me this one?"

"And you call *me* fool," Servera grated angrily. "You have killed soldiers of the United States. For decades we have feared that the Americans would listen to men such as George Rogers Clark and William Blount and move an army of frontiersmen with long rifles down the Mississippi. Had they done this, we would not have had the forces to stop them, and New Orleans would now be an American city. And here you want to compound the murder of their soldiers by stealing an American woman? What would you do with her? Would you 'question' her as you did this Choctaw?"

"What I will do with this little bird is for me to decide," Othon said, facing Servera.

Through slitted eyes Renna saw Othon's arm muscles tense. She knew that he was preparing for some sort of action.

"We will free this American woman," Servera declared. "We will leave her with friendly Choctaw, and we will explain that we came upon the scene of the battle to find her injured . . . by a Creek war party. Is that understood?"

"Ah, young man," Othon said, "you do take too much upon yourself."

"Watch him!" Renna cried, for she had determined that her best interests lay with the Spanish officer, not with the man with the pockmarked face.

Her warning came too late. Othon lowered his musket and fired with blinding speed. The ball caught Lieutenant Servera in the chest and knocked him backward. He sat down heavily, lifted one hand to his breast, and looked down with wonder at the quick spread of blood onto his tunic. He fell slowly onto his side even as the surviving Spanish soldier scrambled for his musket, only to be stilled by one quick blow from the tomahawk of the Creek warrior who wore Philip's scalp at his waist.

Othon, pistol in his hand, was eyeing the two Creek. "Good work, Bloody Tooth."

"At last we are rid of the Spaniards," Bloody Tooth replied.

"Bloody Tooth, you are a great warrior," Othon proclaimed. "Perhaps you and I see things in the same way. Is that true?"

"You will share the white woman," Bloody Tooth demanded.

Othon moved the muzzle of his pistol to line it up on Bloody Tooth's belly. "My Creek brother is a great warrior and, I pray, a wise one. Is he wise enough to leave my prize to me, without question? Or must we have the same kind of discussion on this matter that was just conducted between Lieutenant Servera and myself?"

The Creek saw that the Frenchman's finger was on the trigger. "You will share the white woman when you are finished with her?"

Othon shook his head. "No, my friend." He pointed to the Choctaw girl. "There is still warmth in that one. And if she does not please you, there are others in the village. A warrior of Bloody Tooth's ability should have no problem obtaining a Choctaw woman for his pleasure."

"You are not concerned, as was the Spaniard, about keeping the peace?"

"My Creek brother," Othon said with a smile, "if it is your pleasure to kill Choctaw, male or female, far be it from me to stand in your way. Now why don't you fellows go on about your business and leave me to give my attentions to the pale-haired woman?"

The warrior approached the Choctaw girl. Renna tried not to watch when the tall, brawny Creek ripped off his leggings and breechclout to reveal rampant manhood. She averted her eyes, but the anguished moans of the Choctaw girl caused her to look. The Creek was making the beast with two backs with an energy that caused the weakened, dying girl to roll her head in pain.

"Ah, you *are* interested," Othon approved, seeing Renna's eyes widen with shock as the second Creek took his turn.

"These Creek are animals," Renna said. "You are French. Are you, too, an animal?"

Her only answer was a laugh as Othon turned his face to watch the action. The two Creek were quickly finished with the girl. As they pulled on their clothing, they laughed and joked about the lack of movement on the part of the helpless Choctaw woman.

Bloody Tooth gathered his weapons. "We go, Frenchman, to find more lively sport," he said. "What is left here"—he pointed at Renna—"is my gift to you."

"I am deeply appreciative," Othon said sarcastically, nodding as the Creek disappeared into the forest.

Renna watched the Frenchman warily. He squatted in front of her, put out his hand, touched her pale hair, then ran his rough fingers along her cheek. She said nothing, nor did she give him the satisfaction of seeing her cringe from his touch.

"Ah, little one," he breathed, "we will have such a beautiful time together."

"If you touch me again," Renna warned evenly, "pray that you will always be a light sleeper."

He laughed with delight and reached out to squeeze her breasts. She kicked, aiming at his genitals, but he had anticipated her move, caught her foot in one hand, and twisted it until a grimace of pain came to her face.

"Yes, a lovely time," he said. "Do you know, little one, what I have planned for you?"

She did not dignify the obvious question by answering.

"But I fear you do not," he said sadly. "And to make it fully enjoyable for me, it is vital that you know." He rose and gazed down at her. "Fortunately the means of my demonstrating my intentions to you are at hand."

He walked to the Choctaw girl, who lay on her back. She had managed to pull down her deerskin skirt to cover her nakedness, but she had not been able to muster the strength to flee.

Othon looked at Renna. "I fear that she has lost so much blood that she will not have the vitality to respond to my attentions. We shall see." He began slowly, and at first it seemed that he had guessed correctly.

"Animal! Animal!" Renna cried out in revulsion as she watched the Frenchman with the numbed fascination of a snake-charmed rodent waiting for the lightning strike of poisoned fangs. And then she began to pray, first to her mother's God, and then to the Master of Life as the Frenchman found pain centers still sensitive enough to penetrate the lethargy of the dying girl. Renna's screams blended with the agonized screechings of the Choctaw.

She had heard and had shuddered at the tales of old, when an Iroquois warrior's worst fear was to be captured and turned over to the women of the enemy tribe. In those days, women were the masters of torment, capable of keeping a man in agony for days before he died. It had always been difficult for her to believe such stories, for the Seneca had long since ceased such savagery, and Renna was also a product of gentle Emily, her mother, and the sophisticated Beth. Being both Seneca and white left her more vulnerable to the horror that she witnessed. She tried to turn her head away, tried to keep her eyes closed, but each new moan or wail of terminal torment drew her gaze back to the Frenchman who was so deeply immersed in his abominable pleasures that his eyes were glazed, his face slack and expressionless.

With a frenzy of strength Renna struggled against her bonds, and when she felt one of the thongs slip, her heart leaped in hope. Praying, panting in terror, she pulled and wriggled until her own blood lubricated the rawhide and one hand came free.

Othon had reduced the Choctaw girl to semi-consciousness. Renna would have thought, had she not been in a state between shock and madness, that she was beyond being horrified further; but as she crept quietly toward the trees she looked over her shoulder to see the Frenchman mount the dying woman. Her gorge rose, and she nearly betrayed herself by gagging, but she swallowed and continued to crawl toward the shelter of the trees. Behind her she heard the Frenchman's voice rise in an eerie chanting and then there was one last coughing sound from the girl.

Renna climbed to her feet and ran, for she was being pursued by a devil from hell. She ran in total panic and realized that she was moving toward the river only when she slid to a halt on the edge of a bank overlooking a muddy flat leading to the water's edge. She looked around wildly, but she was alone, at least two days' ride from the fort, without weapons, without her horse.

From the forest behind her she heard the bellow of an enraged animal. The sound could only have come from the Frenchman, who, upon finishing his appetizer, realized that the entrée had vanished. The outburst of rage gave her renewed strength. She scrambled and slid down the bank, planning to move northward along the river's edge. But her feet sank into the mud, and walking was difficult.

Ahead, the bank rose high with a rise of ground. The mud flat between bank and water widened. Near the bank the surface became harder and the walking easier. She rounded a protrusion and could only gasp in protest as she was seized roughly. For a moment her perception was limited to a red haze of hopeless fear as she thought that the Frenchman had found her. A harsh voice speaking Creek brought her back to her senses. She was being held by Bloody Tooth.

"Creek Warrior," her words came out in a desperate, breathless rush, "I am Renna of the Seneca, daughter of the warrior-sachem Renno, of whom you may have heard. My father is a friend of your chief, McGillivray. If you will help me to escape the Frenchman, if you will assist me in reaching the fort of the white man that lies to the north, the friendship between our tribes will be honored and you will be greatly rewarded."

"You speak our tongue," Bloody Tooth said in puzzlement.

"We share common ancestors, we three," Renna said, glancing at the other Creek. "We are children of the Master of Life."

"But your hair is not the hair of a Seneca," Bloody Tooth said, fingering her braids. "Your skin is the skin of a white woman."

"We will share her, since the Frenchman does not seem to want her," said Bloody Tooth's companion.

Bloody Tooth seemed to be caught in indecision. Renna took the opportunity to slip out of his grasp. She ran, but the second Creek prevented her from moving directly to the north on the hardened mud near the bank. She circled toward the river and was soon moving as if in slow motion. It was her childhood nightmare made doubly frightening by reality. The soft mud clung to her feet and sucked off her moccasins. She sank nearly to her calves with each step. The two Creek did not pursue her into the mud. They kept pace with her slow movement, laughing at her, pointing at her in derision.

"Now we will have to wash her," Bloody Tooth said loudly as she fell facedown into the mud.

She struggled to her feet. She had only one option— the river. She turned toward the water and struggled through the mud. The Creek, seeing her intention, whooped and ran toward her, sinking into the mud with each step. Ahead of her on the water's edge was a rise in the mud bank. Atop the little mound, perhaps built by silt collecting atop a mass of tangled brush, the mud was dry and cracked into hand-sized, sun-hardened shards. She struggled out of the mud onto the hard surface and halted for a moment to catch her breath. The Creek were closing on her. She seized a piece of brittle driftwood and threw it, catching Bloody Tooth off guard. The stick struck him in the face, and blood gushed from his nose. With a roar of pain he drew back his arm and threw his tomahawk with deadly intention.

Renna saw the weapon being drawn back for the throw. She poised herself to dodge it, but her foot slipped into the crack between the heat-baked plates of mud, and she was falling when the tomahawk struck her in the stomach. She lived only because Bloody Tooth had been off balance during the throw, so the tomahawk had twisted to strike her flat-side first. But the impact caused her to cry out in pain and took her breath, so that she sank down to her knees and was holding her stomach with both hands as the Creek came closer.

Together they dragged her through the mud to the shelter of the bank, sat her down on the hard ground, and stood over her, arguing who would be the first to have her.

Something was very, very wrong inside her stomach. She retched, and the strain of it was anguish. Then she felt an ominous wetness inside her clothing. When she put a tentative hand there, it came away tinged with blood. A spasm cramped all of her stomach muscles, and she grunted with the intense pain and bent over.

Now the Creek had resolved their dispute. Might was right. Bloody Tooth was the stronger, the larger. It was he who bent and with his knife sliced away Renna's clothing to leave her naked from the waist down.

"Oh, no," she whispered as spasm after spasm convulsed her stomach and left her helplessly weak. "Oh, no, not now."

Bloody Tooth, having bared himself, was kneeling. He spread her forcefully, and that force, in opposition to the cramps in her stomach, completed the process. With a hoarse cry of disgust Bloody Tooth jumped to his feet and jerked his clothing back into order.

"Unclean," Bloody Tooth whispered, his face twisted with repugnance.

"Unclean," agreed Bloody Tooth's companion, lifting his tomahawk with the intention of putting an end to Renna's gasps of pain.

"No!" Bloody Tooth thundered. "Do you want the ghost of the unborn to curse you forever?"

The Creek shuddered and backed away. They left her there, lying on the hardened silt of the Mississippi. As the sun climbed toward midday and shortened the shadow of the bank under which she lay, she felt the heat of it and tried weakly to cover herself. But blackness came to her again before she could complete the effort.

* * *

It was the sharp eyes of a Creek boatman that spotted the touch of color on the mud flat below the high bank. He pointed it out to others until it was brought to the attention of the comte de Beaujolais, who sat in a canoe that brought up the rear of the flotilla. With his Spanish escort and the Creek manning the canoes, young Beaujolais, recovered from his fever, had been pushing hard to catch up with Othon Hugues and Lieutenant Servera. There had been no sign of them, however.

Word was passed back as the leading canoes came abreast of the object of their attentions: a dead Indian woman lay on the mud flat. To the Creek and the Spanish soldiers, a dead Indian woman was not a worthy reason for landing and wading across the wide flat.

As the comte's canoe came abreast, he shaded his eyes with his hand against the noonday sun. He could see that the woman was dressed in Indian deerskins and that her lower body was nude. The darkness on her thighs could only be blood. Although he was not exactly a greenhorn—he had traveled the American wilderness with his brothers on an earlier occasion and was familiar with the ways of the Indian—he had never been able to adopt the casual attitude toward death exhibited by Indians and certain frontiersmen. Just as he had never been able to accept the bloody excesses of the French Revolution, neither could he accept that the death of an Indian, male or female, was no great loss.

He was, however, fighting his inclination to investigate, for it was important that he catch up with Hugues and the lieutenant. Then he saw the Indian woman move. He made his decision quickly, ordered his boatman to pull up to the edge of the water. He called out his intentions to the Spanish sergeant who had been left in charge of the military contingent.

"We will find a place where it will be easier to land and wait for you," the sergeant called back.

Beaujolais considered removing his boots, but the thought of stepping on a sharp, waterlogged piece of driftwood dictated that he wade in the mud fully shod. He sank almost to the top of his boots before reaching firmer ground. As he neared the woman she stirred weakly and tried to pull her slashed skirt over her nakedness. He saw that her skin was not the red-brown of the Choctaw women. Her hair was pale, flecked through with gold. She was covering her eyes with one hand against the burning sun as he knelt beside her.

"Mademoiselle?" he said.

"No, oh, no," she moaned. She tried to turn onto her side. He put his hand on her shoulder.

"Mademoiselle, I will do you no harm," he said in French.

"Help me, help me," she whispered in the same language.

"Yes, I will," he said.

She moved her hand, and he saw the blue of her eyes, the sculpted perfection of her face, evident even through her grimace of pain.

"*Mon Dieu*," he whispered. "It can't be. Is it you, Renna?"

Hope soared in her. She looked into his face and reached up as if to touch it.

"It is I, your Beau," he said. "Do you remember?"

"Beau?"

"Yes, Beaujolais. I came to your village with my brothers, with Louis—"

She found the strength to seize his wrist with both her hands, to cling, to weep. He reached down and tenderly covered her with her skirt. Huge blowflies with shiny green, hairy bodies crawled over a bloody mass lying on the hard mud. He averted his face, but something made him look back. He had never seen an unborn fetus, but he recognized the vaguely human shape of it, and his heart broke for Renna. He gently slid his arms under her and lifted her, thinking to remove her from the drying, tragic little mound of tissue and flesh. With her in his arms he looked upstream. The last canoe was almost out of sight around a slight bend. He called out to the Creek boatman waiting in his canoe and instructed the man to catch up with the others and to bring back food, water, and clothing. He set Renna down in a shady spot near the bank.

"Beau?"

"Yes, it is I."

She began to cry. "I lost my baby."

"Yes."

"He was going to kill me."

"Who?"

"The Frenchman."

"The man with the pocked face?"

"Yes."

"Hugues," Beau grated. "Where is he?"

"So nice of you to inquire about me, Count," said Othon Hugues, stepping out from behind a pile of drift brush, his musket at the ready.

"What is the meaning of this, Hugues?" Beaujolais demanded.

"Where is the main party, Count?" Othon asked.

The tone of Hugues's voice, the look in his eyes, made Beau uneasy. He was weaponless. Renna began to crawl away, trying to put as much distance between her and the insane Frenchman as possible. The count continued to converse, stalling for time, glad that Renna had the strength to move away.

"They landed just upstream," Beau said. "The soldiers are coming with food and clothing for this lady."

Othon cocked his head, listening. Beau listened, too, and heard only the sounds of the forest, the song of birds, the murmur of leaves in the slight breeze.

"Hugues, you will help me carry this lady to a more comfortable spot," Beau said.

Sanity had returned to Renna. "Beau, he is going to kill you," she said.

"Do as you are told, Hugues," Beau ordered.

Othon laughed as he lifted his musket. "You were a dead man from the moment you left New Orleans with me, you spawn of an aristocratic harlot. It is a measure of the stupidity of your class that you could believe that the man who lowered the blade on the pretty neck of Marie Antoinette would allow an abomination like you to continue to live."

The musket was swinging to bear on Beau's stomach. Renna scooped dry silt into her hand and flung it into Othon's face. The musket exploded, but Beau had jumped aside to snatch up a stout limb of driftwood.

Othon was wiping dirt from his eyes with one hand. He blinked, hefted the musket by its barrel, and advanced to meet Beau. Beau, a master swordsman, parried a wild swing of the musket with the driftwood limb, then darted in to whack Othon stoutly across the neck with his make-shift weapon. But Othon managed to catch the blow with his shoulder. Even then its force caused a grunt of surprised pain. He stepped back and became more cautious.

The next time Beau parried a blow, his limb broke, leaving only a few inches of driftwood in his hand. He began to back away, searching desperately for another weapon, while Othon laughed, sensing the kill.

Beau had not been blooded in battle, but he had faced foes in more than one affair of honor. His weapon had been the slim épée, the fencing sword. He had inflicted injury and once had felt the prick of the sharp point of his opponent's weapon. He had killed two men. In his travels in America, with a musket in his hand, he had faced a black bear and he had killed the animal. But never had he seen a man transformed into an animal with burning eyes and snarling mouth. He backed away from the mad thing, a being that radiated pure evil, a feral creature from a nightmare, that was intent on killing.

Beau had learned that sometimes insults would anger an opponent and that an angry man is not at his best. "Barbarian," he said, twisting his mouth in disgust. "You are no better than a common criminal, Hugues. You are a beast. Do you actually think that low-class scum like you can best a man, an aristocrat?"

Othon growled deep in his throat.

Seeing that his words were affecting Hugues, Beau continued. "In my veins flows the royal blood of France. And it is well-known that the possessor of such royal blood is far superior in intelligence and weaponry to such common dirt as you."

Othon roared and charged. At that moment Renna

slipped another stout driftwood limb into Beau's hand so that he could meet the challenge. Limb and musket smashed together, and the force was too much for both. The limb broke, and the shock of impact knocked the musket spinning from Othon's grasp. The two men closed. Othon's teeth were bared. An animal growl emanated from low in his throat.

They rolled on the hardened mud, and it became quickly evident that Beau was getting the worst of it. Hugues seemed imbued with supernatural strength. When he straddled Beau and placed his hands at Beau's throat, Renna roused herself and threw herself onto Hugues's back, clawing and tugging. He brushed her aside as if she were a falling leaf. She fell heavily.

Beau's struggles were weakening, and he began to fear that soon Renna would be at the mercy of the Frenchman once more.

Beau was so very near death that his world was going dim. Then four Spanish soldiers came crashing and sliding down the bank from above to rip Hugues away from his victim. It was fortunate that there were four, for Hugues sent two of them sprawling, disabled a third with a kick to the groin, and was subdued only when the fourth Spaniard, joining forces with the two who had fallen but regained their footing, attacked as one, using the butts of their muskets.

A soldier helped Beaujolais to his feet. He was coughing, gasping for breath, and fingering his bruised throat. "See to the lady," he croaked.

Renna was unconscious. She was sprawled limply, her lower body again exposed.

"And what of this one?" asked the sergeant who had led the party. "This one who tried to kill you?"

Beaujolais was tempted to give the order that would have ended the life of Othon Hugues, but, unlike Hugues, he was not an animal. "He is alive?"

"He'll be none the worse," the sergeant said. "A bump on the head."

As if in confirmation, Othon sat up and looked around dazedly. "Melisande," he whispered softly.

It appeared to Beau that Othon's dizziness immediately abated. He looked impossibly strong.

"Sergeant," Hugues said sheepishly, "I am myself
again. In my anguish and pain I must have thought that
the count was the enemy who ambushed us."

"You knew fully well who I was," Beau scoffed.

"Choctaw," Othon said. "They lay in wait for us. The
lieutenant was killed without having gotten off a shot.
Your other comrade fought well, as did the Creek. And
then only I—"

"We can't believe this fellow," Beau said to the soldiers.

"Go there," Othon said, pointing. "You will find some
of our dead."

The sergeant sent two men.

Beau busied himself with the unconscious Renna,
rubbing her wrists, patting her cheeks lightly. She was
breathing rapidly and shallowly. Her flesh was cold. She
was in shock. "We must get her to camp," he said, removing his tunic, then covering her with it.

Othon seized his first opportunity to grab the weapon
of the Spanish soldier who had stayed with the sergeant.
He was raising the musket to kill the sergeant when the
sergeant's musket butt crashed into the side of Othon's
head.

"Now he dies," the sergeant vowed, lifting his musket
to smash it down onto Hugues's nose.

"No," Beaujolais said. "We will take him back to New
Orleans for trial."

"This one?" the sergeant erupted in disbelief. "He
would kill all of us at the first opportunity. Under no
circumstances will I try to take him alive back to New
Orleans. I will obey your wishes otherwise, Señor Count. I
will give you the options of leaving him here alive or
leaving him here dead."

"Then we will leave him alive," Beau decided.

The others soon returned to report that the lieutenant, the soldier, and four Creek were indeed dead. A
crude stretcher was made from saplings and tunics, and
Renna was carried upstream to the campsite, where Beau
washed her and wrapped her in blankets.

When, with the morning, her condition was unchanged, he gave orders to start back down the river. He had only a faint hope that she would live to see a doctor in Natchez, the nearest point of civilization downriver, but he refused to continue upstream with her in a coma.

The sun was still low in the east when they passed the mud flat where Renna had miscarried her baby. The line of canoes filed past, moving swiftly with the aid of the current. And just as the canoe carrying the unconscious Renna came abreast of that spot, Othon Hugues appeared on the mud flat, shaking his fists.

"Spanish soldiers," Hugues called, his voice carrying powerfully, "it will go hard for you if you return to New Orleans without me. I am Othon Hugues, personal emissary of the first consul!"

"Hugues," Beau called in answer, "I would advise you to find a home in a place other than New Orleans. For if you should make it to New Orleans alive, I will put you on trial for attempted murder." He could only suspect, at that time, that Hugues might have had something to do with the deaths of the lieutenant and the others.

"You royal bastard," Othon screamed. "This I promise you: you will face me again, and next time there will be no one to save you. And as for the little one, tell her if she awakens, someday she, too, will see Othon Hugues again. Tell her that then she will know the pleasures that I gave to the Choctaw girl, and she will know what I mean."

It was not necessary to trap opossums. Every Indian boy knew that possums slept during the daytime in hollow trees and wandered the woods looking for food at night. Gao and Ta-na knew of two ways to catch a possum. At night one walked in the woods with a torch, listening for the rustle of the waddling, slow-moving little animals in the underbrush. When a possum took to the trees, the glow of the torch reflected in its eyes. Then one climbed the tree and knocked the possum to the ground, where it was quickly put out of its misery and skinned to be made ready for the cook pot. Until the Gao and Ta-na Trapping Company was formed, neither youth bothered to think about going through the long, messy process of taking the skin whole from a possum and mounting it on a drying board, to be hung on an outside wall of a longhouse until the sun cured it to dryness.

Ta-na's small toe was still sensitive when the boys decided that one particular day was ideal for possum hunting. It had long since been determined that days were much nicer for hunting than nights.

Toshabe had agreed to bake the catch if the boys returned early enough with the carcass. The scholarly Cherokee Se-quo-i had shown the boys how to cut drying boards during the time that Ta-na could only hobble around on his sore toe, so there were half-a-dozen drying boards cut and smoothed, waiting only for hides to be mounted on them.

Gao, the scratches on his face healed, climbed the first few trees to poke around in hollows with a forked stick. The technique was simple: if something soft was encountered, one twisted the stick. The fork entangled itself in the possum's soft hide, and then one pulled the animal out and cast it to the ground to be dispatched.

At the second tree Gao felt something soft. He twisted the stick, heard a flurry of scrambling claws, and almost fell out of the tree when a gray squirrel burst out of the hollow, bounced once on the boy's shoulder, and jumped to another tree.

"We are not after squirrels," Ta-na called from the ground.

"If you think you can do better, I will let you climb the next tree," Gao said shakily.

"Well, don't think that I can't."

"Oh, sure," Gao said, leaping the last few feet to land on the soft leaves.

"I'll show you," Ta-na offered.

But his climbing ability was not to be put to the test that day. The boys walked on, looking for likely hollow trees. They spotted one with a huge hollow near the ground, and Ta-na probed with his stick and felt softness. He twisted and pulled as he yelled out to Gao to be ready. A hissing came from inside the hollow as the animal whose hide was being painfully pulled protested.

"It's a possum, all right," Ta-na said. "Get ready."

"I am ready."

"All right, here he comes," Ta-na said, jerking on his stick to pull out not a possum but a thoroughly aroused, fully adult skunk.

The skunk, spraying, drenched Ta-na from the neck down. Ta-na cried out, cast the stick and the skunk from him, as it happened, directly onto Gao, who was standing at the ready, with his tomahawk raised. The skunk was still spraying, and the stream struck Gao full in the mouth, then spewed downward as the skunk fell to the ground.

Gao was spitting and sputtering and yelling, and the skunk was coming to its feet to point its rear end, tail standing straight up like a banner, at Gao. The taste in the boy's mouth was terrible, and he could scarcely breathe, so aromatic was the air. He flung his tomahawk at the skunk and turned to flee.

"You got him!" Ta-na yelled between gasps for breath.

"I think, Brother," Gao said gravely, "that it got us."

By sheer accident the tomahawk had split the little animal's skull. It lay on the ground, twitching out its life, and the remaining drops of its highly effective perfume squeezed out onto the leaves.

Ta-na waved his hand in front of his nose, trying to get a breath of air. "I suggest, Brother, that we get to the creek as quickly as we can."

It was not yet swimming weather. The water was frigid, but anything was preferable to suffocation. They jumped, clothes and all, into the stream and began to splash themselves. Later, skin blue with cold, their sodden clothing lying on the bank, they scrubbed each other with sand. They shivered and groaned with the cold and then gave up all hope of getting the scent off before they froze to death. They put on their stinking clothes and looked at each other.

"We killed the animal," Ta-na reminded. "Our father would say that since we killed for a reason, we must carry through with that reason."

"Manitous," Gao said, spitting, the taste still in his mouth, "are you suggesting that we now take the hide from it?"

"It is our first pelt," Ta-na said. "It is worth fifty cents in Knoxville." He sighed. "But that is not the main reason why, yes, we must skin it. You know the reason."

"Kill only what you can eat. Kill only to meet your needs. Yes, I know."

"Come then."

Ta-na gagged as he slit open the skunk's skin. Both boys lost their breakfast before the red, naked body of the dead skunk was buried quickly and shallowly in sand. The two youths headed for the village, with the intact skunk pelt carried on a stick. The wind was behind them, so their coming was announced to all those outside their longhouses and to many unfortunates inside. Gao and Ta-na went to the back of their own home and were stretching the pelt on a drying board when El-i-chi and Ah-wa-o came around the corner of the longhouse.

Ah-wa-o held her nose, while El-i-chi tried to hide a wide grin. "I see that the trappers have found game."

"Actually, it found us," Gao admitted. "We were looking for possums. My *brother* here cannot tell skunk from possum."

"I can too," Ta-na retorted.

"Then why didn't you pull out a possum instead of this?" Gao asked, turning his head away from the inside-out pelt and holding the drying board at arm's length.

"Settle that later," El-i-chi suggested. "For now, take that pelt away, far away."

"We will sell it in Knoxville for fifty cents," Ta-na said.

"Then take it to Knoxville," El-i-chi urged. "And take yourselves to a great distance as well. Build a shelter by the creek, where you can wash yourselves several times a day."

"We will starve," Gao objected, his eyes wide.

"Perhaps I can stand the smell of you long enough to bring food to within a few hundred feet of you," El-i-chi said. "Go."

"I go," Gao said, head hanging.

"May I ask, Father, how long it will take to wash away the scent?"

"No more, perhaps, than a week," El-i-chi answered.

"A week," Ta-na muttered, wanting—for the first time since he was a small boy—to weep.

Both youngsters looked back wistfully as they trudged away. El-i-chi stood, arms crossed, face unforgiving.

"I'll take blankets and clothing to them after they've had time to build a shelter," he told a worried Ah-wa-o. He laughed. "Lo, my mighty hunters."

"It will be cold at night," Ah-wa-o said. "Couldn't—"

El-i-chi didn't let her finish. "Wife," he said with a chuckle, "if you want to run after those mighty hunters and tell them that they can come home, please feel free to do so. I will spend the next week or so in Renno's long-house, and then, after the scent has worn off the hunters, I will burn down our house and build a new one."

"I think it would have been simpler," Ah-wa-o said, "if we had told them that we would buy muskets for them when the time comes."

El-i-chi laughed. "With boys, my little Rose, nothing is ever simple."

Later, when he went to the creek with blankets, fire, and food, he found his sons huddling in a brush shelter and shivering with the cold. The forlorn skunk pelt, inside out, looking white and greasy and putting out fresh torrents of scent that were undetectable to the desensitized noses of the boys, was fastened to a tree. The shaman had a suspicion that it would stay there until it rotted away. His mighty hunters, he felt, had had all the skunk they would ever want.

Many times during the next few days the comte de Beaujolais feared that Renna was dying. Her skin would become cold and her breathing so faint that he had to put his ear next to her mouth to hear it at all. He was torn between trying to get her downriver to Natchez and halting to make a comfortable camp so that she would be spared being hauled in and out of the canoe and lying on the floor of the boat in the sun all day. After three days of torment it was Renna herself who helped him make his decision. She opened her eyes as he was carrying her to the canoe at dawn of the fourth day.

"What are you doing to me?" she asked.

"Thank God," he said. He waded into the water and settled her on the blankets that were spread in the bottom of the canoe. "I'm taking you back to civilization so you can get well."

"Beau?" She raised her head with effort.

"Yes, my dear girl?"

She lay back, exhausted by the effort. "He killed my husband. That monster killed Philip."

"I am so sorry."

"And the Spanish officer—"

Beau grimaced. He had feared as much.

"Don't talk now," he said.

"Where—"

"We're going down the river. We will be in Natchez in a few days, and there'll be doctors there."

"Oh, God . . ."

"Hush, now."

"My baby . . ." All that she had left of Philip, his child, was gone as well.

"Hush, Renna. Close your eyes. I will be with you."

"Did you bury my baby?"

He flushed with guilt. "Yes," he lied. "I buried it."

"I'm thirsty."

"Of course."

He gave her water from his canteen. "You'll need food, too." But the flotilla was already under way, and he did not want to be left behind alone in the wilderness with a sick woman.

He called a halt at midday and made porridge for Renna, but she could force down only a little. She slept in the canoe through the afternoon. Still bleeding on occasion, she was very weak.

In camp that evening, after taking more porridge and great quantities of water, she told him the entire story.

"I am very sorry now that I didn't let the Spaniards kill him," he said.

"I would gladly kill him myself," she responded.

Two days before reaching Natchez Renna became feverish, and by the time the little flotilla landed at the city that had become the capital of the Mississippi Territory in 1798, she was delirious. Soon after landing, Beau found a doctor. Renna was bathed, settled in a clean bed, under a stiff linen sheet, and was being fussed over by the doctor and his wife while Beau hovered nervously nearby.

She was having the old nightmare, which she had first experienced as a child of about seven. Something infinitely evil and unimaginably, immeasurably loathsome was pursuing her. At first, running like the wind, she fled the horror, but then something began to pull at her feet. Her limbs became leaden. She was moving in slow motion, each step completed only after torturous straining, and she was moving only inches at a time while the evil entity gained on her. . . .

She awoke moaning. Perspiration, beads of panic, ran into her eyes. A small oil lamp was burning. She was in a real bed, with a clean sheet pulled up to her chin. Beside the bed the comte de Beaujolais dozed in a rocker. She reached for a towel on the bedside table, assuring herself that it was over, that Othon Hugues had been left far behind, far up the river. In a perfect world, a world of justice, he would be dead by now, killed by the relatives of the Choctaw girl he had mutilated or by the Creek.

It was a still, muggy night. She wiped her eyes and forehead and let her arm fall, for that small effort had tired her. She heard the shrill singing of cicadas. An owl hooted once, twice, from far away.

She heard Beau's even, deep breathing and took the opportunity to look closely at him. His face, although browned by the southern sun, was so fair, so well formed. She smiled. Here, then, was the prince whom she had dreamed about before—oh, God—before Philip had ridden down from the north to claim her heart.

"Oh, Philip, love of my life. Oh, Philip."

Until that moment she had not realized the depth of her loss. She had seen him fall, had felt the blood that oozed from the fatal wound at the base of his skull. Logic had told her then that he was dead, but during the events that followed so swiftly, the most powerful instinct of all, self-preservation, had pushed aside her grief. During her days of coma, stupor, and fever, a benevolent numbness had protected her from the enervation of grief by dulling her mind. So it was that in the warmth of a Mississippi night, with an owl hooting lazily and with cicadas trilling happily from the trees just outside the windows of her room, she felt for the first time the impact of Philip's death. The pain was too penetrating, too potent to allow for tears. She lay in stunned silence as her aching heart eroded. Her eyes rested on the face of a sleeping prince but saw the dear, never-to-be-forgotten face of her beloved Philip.

Pale-haired, emaciated, wan in face and in spirit, wearing a faded calico dress given to her by the doctor's wife, Renna Woods walked the streets of Natchez on the arm of a solicitous Frenchman. At first the strolls were brief—a block, no more.

"You know," Beau told her during one of the first of her short, recuperative walks, "that this was originally a French town."

"So I was taught," Renna said in a listless voice.

"By a beautiful teacher whom I once met?" Beau asked. "By Lady Beth Huntington?"

"Yes," she said. "My stepmother." She was silent, musing. She was in southernmost Mississippi Territory, with Spanish Louisiana just down the river. She was weak, so weak that to think of making the trek upriver to reach Fort Jefferson and then across country to The House seemed an impossible dream.

"I must go home," she said. "I must, Beau. By now the people at Fort Jefferson will know some of what happened. Perhaps they've found Philip's . . . uh, Philip's body. I must go home so my family will not mourn my death. I must notify Philip's family, too."

"The doctor says that it will be some time before you recover from your ordeal," Beau said. "I've made the journey upriver. It's strenuous and long and dangerous. The more sensible thing is to take you on into New Orleans, where you will have the best medical care available. We can send letters to your family and his from there."

"Letters that will have to go by ship to the eastern coast of the United States, then back toward the west cross-country," Renna said.

"I see no other alternative," Beau told her gently. "Traveling upriver will be too exhausting for you."

As the days passed, the daily stroll became longer in both time and distance. She was impressed by the vitality, by the bustle of activity in the Mississippi River town. She and Beau met and talked with former British loyalists who had sought exile in what was then a British outpost. The couple was invited to dine in the home of one of the original Spanish settlers. They spoke Beau's native tongue with descendants of the original French founders or chatted with brash, boastful rivermen from Tennessee and Kentucky who were on their way by flatboat to the markets in New Orleans.

Renna's fever recurred just as she was beginning to have a bit of color in her cheeks, and when she was once again able to get out of bed, she made no protest when Beau took her aboard a Mississippi flatboat and made her comfortable in a canvas shelter for the float down the river to New Orleans. The young man was constantly at her side. She had, without realizing it, come to depend on him for all the necessities of life. He brought her food and water. He saw to it that her new clothing was washed and clean. He brushed her pale hair and even became adept at braiding it. When the fever came again, he held her head as she vomited up vile, yellow horrors. And when the nightmare came to her in the darkness, he was there to squeeze her hand and say, "There, now, everything is all right. Go back to sleep. I am here."

Chapter Eight

The crew of a Kentucky flatboat gathered in an odoriferous group to watch the Frenchman and the woman come aboard. The woman was young and obviously had been quite ill. She leaned weakly on the Frenchman's arm but managed a smile for the assembled Kentuckians as the man helped her up the slanted gangplank to the rough-hewn planks of the deck. A bearded, lanky frontiersman in a coonskin cap and fringed buckskins surprised himself by bowing to the woman as the Frenchman led her toward a canvas-covered shelter near the stern.

"If they's ary a thang we'uns kin do fer ye, ma'am . . ." the captain of the flatboat said.

"Thank you," Renna responded. "You are very kind to allow us to accompany you, sir."

"My pleasure, ma'am," the Kentuckian said.

Behind the flatboat captain, two ragged frontiersmen capered, mocking his bow. "My pleasure, ma'am," one of them minced in a falsetto voice.

The captain turned to face his tormentors. "Now, fellers," he drawled, "you'uns wouldn't want me to give this here lady a false impression of Kentucky gents by moppin' up the deck with your sorry hides, would you?"

"A rough lot, indeed," Beau said under his breath. He helped Renna settle down onto the pile of blankets under the shelter.

"They are good men," she said. "I know them." She smiled. "Not personally, not as individuals, but as a type. I imagine that all the older men fought with George Washington, and many were probably with the Kentucky cavalry at Fallen Timbers. You could probably leave your purse full of gold lying about all the way to New Orleans, and not a piece of it would go missing; and if you make them your friends, they would die at your side rather than desert you in time of danger."

Indeed, the rough rivermen vied with one another in supplying the pale, emaciated woman with the choice cuts of meat and the freshest fish. And when illness struck Renna again, confining her to her bed with racking chills, followed by a fever that threatened to consume her altogether, the men hovered around with worried looks, speaking in soft tones, murmuring prayers.

Beau never left her side for more than a few minutes at a time. His devotion impressed the rough frontiersmen.

"Any feller what loves a gal that much," one of them remarked, "even if'n he's a Frenchie, cain't be all bad."

Renna had to be carried to a carriage when the flatboat arrived in New Orleans. While she was being tenderly installed in the vehicle by men from the flatboat, Beau inquired about the best doctors. Soon Renna was in a proper bed in a doctor's house with the learned Spanish physician lifting her eyelids, peering down her throat, and thumping her chest and back. The doctor listened gravely as Beau told the circumstances of the loss of Renna's baby.

"Ah," said the doctor. "Following grave sorrow to the heart, this *niña pobre* suffered severe physical trauma. The result is that her entire system is weakened, thus making her easy prey for the fevers."

"I will pay you so I might have the room next to hers," Beau offered.

"That is not allowed," the doctor replied.

"I have been at her side for a long time," Beau said, his voice hard, his face set. "I do not intend to leave her now."

The days passed . . . a week . . . two weeks . . . Beau left Renna alone in the doctor's little *dispensario* only long enough to check with the office of the French representative in New Orleans to find that in his absence orders had come for him.

Renna was walking, and her improved appetite made both Beau and the Spanish physician smile. Slowly, slowly, she began to regain the pounds that had been consumed by the fevers.

"I feel like a small child just learning to walk," she told Beau and the doctor. "My legs have no more strength than those of a toddler."

"If there is no recurrence of the fever," the doctor said, "you will soon be strong again. A few months, no more."

"Months?" Beau asked grimly.

Renna looked at him closely. "You have to leave, don't you?"

"I have been ordered to St. Domingue," he admitted. "A ship is in port at this time. It will leave within a matter of days for the islands." He watched her face for her reaction.

"If you are ordered to go, then you must go," she whispered.

"Such a course of action would present certain problems," he said.

"I'll be fine, Beau," she said, but her cheeriness sounded forced. "I'm getting stronger every day. When I'm fully recovered, I'll find a group of Kentuckians headed up-river toward home and travel with them to Fort Jefferson."

A look of pain crossed Beau's face, and he glanced at the doctor, who discreetly left them alone. "I cannot bear to think of you by yourself on the river with such men, even if you do believe that they are honorable." He pulled her to him. "You must go with me."

"Beau, I can't," she whispered, although the thought of being left alone in New Orleans clearly chilled her.

"There is no other way," he said. "You have not recovered from your illness. There will be good doctors in St. Domingue. As vice-consul to General Victor Leclerc I will be in a position to see that you are cared for. The letters we have sent to your family will have reached them, so they will no longer be worried about you. Knowing your father, I would think that he just might go to North Carolina and come for you in one of your stepmother's ships."

"He would," she agreed, warmed instantly by the thought of her father. Ah, so many times during the past period of anguish and pain she had called out for him in her mind.

"Then it is settled," Beau said. "We will sail for St. Domingue within the week."

The French merchantman that put down the river to the open Gulf was a trim ship, and the cabins assigned to Beau and Renna were spacious—as ship's cabins went—and comfortable. Fortunately there were no storms blowing in the Gulf of Mexico, so the first days of the voyage were pleasant. The sea air served as a tonic to Renna. Her cheeks began to regain their color. Her appetite impressed even the French officers, men who appreciated good food.

On an evening of favorable winds and a fiery sunset that could only have been the work of the Master Painter Himself, Renna and Beau stood at the rail, watching porpoises stitch in and out of the untroubled surface of the Gulf. He had his arm around her waist. So often had he supported her thus when she was too feeble to walk alone that his touch seemed natural to her. She found herself talking about the events that had occurred far up the Mississippi. In a bleak, unmodulated tone she described her terror as she watched Othon Hugues torment the Indian girl. She talked, then, of Philip, and made to feel at ease by Beau's patient understanding and gentleness, she wept for her dead husband for the first time. Beau turned her to face him and cradled her in his arms, and she put her head on his shoulder and let the hard, racking sobs take her.

"Ah, Beau," she said hoarsely after a timeless interval during which she had given herself over completely to her grief, "you are so good. You are as dear as a brother to me. How can I ever repay you for what you have done?"

She did not suspect that her words knifed into Beau's heart. He had just experienced the ultimate bitterness for a man in love—the hopelessness that comes when he holds the woman he adores in his arms while she weeps for another man. Then, to be told that she looked on him as a brother!

And yet he was not totally dismayed. The seas were wide, and time was long. Wounds heal. One day he knew she would overcome her pain, not by forgetting her dead husband but by the simple process of living. Knowing Renna and recognizing her loyalty, he knew that it would take a long while. In the meantime, as the days of their voyage passed, he listened. He encouraged her to confide in him during the balmy, sunny days and the long, slowly darkening evenings.

"Talk it away," he urged her, when she confessed that her worst fear was to fall again into the hands of Othon Hugues. "Only by facing that which we fear can we conquer it."

The ship sailed into a storm in the Caribbean—not one of the deadly, raging storms that had ravaged so many ships and left the ocean floor strewn with the wreckage and the riches of Spanish treasure galleons, but a respectable storm nevertheless. At its height Renna, frightened, sought out Beau in his cabin and clung to him. At last she went to sleep in his arms. . . .

She awoke in his cabin. Her clothing had been loosened at her throat. She lay on his bed. He was sleeping in a chair. She had spent the night in the cabin of a man who was not her husband, but that was not her main concern as she looked at Beau's face and listened to his deep, even breathing.

What have I become? she wondered, miserable. *I am*

the daughter of Renno, with the blood of generations of sachems in my veins.

Yet she had run to Beau's cabin like a child frightened by thunder. It simply would not do, her acting like some silly girl from Philadelphia or London. A granddaughter of Ghonkaba and Toshabe did not cringe at the imaginary ogres of the darkness, nor did she panic because of a storm at sea. It was time for her to be Renna again, to erase the past, and to conquer the helpless terror she had felt when she was at the mercy of Othon Hugues.

But as she thought of him, vivid and horrific pictures came to her. In spite of her brave front she was still haunted by his pockmarked face. The feeble, protesting moans of the dying Choctaw girl continued to steal into her mind from the dark regions of nightmares and make her feel faint. Because there was in Renna something of grace, a knowledge of good, and perhaps just a touch of God or the Master of Life, she shivered, knowing without doubt that on the banks of the Mississippi she had been exposed not to a "merely" sadistic man but to someone wielding a power infinitely more potent, more evil.

She shuddered and successfully cleared her mind of Othon Hugues. She watched Beau sleep for a few more moments. He had been the dream prince of her youth, and now he had come back into her life too late, for there was no room in her heart for another. He was a true friend, a brother. She felt no guilt for having slept in his cabin, save a rueful acknowledgment that Beau couldn't have been too comfortable sleeping in the chair. She rose, straightened her clothing, and drew her forefinger playfully along the surface of Beau's upper lip and cheeks. His skin was rough with the stubble of a night's growth of beard. He lifted one hand lazily to brush away the irritant. When she laughed, he opened his eyes.

"My dear comte," she said teasingly, "the morning is half-spent, and I have stayed the night in your cabin. Whatever will the ship's officers and crew think?"

"They will be envious," he replied smilingly. He looked at her happily. "They would all like to see your pretty face as they came out of sleep. They are French, after all."

By the time the ship reached the island first seen by Christopher Columbus and his men on 6 December 1492, Renna's youth and vitality had triumphed over her illness. Those who had spent time in tropical and subtropical climes knew, however, that her fever might recur, for that was the nature of the illness. Indeed, if the Good God intended it, she could be one of those unfortunates whose urine would one day blacken with the heat of the fever, and in that event she would die. But many had contracted the fever to which the black slaves from Africa seemed to be immune, and many had lived. Renna, with the optimism of youth, chose to believe that the fever would not attack her again. In fact, the thought of dying from it never entered her mind once her strength returned.

The aboriginal Arawak Indians had called the island Quisqueya or Hayti. When Columbus landed on the northwestern tip he named it La Isla Española. The French pirates from Tortuga who wrested a foothold from the Spaniards on the western point and founded Port-de-Paix christened their territory St. Domingue, and thus it was still called in late 1801 when the comte and his lady landed amid strife and confusion.

Ironically, it had been the French Revolution that had first inspired St. Domingue's half-million Negroes to rise up against slavery and French rule. Crying "Liberty, Equality, and Fraternity," the slaves won emancipation in 1794. For these illiterate, half-savage people, however, mere emancipation was not enough; it did not satisfy the stuff of their dreams. Only their leaders enjoyed the luxuries once reserved for the French overlords. The masses had traded the whip of the overseer not for the master's fine house, ample food, and fancy clothing, but for unabating poverty and hunger. To most, freedom meant only that they no longer had a Frenchman to provide them with the basic necessities. Since freedom obviously meant cessation of work, the fields and plantations that had once fed them were neglected.

Thus, when Pierre-Dominique Toussaint l'Ouverture promised all the things about which the populace dreamed, he was enthusiastically applauded and supported by the masses. In May of 1801, he proclaimed himself governor-general for life and adopted a constitution not at all to the liking of Napoleon Bonaparte, who needed St. Domingue as a way station to his secretly held colony in North America. The populace did not waver in their loyalty to the new governor-general, and since l'Ouverture provided a steady flow of food, they flocked by the thousands to join his army. To meet this renewed threat to French rule, the first consul sent his own brother-in-law Victor Leclerc in command of a veteran army, to restore French dominance.

Leclerc himself had written the orders for the comte de Beaujolais to join him. He had seen Beaujolais in action, and he liked the young man in spite of his royal blood. Beaujolais had shown great talent as an administrator, and Leclerc needed a capable man to run the country while he himself chased down l'Ouverture and his lieutenants.

Leclerc was very well pleased when informed that the comte de Beaujolais was in the anteroom. He rushed out, extended his arms for a quick embrace, and got down to business immediately. He pulled Beaujolais into his office, seated him, and paced the floor as he explained the situation.

"There are five hundred thousand black faces in this colony, Beaujolais," Leclerc said, "and twenty-four thousand mixed bloods who are probably in sympathy with the uprising. There are—or were—thirty-two thousand French settlers."

"It would seem to me, General," Beau said, "that we face intimidating odds."

Leclerc waved his hand to indicate that Beau's comment meant nothing. "It is not the numbers," he explained. "It is this bedamned country. They strike, and heaven help the Frenchman who is their target, for their actions are barbaric. When we give chase, they melt into the mountains. A fellow who calls himself Agussu is particularly troublesome. He is l'Ouverture's right hand and a master of the quick raid—strike hard and quickly and withdraw." He rubbed his palms together. "But we will get Agussu and l'Ouverture, and when we cut off the rebellion's head, the snake of unrest will writhe for a few moments and then die."

He added that at the moment, however, the snake was very much alive.

It was not difficult to find suitable quarters. Beaujolais installed Renna in the town house of a French plantation owner who had taken his family away from the bloody island. The house was staffed with servants—one mulatto man and three females of light skin—who greeted the new masters warily. When assured that they would still have a place to live and that the dwindling victuals in the storage areas would be replenished, the staff showed strong white teeth in happy smiles.

The youngest servant, a girl named Sylvie, was lithe and comely. A member of the third generation of Creoles, her features were those of the Frenchmen who had passed down their blood to her. Her eyes were reminiscent of women shown in the ancient Egyptian artwork brought back to France by those who accompanied Napoleon to the land of the pharaohs. Sylvie's hair was inky black, a mass of silken sheen that she had loosened for only one man in her young life—a man who came to her, even now, with regularity. She spoke French without the Creole revisions that made the argot of the people almost impossible to understand unless one had lived on the island for some years.

Since Renna and Sylvie were of an age and because Sylvie was a gentle, polite, fastidious person, Renna quickly became partial to her. While Beau went about the business of government Renna spent hours asking Sylvie about life and conditions in St. Domingue. As her health continued to improve, Renna told the girl about the United States, the Seneca village, and her family.

Like her father, Renna hated slavery. She realized that it was natural for Sylvie to feel bitterness toward white men. "But, Sylvie," she explained, "the French did not bring your people here to be slaves; the French freed you. Spain brought slavery to the island, to the entire New World. At first the Spanish enslaved the native Indian populations, and when they found that Indians didn't make good slaves—that they died quickly, preferring death to bondage—they bought Africans from Arab and African slave traders."

"And yet," Sylvie said, "if the French went back to their own home, we would be free to run our own country."

"Why is it *your* country? The descendants of the French and Spanish settlers, after all, were here before the first black slaves were brought over."

"Since you are white," Sylvie responded, "you would not understand."

"I am Seneca," Renna told her, but that distinction obviously held no meaning for Sylvie.

There were nights when the demands of Beau's office kept him away from the town house until the gray hours of morning. On such a night Renna woke from her old nightmare: she was running in slow motion through deep mire, and Othon Hugues was just behind her, gaining on her. Her body was damp with sweat when she sat up in bed and gasped for breath. She got up and walked to a moonlit balcony overlooking the garden. She felt a bit of relief there. All was quiet.

She went down into the garden and walked to the low stone wall that looked toward the sea. A cooling breeze moved the leaves of flowering tropical plants, creating a rustling sound that covered any small noise made by her movements, so that she almost stumbled over a couple lying side by side on the grass.

"Who are you?" she asked, startled. She was backing away, but the man, his bare skin blending into the darkness, moved faster and seized her arm.

"Don't hurt her," a female voice said.

"Sylvie, is that you?" Renna asked.

"Yes, mistress." The girl was getting to her feet and pulling her disheveled clothing into order. "Release her, Agussu."

"That will not do," the man growled. "She has seen me, and now, you little fool, you have said my name."

"I don't know who you are," Renna said firmly, "but you are in my garden. I advise you to do as Sylvie says before I call Monsieur Beaujolais and the other servants."

The moonlight glinted on a long blade in Agussu's hand. He lifted it. Renna tensed herself to use the only weapon available to her, a knee to his groin.

But Sylvie seized Agussu's arm and put her full weight on it. "No!" she whispered hoarsely. "She is not like the others. She is my friend."

After Agussu released Renna's arm and lowered his machete, he turned to Sylvie. "If this one betrays me, I will not be able to see you again until we have won."

"She will not betray you," Sylvie said.

"Perhaps it would be best if you did not come into my garden again," Renna said. "I do not take kindly to being threatened in my own home."

"You do not belong here," Agussu grated. "This little fool has told me about you. I advise you to go back to your people. If you stay here, you will die, as the other whites must die."

Renna held her tongue.

"I will go now, Sylvie," Agussu said.

"My mistress will not betray you," Sylvie promised in a small voice.

"No matter," Agussu said lightly. "The Frenchman who can capture Agussu has not yet been born." He laughed. "I am Agussu! With me is the magic of our ancestors. I have been given the power of the old gods."

He blended into the darkness and was gone.

"You had best go to bed, Sylvie," Renna said. "You have your work to do tomorrow."

The girl hurried away.

Alone, Renna again sat on the low stone wall and looked toward the harbor. She could see the mast lanterns of the ships at anchor. Soon she would have to think of boarding one of those vessels. The voyage would take her to Wilmington, to the home of her father's cousin Nathan

Ridley. From there she would arrange transportation to cross the state to the mountains, and home.

She leaped to her feet at a sound from behind her. She was poised to flee when she recognized the familiar form of Beau.

"You handled that well, my dear," Beau approved. He was unarmed save for a thin stick used by the gardener to support top-heavy flowering plants. The stick would have been of no avail against Agussu's machete.

"You heard?"

"Everything. You were not in your room when I came home," he explained. "I saw movement down here. . . ." He came to her and put his arm around her shoulders. "You must think I am a terrible coward, to stand idle in the darkness while that rascal threatened you."

"No, I think you were very wise not to face a man armed with such a terrible blade while you were without a weapon."

"Thank you. I felt the same way myself." He laughed. "I'm sure that your father would not have stayed in hiding."

Renna thought, *Well, you are right*. And then she took Beau's hand, for that thought was disloyal to the man who had saved her life and who continued to care for her so tenderly.

"If he had persisted—"

"Yes, Beau, I know," she said. There was no doubt in her mind that Beau would have fought the big black man, thin stick against the razor-sharp blade of Agussu's machete.

"But we'll catch the beggar now," Beau enthused. "He has passion for our Sylvie, does he not? He is a man, and she is a beauty. He will come back, and when he does, I will be armed with more than a stick."

"I promised Sylvie that I would not betray him."

"You promised nothing. Sylvie told him that you would not speak. Anyway, I did not learn of his presence from you. I wouldn't call it betrayal, for that would imply that this Agussu is a man of honor. *Non*, he is a butcher, Renna. He must have come directly here, to our garden, from his latest barbarity. Tonight he killed an entire family—a French merchant, his wife, and three children, the youngest a babe in arms."

"How do you know that it was Agussu?"

"He leaves his 'calling card.' He is proud of his bloody work. You see, he fancies that he is invincible because he has the blessings, if you can call them that, of the *voudon* priests. He signs his name in blood, the blood of his victims, surrounding it with *voudon* symbols."

Renna was silent. True, she had not spoken her promise. If there had been a promise, it was one that had been implied by her silence. But she was not betraying Agussu. His own boldness, his passion for Sylvie, had been his downfall. Since Sylvie had promised her lover that Renna would not tell of his presence in the vice-consul's garden, she wondered if she should tell Sylvie that Beau had overheard them, so that Agussu could be warned.

She was still pondering the dilemma after Beau had escorted her back to her bedroom. As she sought sleep, she fought the images emerging from the dark recesses of her mind: Othon Hugues became Agussu, and the dying Choctaw girl became a Frenchwoman begging for the lives of her children. Thus, in her mind, Agussu became Hugues, a rabid animal to be killed without mercy.

Agussu returned to the garden only three nights later. The French soldiers who lay in wait concealed themselves until the big Negro was quite occupied with Sylvie in their favorite grassy bower, his machete lying beside them. When the sergeant in command of the detail signaled, the men crept forward to encircle the busy couple. One soldier stumbled, and Agussu jumped to his feet, his weapon in hand. When the rebel leader saw the gleam of moonlight on musket barrels, he roared in rage and slashed downward, almost decapitating Sylvie, who had sat up in alarm.

"Thus I repay those who betray me," Agussu bellowed, lunging to attack.

Two shots rang out, but both missed. The French sergeant, a veteran of many campaigns, rushed forward. Before Agussu could add another soldier to his long list of victims, the sergeant stopped Agussu with a well-placed musket butt to the back of his head.

Renna, deeply saddened, had overseen the burial of Sylvie. It was a day of steaming heat and threatening skies. When she returned to the town house, Beau was waiting for her.

"Agussu has asked to see you," he said.

"I don't care to see him," she replied quickly.

"They're going to burn him," Beau said.

"Burn?"

"Burn," he repeated. "As in a bonfire. They will tie him to a stake and heap wood under and around him, and they'll douse the wood with oil and light it."

"How horrible," she said, cringing.

"Some see it as fitting punishment for his butcheries," Beau said.

"Why does he want to see me?" she asked.

"When I told him that Sylvie had not betrayed him, that I had seen him in the garden, he wept. I think he wants to tell you that he is sorry that he killed Sylvie."

"That will not bring her back to life."

"No. Well, I wouldn't advise your going to him."

"But to be burned," she whispered, with a shudder. "I will go. If that will give him some ease, I will go."

Renna stood before the cell door. Agussu was in irons and behind bars. He lay on a rude cot, his eyes closed. A guard barked his name harshly, then said, "You wanted to speak to this lady, you black bastard, so get on your feet."

"Ah, mistress," Agussu said, swinging his powerful legs off the bed with a jangle of chains. He stood, tall and proud and muscular, dressed only in a loincloth. His skin glowed with perspiration. "I am told that it was not my poor Sylvie who betrayed me."

"No, nor was it I," Renna responded. "It is as the comte told you. He came into the garden that night."

"No matter." He laughed. "These French fools think that they can kill Agussu." The man drew himself to his full height. "I have asked to speak to you, mistress, because I feel that only you can understand what I have to say. Agussu cannot be killed. I was born of woman, but I was sired by a panther. The power of the old gods is in me."

His voice rose to near hysteria, and Renna took a step back.

"Burn me, will they?" he continued in a fury. "They will try, of that I am sure. But I am Agussu! I will call upon the magic of the old gods, and I will become a fly. I will soar above the flames."

"Prepare your wings, fly," taunted the guard.

"And, mistress, I had another reason for asking to see you. I wanted to tell you that your man, the man who was too cowardly to face me in the garden, will be the first to die when I return."

Anger flared in Renna. "In spite of your crimes, I have felt sympathy for you," she said. "I thought that the flames were too severe a punishment."

He laughed. "And now you will be there, to see me writhe and burn?"

Her eyes flared.

"I am content, mistress," he said, sitting down on the cot.

The great pyre was prepared in a square near the municipal buildings. At the center of the pile a log had been buried deep into the earth to serve as the stake to which Agussu would be bound.

Long before first light Negroes began to gather in the square, and throughout the morning the crowds grew. The gathering was orderly. Many had brought food and picnicked on the cobblestones. As the sun neared its zenith, the city's French population began to make an appearance, occupying an area that had been cordoned off for them near the center of the square, upwind from the pyre.

Renna had decided at the last minute to accompany Beau, who, as a government official, was required to be in attendance. When Agussu was led into the square by four Negroes in the uniform of the French, each of them

holding a chain that was attached to one of the rebel
leader's legs or arms, he walked with great dignity. His
eyes moved purposefully over the gathering of Negroes,
then settled with disdain on the French troops surrounding the square. He made no protest as he was pushed
against the stake. Although his powerful arms were chained
behind him, his legs were freed, so that when he writhed,
the pain of his death would be more evident to the gathered Negroes. General Victor Leclerc supervised his
placement.

"I have one last word for my people," Agussu requested.

"Speak," Leclerc ordered.

"My brothers!" Agussu cried, his voice filling the
square, "we have fought, you and I! We will fight again!"

A soldier raised his musket to silence Agussu.

"No, let him continue," Leclerc said.

"I have led you, and I will lead you again, for I,
Agussu, am born of woman and panther. I cannot be
harmed by the white man's flames. Do not weep for me,
brothers, for I will soar above the fires and lead you to
final victory."

At a nod from Leclerc, soldiers lighted the oil-soaked
pyre. Then the French commander moved to stand on the
forward edge of the pyre. "Look upon the criminal Agussu!"
he thundered to the spectators. "He is condemned because he rebelled against those who are the only hope for
you. What have Agussu and his master, l'Ouverture, given
you other than hunger, misery, and death? Your future is
with the French. Work with us. Help us to build a country of which we all can be proud."

Behind Leclerc the flames burst upward with a
whooshing sound. Fire engulfed Agussu with astounding
quickness. A moan of sympathy came from blacks and
whites alike as his hair burst into flame.

Renna turned away, only to look back quickly when
she heard a gasp of wonder and awe from the crowd.

Agussu did not become a fly; he had no wings to soar
away from the chains and the fire. He had only his bull-
like strength. When the torment of burning galvanized
him into action, he yanked the huge stake from the ground

and, bellowing in terrible agony, came charging out of the smoke and flames, the charring stake on his back.

For a moment Renna would not have been surprised to see him sprout wings and soar. His huge legs kicked aside burning branches. The flames in his hair were extinguished, leaving only a smoking, charred mass atop his skull. His lungs, obviously seared from breathing the flames, were pumping in rasping labor. His momentum carried him toward the white spectators' area.

White women screamed and looked ready to flee. But French soldiers caught him, freed him from the heavy stake, picked him up by his arms and his legs, and tossed him, soaring in an arc, back into the flames.

The hushed crowd heard one long, rasping scream and saw sparks shoot up from the area of his terminal struggles. A smell of burning flesh began to waft out over the square.

"Come, we have seen enough," Beau said in disgust, leading Renna away.

The comte had left orders that when the fire had burned down to embers, black laborers would scoop up the ashes and scatter them into the sea, lest Agussu's followers gather his remains and make them objects of inspiration and worship.

The death of the war leader most popular among the masses was a huge victory for the white man's magic. Agussu had promised the ex-slaves that they would be living in the fine homes of the Frenchmen, that they would be eating rich foods at the tables of the white masters, that the white man's women would be theirs. Now he was dead, his promises unfulfilled. For a time, at least, the *voudon hungans* were discredited, the masses doubtful. And in spite of desperate efforts by l'Ouverture to regain the initiative, the French held an obvious advantage.

Leclerc was understandably ecstatic. "When the day comes that armed rabble can defeat the forces of France, the sun will cease to shine," he told Beau. "And now that we have satisfactorily settled this little matter—"

"There is still l'Ouverture," Beau reminded him.

Leclerc waved his hand, dismissing concern. "He is an ignorant man. He will be as easily taken as was this Agussu. It is only a matter of which bait we should use to trap him. Gold? A woman?" He smiled. "That particular bait seems to work well for these fellows."

The general delayed the conversation long enough to take a pinch of snuff from an elaborately engraved gold box and sniff it into his nostrils. He sneezed delicately, sniffed, and swallowed. "In the meantime, my dear Beaujolais, I have a chore for you."

"I am at your disposal, Governor," Beau said with a little bow.

"I have had enough of these Americans who supply the rebels with goods and weapons," Leclerc said. "I want all American goods and property in this colony seized. I want all American merchants and traders thrown into prison. There will be no exceptions, for by bringing all of them into our net, we will be assured that not one of the criminals who give aid and comfort to the rebels will escape. Moreover, I want all ships' captains tossed into the cells with the Yankee traders."

"As I have said, General," Beau stated, choosing his words carefully, "I am yours to command. I would, however, like to question this decision, with all respect."

"Yes, yes, Beaujolais," Leclerc said impatiently. "I understand your concern. But you are a product of the old regime, when *diplomacy* was the watchword." He uttered the word *diplomacy* as if it were profane. "I have no time to pamper criminals who act against the interests of my country. I want the Americans to understand without doubt that it does not pay to support the enemies of France. You may tell Monsieur Tobias Lear as much, in as many of my own words as you can remember."

Tobias Lear was Thomas Jefferson's unofficial observer in St. Domingue. A capable man who had once been private secretary to President George Washington, he did not wait for the comte to seek him out. At Beau's orders, Americans were dragged from their homes, ships, and places of business. An indignant Lear appeared at the headquarters of General Leclerc and demanded to see the governor. He was escorted into Beau's office.

"My dear Monsieur Lear," Beau said, extending his hand in the manner of the Americans. "I know why you have come. Indeed, I was just about to seek you out."

"If you know why I am here, Monsieur le Comte, then why are you allowing this outrage to continue? I remind you, sir, that the United States and France are not at war, and yet warlike actions are being perpetrated against citizens of the United States in this very city. I must protest with all of the resentment that I can muster."

Beau spread his hands. "I understand, Monsieur Lear. Indeed, I agree with you. You must remember, however, that we are at war here on this island. Many have died, and more will die before the flames of rebellion are doused. Perhaps the military, which governs St. Domingue, is overreacting, feeling heady from its successful capture and execution of Agussu; but you must admit that certain citizens of your country have committed if not crimes, at least acts that are detrimental to the interest of France by trading with the rebels and supplying them with food and weapons."

"Perhaps a few, no more than three or four—" Lear began, but he was interrupted by Beau.

"One would be too many, Monsieur Lear. The actions against Americans are being undertaken at the orders of General Leclerc. His orders, sir, will be carried out." He sighed. "There is one other matter of some urgency."

Lear nodded, waiting.

"The representatives of the government of France hereby notify you, Monsieur Lear, that your presence in St. Domingue is no longer desirable. We will release one American ship immediately, and you, monsieur, must be on it when it leaves the harbor."

Lear's face burned for a few moments, then he recovered his poise. "Beaujolais, I trust that you, a man of tact and intelligence, did not initiate this action."

Beau smiled but made no comment.

"France was our friend once," Lear said. "And when

the people of France rose against tyranny, as the people of the United States had done previously, our nation applauded and made it clear that we would stand by France in her time of trouble."

"And then came the Jay Treaty," Beau pointed out.

"A much misunderstood piece of paper," Lear responded. "Men of goodwill have prayed that this misunderstanding on the part of the French would, at last, have been cleared away, that never again would our two great nations face each other in hostility. We prayed thus even when French pirates were seizing American ships, even when there was a clear threat of open war between us. That breach was healed—or at least was on the way to being healed—but now this happens. Now, on a small island in the Caribbean, France raises her weapons of war against Americans."

Beau stood, making it clear that there was nothing more to say. "May there always be men of goodwill in both our countries, Monsieur Lear, to smooth over our differences."

When the leader of the revolt, Toussaint l'Ouverture himself, was captured and sent off in chains to France, it seemed as if St. Domingue had been secured to serve as a Caribbean naval base for French possessions in Louisiana. Beau was busy trying to organize a working government, using a few educated Negroes who were, at least ostensibly, loyal to the French.

By this time Renna had fully recovered. Months of plentiful food, rest, walks with Beau along the shore, good talk, and gentle companionship had erased all physical scars of her ordeal. Her spiritual wounds, too, were less tender. She was not yet in love with Beau, and had not even so much as kissed him. But she was very fond of him. In spite of the tragedies she had suffered, he had a knack of making her laugh. She no longer concerned herself with the fact that she had traveled alone with Beau and now lived alone with him in a large, elegant town house. Whatever assumptions other people made about propriety were their affair, not hers. She had more important things on her mind—it was time for her to leave. She said as much to Beau.

"Yes, I have feared that you would say that," he painfully admitted. "I can't blame you, my dear. I will, of course, accompany you."

"You have your responsibilities," she said. "And you have done more than enough for me already. I will be perfectly safe aboard one of your great French warships. And once I reach Wilmington, I will be among friends and relations."

But, Beau cried out to himself in silence, *how will I live without you?*

As it happened, it would be some time before he was forced to examine that question more fully. Napoleon and General Victor Leclerc had made one fatal strategic mistake. Many soldiers in Leclerc's veteran army were men of color who had served France well in European battles. In command of these troops were two mulatto generals, Jean Jacques Dessalines and Henri Christophe. Stationed far from the source of French strength and recognizing a golden opportunity, the two mulatto generals mustered their mixed-blood troops about them and put out the word to the Negroes of St. Domingue that Napoleon and Leclerc intended to restore the institution of slavery, exempting no person of color. This created a renewed racial war.

The two able mulatto generals introduced European tactics to their ever-growing forces. Christophe especially allied himself with the voodoo priests, who were able to exhort the Negro rebels to superhuman efforts. Meanwhile, yellow fever added to the woes of the weakened French army under Leclerc. When Leclerc himself died of the fever, Christophe declared himself King Henry I in the north of the colony and Dessalines titled himself Emperor Jacques.

The comte de Beaujolais, now senior French official in the island colony, sent urgent word to France to provide him with reinforcements. Now it was Beau who wanted Renna to leave. He arranged passage for her on a well-gunned merchantman scheduled to stop in the Bahamas, and from there she would have little difficulty arranging passage to Wilmington.

"I will not leave you," she told him.

"You must go," he insisted. "Unless help comes quickly, I don't think we can win."

"You cared for me in my time of illness," she said. "I would not be a true friend if I deserted you in your time of need."

In the end he did not agree, he simply stopped insisting that she leave. He admitted that he was being totally and thoughtlessly selfish. He simply could not bear to think of life without her.

It had taken Othon Hugues months to make his way down the Mississippi River to New Orleans. The duration of his journey was partly a result of his own choice. Like Beau and Renna, he could have taken passage on an American flatboat. He could have bought or stolen an Indian canoe and made better time by water. Instead, he chose to walk for two reasons: first, having been bested by a member of the former ruling class, he felt the need to punish not only himself but others. And in the relatively thickly populated Choctaw Nation, he found ample opportunity. Second, not knowing how to swim, he felt safer on terra firma.

He had treated his own bruises. The abrasions left by the mauling he had taken healed. He telepathically called upon Melisande, the Witch of the Woods, for courage and strength, and it was as if she had heard him and inspired him to feats that, once he reached New Orleans, would require long, delicious nights to recount in detail. His victims were varied. If he had opportunity to ambush a lone Choctaw man, so it was. If he discovered women and children alone or in small groups, even better. His progress down the river was marked by a trail of blood, but the Choctaw, having been at peace for decades, were incapable of learning the true nature of the events and blamed the bloody mutilations on marauding Creek.

When, at last, he returned to New Orleans and placed his head on the warm breasts of Melisande and became as a child again, her milk warm in his mouth, the humiliation of his defeats faded.

"The master is pleased with you," Melisande whispered. "You served him well, so very well. You sent him many souls."

Melisande's contacts with Spanish and French society through her fortune-telling had brought news to her of the sailing for St. Domingue of a certain comte de Beaujolais and his paramour, a fever-weakened girl who had come down the Mississippi from the United States.

"For the moment, my love," she whispered to Othon, "they have escaped us, and although I cannot see it all clearly, I feel that they will return to New Orleans."

"And when they do," Othon growled, "ah, when they do . . ."

"In the meantime, love, let us serve the master."

"Just tell me how."

She spoke, referring to the techniques he'd developed during his orgy of death among the Choctaw. "The well-fed peacocks in New Orleans deserve to experience the same fear and suffering," she said. "And since they will soon realize that something deadly moves among them, their fears will be magnified."

At first it was easy for Othon to stalk and kill well-dressed French- and Englishmen and the occasional woman. For his own amusement he captured and enjoyed Creole girls, choosing only those of great beauty. But his most intense pleasure came when he could carry to his underground hideaway a young French or Spanish girl of good family.

Each time he enjoyed, then killed, later extracting from his victim something in the form of a trophy. For example, Melisande liked to use freshly cleaned skulls in her ceremonies with her Creole and Negro followers, while the native voodoo practitioners made use of the long, beautiful hair of Othon's female victims. More than one priest exhorted his flock by waving a human femur at them.

As Melisande had predicted, the people of New Orleans became aware that they were living in a reign of terror. At nights the streets were deserted. The Spanish government postured and shouted promises but was helpless to stop the murderous monster that stalked the nights.

President Thomas Jefferson had sent for his secretary of state late in the day. James Madison's usually neat hair was slightly mussed and his customarily immaculate clothing just a bit limp.

"James," Jefferson said, "this year started out with my being given what was, most probably, the world's largest cheese."

Madison laughed. He remembered the occasion well. The cheese—1,230 pounds of it, a wheel four feet in diameter and fifteen inches thick—had been made from a single day's milk supply of "all the Republican cows in Cheshire, Massachusetts."

"With an event of such significance occurring on the first day of the year, I thought that the rest of the year would be anticlimactic, even peaceful." He sighed. "I have just talked with Tobias Lear."

"I think, Mr. President, that Mr. Lear might tend to overestimate the importance of the incident in St. Domingo." Madison used the American pronunciation of the French colony. "He was, after all, personally involved and viewed his expulsion as a personal insult."

"How do you evaluate the affair, James?"

"Actually, although I deplore the imprisonment of our citizens and the seizure of their property, I think that in the long run the situation in St. Domingo will work to our advantage. The mere fact that the French on the island feel it necessary to take such drastic measures to keep American citizens from trading with the rebels indicates to me, sir, that the claims of French victory are premature."

He paused, tented his hands, and stared at Jefferson, who was turned in his chair to look out a window. Madison took advantage of the comfortable silence to remember when he had been asked by a Russian diplomat to describe Thomas Jefferson. He recalled now what he had told the Russian. "The president is a rather spare man, tall of stature, not so much grave as sedate. He can smile. He lacks any hint of ostentation or pomp."

Madison had not mentioned to the stolid Russian that Mr. Jefferson had a sense of humor and could tell an amusing story with charm and well-chosen words.

As the president turned back from the window, Madison continued. "I would, sir, advise that you send a message to Mr. Livingston in Paris, informing him of what has happened in St. Domingo. I would ask our worthy ambassador to indicate to those with whom he confers that in the event of continued rebellion in St. Domingo, a French sea-lane to New Orleans would be extremely insecure."

Jefferson nodded. "I was just thinking of the vastness of the American continent, of the distances involved. It is almost impossible to remain abreast of events in far-distant places, such as New Orleans and St. Domingo. For all I know, the French might have started arriving in Louisiana."

Madison nodded grimly. "In the time that it has taken Tobias Lear to get back here from the Caribbean, the situation in Port-au-Prince might have changed drastically."

"And water travel is swifter than travel by land," the president pointed out. "I've sent an agent to New Orleans—or at least I've requested that the Seneca Renno, a man trusted by Washington, go to New Orleans. This request was made months ago, but I have heard nothing from the sachem. This concerns me, since our representatives in Europe have rushed the dreaded word to us that the rumored cession of Louisiana to France is, indeed, 'a transaction of pretty long standing.'"

The men sat in thoughtful silence. Then Madison spoke. "If Livingston speaks of the French sea-lanes to New Orleans, might not Napoleon take that statement as a threat? You have said, Mr. President, that you would view French occupation of the mouth of the Mississippi as an act of defiance. Sooner or later France must be informed of your feelings."

"We will wait, James, for word from Livingston regarding France's attitude toward our offer to purchase New Orleans." He rubbed his face tiredly. It had been a long day. "James, why can't Napoleon see that if he takes possession of New Orleans, he forces us into alliance with England? Spain—poor, old, weak, feeble Spain—would have stayed quietly in New Orleans for years. I am convinced that their new truculence, this threatened closing of the river to American trade, is at the prompting of France. Well, if we must, we will marry ourselves to the British fleet and nation. We will build ships, and we will forge cannon, and with England, we will make it impossible for France to reinforce her settlements on this continent."

"And in so doing," Madison inquired, "assure that we will forever share the continent with the British?"

"That is not my desire," Jefferson said with feeling. "My actions will be forced on me by France, unless they agree to let us purchase New Orleans and, hopefully, East and West Florida."

"I have been wondering, Mr. President, if we might be putting too much importance on New Orleans and the Floridas and ignoring the remainder of Louisiana," Madison said.

Jefferson gave the secretary of state a thin smile. "Ah, James, forget the balance of Louisiana? Never. But it's a matter of priorities, my friend, priorities. New Orleans is the key. Kentucky and Tennessee will scream for war if Spain closes the river to their trade. We will leave the question of the great West for the moment. If France should agree to sell New Orleans, if she should give up control of the Mississippi, then she will not, in the future, be able to build a colonial empire strong enough to withstand a determined United States. Our destiny, James, is to expand. Once the fate of New Orleans is settled, then we can turn our energies to the rest of Louisiana."

Madison looked at Jefferson with new respect. This was the man whom many had called a dreamer, a pure theoretician. But Madison had learned a lot about Thomas Jefferson during their relatively short time of working together in Washington. Jefferson was a dreamer, perhaps, but a dreamer who had ordered American warships into the waters made hazardous by the Barbary pirates . . .

a dreamer who not only had the gall to try to coax control of the most important waterway on the continent from France but was looking ahead to a time when a more secure, more powerful United States could begin to plan for—not dream of—settlement in the great West.

If the news arriving from France only days after Madison's conversation with the president discouraged Jefferson, he gave no sign of it. A dispatch had come from Robert Livingston in which he stated that the French were no longer trying to conceal the agreement of cession with Spain. They had openly told Livingston that they intended to take possession of New Orleans and Louisiana, and no offers from the United States would be considered before that time.

"There never was a government," Livingston wrote, "in which less can be done by negotiation than here. There is no people, no Legislature, no counselors. One man is every thing. He seldom asks advice and never hears it unasked. His ministers are mere clerks, and his Legislature and counselors parade officers."

"Hail, King Napoleon," Madison said in disgust, upon reading the letter.

Chapter Nine

Renno and Little Hawk, mounted on horses that had been bred by Beth, left Huntington Castle to travel leisurely toward the west. They took time to hold informal council with Cherokee village chiefs until they had passed the ill-defined boundary into the hunting grounds of the Chickasaw.

There was no particular urgency, so they enjoyed little side trips of exploration across likely-looking ridges. Both looked forward to visiting with Renna and Philip at Fort Jefferson. Military couriers had detoured past The House twice with letters from Renna since the day of her departure. The newly wedded couple were, Renna had reported, fat and sassy and eagerly praying for a visit from the entire family.

It took only a few days on the trail to convince Renno anew that although traveling lazily on horseback had its advantages, he preferred to be afoot so as to cover the long, trackless miles in a direct line. Such an ideal was impossible when he had to find a trail and grazing for the horses. On the other hand, the relative ease of riding demanded little in the way of effort or concentration, so he had time to be more attentive to Little Hawk.

Little Hawk, although he retained the lithe slimness of a boy, had become a man. He was as tall as his father. His hair, sun-bleached to be more conspicuously blond, was lighter than Renno's. His blue eyes had the farseeing look of an eagle. There were times when Renno would feel an electric shock of eerie recognition when he looked at his son. He had seen the same fair hair, the steely eyes, and the proud stance and sculptured features more than once in spirit form when he had received counsel from the manitou of his ancestor the first Renno.

Ah, Great-grandfather, he would think, seeing Little Hawk dart from tree to tree during the day's hunt for an evening meal or seated on the ground across a flickering campfire. *You have returned to this world in the skin of my son.*

There was in Little Hawk much of the playful boy, evidenced by mighty splashings and cavortings in a clear stream at the end of a day's travel or in the wonder on his face as, on the flat floodplain of the Father of Waters, they halted their horses to watch a top-heavy storm front move toward them, trailing columns of dense rain. But there was also Little Hawk the man, and this new quality in his son fascinated Renno so profoundly that he slowed their pace just to take time to observe and to feel proud.

To Renno's intense satisfaction, Little Hawk was in the process of learning that a father can also be a friend. This was a matter of true significance.

Little Hawk could bend Renno's English longbow with an ease that matched his father's, although his bolts had yet to match the accuracy of either his father or his stepmother. His aim with a thrown tomahawk was deadly, and he was an instinctive shooter. In his hands a musket or a pistol became an extension of himself. He pointed the weapon as he would his finger, and the projectile went where he willed it to go.

In a time of peace, there was no need for Little Hawk's skill at arms, but Renno realized with great pride that in the event of trouble or war, he would be pleased to have at his side this young man who so recently had been his little boy.

And so a new relationship was bonded during that leisurely tour from the eastern area of the Cherokee Nation to the Mississippi. It was no longer man and boy who arrived at the log-palisaded fort on the bluff overlooking the big, muddy river, but two warriors who happened to be father and son. And father and son suffered a similar mixture of rage and grief as they stood with Captain and Mrs. Talbert beside the grave of Philip Woods.

"They were such a beautiful young couple, Sachem," Fran Talbert said tearfully. "So full of life. I just can't bear to think—"

Renno and Little Hawk had heard the story first from Captain Talbert—how Philip's patrol had been overdue, how another patrol from the fort had found the scalped and decayed remains of the officer and his men, Sergeant Sam Lemon among them. Of Renna there had been no sign. The Choctaw who lived near the site of the massacre had reported an incursion by Creek.

"Strange, though, Sachem," Talbert mused. "It's not unusual for a small Creek war party to penetrate all the way to the river and take a couple of scalps. But what happened at Philip and Renna's camp didn't look like the work of an Indian war party out to count coup. One thing in particular puzzled me: the Choctaw had removed her body before our men got there, but they said that one of their women had been mutilated at the campsite. And for a time afterward, someone pretty mean was killing people in the way that girl had been killed, with torture and mutilation. The Choctaw shamans say that the evil one came among them. The killings moved off down the river after a while, then stopped."

Talbert paused. Renno, lost in his own speculations, waited.

"But the whole thing's peculiar," Talbert continued. "Long about the time we figure Philip and the others were killed, the Indians saw a bunch of canoes moving up the river. The boats were manned by Creek, but Spanish soldiers were with them. Now again, it ain't too unusual for Spaniards to come up the river on their way to New Madrid, but this bunch, as far as I can tell, didn't even make it as far north as Fort Jefferson. They turned around and went back down the river."

"Do you think it was the Creek with the Spanish force who killed Lieutenant Woods?" Renno asked.

Talbert shrugged. "I definitely would have thought so if the killings started moving south when those canoes turned around and went back down the river. But we can't be sure of the timing. You know how Indians are." He obviously had forgotten, for the moment, that he was speaking to Seneca, since both Renno and Little Hawk spoke English with the accent of an upper-class Britisher. "They don't have the same sense of time on a day-to-day basis as we do. They tend to mark events according to the moon or the season. The ones I talked to said *maybe* our soldiers were killed at about the same time the canoes were carrying the Spanish soldiers on the river. But they said, on the other hand, that *maybe* that was not true, that *maybe* the torture killings did not stop when the Spaniards went back down the Mississippi."

Alone with his father, Little Hawk was reluctant to lift his eyes lest he weep. "We will go there, to the place where it happened."

"If you think that something would be gained, we will go," Renno agreed, speaking not to a boy, nor to his son, but to a fellow warrior. "It seems, however, that Captain Talbert has gotten all possible information from the Choctaw of the area."

"Renna is not dead," Little Hawk said flatly.

"I pray that Renna is alive by the will of the manitous," Renno replied, but privately he wondered if she would not be better off dead than at the mercy of a man, or men, who would mutilate a young Choctaw girl and do worse things to others—male and female—in a zigzagging line of travel that extended southward from Philip's last campsite.

"If she is not dead, where is she?" Little Hawk asked.

Renno looked thoughtfully at the sky. "It would seem that the trail leads southward."

"The Creek are to the east."

Renno smiled grimly. "The Creek Nation is vast, the people many. If I had assurance that she had been taken east, we would go east, even if the chances of finding her were slim. But I must agree with Captain Talbert, who thinks that what happened was not the work of Indians—at least not Creek acting alone. I think, my son, that any chance of finding your sister lies in locating the man or men who killed Philip and the others. It is my guess that they did not travel east into Creek lands."

He was feeling a sense of urgency for the first time since leaving home. Until then the passage of days and weeks had seemed unimportant, but now even hours began to pass too swiftly. So much time had elapsed since Renna accompanied Philip on his patrol. How many more days, weeks, months, did Renna have? By nightfall, the sachem felt certain that she was alive. He felt that if his daughter was dead, he would know somehow.

Captain Talbert offered to board the horses, so long as they were available for use, and Renno agreed. He spent the money that he had taken from the French pirate ship the *Sans Doute* to buy passage for two on a Kentucky flatboat carrying tobacco, smoked hams, and corn to New Orleans.

Renno had visited New Orleans on two previous occasions. Once, due to circumstances not entirely of his making, he had sailed southward to the Gulf of Mexico, leaving large sections of the city in flames behind him. Upon their arrival, the sachem was pleased to see that the destroyed frame buildings had been replaced with graceful brick structures, making for a more permanent and a more beautiful city.

They were a handsome pair, father and son, dressed in frontier buckskins as they left the flatboat. Renno led the way to a waterfront grogshop. Smoke swirled through the dim interior. Voices in three languages vied for service. The arrival of two new rivermen from the United States drew a curious glance from the innkeeper and speculation from two tarts who were attracted by Little Hawk's vibrant youth. As the two women approached him, he smiled uncertainly. Renno gave them a slight bow and said, "We do not desire your company."

One of the women vented a flow of insults in rapid French.

Renno smiled widely and said in the same language, "I see, mademoiselle, that you have allowed the Creole influence to affect your pronunciation. Or is lack of skill with the language and your rudeness merely indicative of your absence of breeding?" He pushed past, brushing the tarts aside.

Renno had the ability to abandon his usual British accent and use the inflections, tones, and colorful figures of speech that were a product of the southwestern frontier. For the first time, Little Hawk saw his father in the guise of a long hunter who had settled down in Tennessee to raise hogs and corn. Ostensibly he had taken his produce to market on the watery highway that was the Father of Waters. In that role he talked with other rivermen, with Spanish and Creole dockworkers, and sailors off Spanish and French ships. By the end of the day he had collected a fine assortment of rumors regarding French-Spanish agreements about Louisiana.

For two more days father and son, as frontiersmen, walked the streets of New Orleans. Little Hawk was impressed by the fine homes of the prosperous French and Spanish merchants who profited from the river trade with the Mississippi Territory, Tennessee, Kentucky, and points north. The houses were as fine as anything he'd seen in Philadelphia.

The people of the city also attracted Little Hawk's attention. He had seen beautiful women in Philadelphia, and his stepmother was a beautiful woman, as were his aunt Ena and sister, Renna. But he'd never seen such a parade of beauty as he saw on the streets of New Orleans. Nor had he ever seen such fancy, and fanciful, modes of dress.

At first Little Hawk protested when Renno told the owner of a nicely decorated shop to equip both of them with the clothing and accessories necessary to move about in New Orleans society. A wink from Renno halted his objections, and once Little Hawk got into the spirit of it, it was fun to pose before the full-length pier glass in a morning suit, an evening suit, and a street suit.

Soon the new clothing was hanging in a wardrobe in a room in one of the city's finest hotels. The two gentlemen who came down to the dining room for the evening meal were unrecognizable as the frontiersmen who had walked the streets and entered into conversations in the waterfront inns. Over after-dinner cigars in the hotel's salon, Renno posed his questions to a different class of New Orleans society. There he found the same rumors of impending change, but no direct statement that a new agreement existed between France and Spain.

When Renno chose to be charming and friendly, his smile was engaging, his manner pleasing. With an ease that awed Little Hawk, the white Indian became a part of a conversation group and after a few moments exchanged introductions, stating proudly, Little Hawk thought, that Master Hawk Harper was his son.

Little Hawk had noticed that Renno was especially attentive to a well-dressed, well-spoken man of olive skin and dark mustache. When the introductions were made, he understood why. The man was Señor Alonzo Almandor, commandant of the New Orleans *guardia*. Señor Almandor was concerned about a series of unusually brutal murders that were disturbing the peace and tranquillity of his city.

Little Hawk expected his father to confide in the commandant that similarly barbaric killings had been performed in the Choctaw Nation, but Renno offered no such comment. He merely asked questions. Once he caught Little Hawk's eye as Almandor described the mutilation of the body of a young girl. Little Hawk nodded in understanding, even as his heart became heavy. Although Renno had begun the trip to New Orleans at the request of President Thomas Jefferson, Little Hawk knew that they had continued down the Mississippi, instead of going into the Creek Nation, only because Renno guessed that Renna might be with the man or men who had left a trail of atrocities pointing toward New Orleans. To think of his sister being the prisoner of such animals almost made him physically ill.

"Señor Commandante," Renno was saying, "once I traveled to Jamaica, where I had occasion to learn something of the black arts."

"Ah, *voudon*," Almandor said. "You are not the first to suggest that *voudon* may have a part in these horrors."

"I am especially impressed by the fact that in each case a part of the victim's body is missing," Renno continued. "But then I'm sure you are aware that the *voudon* masters make use of human body parts in their ceremonies."

"Indeed," Almandor said.

"The fates must be with me," Renno said, "for we are well met, Commandante."

"How so, señor?"

"As it happens, I have come to New Orleans in search of my daughter, who was last seen at Fort Jefferson, south of Chickasaw Bluffs. I have reason to believe that she might have been brought to New Orleans against her will."

"Her name, señor?" asked the commandant.

"She is called Renna. She is Mrs. Philip Woods."

"Ah," the commandant said, "but she was not brought here against her will, señor."

Renno leaned forward, fully attentive. Little Hawk's heart pounded.

"This girl, this woman, fair hair, beautiful, called Renna, was it?"

"Yes," Renno said.

"She was brought here, quite ill, by the comte de Beaujolais, who was a special envoy from the first consul of France. He is the younger brother of Louis Philippe, duc d'Orléans. Your daughter was put under the care of doctors, and when the comte sailed for St. Domingue, Mrs. Woods sailed with him."

"Could he possibly be speaking of Beau?" Little Hawk asked.

"Beau?" asked Almandor. He laughed. "As a matter of fact, young man, I heard Mrs. Woods call the comte exactly that."

Little Hawk blew out a deep sigh of relief.

"And so, my friends," Almandor said, "your worries are over. You know that she is in good hands with Beaujolais. He had orders, you see, to take the position of vice-consul in St. Domingue, as second-in-command to the brother-in-law of Napoleon himself."

"Thank you, sir," Renno said.

He asked further questions—the date of Renna's sailing, the nature of her illness, and how she came to be in the company of the comte—but Almandor could not answer all. He gave no indication of knowing anything at all about the gruesome events in the Choctaw Nation, which had resulted in making Renna a widow.

Immensely relieved, Renno concentrated on completing his mission for Thomas Jefferson. Posing as a prosperous Tennessee landowner and calling on his contact with Alonzo Almandor, he was invited into the homes of the city's rich and powerful; but after almost a month in New Orleans he was still unable to determine the truth or falsity of the rumors regarding a French takeover. He was able to ascertain that there had been no unusual sea traffic from France. There seemed, in fact, to be a decided lack of French presence in the city at the moment. The comte de Beaujolais had been an official French representative, but he'd been ordered to St. Domingue.

Renno learned that there had been another French newcomer in the city. He was described as a common fellow with a pockmarked face, and he wore the drab, black clothing of the revolutionary. But he had faded out of sight after leaving New Orleans with the comte for a trip up the Mississippi.

Renno found it very interesting to learn that the comte had made a trip up the river. That accounted for Beau's linking up with Renna. The sachem was even more interested in the Frenchman who had accompanied the count but had not returned with him.

"His was an odd name," he was told in another meet-

ing with Commandant Almandor. "Let me see. Was it
Arturo? No. Something quite French. You know how the
French sometimes swallow the ending of a word, eh? Ah,
I have it. Othon Hugues." He pronounced the name
O-ton You-g, doing a creditable job of swallowing the final
g sound. "I know little about the fellow, actually. Perhaps
I should have questioned the count about him." He
shrugged. "Little matter. This country has without a trace
swallowed men of more consequence than this Othon
Hugues. I must confess, Señor Harper, that I am more
concerned with what is happening to my city."

There had been more killings since the sachem and
commander had first met. The most recent victim had
been a young Spanish girl of fine family. New Orleans was
in a state of angry panic.

Renno had no intention of becoming involved in Alonzo
Almandor's problems. He had decided that it was time to
consider going home. "I think we'll take the river to
Natchez," he told Little Hawk, "and from there go overland to Nashville on the Natchez Trace."

"The horses are at Fort Jefferson," Little Hawk
reminded.

"I believe we can spare them," Renno said. "I will write
to Captain Talbert and ask him to accept them as our gift."

Little Hawk was also ready to start for home. Soon he
would be leaving once more to travel in a different
direction—northeast—to New York and the new military
academy to which he had been appointed by the president. But the city still held charms for him. He enjoyed
the odd, spicy foods, such as the tasty concoctions using
crawfish as a base. He liked walking the streets to admire
the women of New Orleans in their finery.

"With your permission," he said, "I would like to buy
gifts to take to my mother, my grandmother, and the
others."

So it was, with money in his pocket, he went out from
the hotel into the city and failed to return.

Renno had a farewell dinner with Almandor in the
hotel dining room. He went to the room he shared with

Little Hawk shortly after eleven and retired. He awoke with the pearl light of dawn coming in the window and noticed immediately that Little Hawk's bed had not been used. He felt a surge of concern. He arose, dressed quickly, and checked the dining room to see if, having stayed out quite late, the boy was enjoying an early breakfast before retiring. But Little Hawk had not been seen by any of the hotel staff since the previous afternoon, when he left on his shopping trip.

Renno was not one to fear the worst, but something terrible had happened to one of his children, and now another was missing in a city being terrorized by an inhuman killer. It seemed to Renno, as he went into the streets to go immediately to the headquarters of the *guardia*, that he could feel the presence of the evil gods of the old religion that flourished in the city. There were those who scoffed at the claims of power by the voodoo priests. The white Indian, having fought the magic of the voodoo masters of Jamaica, also vividly remembered how the evil Seneca shaman Hodano had so effectively combined his own powers with those he had learned from the Jamaican masters. The sachem knew that those who served the old, dark gods of Dahomey, where voodoo had originated, could be dangerous enemies.

"I wouldn't concern myself, Mr. Harper," Alonzo Almandor said, surprised to see his dinner companion again so soon. "New Orleans offers much to a man of your son's age. I suspect that he will come back to the hotel shortly and not much the worse for wear, except for having drunk too much and, perhaps, having loved too much."

Renno did not bother to state that his son did not drink. As for the other? Well, Little Hawk was no longer a child. Once again Renno took to the streets. By midday he had covered all the waterfront grogshops. No one with whom he spoke had seen a young man of Little Hawk's description.

Little Hawk, after leaving the hotel for what he had intended to be a short shopping trip, had been distracted by a group of street musicians. Two Spanish Gypsies played guitars while a woman in black, swirling skirts made the cobblestones ring with her dancing feet. He found himself clapping and crying, *"Olé, olé,"* with other spectators as the dancer's ruffled skirts showed hints of trim ankles and shapely calves.

He tossed coins when the music stopped for a moment and was preparing to move on when he sensed that he was being watched. He lifted his face, and his eyes caught those of a odd woman dressed in rich, purple silks, her ebony hair covered by a delicate lace scarf. At first glance she was just another woman, her face unremarkable, her nose a trifle too large. But the eyes, the eyes . . . They were dark pools set remarkably far apart, exotically tilted and compelling. They became Gypsy eyes, much like the eyes of the dancer who was, once again, clicking out rhythms to the sound of the guitars. As Little Hawk stared more intently, her eyes uncannily resembled those of Naomi Burns—a young, laughing girl he'd met while making his way alone from Philadelphia to his home.

At first there had been no similarity between the odd woman who had caught Little Hawk's eyes and the daughter of a Tennessee settler whom he had visited only once but who had made a decided impact on his memory. Naomi Burns, the first girl he'd ever kissed . . .

He felt deliciously intense regret and knew in his heart what he had missed by not going back to the Burns farm to see Naomi. He felt it as strongly as if he were experiencing the touch of her lips and the soft, female warmth of her body pressed to his.

Then the face before him changed. The odd woman's olive skin became pale, her dark hair lightened, and her eyes became the seductive, irresistible eyes of Naomi grown into woman. He was breathless as the woman moved toward him, extending one gloved hand.

"Come," she invited. "Come with me, my dear."

In her early apprenticeship to the master, Melisande had suffered cold and hunger and the ultimate loneliness of the outcast. Then the evil one had sent Othon to her, and for years that was satisfaction enough. Together they had fulfilled the master's desires while satisfying mutual needs. She was not lonely anymore, not even when Othon was distant from her. Of late, however, it seemed that Othon was living in a world of his own making and of his own choosing. He was serving the master, true, and she participated, receiving the booty that he brought to her following each of his excursions into the moist, sultry New Orleans nights . . . but there was a void in their relationship.

She did not realize what she had been missing with Othon until she saw the man who was little more than a boy, the one with blond hair, piercing blue eyes, and the proud, athletic carriage. Although she had been giving Othon strength and solace in the unique way made possible by the master, she had been receiving nothing in return. Othon's insatiability had made her into a woman who needed frequent attention. Seeing the beautiful boy reminded her of the time when Othon was young and had ignited her passion.

The master had given her the ability to alter the will of any man who gave her the opportunity to gaze deeply into his eyes.

"Come, little one," she had whispered as she led the boy away from the crowd surrounding the street musicians.

Nothing in Little Hawk's experience had prepared him for the dizzying heights of passion that he attained in a haze of dreamy sensuality. With a strength and stamina fueled by his youthful vitality, Little Hawk swam deep into the woman's eyes and became a part of her melting flesh.

She became all things to him. She was Naomi, but she was more. She whispered to him in warm, erotic tones, teaching, guiding. She possessed him and laughed lovingly at his heated reactions. He slept and woke to her warmth.

Finally a time came when he smilingly pushed her away. He was spent. It was as if he had run with the wind for a day and used up all his reserves. She soothed him, and he slept again. . . .

He awoke alone in a large, rumpled bed. He could hear movement through an open door to an adjoining room. He heard a splash of water, then the woman's voice humming an odd, minor-key melody. Everything that was Little Hawk—body, soul, emotions—told him to go to her. He knew her now. He could picture her washing herself, her bountiful feminine plushness unencumbered by clothing. The heat of lust flushed his face, and he threw off the sheet that was covering him. A musky, carnal smell caused him to wrinkle his nose. He sat up and swung his legs off the bed to go to her.

Come, come, she was saying without sound, the words echoing in his head.

"Naomi?" he called.

Yes, little love.

Again the words were in his head. He looked toward the open door.

Come. I will allow you to wash my back.

He flushed more deeply with the need for her. He was about to join her, but another voice halted him in his tracks. It, too, echoed in his mind.

Os-sweh-ga-da-ga-ah Ne-wa-ah, the voice called. *Look around you. Look!*

He knew that voice. For a moment it was as if he could see her, his mother, the fair Emily. He had been only a child when she died after giving birth to Renna. She was more beautiful than he remembered.

Little Hawk, my son, look around you.

"Ah, Mother," he whispered, aching.

Look around you.

"Come, my little lover," Melisande called. "Why are you tarrying?"

He shook his head and, after great effort, banished from his mind's eye the image of the woman naked in her bath.

Yes, yes. The misty form nodded her pale head. *Look around you.*

His gaze settled on the top of a low table at the side of the bed. A grinning skull stared at him with black, empty eye sockets. Startled, he took a step away. Bats hung on the wall, looking as if they were alive until, with growing wonder, he moved closer to examine them. Next, on a raised platform against the far wall, he noticed human bones arranged in an odd pattern. At the center of the pattern lay four hanks of hair so long and fine they could only be women's, one dark, one blond, one auburn, one light brown.

"Come! I have called you," the woman said with a touch of anger.

Run, my son, urged the manitou. *Do not be ashamed. Run now, for you are not yet ready to face* this *evil.*

That silent voice inside his head possessed a frantic undertone that he could not ignore. His clothing lay in an untidy heap on the floor. He seized breeches and shirt in one hand, his boots in the other, and fled into the parlor. He was at the door when he heard *her* voice. He turned. She was a pink-tinged vision of woman as she stood naked in the hallway.

"Look at me," she said.

Do not look into her eyes, pleaded the voice of the manitou.

"Obey me, you fool! Look into my eyes." Her voice changed into the honey of fulfillment and desire. "Would you go? Would you leave your Naomi?"

Off guard for a moment, he looked at her face. The almond eyes seized his, and before him stood an innocent adolescent girl with budding breasts, slim waist, and slightly expanding hips. She took his arm and guided him back into the bedroom.

"My darling . . ." It was not the voice of Naomi Burns. "You will stay with me, my darling."

The voice of the manitou spoke in Seneca, *Become aware then of her works.* The stench of the dead was heavy in his nostrils. The grinning skull on the bedside table now had shreds of decaying flesh attached to it. The bones arranged into an odd pattern miraculously flowed with blood and had reassembled themselves into the bleeding, mutilated body of a young girl.

With a gasp of fear Little Hawk threw open the bedroom door and ran through the parlor, which, he now realized, was filled with other horrors. The door leading to the street was locked.

Behind him the woman was screaming at him. "You dare to reject me?"

He felt a searing pain in his chest. He turned. She was standing before him, nude, odd, old, and flabby. "Feel thisss," she taunted, hissing the final sound.

His head seemed to swell and threatened to burst. He dropped his clothes and boots to press his palms to his temples. He squeezed his tearing eyes shut.

No! shouted the manitou, materializing between Little Hawk and the woman.

The pain in his head suddenly ceased. He scooped up his clothing and crashed through a parlor window, shattering glass and frame, landed on his shoulder, and rolled to a stop.

He lay stunned for a moment. A man and a woman who had been walking on the other side of the street halted and stared at him in amazement. He looked down at his nakedness, leaped to his feet, hopped around as he pulled on his breeches, and shrugged into his shirt without lacing it. He heard a shriek of rage from inside the woman's house, and, boots in hand, he ran down the street as if he were being pursued by all the fiends of hell. When he finally stopped running and turned to look behind him, the street was empty. He sat on the curbing and pulled on his boots.

My little love, purred a soft, seductive voice in his head, *why do you flee me?*

Memories of the night of pleasure battled more recent images of evidence of death and decay.

You disappoint me, little love, but I will forgive you. I await you.

Into his mind came fevered urges and flashes of the night's escapades. He stood and ran again, trying to outdistance the whispering, alluring voice. He would never be sure whether it was purely coincidental or the work of the manitous when, rounding a corner, he ran head on into his father, knocking him over.

"As it happens," Renno said when they had stopped

rolling and Little Hawk lay atop him, their faces close, the boy's eyes wide and staring, "I was hoping I'd run into you."

In retrospect Little Hawk could not understand what had happened to him. Confusing memories continued to do battle. He could not separate the odd, hard-eyed woman he'd encountered in the street from the alluring young lover who resembled in looks, if not in her demure shyness, the first girl he'd ever had the pleasure to kiss. And finally, with the manitou of his mother standing between the woman and himself, blocking the terrible pain, his tormentor had looked old, lank haired, big nosed. So, not knowing the truth, how was he to tell his father why he had disappeared for a day?

Little Hawk was grateful that Renno did not demand explanations. They returned to the hotel without making much conversation, and Little Hawk bathed and changed into fresh clothes. Then they repaired to the hotel dining room.

"When you are prepared," the sachem said as the boy uncharacteristically picked at his food, "I would accept a reason, however vague, of why you did not notify me that you would be gone overnight."

Much later in the day as Renno and Little Hawk strolled along a street of magnificent private homes, taking a last look at New Orleans before starting the journey north, the boy was finally able to speak. Little Hawk had said nothing for hours, and Renno had honored his son's introspection. Now he began the conversation in a way that Renno, at first, had difficulty understanding.

"I feel soiled, Father," he said softly.

"So," Renno said. *It was only that, then,* he thought, relieved. *The boy yielded to the temptation offered so readily by the harlots of New Orleans.*

"I'm still not sure what happened," Little Hawk admitted after long moments of silence. "I know only that I do feel soiled and that I'm angry."

"The Master of Life built into each man that which draws him to a woman," Renno soothed. "And while it is true that there are ways less high-minded than others to indulge this natural urge, in most cases the results wash off."

Again, Little Hawk remained silent while they walked a long city block. When the young man spoke, Renno could scarcely hear him.

"My mother came for me."

Renno's heart pounded. "Tell me," he said, "if you feel you are able."

And, with the memory of Emily's face before him, Little Hawk told all. He spoke of the odd feeling he'd first known in the street when he looked into the woman's eyes. He generalized about what happened to him there in the musty, darkened bedroom but explained in full detail the events that occurred when the manitou of his mother appeared.

Renno felt a chill of apprehension as his son described the contents of the woman's house. He recognized the paraphernalia of a practitioner of voodoo, and he voiced a silent prayer of thanks to the manitous for having saved his son from such a person.

"You need not feel ashamed," he said when Little Hawk had told all. "The black arts, the magic of evil were used against you."

"I felt the presence of something," Little Hawk confessed. "I couldn't quite define what it was, except that it was unsettling."

"Take me to this house," Renno requested.

Little Hawk looked at him quickly, doubtfully, but he had heard from his uncle El-i-chi and his grandfather Roy of the white Indian's epic battles with the evil shaman Hodano. And yet, even as he walked side by side with his father, the man who had defeated the voodoo masters of Jamaica and the evil medicine of Hodano, Little Hawk was uneasy.

The window through which the boy had escaped so precipitously had not been repaired, but draperies had been pulled from the inside to cover the opening. The house was silent and gave the impression of being long deserted. Without hesitation Renno pushed aside the draperies, then climbed into the room, where he saw ranks of skulls along shelves on the wall, long hanks of female hair, and gleaming human bones cleaned of all traces of flesh. It was just as his son had described. He stood in the center of the room and opened himself to spiritual contact. As he prayed silently for guidance, he sensed the presence of a dangerously malevolent power. The white Indian edged forward toward a closed door, then opened it carefully.

The witch lay sleeping. She was nude. In one of her hands was the articulated finger bone of a human being. Around her waist she wore a sash made of human skin studded with human teeth. The stench of decay and death in the room took Renno back in time and a thousand miles away, to the dark woods of the Ohio Territory and the lair of Hodano.

He reached for his tomahawk but found only his stiletto. His very being cried out to him to kill the evil that lay unprotected on the rumpled bed, but this was not his city and, now that his son was no longer in this being's power, not his fight. He would inform Alonzo Almandor about the obvious evidences of death and voodoo in the witch's home. This was probably the base of the cabal the city guards had been seeking. He turned to go.

The sudden flare of alarm that galvanized him into swift movement came from either the manitous or his instinctive survival mechanism. He twisted away from the open hallway door and ducked into the bedroom. An ax swished by his shoulder. He leaped aside, stiletto in hand now. He saw blurred movement, dodged another blow of the ax, and got his first glimpse of the man wielding it. He was a big man, taller than Renno, with broad shoulders and a powerful body and a face deeply pocked by childhood disease.

The white Indian stumbled over something, but he regained his balance before he fell. His hand closed over the skull on the witch's bedside table, and he hurled the skull at the pockmarked man, bent to avoid the blow of the ax, and slashed with the stiletto only to cut empty air. His opponent possessed catlike quickness and was amazingly agile for such a large man.

Behind Renno, the witch, awake and alert, picked up the small table and lifted it to smash down onto his head.

"Behind you!" shouted Little Hawk, who, having heard the sudden burst of noise from inside, had conquered his revulsion and fear and had entered the witch's lair.

Chapter Ten

Beth Huntington Harper received word of the death of Philip Woods in a long letter from her husband, which had been carried cross-country by military courier. Because of the distances involved, weeks had passed since Renno and Little Hawk had arrived at Fort Jefferson on the Mississippi to discover that Renna was missing.

Beth felt distraught and very much alone. Toshabe, although always polite and considerate, lived in a different world. There was regard between them, but no real closeness, so the two women, although similarly grieving, could not share comfort. Ena was . . . Ena. When the onetime warrior-woman visited The House, the talk was invariably of the weather and tribal matters.

Beth, as the village's schoolmistress, had the children, mainly Gao and Ta-na, for company and distraction for a part of the day. As for Ena's twins, Ho-ya came less and less often to his lessons—he considered his training under the supervision of his father and other senior Cherokee warriors to be more important than reading, writing, and arithmetic—whereas We-yo was becoming quite the lady. She was a blossoming adolescent, and due to Beth's influence and We-yo's admiration for Cousin Renna, she showed signs of combining the best aspects of the two diverse societies that influenced her.

During this time of grief and concern, Beth had her teaching duties to occupy her, and she had We-yo to assure her continually that Renna would be fine, that the manitous who often protected Renno and El-i-chi would safeguard one of their own. When Roy Johnson heard the awful news, he came riding faster than usual into the village. Beth was pleased to see him, for she had come to look on Roy as a member of the family.

"Well," Roy said, giving her a hug, "it's always a damned shame when a good young man dies. Such a waste. But all you can say is that maybe the Man Upstairs knew what He was doing. Maybe He had a use for Philip. As for Renna, well, I've done a little unaccustomed praying since I got your letter." His eyes filled with tears. "I'll tell you this: if anyone can find her, Renno will."

Wanting to maintain a semblance of life as usual in the face of the tragedy and knowing that Roy liked to visit with his old friends, Beth hosted one of her famous dinners, inviting the entire family. El-i-chi asked to hear the political news and rumors circulating in Knoxville. Roy obliged, holding the floor for a while, as the serving girls filled and refilled plates for the boys and for Rusog, all of whom found eating to be more rewarding than talking, at least at that moment.

"Well, over in France," Roy began, "Napoleon has made himself consul for life. It appears that he's the big hoss in Europe right now, because England signed a treaty a couple of months back returning to Napoleon all the territory that England had taken. There's some saying that England and France will be going at it again before the end of the year."

"And what do you hear about Louisiana?" El-i-chi asked.

"Well, there's nothing concrete—least not yet. The Spaniards are threatening to tear up the Treaty of San Lorenzo. That means they'd be closing the Mississippi to all trade with the frontier states and territories."

"They've threatened that before," El-i-chi remarked.

"Seems a bit more serious this time," Roy told him, "what with the rumors persisting that Spain is going to turn New Orleans and all the Louisiana Territory—over to France. And the rumors in Kentucky and Tennessee are predicting war. Andy Jackson's just been elected major general of the Tennessee Militia, and you know old Andy. He's fired up and ready to march down to New Orleans right now. President Jefferson's not quite so keen for war. Robert Livingston, Jefferson's special ambassador, is in Paris to talk it over with the French government."

Roy paused to fork a bite of rare roasted beef into his mouth, then followed it with a hunk of Beth's Yorkshire pudding. "I'll tell you this, though, judging from what I read in the eastern papers: if Napoleon gets New Orleans from the Spanish, there won't be many men in Washington and none west of the mountains who won't be ready to go down the Mississip' and take it away from him. You can mark that down in your little book and bank on it."

Later that night, after the others had gone, Roy and Beth sat on the front porch. The pecan trees that lined the long, straight lane leading to The House were getting to be near bearing size. Fields of corn rustled in a pleasant evening breeze. Overhead, the Big Bear, who would soon spill the colors of autumn onto the foliage, glowed brightly. The hazy, gleaming pathway of the manitous arced across the sky in its brightest glory.

"I reckon Renno and Little Hawk got down to New Orleans right quick," Roy mused, for those who were not with them were on his mind as constantly as they were on Beth's. "If he had thought that Renna had been taken by Creek, he wouldn't have gone on down the river, you know."

"I know. But I just can't—I mean, if not Indians, then who?" Beth asked.

"We'll just have to wait till Renno brings her back to find out," Roy said. "Being her father's daughter and her uncle El-i-chi's niece, she'll have quite a story to tell, you can bet on that."

*   *   *

Renna's story was still unfolding. After the capture
and deportation of Toussaint l'Ouverture, the French offi-
cials in St. Domingue were lulled into a false sense of
security by a period of quiet. Beaujolais, temporarily the
senior French official in Port-au-Prince, began to organize
efforts to institute public programs that would lift the
ex-slaves of the country from their abject poverty. His
well-intentioned efforts resulted in frustration. He received
only grudging help from French civil servants, and the
leaders of the Negro population reacted with strict and
formal politeness that did not conceal their distrust and, in
many cases, hatred for anyone with a white face.

As for Renna, she seemed to have lost track of time. She
knew that weeks and months were passing, but still she delayed leaving St. Domingue. It was not that she was in love
with Beau. She was grateful to him for saving her life, and she
enjoyed his company, for he was a good and considerate
friend. His sense of humor continued to ease her recovery
from the dark events that had so altered her life. Tragic
memories faded into the dim recesses of her consciousness.

Beau encouraged her to participate in his decisions,
talked over his problems with her, and took her with him
on tours of the city as he tried to better the lot of the
masses. The feeling of being needed, as much as anything,
prompted Renna to procrastinate in making a decision
about going home. Her sympathy for the suffering people
of the country prompted her to work in the local clinic,
where skilled medical personnel were in short supply.
There she came into face-to-face contact with the people
of Port-au-Prince.

They were a curious lot, the people of the city. They
came into the hospital wearing *gris-gris* bags around their
necks and clutching magic charms that had failed to cure
their ailments. They turned to the white man's medicine
out of desperation and, quite often, too late. When a
Negro child died in hospital, a fierce-eyed *voudon mamalois*
and *papalois* came with the victim's relatives, preaching
openly and arrogantly that the white man's medicine was
poison to the people of Hayti, that the only deliverance for
the people lay with the old gods.

Ambitious Negro men and women who received the white man's education wanted to do their part in lifting the nation out of ignorance and suffering. From them Renna heard quietly spoken tales of savagery and superstition, of the drinking of human blood and the sacrifice of innocents. And she remembered the stories told by her uncle and her father about the voodoo masters of Jamaica.

And as if there were not enough hunger and disease and dying in the steamy hills of old Hayti, war came again, led by the two mulatto generals who had come over with Leclerc.

"The Frenchmen," thundered both Jean Jacques Dessalines and Henri Christophe, "own the best plantations. The white men live in the finest houses. They eat the fruit of the land, the product of your labors, and they plan to return you to slavery so that they can continue their privileged existence forever."

After General Leclerc's death by fever, General Jean Baptiste Rochambeau was sent from France with orders to command the French forces and to be titular head of government. Beau was not displeased.

"I'm relieved, actually," he confided to Renna. "The rebellion is getting to be a bit much for me. I suspect it's going to be too much for all of us."

Never had the war in the hills been more bitter. Using skills taught to them by the French mulatto generals, the ex-slaves and freedmen grew ever more daring, ever more effective. To Beaujolais's chagrin and Renna's puzzlement, the rebels were being supplied by American merchants: food grown in the United States fed the black armies; arms manufactured in the United States and in England killed Frenchmen.

Although it was not possible to put aside all concern for conditions—unwary whites who entered certain sections of the city without proper protection were vulnerable to injury or death—Beau had found a way to escape from responsibility and worry for short periods of time. He had purchased a sleek little sloop from a departing plantation owner whose irrigation system and plantation machinery had been destroyed by the rebels. He had rechristened her the *Seneca Princess* in Renna's honor, and when he needed to find peace of mind, the sloop provided it.

When General Rochambeau called Beau to his office, he gave him orders that would once again change Renna's life.

"You are not without military experience, Comte," General Rochambeau said. "I have just been looking through your papers. You were with the first consul in Italy?"

"That I was, sir," Beau replied.

"I think you're aware of the situation, Comte. We face two principal armies. In the north, the traitor Christophe has declared himself King Henri. Dessalines, in the south, fancies himself to be Emperor Jacques. I want you, Comte, to take command of our troops at Cap-Haïtien. Working together, we have, I believe, the force to overwhelm the traitors."

Neither Beau nor Renna had accumulated many personal belongings since coming to St. Domingue. Instead of making the dangerous and arduous overland journey to Cap-Haïtien, Beau decided to sail the *Princess* around the northern cape to the north shore.

Port-au-Prince was situated at the apex of the Gulf of La Gonâve, one hundred miles from the end of the two long peninsulas extending toward the west, like the upper and lower jaws of an alligator, with the city and the island of La Gonâve caught in its throat. To reach Cap-Haïtien, the *Princess* would sail west, make her way around the western tip of the northern peninsula, and then eastward to the city of Cap-Haïtien.

They loaded all their possessions and took the sloop away from the dock on a morning like all others in St. Domingue, meaning that it was steamy and muggy, with the temperature promising to reach into the nineties as the day progressed. Renna followed Beau's orders, working strongly and efficiently to help raise and set the sails, and soon they were rewarded by the cooling breeze of motion. Salt spray joined with the breeze to cool her. She smiled back at Beau, who saluted and called out instructions to trim the sails.

There was a feeling of being on holiday. They ate fresh fruit, cheese and black bread, and boiled eggs and salt pork. The *Princess* sailed out of the Gulf of La Gonâve into a series of squally rainstorms, which lowered the temperature to a level of comfort and even to a chill at night when the sloop drifted on her sea anchor.

Renna and Beau lay side by side on the sloop's deck. The passage of a line of squalls had temporarily washed the air of its usual humidity, and the colors of the sky were glorious. The starlight was brighter than the glow of the lantern burning at the masthead. The waters of the Windward Passage between the Isle of Hispañola and Cuba were as heavily traveled as any sea-lane in the Caribbean, so a riding light was necessary.

"One never gets quite dry when sailing in a small boat," Beau mused idly.

"I don't think I have been completely dry since arriving in Port-au-Prince," Renna said. The blanket on which she was lying was damp. She had changed into men's clothing as soon as the *Princess* had cleared Port-au-Prince, and both her breeches and shirt held some dampness from the most recent rainstorm.

"It makes me long for a crisp, autumn day in France," Beau said. "A log fire in a huge fireplace . . . a comforting shawl pulled snugly up to my chin as I sit and look into the flames . . ."

"We used to build huge bonfires in the autumn," Renna reminisced, "just for the fun of watching them burn. In the evenings, after the sun went down and the air got chilly, we'd sit around the fire and listen to the storytellers."

"Sometimes I think that these islands should have been left to the original inhabitants. They, most probably, have become acclimated to the incessant heat, the smell of rot, the heavy, dank air." He sighed. "And now here we are. Belowdecks we have the climate of the islands—hot, humid. On deck we shiver because our clothing is damp and the night air cool." He laughed. "We humans! We are never satisfied."

"Beau, I think we should leave this particular island," Renna said, startling herself, for the unbidden remark had come as if from some sleeping but aware portion of her mind.

"I know," he agreed. "I have been selfish. Perhaps it is time for you to go."

She sat up, crossed her legs under her, and leaned toward him. Star glow lighted his handsomeness, and again she spoke words that surprised her. "But I won't leave you."

The dim, misty light illuminated his face as she'd seen it when she was but a girl, when his almost too-pretty manners had caused flutterings of awakening passion in her. "Ah, Beau," she said. "Do you remember how I blushed when you first kissed my hand?"

"With infinite fondness," he said. He put his hands under his head and turned to look up at her shadowed face. "I remember the first time I saw you, Renna. I remember saying gallant and foolish things, which, at the time, were meant to be mere flirtings. Now, when I think back on it, I realize that my heart knew you then, knew that you were the only girl whom I would ever love."

"Yes, my Beau is the master of the flattering word," she whispered, leaning toward him as if drawn by magnetism.

He sat up and put his hands on her shoulders. "I have been waiting for you, my love. I have respected your grief while castigating myself for not coming for you before Philip won your heart. It will be impossible for you to forget Philip—and I accept that obvious fact—but I say to you in all goodwill that he is dead, while I am alive. And you are alive. And I do love you."

"I loved you once when I was a child," she whispered. "I dreamed that you would carry me away to your castle in France, where we would live happily ever after."

"Alas, I have no castle," he said, pulling her toward him.

She came into his arms, leaned against his chest, and gave him her lips.

"Make room for me in your heart," he whispered,

breaking the kiss to turn her so that she lay in his arms, her face upturned.

"Can you be patient with me?" she asked. "Where there are respect and friendship and fondness—"

He laughed. "Little goose, you have just defined the most important qualities of love."

"Well, then," she said, sighing.

They knew each other for the first time on the gently rolling deck of the *Seneca Princess*. The act seemed entirely natural to Renna. She felt no guilt. The man to whom she was giving herself had been the perfect gentleman under circumstances that must have been extremely frustrating for a man in love.

Although he trembled with desire, he was gentle and did not rush. He courted her, pampered her, and roused in her a need that, at last, he could feel.

In response to his ardor, she experienced completion, but she wept, for pleasant though it was, something was lacking. As he held her in his arms, soothing her, kissing her perspiration-dampened cheeks and neck, she realized that she had missed the fiery and youthful ardor that she had known with Philip.

Beau was chuckling.

"Why, sir, all the mirth?" she inquired.

"Ah," he said, "I laugh because I have you, my lady. I know you, you see. You are the daughter of a sachem of the Seneca, and your father is a very proper man. Now that I have taken advantage of you, your father will force you to marry me, whether you want to or not."

She laughed with him. "My father would have taken his tomahawk to you after that night I slept on your bed in your cabin on the voyage to St. Domingue."

"Alas, then, that he wasn't present to fulfill his fatherly duty. To avoid the tomahawk, I would have married you immediately."

She was silent for a long time. When she spoke, her voice was soft, musing. "Beau, should we marry?" She put her hand over his mouth to shut off his quick response. "Oh, I know you say that you love me, and I should consider myself lucky having a man like you to want me.

But would it be wise? I grew up in a Seneca longhouse, you in a palace. You are in favor with one of the most powerful men in the world, and even you say that there will be war again between France and England. Your duty will be to go home, to fight for your country. What is my duty? I have been too long away from my own family."

Beau nodded. "It is true that we will be faced with difficult choices. My answer will be to try to teach you to love me as I love you. If I am successful, then the choices will be easier, for neither of us will be able to abide the thought of separation."

He lifted her face and kissed her. "Now, however, we lie drifting on azure seas, with no human eye within watery leagues, and I have just discovered a great need to make love, once more, to the woman I adore."

To her confusion and surprise, she felt a surge of excitement so intense that she quivered. And when he came to her for the second time, she was reaching for him, moaning softly, with no thought of the dead in her mind and with no rueful nostalgia for what she had previously thought to be the lost passion of youth.

The docks at Cap-Haïtien showed the results of neglect, a condition that was becoming general in the colony. Many Negroes had fled the town. The main body of the French troops garrisoned there were afield, chasing the hit-and-run units of King Henri I's army, determined to make him Henri the Last.

Although Beau, true to the spirit of the Revolution, professed to be a nonbeliever in God, and although Renna was not a Catholic, a priest united them in marriage on the day of their arrival in Cap-Haïtien. The priest explained that he was relaxing the rules of the Church because of the state of emergency.

"Rebels are slowly surrounding the city," the cleric warned. "The French citizens who were free to leave have already departed. Those of us who stay will probably be used as living sacrifices by the unholy worshipers of the devil."

"Most probably," Beau told a laughing Renna later,

"he performed the ceremony not because he expected all of us to be killed soon, but to erase our sin."

"What sin?" she teased. "Did you sin? Where was I when you sinned, Monsieur le Comte?"

He pushed her back onto the bed and lowered his weight atop her. "As I remember it," he said, "you were in a position much like this."

"No," she corrected, putting her hand between them to guide him, "it was more like this."

In the night, after long hours of talk, talk, and more talk, she clung to him. "Oh, Beau," she said, "how could I ever have doubted my love for you? I am so grateful that you didn't come to hate me during that long, wasted time when I was so wrapped up in my own sorrows."

French army headquarters in the north was a fenced compound on the outskirts of the muddy, decaying town. A dozen families had taken refuge there because it had become unsafe for unprotected women and children to dwell in the town itself. Beau had orders to join the army in the field, so he settled Renna in a cottage with windows that faced the sea breeze, and then he was gone.

He left Cap-Haïtien with a group of half-a-dozen mounted men and rode into the chaos of war north of the city. French intelligence had not been successful in keeping track of the major rebel forces at any time during the hostilities, and in the feverish last days of the war French units suffered disastrously.

In the north, Henri Christophe had amassed all his forces to drive the French out of Cap-Haïtien. Now he had the only French army in the north pushed back against the sea.

Beau lost two men when they rode into a rebel ambush. Seeing that the enemy had taken possession of the road leading to the reported position of the French army, Beau ordered a roundabout route and got close enough to the shore to hear the sounds of a furious battle. Even as he tried to find a way to get through the rebel positions to join the French soldiers, the firing reached a crescendo, faded, continued for a time with sporadic single shots, then was silent.

He climbed a tall tree and was able to look over a small ridge to the seaside. It looked to Beau as if the entire French force was dead. Rebels were looting the field, gathering weapons, supplies, boots, and clothing from the corpses. A single shot sounded when a rebel found one French soldier still alive, moving feebly. The rebel had remedied the situation with a musket ball to the soldier's head.

Beau scrambled down the tree and, calling out orders, ran for his horse. The four men who had survived the rebel ambush asked no questions, and when told what had happened, they spurred their horses, for each of them had family at risk in Cap-Haïtien.

They saw the smoke from a distance and the flames as they rode hard for the compound. The fence had been demolished. Headquarters buildings and barracks were in flames. A dead nun lay in the mud outside the burning schoolhouse, and a woman with a headless child clutched to her cold breast was sprawled at the nun's side.

The cottage where Beau had left Renna still stood, although it had been ransacked. Inside, he saw pieces of Renna's clothing scattered about, and the bed had been turned over. Fortunately, no blood could be seen. Beau would not accept the overwhelming possibility that Renna might be dead. It did not seem fair that, having just earned Renna's love, he was about to lose it so quickly.

When he heard shots from outside, he ran to a window. A group of ragged Negro townsmen armed with ancient muskets, machetes, and swords was charging back into the compound. He heard a horse whinny in pain and saw it go down onto its knees, blood springing from a machete cut on its neck. A burly Negro swung his blade again, and the horse collapsed. Because the horse belonged to the hated whites, in the heat of battle it was more satisfying to kill a valuable animal than to steal it.

Two of the men who had ridden with Beau were making a stand that was obviously doomed to fail. Beau lifted his musket and dropped an onrushing rebel. A black wave of humanity swarmed over the men. One of the enemy who had noticed the smoke and flash of Beau's musket yelled out, waved a hand, and led a small group of men toward the cottage.

Beau's every fiber cried out for Renna, and he knew that he would be of no help to her unless he survived the fray. He ran out the back door of the cottage and was soon hidden in the dense jungle that lay between the compound and the main portion of Cap-Haïtien. He had no plan other than to stay alive for as long as possible. He made his way to the outskirts of the town. Looting and death ruled. He found a secure hiding place to wait for the coming of darkness.

With night the carnage in the town eased off. Fires burned here and there. Rebels dressed in the white man's finery, drunk on the white man's brandy and rum, roamed the street, firing their weapons in a frenzy of victory. Beau kept to the shadows as he crept toward the church where he and Renna had been married. He had a vague hope that not even the worshipers of the old gods of dark Africa would desecrate a place of God, and at first it appeared that he was right. The church was intact; the front door was standing open. A glow of candlelight came from the altar. All was silent within. He moved slowly and cautiously into the interior darkness, guiding himself by the burning candles. He stopped, heart pounding, at the sound of harsh, shallow breathing. Almost atop the altar, Beau squinted into the semidarkness to discover the source. He looked up and with a shock saw that the carved figure of Jesus Christ on the life-size crucifix had been replaced by mortal flesh.

He climbed atop the altar and reached up. The priest who had united him in marriage with Renna had been nailed to the cross.

"Who . . . is . . . there?" the crucified priest rasped.

"Have patience, Father," Beau said. "I'll lift you down."

"No, no, please."

Beau held up a candle. The glow illuminated the priest's face. "Father—"

"Please, no," the priest said. "Leave me."

Then Beau understood why. The priest's stomach cavity had been opened, and inside had been thrust a dead chicken.

"I'll pray for you, Father," Beau whispered.

"Leave me. Go, before . . . the . . . the—devils—"

"All right," Beau said. "But have you seen my wife or have you heard of her?"

"I am sorry . . . my son—" And, with a convulsion that ripped one hand away from the cross and left him dangling, the priest was dead.

"*Why* are you sorry? For what?" Beau cried in anguish, for there had been infinite sadness in the priest's apology. Did it have anything to do with Renna's fate?

He ran from the church. The fires made rosy patterns against the blackness of the tropical night. He had little choice if he cared to stay alive, and he would stay alive as long as there was any hope at all that Renna was not dead. He left the town and warily circled down toward the waterfront.

The rebels had attacked the compound only hours after Beau's departure. The small French garrison fired from loopholes and piled up the careless enemy's black bodies outside the fence. The noncommissioned officer in charge sent a messenger galloping to the north to inform the colonel and the new commander that headquarters was being attacked.

Meanwhile, a sergeant addressed an assembly of women—including Renna—and children in the church. "We have nothing to fear," he assured them. "The comte will return quickly with our army, and they'll make short work of the rabble outside the gates."

An hour later the fence was knocked down, and half-naked black men waving guns and blades swarmed into the compound. The garrison met them with perfect French army technique, firing from ranks, kneeling to load, and rising to fire again.

When Renna saw the alarming attrition rate, she realized that there was no hope of rescue. Even if the messenger had found Beau and even if Beau had been able to start back immediately with a relief force, it would be too late.

Her decision was made when she saw a group of Negro women run through the great gaps in the fence with the head of the messenger on a spear. She left the church and back at the cottage changed into men's clothing for ease of movement. She gathered a bit of clothing, some food, and Beau's spare pistol, shot, and powder. Then she sneaked out the rear door, crawled through a breech in the fence, and ran into the jungle.

From an overlook near the sea she saw the rebel army swarm into Cap-Haïtien. All the French citizens had either left the town or were at the compound. The rabble smashed their way into French houses and broke down the doors of French-owned stores. Renna, knowing that they'd be preoccupied with looting for a while, made herself comfortable and waited.

Under the cover of darkness, Renna cautiously made her way to the shore and waded in shallow water to the docks where the *Seneca Princess* was moored. The waterfront was deserted. Everyone in Cap-Haïtien desired his share of the white man's luxuries and wanted to be a part of the victory celebration. This left her the most important luxury—life—for the *Princess* would be her means of escape.

She had the help of a favoring, offshore wind when she loosed the mooring lines and allowed the sloop to drift away from the dock. Tide and wind carried her to a safe distance from shore before she hoisted a sail and tacked eastward. At a distance of some ten miles from Cap-Haïtien, she noticed the glow of many fires and eased the sloop toward land until, almost in the surf, she saw black skin shining in the firelight. Her heart lurched when she realized that the mounds beside the fires were naked dead men with white skin.

Although the French army in the north had been defeated and the French army headquarters at Cap-Haïtien had been gutted, she, Renna, was alive, and therefore she believed that the man she loved was alive as well.

As she sailed back toward the town, guided by the

fires that lighted the sky, she tried to put herself into Beau's mind. He would have come back to headquarters to look for her; he would have found death and destruction. What then? He would have gone to the cottage, and not finding her, he would have stopped to think. And just as the *Seneca Princess* had sprung to her mind when she was in danger, when the world was burning around her, so would Beau have thought of the boat.

She moved as near to the shore as she dared, lighted a lantern, and kept it on the side toward land as she tacked back and forth. The wind freshened, and the *Princess* got a bit frisky, taxing Renna's strength and ability. Her palms were raw from rope burns when she saw a flash from the shore and heard a gunshot. She lowered the sail. Was it some rebel who had caught a glimpse of sail in the moonlight, or was it her husband?

She waved the lantern in an arc.

"Renna . . ." His voice was faint.

She was not even surprised. An island was in flames, and the proud French army was defeated, but her Beau could not have been killed. She would not have allowed it. She drove the *Princess* shoreward.

"Renna."

She could hear him clearly now.

"That's far enough," he called.

She dropped sail and let the sloop drift. Soon she heard the splashing of a swimming man. She helped Beau over the stern of the boat and clasped him to her, heedless of dripping seawater. "Oh, Beau! Thank God!"

"Quickly," he said, pushing her away. "My musket shot may have attracted attention."

Indeed it had. Even as they worked to raise sail and point the *Princess* seaward, gunfire exploded at them from shore. They heard wet, plopping sounds as balls pierced the sail. The *Princess* was leaping for the open sea on the freshening breeze, leaving the sounds and smells and sights of death behind.

By morning St. Domingue was only a smudge low on the horizon behind the *Princess*. Beau had set a dead-reckoning course for the eastern shore of Cuba. There was no question in his mind that he had decided wisely. To go back, to try to make it into Port-au-Prince, would put Renna in jeopardy again. Even if he had not felt that it would be an empty gesture to re-join the doomed French forces in St. Domingue, he would not have risked having Renna fall into the hands of savages who would crucify a priest, a man of peace, in his own church.

The small amount of food that Renna had brought was quickly gone. Drinking water was provided by frequent afternoon showers, but hunger came to be a constant companion by the end of the third day. When Beau's efforts with hook and line produced a long, fleshy Spanish mackerel, they chewed eagerly on the raw meat, while cutting up the rest into long, thin strips to be dried in the sun, where it quickly began to emanate a disgusting smell. Renna would always be thankful to the manitous for sending a Spanish ship into their path before it became necessary to eat the stinking, sun-discolored flesh.

After Beau's identity had been established, he was welcomed aboard the Spanish merchantman. The ship was going to sail to New Orleans after stopping at ports of call in Cuba. The comte de Beaujolais and his charming wife were to be given every comfort the ship could offer, for now, more than ever, Spain and France were firm allies, and a friend of the first consul was worthy of the finest treatment.

"You will be interested to know, Comte," said the captain of the vessel, "that I carry orders to the governor in New Orleans abrogating the Treaty of San Lorenzo. This action withdraws the right of deposit for the arrogant Americans who have, in the past, sent their trade goods down the Mississippi."

"But that will mean war, Señor Capitán," Renna said.

The captain shrugged eloquently. "That, my dear lady, is not my concern, nor, any longer, the concern of Spain. I believe you will hear, very shortly, Comte, that your nation has once again put down its roots in Louisiana."

Upon their arrival in New Orleans, Renna and Beau kept abreast of the situation in St. Domingue. Although the reports were sketchy, Beau gleaned from them that the French fought on. The economy of the colony was in shambles, and its rich plantations were being reclaimed by the tropical bush. Glad to be alive, happy to have survived the bloody rebellion on the steaming Caribbean island, Renna and Beau were too involved in themselves and their own love to devote much thought to the overall meaning of the events in which they had been participants. In Washington and in other capitals, however, men eagerly sought news from the Caribbean.

James Monroe, like Thomas Jefferson and George Washington, was a Virginian. He had come by stage to the young nation's new capital from Fredericksburg. Having just finished his second term as governor of Virginia, he was considering taking up the practice of law once more. His summons to visit the president of the United States had come as a surprise to him. Now he tapped on the doorjamb and, without waiting, stepped into the office of the president.

Jefferson sprang to his feet and moved rapidly around his desk to extend his hand. "My dear James."

"Mr. President, good morning."

"Please take a chair. Did you have a pleasant journey?"

"One day, perhaps, this nation will be rich enough to build roads whereon ruts are limited to no more than two inches deep," Monroe said.

He was a long-faced, gray-haired man of dapper appearance. His linen was gleaming white, bunched at his throat in the opening of a black frock coat with the fashionable peaked collar that covered his nape to the hairline.

"I suspect, Thomas, uh, Mr. President—"

"Please," Jefferson interrupted. "Thomas is more than adequate between old friends."

"Am I correct that certain communiqués from Madrid and Paris have something to do with my having been asked here?"

"Always one step ahead, eh, James?" Jefferson asked with a chuckle.

"The 'secret' Treaty of San Ildefonso is no longer

secret, Mr. President." He sighed, settled back in his chair, and crossed his neatly encased ankles.

"I've sent Robert Livingston to Paris," Jefferson said. "Are you familiar with events in the Caribbean, specifically in the French colony of St. Domingo?"

"I am," Monroe answered. "I think I understand your meaning: if Napoleon is to occupy New Orleans and Louisiana, he must have a secure sea-lane from France. St. Domingo has been a strong point for the French in the Caribbean, directly on the route from France to the mouth of the Mississippi. If this rebellion is successful, as it seems that it will be, the little general will have no base in the Western Hemisphere for his warships. His merchant shipping would be vulnerable to English or, indeed, to American interference."

Jefferson nodded in confirmation. "I've instructed Mr. Livingston to offer to purchase the Isle of New Orleans and certain other territories at the mouth of the Mississippi. I think, James, that we'd find this course less expensive than going to war with France."

"Indeed," Monroe agreed. "And, Mr. President, where do I enter into this equation?"

"I want you to go to France to assist Robert Livingston," Jefferson replied. "I believe that you, being a Virginian, know as well as I the importance of keeping the Mississippi open to American traffic. And I think, James, that you value peace as much as I."

"My authority, sir?" Monroe asked, with a wry smile that was answered by Jefferson's.

Both men knew the reason for Monroe's question: George Washington had sent Monroe as his ambassador to France in 1794. The various judgments about Monroe's work had been mixed. He had done nothing to justify the Jay Treaty to the French, although he was aware that France regarded the treaty as betrayal of an old friendship and even a cause for war. In fact, he had told the French government that the Jay Treaty would never be ratified by the Senate and that George Washington's administration would be overthrown by the treaty's opponents. The French, he had said, could expect much more sensible treatment from a new president.

Jefferson knew that George Washington had considered Monroe to have been disloyal to a political ally and a friend and that Washington had never forgiven Monroe. But Jefferson knew the high regard in which James Monroe was held in France. To avoid war, Jefferson was willing to take risks.

"Your authority, James, will be that of envoy extraordinary and minister plenipotentiary. You will have my instructions to make all efforts to affect a peaceful transfer of New Orleans and the mouth of the Mississippi to the United States and, moreover, to work with Charles Pinckney in Madrid to secure from Spain the cession of East and West Florida to the United States."

Monroe shook his head. "You do not lack optimism, do you, Thomas?"

"Perhaps," Jefferson said with a stiff smile, "there is in me just an iota of the faith that many people say I lack."

Chapter Eleven

When Little Hawk yelled out a warning, Renno jumped to one side. The small bedside table smashed down onto the sachem's left shoulder and disintegrated in Melisande's hands. Othon tried to take advantage of Renno's momentary unsteadiness. If Hugues had had a balanced weapon instead of a wood-chopping ax, Renno's feint with his stiletto and his quick move away from a swishing, roundhouse swing of the ax might have come too late. As it was, the blade of the ax struck the wall and cut through plaster and lath.

Melisande jumped onto Renno's back to claw and bite at his neck. He jammed an elbow hard into her stomach and threw her off.

"Keep the she-wolf away," Renno told Little Hawk as he ducked under the return swing of Othon's heavy ax.

Little Hawk edged warily toward the witch. She sat flat

on the floor, shaking her head dazedly. Her voluptuous nakedness caused the boy's libido to flare for a moment. But when she smiled at him and he saw her shining black teeth, a shiver of dread coursed through him, for during the glowing hours with her she had not allowed him to see that aspect of her. She sidled away from him now like one of the crabs that he had chased as a boy on the beaches near Wilmington. Her destination was the bed. Her hand snaked under the mattress and came out with a wicked knife.

"Come to me, little one," she intoned.

He avoided the direct stare of her eyes, knowing their power. He drew his own knife.

"After what we have been to each other, you threaten your Melisande?" she whispered, smiling, catching enough eye contact to cause her teeth to change from black to healthy white. He shook his head and lowered his gaze to her full breasts.

"I prefer not to have to harm a woman," he said. "Please put the knife away."

"I think not," she retorted, and her black teeth gleamed at him once more. "I think you and I will hold stalemate until Othon kills the intruder."

Renno and Othon circled each other, restricted in their movement by the limited space in the small bedroom. Renno bent swiftly and snatched up a leg of the table that the witch had smashed over his shoulder. The wood was no match for Othon's ax, but it gave Renno a weapon with more reach than his Spanish stiletto. He made good use of it quickly by avoiding a thrust of the ax, coming in low, and landing a thudding blow to the Frenchman's shin that elicited a bellow of pain and rage. Othon limped back. Renno, hearing a thin, eerie scream from the witch, stole a quick glance at his son.

Little Hawk started forward as Melisande slashed a pattern in red across the pale skin of her chest with the tip of her sharp blade. As she began a hissing, whispering chant of incantation, she wetted her hands in her own oozing blood and smeared it over her face and arms. A distorted form began to materialize in front of Little Hawk, and seconds later, a malformed imp with evil, gleaming eyes capered toward

Renno. Another and another materialized out of thin air, all chattering like monkeys and flexing long, curved claws at the end of their crooked fingers. All of them leaped toward Renno to cling, climb, and hinder his movements.

Renno brushed off the first imp and sent him tumbling. But there were two more of them, each clinging to a leg as Othon Hugues roared in satisfaction and attacked. His swing missed and slashed into one post of the testered bed, breaking it, causing the canopy to collapse.

Renno kicked the imps away. He knew, then, the reason for the feeling of oddness in the house. He had faced the manifestations of evil before. Understanding the nature of his new enemy, he banished the imps from him by an effort of will just as, long ago, he had rebuked Hodano's spirit wolves. The imps, enraged by their sudden impotence, cavorted around him, gibbering wildly.

But Melisande's magic seemed to affect Othon as well. He suddenly displayed a surge of superhuman strength and strode forward, swinging the ax in sweeping arcs. On either side the sharp blade played havoc with the remains of the bed and with the wall. The sheer power of the advance pushed Renno back. Once he timed his lunge and broke the table leg across Othon's stomach, but the Frenchman merely grunted, then grinned maliciously.

"Now, little one," said the witch to Little Hawk but loudly enough so all could hear, "watch your father die."

Little Hawk launched himself toward the end of the shattered bed, intending to attack the big Frenchman from the rear. As he hurtled through the air, the witch laughed, and Little Hawk felt the sharp claws and the pointed teeth of the imps. At least eight of them swarmed around him, grabbing his leg, climbing to his thighs, clawing upward with their hands toward the softness of his stomach. He grunted in pain and began to flail at the imps with his fists and his knife. He felt steel slice flesh, but there was no blood, and the gashes made by his blade healed instantly even as the imps sapped his strength. They caused intense pain with their razor-sharp claws and teeth, and the effort expended in the futile fight against them began to weigh heavily on him.

Renno heard the gibberings of the imps and looked just in time to see Little Hawk fall under the tangled mass of misshapen bodies. He feared for his son's life. He himself had faced powerful men like Hugues before and knew how to turn strength back against itself. Little Hawk did not. Renno was confident that in one or two more minutes he could put an end to the fight with the Frenchman; he knew, also, that his son was powerless to overcome the material manifestations of evil evoked by the witch. For Little Hawk's sake, he decided to break off the fight.

As the Frenchman moved steadily forward the sachem waited until the proper moment, and when the ax thudded into the wall at the end of a swing, he lashed out and felt his Toledo steel blade contact flesh. Blood gushed from the Frenchman's laced shirt. Renno glided past Othon and scored with his blade once more, but not fatally. Hugues, roaring like a wounded animal, whirled to face him.

Renno kicked out, his heel contacting Hugues's knee. An ordinary man would have been disabled, with cartilage and tendons smashed and torn. Hugues, however, merely roared in pain and retreated for a moment, giving Renno enough time to get to Little Hawk's side, brush away the imps, and lift his son to his feet.

Little Hawk clutched his knife and made one last slash at a capering imp, and then the witch's laugh rang out. She was squatting on the floor. Little Hawk's arm drew back, coiled, then lashed out. His blade flew toward Melisande. Her dark eyes widened, and her black teeth showed as she snarled in defiance. The knife curved aside inexplicably to drive its sharp point into the bed beside her head. And then Renno was pushing Little Hawk ignominiously out of the bedroom and shoving him through the open window into the sun on the street. The white Indian came right behind him.

The sachem looked back for a moment. Imps clung to the broken window frame and tittered. From inside came a wail of anger and frustration from the witch.

Othon pushed Melisande aside and ran to the broken window. The man who had drawn his blood was standing on the cobblestones of the street. Othon climbed through the window and onto the stoop, then staggered, his strength leaving him.

"Melisande!" he called out.

She came to stand behind him in the window. "Let them go," she muttered. "He is protected by the spirits."

Othon bellowed in rage. Was his entire life to be one of total frustration? The man standing not thirty feet away, knife in hand, had injured him, and yet the master stole his strength, leaving him weak and helpless. He moaned with hatred and pain as Melisande helped him back inside.

"That one will come again," she consoled. "And we will be ready."

"I pray that he does, and his whelp as well."

"Come, I will heal your hurt," she offered.

"Scratches," he dismissed, for as he put his arm around her his strength returned.

"Nevertheless," she said tenderly, guiding him toward the bed, "they need attention."

She pushed aside the fallen tester and eased him down so she could use her magic on the cut on his back, then on the slash along his side toward the front. As she worked, chanting the arcane words, he nourished himself from her fecund breasts and felt the potency build again in his body.

"Now we must hurry," she said.

"To go after him?"

"To leave this house."

"This is our home," he protested. "We have consecrated it to the master." He moved his hand in an arc, indicating the grisly evidence of his frequent nighttime excursions on the streets of the city.

"The man who fought you so well will, of course, report what he has seen to the authorities," she explained. She laughed. "I'm afraid, my love, that it would be difficult to explain your souvenirs to the *guardia*."

"What sort of being is our master, to allow us to be humiliated continually?" he asked.

"Speak not of the master in such tones," she warned. "He guides us well. Here in New Orleans we have been learning how best to serve him. Perhaps we have grown too soft, living in such comfort. He has told me, my dear one, that we must explore more of this great land. In a dream he showed me how you struck terror into the hearts of the Choctaw along the river. And yet that area you traversed is only a tiny portion of this giant country. In the dream he has told me to go forth from this city so we may avail ourselves of unique opportunities."

"What of my duty to France?" he asked.

She laughed harshly. "Why do you speak of duty to France, when you have not even paid it lip service during the time you have been so preoccupied with your own pleasures? You can do your duty to France while enjoying yourself by killing all those who oppose French control of Louisiana. Of those there are many."

He nodded, seeing the wisdom of her words. Grand plantations were spread around the city, and less imposing homesteads were interspersed among them. The great and small houses were populated mostly by Spaniards, but a few people were of French blood, descendants of the early French settlers of Louisiana. The propertied Spaniards would, of course, resent giving over Spanish control to the French. Yes, he could serve France while serving the master, all the while doing that which gave him the most intense gratification.

They vacated the house within minutes, carrying little. As Othon joined Melisande on the street, smoke billowed from the damaged bed, and as they walked away the whole house burst into flames. There would be nothing left to be used as evidence; the human relics that Othon had collected would be destroyed.

The couple did not leave the city immediately. Melisande's magic was strong enough to alter their appearance and there was work to be done. Due to her years in the solitude of the French forest, she had, during her time in New Orleans, learned to value the occasional company of people. Together Othon and she began to gather a force of men and women who had been rejected by society. Spanish renegades responded to Melisande's commanding eyes, and mulatto freemen joined their group, along with prostitutes who were willing to take to the wilderness to escape their sorry lot in the city.

To finance the venture, Othon led his growing band in looting isolated farmsteads. He waylaid coaches on the roads and robbed the passengers, killing all to prevent the spreading of information about him and his men. These profitable activities drew other malcontents to him. Murder, rape, and rapine created a wide region of fear around the city.

In New Orleans, the Spanish governor summoned Alonzo Almandor to him and ordered the immediate formation of a special militia to eradicate the brigands who were rampaging through the countryside.

Othon and a half-dozen specially picked men waited in the dense greenery beside a well-traveled highway that led toward the city. Soon he heard the snap of a whip, the rumble of the wheels of the coach, and the snort of horses. As the coach came into view, he nodded a signal, and two men pushed at a tree that was almost cut in two. The tree toppled with a swishing of branches and leaves to block the road. The driver cried out to the horses and hauled back on the reins, and the coach came to a lurching halt. Othon ran forward to throw open the door to the coach and almost lost his head as a musket fired. The ball missed him by a fraction of an inch, but the hot blast of burning powder singed him.

"*Guardía!*" a renegade yelled in warning as Othon fired his pistol into the dark interior of the coach to be rewarded by a cry of pain. "The *guardía* come!"

He glanced down the road behind the coach and saw a dozen mounted men pounding forward at full gallop, raising a cloud of dust. He cursed, raced back into the greenery, and led his band to the edge of a swamp and away. No man on horseback could follow.

Melisande awaited him in the camp that had been established near a lake of clean, fresh water. She saw the scowl on his face and rose to clasp him to her breast.

"It is nothing, my love," she whispered, soothing him with her hands. "A momentary setback."

"You know?"

"I saw. We are right in being here, love, for the sight is more clear to me here than in the city." She was removing his tunic as she spoke, loosening his shirt.

"You saw, then, that the *guardía* ambushed us?"

"No matter," she assured him. "We will leave this place. The master has spoken to me of many things." He was in her arms on the blanket, drawing strength. "Ah, my dear one, how you will crow when I tell you the things that I have seen!"

"Speak, then," he urged.

"The aristocrat who foiled you on a Mississippi mud bank, depriving you of a tender, young morsel of a girl . . ."

Othon growled.

"The master will deliver him into your hands."

"When?"

"In time. And that is not all, my love. The master also brings with the French blue blood that little beauty who has haunted your dreams since you lost her."

"Ah," he breathed. Satisfied, his strength renewed, he pulled himself up and out of her arms.

"There is more."

"Soon my cup will be full," he said with a smile.

"The man who wounded you in New Orleans—he, too, will be delivered into your presence."

Othon lifted his clenched fist to the sky and laughed deeply.

The next morning they started up the Mississippi in stolen boats, carrying with them the loot taken in their raids. They avoided the eastern bank, lest some Choctaw recognize Othon. It was Melisande who, after long days of travel and sultry nights of planning, chose the campsite on the western bank.

"Here we will make our city," she announced, "and soon our dominion will extend far to the north and even farther to the west. Here we build our empire, my love, under the protection of the master."

She presented a grandiose vision of the future. It was as if Othon had been waiting all his life for the total freedom of action that was granted to him in the trackless wilderness. The region had never been affected by the laws enacted by civilized men. He was like a child in an East Indian myth who, taken from the she-wolf who had suckled and reared him, escapes the unaccustomed bonds of being an unwilling child of man and returns to the wilds to rip raw flesh with his teeth.

The master delivered into Othon's hands a Kentucky flatboat laden with corn, smoked hams, good Kentucky whiskey, and live chickens. Food, drink, and amusement kept his followers and him content for days. His empire would be built by preying on the river trade. No witnesses would be left alive to tell of the well-concealed town of log cabins and lean-tos that grew not far from the bank of the great river.

Melisande had not forgotten her lover's duty to France. She controlled his thoughts and twisted them to her own use, so Othon came to believe that by establishing a holding on the west bank he was taking possession of the lands in the name of France. By harassing American river traffic he was being loyal to his original mission.

Being visiting royalty in New Orleans, the comte de Beaujolais did not lack for company or entertainment. He and Renna accepted the insistent invitation of an old acquaintance, a Spaniard with the blood of kings in his veins, and soon Beau and his beautiful wife were ensconced in one wing of the friend's house with shaded courtyards and long, quiet verandas.

The day after their arrival Beau visited with the governor and learned that although the Treaty of San Ildefonso had been made public, the French were still without an official presence in the city.

Beau, puzzled, told Renna that he should sail at the first opportunity for France to report the events in St. Domingue. He knew the importance of the island colony to his homeland, and he was concerned that the French authorities, ignorant of the revolution on that tropical island, might send unprotected ships toward New Orleans and Louisiana. The vessels would be at risk to pirates, Americans, or Englishmen due to lack of naval protection

or, equally disastrous, the ships might unwarily sail into
the fine harbor at Port-au-Prince and be taken by the
ex-slaves under the command of the French mulatto
generals.

Renna, having developed a maturity beyond her years
in the relatively brief span of time since leaving her father
and stepmother's house in the Cherokee Nation, was fully
aware that she had been extraordinarily lucky in having
two fine men love her. Philip was a warm softness hidden
in her heart. She would always remember his tenderness
and concern for her as they, both just past childhood,
experimented with the mysteries of love. It was as if
Philip and she had grown up together during a miraculously beautiful interlude that had ended so heartbreak-
ingly quickly. She would always be grateful to him for
having taught her how to love. It did not dishonor his
memory, she believed, to put that knowledge to work in
loving the Frenchman who had become her second husband.

Beau was older and more cosmopolitan than Philip
had been, but then she, too, was older, having turned
sixteen.

The word was out that Louisiana was again French,
and since Beaujolais was the only Frenchman of official
rank in the city, the handsome young couple was much in
demand socially. Beau had no difficulty drawing on his
position for credit, and Renna spent pleasant days rebuild-
ing her wardrobe. She took great pleasure in buying new
clothing and accessories for Beau.

One late September day in 1802, she brought some
material home for his approval before having it made into
a garment. For once, no social obligation drew them out of
the guest quarters of the *casa*.

Having praised her good taste, Beau sat beside her,
poured wine for both, and kissed her on the cheek. "You
did well for me," he said.

"I like doing things for you." Her smile was his joy,
her face his living portrait of beauty.

"When we sail for France I will bribe the captain to
give us the finest cabin aboard, and I will take you inside,

lock the door, and make love to you night and day to pass the time during the crossing."

She feigned a look of shock. "And I thought that young Seneca and Cherokee warriors, talking of their great feats of coup, were the world's most accomplished braggarts."

"Well, maybe not all day and all night every day."

She pinched his cheek, then kissed him on the lips. "Beau?"

"Umm."

"Were you ever homesick?"

"I had no home," he answered. "Not after they sent my father to the guillotine."

"Ah, poor dear."

"Do you ask because you are? Homesick?"

"It's been so long since I've seen my father, my brothers, my stepmother. I'm sure that they must have, by now, received letters telling them that I am alive—"

"More alive than any woman I've ever known," Beau whispered, nuzzling her ear.

"Stop it, beast," she said playfully. "—that I'm alive and well and married to a lecherous Frenchman who gives me no peace—"

"You taste very good," he said, brushing his lips tantalizingly down her neck.

"—and refuses to take me home to see my family."

"Can you wait until after we go to France and report all to the little corporal?"

"Ah-ha!" she said. "So now it comes out. The old aristocratic contempt for the self-made man who was not nobly born."

His expression darkened. "You come so close to the mark that you make me uncomfortable." He sighed. "There is no doubt that he is a great man, our Napoleon. He has given honor back to France."

"You feel that you must report in person to him?"

"I owe that much to him," he said. "After all, he kept my brothers and me from the blade that took my father's head. He gave me my position as an envoy of France, and through his efforts a part of the family estates have returned to Louis, my brother. Once again I have a home

that I might return to if I so desire." He held her close.
"Ah, my Renna, you'll love France. The very air is special.
In the winter the cold is invigorating, and the spring sun
brings new life. And the summer—ah, the summer! And
the quiet, misty autumn mornings when the leaves begin
to turn on the chestnut trees—"

"You *do* get homesick!" she accused.

He looked at her with concern. "I suppose it is the
nature of marriage, when man and wife come from dispar-
ate backgrounds, to tear one spouse from his or her
home. You do choose to stay with me?"

"Of course, silly."

He shrugged. "Then we have only to decide which of
us is to give up his home for the other."

"Do I really have a choice?" she teased.

"You have only to ask," he said, bowing, "and I will
go with you to live forever in a Seneca longhouse."

"Beau, now you're teasing *me*."

"But only after I go to France and report to the
general."

"Already you've promoted him." She leaned against
him and enjoyed having his gentle hands around her
waist.

"Will it please you to model that boudoir garment of
black Spanish lace for me?"

"Well . . ."

"For me?"

"You've heard how my great-grandmother was kid-
napped by a Frenchman and taken off to France?"

"At least once," he answered.

"I will model the lace garment for you only if you
promise that you will not soil it with sweaty, male hands."

He moaned. "You demand more strength of character, more power of will, than this weak mortal can muster."

"Well then, if not that, promise me that you won't
take me off to France and keep me there forever without
seeing my family."

"Willingly," he agreed. "Now, the black lace?"

"Willingly," she responded.

*   *   *

Renna was secretly pleased when weeks passed without the arrival of a ship that could carry them to France. Vessels came from other ports in Spanish America with news that had made its slow way from Europe or from ports in the United States. Through this grapevine Renna and Beau learned that Napoleon had made himself consul for life, assuring that France was more surely ruled by one man than she had ever been under the monarchy. In North America, Ohio had been admitted to the union as the seventeenth state of the United States. In a weeks-old newspaper Renna read that a new academy to train officers for the United States Army would soon open, and that article made her yearn to see her brother and the rest of her family, for the last letter she'd received at Fort Jefferson had told of Little Hawk's appointment to the academy by Thomas Jefferson.

Beau, too, seemed content to mark time on official matters. He spent many hours with the Spanish governor, planning for the smooth transfer of power, for the change of flags once again over the old city on the Mississippi.

Renna was no longer plagued by the nightmare in which she was mired in deep mud and unable to escape the tortures that she had seen a pockmarked man inflict on a Choctaw girl. She was grateful that the series of barbaric mutilation murders that had terrorized New Orleans had come to an end. Unfortunately, the perverted perpetrator was still as much a mystery as ever. It was safe once again for a lady to take to the street to examine merchandise at little shops. It was on such a trip that Renna came face-to-face with a splendidly dressed, bronzed, blond-haired young man who looked at her questioningly and then uttered a cry and swept her into his arms.

Renna gasped his name in Seneca as she was hoisted from the sidewalk and whirled wildly. He was saying, "Sister, Sister, Sister."

Then, after exchanging kisses and trying to talk at once, they laughed happily. Renna cried out in joy when she learned that her father was also in New Orleans. "Don't say any more," she said, putting her hand over Little Hawk's mouth. "There is time to tell all, although

there is much to tell. Now, at this very moment, take me
to our father."

Renno was packing the belongings that he would take
up the Mississippi to Natchez and then along the Natchez
Trace to the Cherokee Nation and Huntington Castle when
he heard footsteps in the hallway outside the room. He
was alert and ready, his hand on his tomahawk, when the
door was flung open.

He saw standing there in the open doorway a lovely
young woman in a colorful dress of French design, a black
lace mantilla over her cornsilk hair. He fell to his knees,
lifted his hands, and chanted a quick prayer of thanks to
the Master of Life, so happy was he to see his daughter
alive and well. Renna stood there, a glad smile on her face
and tears in her eyes, until her father had finished his
thanks to the manitous. Then she flew into his arms and,
quite properly, she being the youngest *and* a woman,
asked the first of what would be a thousand questions that
needed answering all at once.

"What are you two doing in New Orleans?"

After the public disclosure of the impending cession
of Louisiana to France, Renno had no need to stay in New
Orleans to collect information for Thomas Jefferson. With
his daughter in his arms, nothing, he felt, could prevent
him from leaving for home as quickly as possible.

He listened with growing admiration for this beautiful
young woman who had been his little girl as she described
the events since Philip's death. The sachem's face froze
into a cold mask of anger when she described the Frenchman
who had tortured a helpless girl before her eyes and had
promised her the same treatment.

Renno had already known that a Frenchman with a
pocked face had accompanied the comte de Beaujolais
upriver. It was, he mused, a large country but a small
world. The barbarian who had so frightened Renna could
be none other than the powerful man who had fought him
with the support of the evil ones in the witch's house.

Renno had, of course, reported what he had seen in

that bizarre house to Alonzo Almandor, but a quickly organized raid had found only smoking ashes. The neighbors could tell Almandor only that they had often heard odd sounds coming from the house and that they had seen eerie, flashing lights. If anyone knew what had become of Othon Hugues and the witch, that knowledge was not shared with the *guardía*.

Renno's first desire was to avenge the death of young Philip, whom he had come to respect and love, but other factors had to be considered. It was a certainty, considering the link of mail communications between Fort Jefferson and Nashville, that Beth had already received word about Philip's death and Renna's disappearance; but it was not all that certain that mail from New Orleans or St. Domingue had made its way to a United States port city and then cross-country to Knoxville and The House. Beth and the family would be mourning unnecessarily. And there was no easy way to rectify the situation; Renno and his children were, even by the swiftest means of travel, long weeks away from home.

When Renno first heard that his daughter was now the comtesse de Beaujolais, he felt his heart tighten. Beaujolais had impressed him favorably when, as a boy, he had visited the village with his brothers. But Beau was French; it was natural for a man to want to return to his home. If Beau took Renna to Europe, the tyranny of distance would make it unlikely that Renno would ever see her again.

"You're married to old Beau?" Little Hawk asked incredulously. "That fancy-pants Frenchie?"

"My fierce hawk," Renna said haughtily, "don't judge Beau until you know him as he is now."

Renno saw quickly that the callow youth who had visited the Cherokee Nation was now a man. He liked Beau's firm handclasp. Beau laughed in pleasure when he was treated to the Seneca warrior's arm clasp of greeting and brotherhood by both Renno and Little Hawk.

There was talk, seas of talk, for each had much to impart. Renno listened with the interest of a fighting man to Beau's account of the deadly little war in St. Domingue and made a mental note to call this to Mr. Jefferson's attention when he made his report by mail to the president.

Renno's need to go home was negated by the pure joy of being with his daughter and her husband. As the white Indian came to know Beaujolais better, he felt certain that Renna had made a good decision in marrying him. If it meant her separation from her family, then that was the will of the manitous. The important things were Renna's happiness and welfare. Since Beau was an intimate of the most powerful man in Europe, his future seemed assured . . . if one put aside pessimistic fear of another great war between France and England.

There came a time in the talking when the subject was a man who had touched all of their lives. Renna shuddered and clung to Beau as she listened to Little Hawk's account of the battle in the house of the witch.

Beau muttered French words of condemnation for Hugues as Little Hawk told of the spirit imps.

"I do not believe in such things," Beau confessed.

"Let us pray," Renna said fervently, "that nothing will happen to force you to believe."

"This Hugues," Beau said, "is a low sort, a typical product of the Revolution. In the bloody early stages, the Revolution offered opportunity for advancement to such men, who were willing to do anything in the name of liberty, equality, and brotherhood. As the political situation returns to normal, with a king on the throne of France—although he calls himself first consul—men like this animal Hugues will be discarded."

"Señor Almandor thinks that Hugues and the witch were committing the mutilation murders here in New Orleans," Little Hawk said.

"Well, he has fled," Beau said. "Soon Frenchmen will be protecting the streets of this city. If the monster comes back then, he will find it more difficult to commit his atrocities."

Thus did Beaujolais easily dismiss Othon Hugues and his odd female companion. Renno, however, could not entirely banish the Frenchman and his witch from his thoughts. He did make a conscious choice, though, to ignore the nagging need to seek out Hugues, wherever he was.

When Renno announced his intention to start for home, Beau, after a long discussion with Renna, said that he could make his report to Napoleon by letter, after all. That way, the family could travel together to the Seneca village. Had there been even the smallest doubt in Renna's heart of Beau's love for her, it would have been dispelled by his decision to travel north with Renno and Little Hawk.

"You asked me to take you to see your family," he explained. "I simply decided that it should be sooner than later."

Renno clapped Beau on the back and gave silent thanks to the manitous.

Beau said, "I have seen quite a bit of this vast continent of yours. I want to see more."

"The husband of my daughter is welcome to travel my trail," Renno said formally. He grinned, caught Beau's arm in the warrior's clasp. "We'll see new country together."

Beau spent long hours laboring over his report to Napoleon and included an account of Othon Hugues's actions and subsequent desertion. Beau stressed the hopelessness of the situation in St. Domingue, saying that only massive reinforcements could prevent the total victory of the mulatto generals and their native armies.

As it happened, a French trading vessel came up from St. Domingue the next day, bringing news that General Rochambeau was still in power but under very difficult circumstances. The captain confided to Beau that he was carrying on to Paris urgent dispatches from Rochambeau, demanding reinforcements. He agreed to deliver Beau's message to the first consul along with those from the general.

Any man who had ever made a two-way journey to New Orleans from the Kentucky-Ohio-Tennessee area would have been quick to state that going down the Mississippi was far preferable to going up the Mississippi. Many flat-

boats laden with the abundant produce of American frontier settlements put into the muddy current of the Ohio or
directly into the Father of Waters. From that point, getting to New Orleans was merely a matter of avoiding the
knife-sharp, water-hardened snags; staying off shifting sand-
bars, which changed locations with the seasons; watching
for unexpected floodwaters, which surged into the Mississippi from its numerous tributaries; and keeping an alert
eye on one's scalp and other belongings when the flatboat
was tied to the bank at night.

Going home? That was a different story. The weight
of the rains draining from half a continent pushed against
any vessel seeking to travel to the north. The riverside
swamps and mud flats made it impossible to propel a boat
by pulling it from the bank. Sails were not always practical, since the wind seldom blew from a southerly direction
for any length of time. As a result, the large flatboats
never returned to the places where they were built. Instead they were sold for their timber in New Orleans.

Some travelers had learned that small boats could be
propelled by manpower against the eternal, relentless current, while other experienced rivermen who had floated
so easily down a thousand miles of river opted to make the
long trek homeward on horseback or by shank's mare—
their own legs and feet.

Renno had chosen to combine travel by canoe and by
land. After a serious conference with Beau and Renna—
the subject of which was lessening the weight of their
communal baggage—a small fleet of canoes left New Orleans. The destination was the bustling city on the Mississippi frontier, Natchez. Renno had hired Choctaw boatmen.
The small hoard of gold from the *Sans Doute* that he had
carried with him was almost depleted, but Beau gamely
shared the expenses, so there was plenty of coin with
which to pay the boatmen and to buy horses for the long
journey up the Natchez Trace.

Four days out of New Orleans Renno picked a campsite on the eastern bank near the Choctaw village of a
petty chief called Iron Legs. Intrigued by the man who

called himself a Seneca and spoke the Choctaw language, Iron Legs invited all the whitefaces to a feast. Since it would have been both impolite and ill-advised to insult the Choctaw chief by refusing, the four travelers joined the man in his lodge. There they saw the basis for the chief's name: for the occasion he was proudly wearing the lower half of a medieval suit of armor. His legs were covered from the thighs down by rusting metal—cuisse on the thigh and jambeaux over his shins, joined by knee pieces that squeaked when he moved. He seized all opportunities to demonstrate the resonant qualities of the metal, striking it with his fist to illustrate a point, tapping on it idly with a dagger as he listened to Renno's tales of New Orleans.

The food was excellent, for of all the tribes in the Southwest Territory—meaning that part of the eastern half of the continent that bordered on the Mississippi and was under at least partial United States control—the Choctaw had been most successful in adopting the agricultural methods of the whitefaces. Even there, in the far western portion of the Choctaw Nation, the fields were cultivated with iron plows. It had been an excellent year for crops. Iron Legs's village was prosperous, the people well housed, well clothed, and well fed.

During the meal, the Choctaw chief spoke of Tecumseh, who had recently visited the village on a recruiting mission. "Will your people join the Shawnee in his holy war?" he asked Renno.

"No. The Seneca and the Cherokee of my brother Rusog will honor the peace that exists with the white men of the United States," Renno answered. "Since I have not come to counsel with Iron Legs but to enjoy his hospitality, I will not ask Iron Legs the intention of his people."

Iron Legs mused for a moment. It was one thing for young bucks to go a-roving, to raid an isolated Creek village, and to take a scalp or two. But war? That was another matter. In fact, even the old custom of raiding one's neighbors had almost faded away in the Choctaw Nation. They had become a tribe dedicated to peace and, to a large degree, to progress as defined by the whiteface.

When Iron Legs answered, his voice took on the tone of the orator. "The Seneca of the sachem Renno and the Cherokee of the chief Rusog are not the only men of wisdom. We in this land have long since come to terms with our whiteface neighbors to the east. We accept that their lands are theirs, although these territories once were the hunting grounds of Creek and Choctaw, and long ago of the Chatot, the Biloxi, the Yamasee, and the Napochi. Our lands are ours, and this is guaranteed by solemn treaty. The Shawnee have reason to urge war, as do many of our brothers. But Tecumseh's war is not our war. We will continue to live at peace with our neighbors."

"I have heard Tecumseh speak," Renno said. He was Seneca. He was Indian. And no true Indian could resist the opportunity to engage in an exchange of oratory. "I have heard him dream the dreams of one giant alliance of red brothers, reaching from the Great Lakes of the north in the land of snows to the Gulf of Mexico, and from the eastern boundaries of the Cherokee and the Creek and the Choctaw to the Father of Waters and beyond. And yet I hear few men speak of dreaming the same dream, for, like you and me, my brother, we know the price of war and the war-making ability of the whitefaces, who breed as do the rabbits of the fields and overwhelm the battlefield with thousands upon thousands of well-armed soldiers. And yet it is not fear of the whitefaces' prowess in war, nor their countless numbers that makes my decision. I see that the spread of the whiteface is inevitable. I see also his machines and his riches, and I know in my heart that our old way of life must give way to the new."

As he spoke on, Renna translated the words for her husband. Beau listened to Renna's whispers with an expression of growing admiration. Little Hawk, having heard it all before, stifled a yawn behind his hand.

Iron Legs, while listening to the Seneca's oration, sneaked glances at the young woman. In recent weeks a new source of riches had opened up to him: from time to time he sold a young maiden to a new friend and ally who had established a settlement not far up the river on the western bank. Iron Legs never sold women from his own clan or village, but under his command were those who, for just a small portion of the gold that he was paid by his new ally, would kidnap a maiden from three or four days' march away. The girl would be delivered to Iron Legs, who would bring her to the town across the river. This new friend, a great admirer of feminine beauty, would certainly pay gold in multiples of the usual price for this fair-haired, sky-eyed whiteface woman.

Chapter Twelve

Beth was awakened one morning by the honking of wild geese. She pulled a woolen shawl around her shoulders and walked out onto the second-floor veranda. The birds were flying toward the south in a low, V-shaped formation that waved up and down like a reed floating on the small ripples of a lake. She shaded her eyes against the brilliant autumn sun and watched until the birds were lost to her sight. She stretched, yawned, and took a deep breath of the delicious late-September morning. Was there a hint of winter in the air? The afternoons were comfortably warm, and yet something was different—a more tangy smell than earlier in the month, as if the air itself had traveled from strange, far-off northern places, bringing with it a bouquet of lovely things unknown, things only to be imagined.

Well, she thought, the birds knew. The early-morning low fliers were seeking the warm climes of the South.

Somewhere to the north, in their summer nesting places the snows had arrived early, and winter was beginning its slow, inexorable march toward The House.

"So, then, my husband," she said aloud, speaking softly, "it is time for you and your son to return."

Little Hawk had weeks of travel ahead of him in order to report to the new military academy fifty miles north of New York City on the Hudson River at West Point. During the War for Independence, Mad Anthony Wayne had rushed with his army to the fortress at West Point to prevent Benedict Arnold from turning it over to the British.

Beth knew her husband to be a man who recognized and lived up to his responsibilities, so her hope was that Renno and Little Hawk were already nearby, perhaps close enough to look up during the day and see the same formation of wild geese that had passed over The House shortly after dawn.

Ah, but there were other considerations—Renna, for example. Family loyalty was counted by Renno as the most profound responsibility. To find Renna alive, he would be willing to travel the globe. It was possible that he had measured the relative importance of getting Little Hawk to President Jefferson's military academy against Renna's welfare and safety. If so, the academy would have come up on the short end.

Depressing thought, that. She went back into her bedroom, freshened herself, and dressed. *Curse this huge, empty continent,* she thought. There were many advantages to living in a small country such as England, with no place more than seventy miles from the sea. In England a cross-country tour could be accomplished in days—not weeks, months, or years.

She had company for breakfast. Two very young gentlemen dressed in clean clothing came calling. Their dark, thick hair was wetted and brushed. Gao and Ta-na had learned to fancy the sweet rolls that Beth had taught Cook to make, and the boys seemed to have either extrasensory perception or extrasensitive noses, for they usually managed to show up at baking time. On that morning they arrived when Cook rewarmed the rolls for breakfast, sending a savory aroma of cinnamon and brown sugar wafting toward the village.

Neither boy noticed that Beth ate none of the sweets,
nor did she call attention to the fact lest the two reluctant
scholars become aware that the rolls were served at breakfast in The House only on school days. Having enjoyed a
reward in advance—as much of the heavy, sweet, spicy
pastry as their stomachs could hold—they were both too
honorable, or simply too stuffed, to complain or fidget
during a morning of instruction.

You're sly, Beth, she thought. *Crafty. Lonely . . .*

"Aunt Beth?" said Gao.

"Yes, young sir?" Beth acknowledged.

"I'll bet you wouldn't want to skip lessons this morning," Gao said.

"You would be right," Beth replied. "I wouldn't."

"That's what I thought," Gao said, crestfallen.

"What Gao means—" Ta-na began.

"What I mean is not for you to say," Gao broke in.
"It's just that the mulberries should by ripe by now."

"Ah," Beth said. "But they were green only—when
was it?—last Thursday?" She smiled. "It seems to me,
Master Gao, that we skipped lessons last Thursday morning to go to the mulberry tree, and as I remember it, the
berries were green nubs, nothing more."

"Well, they ripen fast in weather like this," Ta-na
pointed out.

"When they get ripe," Gao said, "if someone doesn't
get there quickly, the birds will eat all of them."

Beth mused for a second or two. It was a splendid
day, truly a day that the Lord had made. She nodded, as if
to convince herself. "Good. Let us rejoice and be glad in it."

"Huh?" Ta-na asked.

"Yesterday's Bible lesson," Beth reminded. "Perhaps,
if your memory is so short, we should take up those same
verses again instead of going on a nature outing."

"It's just that I didn't understand you at first," Ta-na
said quickly. He drew back his shoulders and thrust out
his chest, taking the posture for reciting from memory.
His brow was furrowed in thought, his dark eyes squinted.

Beth's heart fluttered for a moment, for in that studious pose he looked very much like a copper-skinned, black-haired miniature of his father.

"Puh-salm one-eighteen," Ta-na said, "verse the twenty-fourth. 'This is the day which the Lord hath made; we will rejoice and be glad in it.'"

"Very good," Beth approved. "But one does not pronounce the *p* in *psalm*."

"Yes, ma'am," Ta-na said. "Salm."

"That's it," Beth said, smiling fondly and shaking her head.

"Hateful language, English," Ta-na said, sounding exactly like Renno using his aristocratic British accent.

"I will rejoice and be very glad if we go to the mulberry tree to find that the berries have ripened," Gao said, just in case Aunt Beth had forgotten the subject of the conversation.

"Let me think," Beth said. "Shall I let you two bandits steal another school morning from me?"

"I believe the berries must be ripe," Ta-na said in all seriousness.

"Then I suppose there's nothing to it but to go and see," Beth said.

Gao shot out of his chair, whooped, and did a little stomp dance of joy. Beth looked at Ta-na and said, "It's a good thing that Gao is so sedate, isn't it? If he got excited about something, he might shake my house down about our heads."

The mulberry tree—a seventy-foot-tall, heavy-limbed oldster of a red mulberry tree—was a good mile south of The House. Every boy who had ever lived in Rusog's village or the village of the Seneca knew about this particular tree, for of all the mulberry trees within a radius of miles, it bore the fattest and the sweetest berries.

Beth took along a pail. A hot mulberry cobbler would taste good at the evening meal. And, ah, she thought, how Renno loved it. The renewed realization of his absence darkened the beautiful day for a few moments, but the energy and eagerness of the two boys soon brightened her spirits.

She wore an older dress, sturdy boots, and a sunbonnet. As she broke into a run to keep up with the boys, she laughed happily, took off the bonnet, stuffed it into the pail, and let her flame-colored hair down to stream over her shoulders. Once across the little creek, Gao gallantly turned and reached back to take her hand and help her jump over the water, although she was perfectly capable of doing it on her own. The boy looked up in wide-eyed appreciation at her loose red hair.

"Your hair is very beautiful, Aunt Beth," he said.

"Thank you, Gao. It's so nice of you to say so."

"I really mean it."

"I'm sure you do."

"You're really beautiful yourself," he added.

"Well, thank you again."

"Come on, you slowpokes," Ta-na yelled from up ahead.

"Aunt Beth—"

"Yes?"

"I just want you to know that if anything ever happens to Uncle Renno, I'll take care of you." He was standing very straight, his dark eyes unblinkingly locked to hers.

She had no inclination to laugh at him. "That makes me feel very secure, Gao," she said in a tone as serious as his. "I am greatly in your debt."

"Well," he said, poised to run, "I just wanted you to know."

As Beth followed the boys along a well-worn trail into the deep woods, she was thinking about the importance of small things. Once she had been welcome at the court of King George, and every fashionable home in London had been open to her. Once peers and dandies had vied for a chance to dance with her and to woo her, but never had she been more flattered than she was by Gao's solemn promise to take care of her.

She had given up Paris gowns and had traded the wine-sipping, snuff-sniffing society of London for a big, empty house near cojoining little Indian villages. Instead of bewigged, bejeweled, perfumed lords and ladies coming to call, she received rough frontiersmen from Tennessee, Cherokee Indians in breechclouts and deerskin shirts, and Seneca women in traditional costume. And, by the holies, she did not miss any of what she had forsworn to be the wife of a Seneca sachem.

The mulberry tree had its own private clearing. It was as if the virgin forest had honored the fruitfulness of the tree by pulling back and giving it its full share of sun and breeze. A yearling deer had been grazing on the tall, green grass that carpeted the tree's meadow. As Gao and Ta-na burst from the forest the lovely creature lifted its head high and pranced off proudly. Ta-na nocked an imaginary arrow to his nonexistent small bow and went through the motions of shooting. Had he carried his weapons, he would not have loosed an arrow; he had learned his lessons well from his fathers and other warriors, and he knew that his weapon was inadequate for killing the deer. If he had hit the animal with anything less than a full-sized arrow, he would merely have inflicted a painful wound.

The boys had shinnied up the trunk of the tree to a low fork and from there to smaller branches. They were busily stuffing their mouths with juicy, red, ripe berries when Beth reached the trunk.

"I say," she called up, "you will leave a few for me and the birds?"

"There's plenty," Gao assured her. "Do you need a hand up, Aunt Beth?"

"No, I think I can make it," she said.

She had often been tempted to adopt the short, comfortable *o-fa-sa* skirts of the younger Seneca women. She had, in fact, worked with Toshabe and Ah-wa-o to make an *o-fa-sa*, devoting hours to decorating it with the very small seed beads that were one of the most popular trade items that any peddler could bring into an Indian village. And she had fashioned *ka-ris*, women's leggings of bright red linen. Worn together, the *o-fa-sa* and the *ka-ris* were ideal for outings like the one to the mulberry tree. But Beth was a product of a different culture. To an Indian girl, a show of leg was not shocking. Beth, however, had been indoctrinated by the modesty of the upper class in England, where a glimpse of stocking was scandalous. She couldn't quite bring herself to walk around with her shapely legs bare or outlined in leggings.

She did make some concessions in her dress to better enjoy the semi-outdoor life she led. As she stood now at the foot of the mulberry tree and looked up at two grinning urchins whose hands and faces already showed purpled joy from eating berries, she was dressed in a short-sleeved blouse and half chemise, with a roomy calico skirt over unadorned, knee-length pantalets. Her stockings came only just past the top of her boots. The summer heat in her adopted homeland would have prostrated half the population of England if such temperatures ever invaded that tight little island, which lay on a latitude with northern Canada. As a result, she had directed her seamstresses in making skirts and dresses of thin material, with special smallclothes made of filmy lawn. She wore fashionable layers of petticoats only on formal occasions at The House.

Now she bent, reached down, and gathered the back hem of the skirt into her hand, drew it up between her legs to the front to stuff it into the waistband, and formed baggy bloomers. Her legs were exposed from the knees down to the top of her hose, but she had no desire to climb a tree in a long skirt and risk breaking her neck. She tossed her pail up to Ta-na, who caught it and hung it by its bail over the nub of a long-rotted limb.

"Are you sure you don't need a hand, Aunt Beth?" Gao asked.

"Just you watch this, sir," she said, pulling herself up to the low fork and proceeding to climb one of the two main trunks of the huge, old tree until she was just a bit higher than the boys, who were perched on limbs radiating out from the other main trunk.

"I told you they'd be ripe," Ta-na said.

"Yes, you did," Beth agreed, sampling a berry.

Above them, high in the small branches of the seventy-foot tree, birds fluttered and chirped their annoyance at the human intrusion. The sun filtered down through the shiny leaves. A breeze came from the south, bringing warm, moist air all the way up from the Gulf of Mexico

and belying the hint of winter that she fancied she had
noted early that morning.

"They are very good," Beth said.

"Umm," Ta-na agreed, stuffing a handful of the juicy,
red-purple berries into his mouth.

"Remember that we have to pick enough to make a
cobbler," Beth said.

"I'll start now, Aunt Beth," Gao offered, reaching for
the bucket. After a breakfast of honey-sweetened corn
mush, cold meat, summer melon, and liberal amounts of
pastry at The House, there was only so much room left
inside the boys' bellies for even the ripest and tastiest of
treats.

Soon the pail was half-full, with Gao and Ta-na taking
turns climbing to skimpy, fully laden branches at dizzying
heights for the largest berries. When odd sounds drifted
up, Beth looked down from her perch on a large limb a
full twenty feet off the ground.

As it happens, bears like mulberries just about as well
as anything in the world. They prefer ripe mulberries to
fat grubs dug out of a rotting log and to mice, and bears
like the little fruit almost as much as they enjoy fresh fish.
Generations of bears had also been well acquainted with
the mulberry tree, just as it had been known by generations of Indian boys. Two yearling black bears chose that
particular day to have a hankering for mulberries, and it
was not the first time that bear and boy had met with a
similar purpose. But it was the first time that Gao and
Ta-na had seen bears there and very definitely the first
time for Beth.

From the look of the yearling siblings, male and
female, they had only recently been cast out by their
mother. They reared high, scratched the bole of the tree,
and voiced interest and concern that the tree was already
occupied. It was the female yearling who decided that there
was room in the tree for all. She leaped high, seized the
bole of the tree with her claws, and scrambled into the fork.

"Gao! Ta-na!" Beth cried in a quavering voice. Both
bears were ascending toward her perch on the western-
most fork of the tree.

Gao climbed down from the high branches and began to yell at the bears. But the yearlings had not yet encountered man and therefore held no fear of the odd-smelling animals perched on high. The animals merely called back to him in high-pitched, sheeplike voices and continued their ascent.

Beth decided that she could climb higher, after all, and started to pull herself toward the smaller branches. The bears, having reached limbs laden with berries, settled down to munch. They paid little attention to their neighbors.

"Just stay where you are, Beth," Ta-na advised. "They'll go away soon."

"They're only overgrown cubs," Gao added. "I will climb over to you and scare them away."

It was a daring feat to take the only aerial pathway between the two main trunks of the tree. Beth, now a full forty feet off the ground, held her breath while Gao swung from tiny limbs that seemed ready to break. He made a leap and seized a limb just above her, causing the branches to sway sickeningly. Then he climbed down past her and began to throw twigs and small branches at the bears. The male bear ignored him, but the female looked up and sent out an eerie growl rumbling in warning.

"Hie, hie!" Gao yelled. He broke off a dead branch and hit the female on the nose with it. She roared and started hunching up the trunk toward him. In alarm, Gao climbed swiftly. The bear followed. "I think we'd better go higher," he told Beth.

Beth had never been particularly daunted by heights. She could stand on the brink of a high cliff in the mountains and gaze out without fear at the vista. But as she climbed higher and higher and the branches got smaller and smaller, she felt her legs getting weak, and a peculiar unsettled feeling roiled in the pit of her stomach.

The bear, feeling the tree sway with the combined weight of woman, boy, and animal, stopped, showed huge, yellow teeth in a snarl, and retreated back down to join her brother in ripping leaves and berries from small branches.

"Perhaps, Gao," Beth suggested, "we'd best let them eat their fill."

The problem was that none of them had any idea how much time a yearling bear required to eat all the berries it wanted. The female, deciding that the best berries were on the other trunk, joined Ta-na on the eastern half of the tree. As she worked her way up, she sent the boy to unstable, swaying heights.

After perhaps an hour of clinging precariously to branches no larger than her wrist, Beth sought a more secure perch. She watched the bear carefully as she descended to a larger limb. And then it began to rain. Beth had not noticed that the sun had disappeared, that the beautiful morning had lengthened into midday with clouds climbing the sky from the southwest. At first the gentle rain made a charming pitter-patter on the leaves. And then the drops, having become plain old unromantic water, began to drip into her hair and down the neck of her blouse. When the main force of the storm came to pound away with flashes of lightning and mighty claps of thunder and a driving wind and a torrent of cold rain, she hoped that the bears would seek shelter—preferably very far from the tree. Unfortunately, the two yearlings, completely unimpressed by the light, noise, wind, and wetness, continued to rip berries from the small and tender branches.

When the storm front passed, taking the lightning and thunder with it, the air was decidedly cold, and a steady, soft rain kept the leaves of the tree pouring water down onto three miserable, shivering, and thoroughly wet human beings.

"I think," Gao said grimly, "that the rain has set in for the day."

Beth wiped water from her face, then looked down at the male bear, who was still gorging himself on the limbs below. "And *I* think," she said with steely, British grit, "that this ludicrous situation has lasted quite long enough. Gao, Ta-na, you will please close your eyes. You will not open them until I tell you to do so."

"What are you going to do?" Gao asked.

"Never you mind," she said. "Just do as I say. Turn your head away and close your eyes."

Beth removed her long skirt. The thin lawn pantalets were wet and clung to her skin. She climbed down the tree, clutching her skirt in one hand. The male bear gave a warning growl, but Beth, undeterred, braced herself in a fork and shook her skirt with both hands at the bear.

"Shoo!" she said. "Scat! Go away!"

The bear growled.

"I will not have that," Beth said firmly, although her hands were shaking as she moved closer. "We are perfectly willing to give you the bloody tree, but you must allow us to climb down. Now, scat!"

The wet, flapping, unfamiliar thing slapped the male bear in the nose twice. His growl turned into an immature howl as he backed away and, looking from side to side and protesting, climbed backward down the tree. Beth followed him all the way, flapping her wet skirt at him.

The male yearling slid to the ground and ran a few feet, then paused to bawl piteously. The female answered from high in the tree and, with a great shedding of leaves, twigs, and bark shredded by her claws, came sliding down, too. She fell the last few feet, rolled to her feet, and started threateningly toward Beth.

Beth flapped her skirt and said, "You, also, shoo!" Then she stepped into her skirt, pulled it snug to her waist, and called to the boys.

Gao came behind her, grinning with pride at his aunt's courage. "Hurry, Ta-na," he called.

Ta-na started down the tree. Beth, her flaming hair clinging wetly to her skull and dripping down her back, called up, "Don't you dare come down without the pail, Ta-na."

During the time that they'd been treed by the bears, Ta-na had filled the bucket, just to have something to do. He descended, pail in hand. The two bears had wandered off but were looking back over their shoulders reproachfully.

"Now, you two," Beth called to them, "you may have the tree."

The bears stopped, turned.

"Come along, then," she invited. "Don't start being silly now, after all the trouble you've caused."

As if the female yearling understood, she led her brother back to the tree and leaped up to hunch her way to the first fork.

"Beth talks with bears, just as Renno does," Ta-na said, awe in his voice.

That night Ta-na and Gao took turns in telling the story during the evening meal. El-i-chi roared with laughter, picturing his sons and their aunt swaying high in the tree, wondering whether to risk the claws and teeth of the bears or the frail, thin branches forty or fifty feet off the ground.

The shaman made it a point, the next day, to visit Beth. He found her in the garden, directing the autumn mulching of her roses.

"I see you, Bear Woman," he said in Seneca.

"I see you, Brother," Beth replied. "But I see no Bear Woman."

"Bear Woman Who Wears Thin Leggings Under Skirt," El-i-chi clarified.

Beth blushed furiously. "Those little rapscallions! Who peeked?"

"It would be very difficult for any young boy to keep his eyes closed while his aunt is taming bears," El-i-chi said obliquely, grinning.

"El-i-chi, I will hear no more of this, this—" she sputtered. "Thin leggings, indeed. I had to do something, didn't I?"

"Bear Woman was very brave," El-i-chi said. "It has been decided that Bear Woman must be honored at a feast tonight in the village compound before my mother's house."

"Oh, come now, El-i-chi," she groaned. "A bit of ragging is permissible, let's not overdo it."

"When the sun touches the trees to the west," El-i-chi continued formally, "the feast will begin. Perhaps Bear Woman will appear in her very thin leggings?"

"Off with you," Beth said, smiling back at him. "I will not, of course."

"As you will," El-i-chi said.

She thought no more of it until, an hour before sunset, she heard the sound of rattles and drums and chanting from the front walk and went onto the veranda to find half of the young ones of the village decked out in ceremonial dress.

"We have come to escort you to the feast, Bear Woman," said Gao.

She sighed and decided that she might as well go along with the joke. She'd have no peace until she participated. She would let them have their fun at her expense. The humor of the Indian was not always quite understandable to a white, especially an Englishwoman, but it was all in a spirit of goodwill, so she allowed Gao and Ta-na to take her hands and lead her to the compound, where cooking pots were steaming, fires were smoking, and the entire village and part of the Cherokee Nation had gathered.

Ena met her and put a garland of fall flowers around her neck, kissed her on the cheek, and said, "Be brave, Bear Woman."

She led Beth to Toshabe's longhouse, where Ah-wa-o had Seneca clothing laid out for her. Since Beth had decided to go all the way with the joke, she donned skirt and shirt, moccasins and beaded headband, without complaint.

Back outside, Rusog gave a splendid oration, speaking first in Cherokee, then in English so that Beth would be sure to understand the extravagant words of praise for her bravery and quick thinking.

Next, El-i-chi presented her with a necklace of bear claws, and it was only then that she realized that she was not serving as the butt of a tribal joke. The bear was, after all, the sacred totem of El-i-chi's clan. The gift he had given her was presented in all seriousness. He orated a bit himself, then winked at her as the women burst into song.

Someone had improvised a chant about Flame Hair, brave Flame Hair, who had become Bear Woman. She didn't understand all the words as the young women chanted in shrill, singsong voices, but when Ena moved to stand beside her, took her hand, and squeezed it, Beth felt an outpouring of affection for those whom she had always regarded as her husband's people. She had thought that she knew the Seneca well. She had known them as human beings, with a human being's innate complications; but there were many aspects of their lives that she had considered to be simplistic.

When the women's song was finished, the feast was served. Beth was honored with the first plate of food.

"Ena," she asked later, after she had eaten of all the delicious dishes, "was all this planned just to have some reason to celebrate? Was it all an excuse to get everyone together for a feast?"

Ena put her hand on the bear-claw necklace. "Ask Renno what this means when he returns."

Beth looked down at the crude necklace. "I am aware that this means much to the Seneca."

"Almost more than anyone can explain," Ena said. "But perhaps you are partly right in saying that we were needing an excuse to hold a feast and celebrate. Look at you: for the first time you acknowledge that you are the wife of a Seneca sachem. For the first time you don the *a-te-non-wa-ran-hak-ta.*" She touched the headband in case Beth had not remembered the Seneca name for it. "For the first time you look like one of us. So we took this opportunity, this excuse, to get to know you better."

Beth blushed. "Ena, I didn't realize—I never intended to—"

"By allowing them to honor you with the feast and the gift and by accepting"—she smiled—"without protest the Seneca name that El-i-chi chose for you, you have said, yes, I am one of you."

"Will you tell everyone for me how greatly honored I feel?"

"No. I will allow you to tell them yourself." Ena rose, called for attention, pulled Beth to her feet, then sat down.

Beth searched for the Seneca words. She could carry on extensive one-on-one conversation with someone close to her, such as Renno; but suddenly, facing the smiling, curious faces, she was almost speechless. Finally she found the words. "How much you please me," she said, "and for what? For little. I was treed by bears, and I was cold and wet, and I wanted to climb down the tree without being attacked and go home. That's all. But how you do honor me."

Ho-ya chose that moment to come capering out onto the commons with a pair of Beth's pantalets pulled up over his breechclout. Roars of laughter exploded from the villagers.

"Bear Woman Who Wears Thin Leggings Under Skirt," voices called out.

"Ho-ya, you scamp!" Beth cried. Blushing furiously, she turned to El-i-chi. "Couldn't you have left off the last part of my new name?"

El-i-chi grinned. "Is Bear Woman still honored?"

Beth threw her head high and tossed her red tresses. "Bear Woman is still very much honored," she called out loudly in Seneca, "but Bear Woman does not willingly display to others the thin leggings under skirt."

That night, after readying herself for bed, she said her prayers and included a plea for forgiveness of her past pride. She had worn the Seneca clothing home. It was comfortable. If showing her legs was immodest, then so be it. She was now officially a member of the Seneca tribe and felt, for the first time, that she had been fully accepted into Renno's family circle.

Her prayers finished, she lay awake, visualizing the vast distances that lay between The House and the river, then the watery, curving path of the Father of Waters as it made its way down toward the Gulf of Mexico.

"Renno," she whispered, "it is time to come home."

Chapter Thirteen

The people of the village of the Choctaw Iron Legs lived in the old way. Their main concession to white civilization was the use of metal gardening utensils. The houses assigned to the chief's four guests were of the traditional type. Around posts buried into the ground and lashed together by liana vines were packed mud-thatch walls. The roof was formed of pine bark, with holes left at the gable ends for the escape of smoke. Beds made from cane stalks were raised about three feet from the earthen floor of the dark, windowless cabin.

Beau and Renna discovered quickly that although they had been given a separate cabin, they were sharing their bed with uninvited guests—fleas. Big brown fleas and little black fleas vied with one another in swift assaults. Beau was the first victim. Renna heard him scratching then muttering.

"Beau, whatever is the matter?" she asked.

"I am being eaten alive," he said.

A sharp nip at her bare ankle revealed the nature of the problem to Renna, and after that first blood-seeking insect had discovered her, others followed immediately.

"We can't have this," she said. She got off the high bed and slipped her feet into her moccasins. "I'll be right back."

"If you're abandoning this pest-infected hut, wait for me," he said.

"I'll be back in just a few minutes with a remedy," she promised.

After some fumbling in the dark she found her sheathed knife. She bent to get through the low doorway and crossed the village commons to a magnolia tree with low, bushy branches. She cut a few small limbs with their huge, slick leaves, then made her way back to the cabin. Beau had lighted a candle to try to determine the nature of the bugs that were chewing on him. By the light of the taper Renna removed the magnolia leaves from the limbs she'd cut and spread them under the blankets on both beds.

"There," she announced. "No more fleas."

Beau lay down and immediately sat up, reaching for his leg to scratch. "I think there has been some miscalculation."

"You'll have to get rid of the ones already on you," she told him. "But no more will come near the leaves."

"I pray, my dear, that you are right," Beau said with a sigh.

She was right. Each of them scratched a bit, picked off a few fleas, and then it was possible to sleep. Beau snored softly. Renna, turned on her side to face him, smiled to herself and let her eyes close slowly, so slowly that sleep came to her with the movement of her lids, softly, warmly, sweetly.

Shortly after his guests had gone to bed, Iron Legs removed his ceremonial armor and made his way to the riverside, where two young men awaited him. The three of them got into a canoe and put out into the current, the young men rowing hard to travel diagonally upstream across the river. When at last the canoe had reached the shelter of the western bank, Iron Legs called out a signal. An answer came from a dark cove, and the canoe was steered to land at a roughly built dock.

"Iron Legs has come to see the *alikchi*."

The sentry at the crude dock was Creek. It was no secret that he had no love for Iron Legs or any other Choctaw, but he knew that Iron Legs occasionally had business with the white chief with the pockmarked face. The Creek snorted to show his contempt for the name used by Iron Legs to designate Othon Hugues.

The sentry knew all about the Choctaw *alikchi*, or doctor. An *alikchi* was nothing more than a shaman, and the remedies and magic of a Choctaw shaman were, in the Creek's opinion, weak medicine. The Choctaw *alikchi* was a fraud who knew only the use of emetics, cathartics, and sweating. If that so-called magic failed, the *alikchi* claimed to be battling witchcraft, which made the death of the sick person inevitable—even if the *alikchi* had to commit the murder himself to prove his diagnosis correct. And then the fraud would choose some helpless old woman—with no young men left in her family to protest and protect her—and claim that she was the witch.

No, the Creek thought in disgust as he watched Iron Legs and the two young men head away from the river, to call the pockmarked one an *alikchi* was comparable to calling the rattlesnake a big worm. As for witchcraft, if one wanted to see witchcraft, one had only to stay in the vicinity of the long-haired woman with the gleaming black teeth for a few weeks.

Perhaps, the Creek warrior told himself, the witch would be hungry or bored and in need of amusement. Perhaps she would cause the detestable Choctaw chief Iron Legs to fall down in terminal agony as if he had been bitten by the little red-and-black-banded snake, which chewed at its victim instead of striking.

Such a consummation was not to be realized on that night, for soon the chief and his boatmen were back. With them were a dozen armed men, all members of the renegade band. The pockmarked white chief was not among them.

There were Creek and Spaniards and from the west four newcomers who called themselves Natchitoches. The sentinel recognized a brother Creek and edged close to him while canoes were being dragged to the edge of the water.

"What game is afoot, Brother?" the Creek sentry asked.

"The game that gives our white chief pleasure," was the answer.

The sentinel made a censorious sound with his lips. All this for another Choctaw girl. If he were the one who had the dominance of the witch's power to back him, he would not waste his time on Choctaw girls. They were more often ugly than not. As infants many of them had been subjected to heavy weights on their foreheads so that their heads were distorted to resemble the bricks used by the Spanish builders in New Orleans.

If he were chief, the Creek sentry mused, and made invincible by the witch, he would choose his female playmates from the tribes west of the river—or better still, he would go home to the lands of his ancestors, where the Creek girls were pretty.

Soon the little flotilla was lost to sight on the darkness of the river. Time once more hung heavy on the sentinel's hands.

To the disgust of the armed renegades from Othon Hugues's settlement, the Choctaw chief ordered them to wait on the outskirts of his village. He went on ahead and twenty minutes later came clopping back with his leg armor in place.

"They are all asleep," he informed the short, stocky Spaniard who was Hugues's field leader. "Three or four men will be needed to take the girl and her Frenchman. The rest should lure the Seneca sachem and his son out of their lodge into ambush."

"You are concerned about two men?" asked the Spaniard. He laughed derisively. "It is unnecessary to resort to trickery and ambush to take two men."

"That decision is yours," Iron Legs said, "but to assure that I am paid the price on which the white *alikchi* and I agreed, perhaps you will hand over the gold now, before you go into the lodge where the two Seneca sleep."

"Iron Legs grows timid in his old age," the Spaniard taunted, laughing again. "You will get your gold. Don't worry." He turned and gave orders in a quiet voice.

Four men separated from the rest and followed one of Iron Legs's young warriors to the lodge assigned to the woman and her Frenchman. Two of the kidnappers were brothers from west of the river, Natchitoches of the scrub oak and grassy woodlands. The other two were Creek.

"We will detain the Frenchman," offered the elder Natchitoches brother.

"The command of this force," said the Creek warrior whose gray hair and rotten teeth testified to his many summers, "has been entrusted to me. We two Creek will handle the man. For you the task is to take the woman to the canoes without bruising her or hurting her. The white chief does not like his women damaged." He chuckled. "At least not by others before it is his pleasure to do so."

The Natchitoches brothers did not protest, although they were no strangers to war. They had come toward the east to see the big river and had attached themselves to White Chief Whose Face Hurt because the food was plentiful, because there were women for all, and because at least once a week the witch herself repeatedly poured rum into a man's drinking gourd until he was so inebriated, he could no longer hold the vessel. The damp, dense forests of the eastern bank of the Father of Waters were not to their liking, but the white chief had promised extra rum for all those who participated in bringing the pale-haired white girl to his lodge.

To the two Natchitoches brothers, it was an honor to have been chosen by Hugues's Spanish field leader to assist in the capture of the prize. As neighbors of the fierce Comanche they had, the brothers would have boasted, faced enemies more dangerous than a sleeping Frenchman.

The party of four crept through the door into the guest lodge. Since it didn't matter if the Frenchman was injured, the older Natchitoches brother prevented any possible protest from him with a solid blow to the temple with the flat side of his tomahawk.

*   *   *

The sound of the impact caused Renna to sit straight up in bed. The only light in the lodge came from the low door opening, so she could see nothing; but in that moment of awakening she sensed the presence of something or someone other than the sleeping Beau. She said softly, "Beau?"

A blanket was thrown over her head, and she screamed, but the sound was muffled by the heavy wool. She lashed out with her fists and cut her knuckles on her assailant's teeth. She heard a gasp of surprise, and the one holding the blanket lost his grip.

Renna screamed again, and the sound escaped the blanket. She kicked, and her feet contacted stomach and elicited a grunt. She struck out and, feeling a nose under her fingers, gouged parallel grooves in the skin with her fingernails. But the blanket was being pulled tighter around her, and someone was lying across her legs to pin them down while another held her arms to her sides. Soon she was helpless, and worse, the blanket was wrapped so tightly around her face that she was having difficulty breathing.

She felt herself being trussed up with rope or thongs, her hands behind her back, her ankles together. Then she was lifted and carried. The kidnappers broke into a jog, and she was jolted by the motion. And then she was half dropped into what she guessed was a canoe. She strained against the bonds, but they were too strong. She could do nothing except concentrate on trying to draw enough air through multiple folds of blanket to fend off unconsciousness.

At first Renno was unable to identify the sound that had penetrated his sleep. He lay quite still and heard the rustle of a night wind in the treetops and the call of an owl. Then he heard the sound again—metal, a clink of metal. His hand went to the pack he was using as a pillow and closed over the handle of his tomahawk. The clinking sound came again, closer. *Iron Legs*.

The white Indian made a soft hissing sound. Little Hawk stirred but did not waken. Renno tensed as he heard a muffled scream from outside his guest cabin. He hissed again and slipped from the bed, his feet finding his moccasins. He touched Little Hawk on the shoulder, and his son sat up, obeying the signal for silence—a touch of Renno's finger on the young man's lips. The sachem pressed the haft of Little Hawk's tomahawk into his son's hand.

Renno pulled his son away from the bed and to the far side of the lodge. He faced the door, outlined by the moonlight from outside. He felt Little Hawk tense and could almost hear his son's heart pounding as dark forms blocked the opening. Four men entered. Two moved toward the bed vacated by Renno; two went toward Little Hawk's bed. There was a thud as a blade struck the blankets on Renno's bed.

With startling suddenness, the roaring, challenging snarl of an angry bear filled the dark lodge. Before the sound had faded, two intruders were dead as father and son leaped forward, swung their blades, and felt the solid impact of tomahawk on skull. Renno dispatched a third man, who was near his bed, with an upswing to smash the blade under the enemy's chin. Then he whirled toward the sound of harsh breathing and of struggle. Renno could not strike, for in the darkness he could distinguish only the mass of Little Hawk and the fourth man locked in mortal combat.

When the sachem sensed movement at the door, he turned. After the sharp blade forged by Se-quo-i smashed into a Creek nose, a cry of question came from outside. Leaving Little Hawk behind was the hardest thing Renno had ever done. His every instinct told him to remain with his son, to distinguish, somehow, between Little Hawk and the adversary, and put an end to the grunting, deadly battle. But more of the enemy were outside and needed immediate attention.

He dived through the open door, hit the ground on his shoulder, and rolled to his feet in time to escape the blast of a musket. The explosion momentarily lighted the night. Fortunately, Renno had not been looking directly at the musket muzzle. The man who had fired the shot was temporarily blinded by the brilliant flash and died without seeing the blow that killed him.

"So there was no need to ambush this one, eh?" grated a voice that Renno identified as Iron Legs's.

The cry of a soaring hawk came from behind Renno. He saw a pale blur of motion emerge from the lodge, and his heart swelled with pride.

"To my side," the sachem said in Seneca, and Little Hawk stood with him.

A musket blasted. Little Hawk, again giving the cry of his namesake, lunged forward, pushed the barrel of the rifle aside, and buried his blade in bone.

The last man to die was the Spaniard who had underestimated the Senecas' fighting ability. As Renno poised to face this adversary, the Spaniard cursed, fired at a shadow, then threw his musket aside to take up his blade. The moon came from behind a small cloud to light his last sight on earth: the snarling face of an avenger, pale in the moonlight. He saw a flash of blade and tried to counter the strike, but Renno's tomahawk took him just under the ear. The blow had been struck with all the force of Renno's right arm. It severed tendon and flesh and blood vessels.

"Hold, Seneca!" Iron Legs pleaded. "This is not my fight."

Brighter moonlight reflected off the leg armor. The two young Choctaw who had taken Iron Legs across the river had backed away from the swift and deadly action. It was clear that neither wanted to challenge the two Seneca who had left eight men lying dead in the time that it would take a normal man to reload a musket.

"Pray, then, Choctaw," Renno advised, "that no harm has come to my daughter." He seized Iron Legs by the arm and pushed him roughly toward Beau and Renna's cabin.

"It was the Spaniards and the Creek," Iron Legs claimed. "I wanted to warn you, but they would have killed me. I am an old man, Seneca. I gave you my hospitality. It was the Spaniards and the Creek."

Little Hawk ran ahead, ducked into the lodge, and emerged immediately. "Empty."

Renno drew his stiletto and placed the point of it under Iron Legs's chin. "Tell me, and tell me quickly," he seethed.

Around them the village was awakening. Curious women in night shifts, or less, peeked out of the lodges. Men, most of them unarmed, were moving toward the gleam of Iron Legs's armor.

"If you harm me, Seneca," the Choctaw chief warned, "my people will kill you."

Renno twisted the blade of his stiletto, and Iron Legs squirmed, for the sharp point had drawn blood. "Speak quickly," he said, and something in his voice caused the Choctaw to shudder.

"They will take her and the Frenchman across the river," he said.

"Where?"

"On the western bank, past the shoulder of land where the river curves to the west. Go inland to a hilltop, and you will see where the white chief has built his village."

"A white chief? Has he a name?"

"It is a name difficult for my tongue."

"Why do you threaten our chief, Seneca?" demanded a Choctaw man who was edging closer.

"Because your chief sends murderers into my lodge in the middle of the night," Renno grated. "Because your chief has allowed others to carry off my daughter and her husband."

"My people," Iron Legs proclaimed in a loud voice, "do not stand idly by while this Seneca insults and threatens your chief."

"Seneca," said the Choctaw man who had moved close, "perhaps you had better release Iron Legs from your grasp."

Renno slid the knife ever so slightly across the Choctaw chief's throat. A trickle of fresh blood ran down Iron Legs's neck. "Does Iron Legs want me to release him?" Renno asked almost sweetly.

"My people," Iron Legs croaked, "it is all right. The Seneca will not harm me."

"What is the name of this white chief?" Renno demanded.

"It is difficult," said Iron Legs. "It is like . . . how do

the whitefaces call this?" He fingered the leather thong that pulled his shirt together below his chin.

"A thong," Renno answered. "The white man's name is Othon?"

"That is it."

"Othon Hugues, a Frenchman?"

"Yes. Now will you release me?"

Renno had listened to his daughter's recounting of the acts of Hugues and had seen the latent fear in her eyes as she spoke of the Frenchman. He had also seen the horrors contained in Hugues's house in New Orleans. His fury rose up in him and could not be controlled. He drove the stiletto deeply into the Choctaw's stomach, angling the blade upward between the V of ribs. Iron Legs's life rushed out of his body in a long sigh. Renno jerked his blade away and let the chief fall with a clatter of armor. Then he turned toward the Choctaw villagers.

"This man delivered my daughter into the hands of the evil ones," he said. "If there are any who dispute the justice of my act, step forward now."

"Father, let's go," Little Hawk urged.

"Yes," said Renno, backing away.

No Choctaw tried to stop them. They found a two-man canoe pulled up on the shore, grabbed the paddles, pushed the boat into the water, and rowed quickly into the current, angling strongly toward the western bank. They were no farther than two hundred feet from the bank when they heard wild war cries behind them. A large group of Choctaw burst out onto the bank and began to pile into canoes.

"I think that they have finally realized that you killed their chief," Little Hawk said.

At least a dozen canoes were moving up the river after them. The Choctaw, living on the Mississippi, were known as experienced boatmen. Renno increased the pace of his paddling, and his efforts were matched by Little Hawk's, but the Choctaw canoes were gaining.

"We must lose them on shore," Renno said, turning the bow of the boat toward the eastern bank, which they had just left.

"My arms and shoulders are aflame from this unfamiliar labor," Little Hawk grunted. He sighed with relief when the canoe grounded in mud.

Father and son leaped out to wade ashore, climb the bank, and disappear into the dense undergrowth. They heard the Choctaw landing behind them, whooping and calling back and forth. Renno and Little Hawk pushed their way through the riverside thickets and into the woodlands. Soon the sound of voices was no longer heard. After traveling parallel to the river for approximately two miles, Renno led the way back to the water. They were surrounded only by night sounds. Below them the river curved around a shoulder of land. They had passed the bend that Iron Legs had described to Renno.

"I think we'll have to go farther upriver," Renno said.

Without a boat there was only one way of crossing the wide, muddy stream. They hurried north as the moon started falling down the western sky. When Renno thought they had gone far enough, he and his son pulled dried logs from a pile of drift and, pushing the logs ahead of them, waded into the current.

It was a long swim. Occasionally they rested and allowed the current to carry them, but most of the time they used their legs to propel the logs toward the western bank. When it appeared that the current was going to sweep them past the bend, they abandoned the logs and swam strongly. As it was, they landed just on the tip of the shoulder of land and had to move upstream to find the dock.

A sentinel lay there sleeping. Renno heard the man's deep breathing before he noticed the sun-bleached timbers of the dock in the light of false dawn.

Little Hawk touched Renno on the arm and pointed. The sachem, who already had reached for his stiletto, hesitated, then nodded as Little Hawk crept ahead. It was difficult for Renno to wait while another took the point, for he had always been the leader, always the first to risk danger. But this was his son, the future sachem of the Seneca, and Little Hawk had already proven that he was of the blood of the white Indian.

The wait seemed long to Renno, although not more than five minutes could have passed before he heard the soft call of a mourning dove. He moved to the dock. Little Hawk was silhouetted against the sky. At his feet lay the sentinel, whose sleep had become eternal.

The path leading inland from the dock was well used. It angled up a sharp slope to the top of a ridge. Below them, in a natural bowl, lay the renegades' town. They could see all of it from their position. There were no lights, but dying fires showed still-glowing embers in front of several huts. A dog barked lazily and steadily.

"There," Renno said, pointing. In the central commons was a vertical slash in the darkness, where a man was lashed to a stake. The embers of fires glowed in three places around it.

Little Hawk whispered, "That would be Beau."

"They will not have done him serious harm as yet," Renno said. He looked up at the eastern sky. A feeling of early morning was in the air—a softness, a coolness. Soon the intense darkness following false dawn began to lighten. He made himself comfortable lying on his stomach as his eyes searched the town below.

One structure stood out from the others. It was built of rough-sawn planks, similar to those used in the construction of a Kentucky flatboat. Its peaked roof was covered with tin. Renno's guess was that the largest house would be Hugues's, but he could not be certain that Renna would be within. She could be prisoner in any of the huts surrounding the commons. If he was going to move, he knew he had to act swiftly, before the sun roused the entire village.

"Watch my back," he told Little Hawk. "I will enter the large hut."

Little Hawk nodded.

They walked down the slope toward the village as if they belonged there, but avoided making any undue noise. A lazily barking dog continued its serenade to the fading night. Earthen rifle pits had been constructed to defend the place from attack, but there were no sentries. The stench and the litter marked the village as a place of filth and disorder. Once, Renno's foot slipped on a greasy bone that had been tossed from one of the huts.

At the edge of the commons the white Indian paused to remove his stiletto from its sheath. His intentions were to free Beau, learn Renna's whereabouts from the Frenchman, and be out and away before the villagers began to awaken.

"Wait here," he told his son, but even as he spoke, he felt that he was too late.

Shadows were being dispelled by the light of dawn. Indeed, as he took a step toward the commons a tall, thick-chested man naked to the waist emerged from the big hut. There was enough light to see that his face had been scratched deeply in four grooves running down one pockmarked cheek. Renno backed into the shadows and froze.

"Pedro, where in blazes are you?" Othon Hugues bellowed in French.

A sleepy voice muttered from within the hut beside which Renno and Little Hawk were standing. They glanced toward Beau. Hugues's voice had roused the French nobleman, and he turned his head toward the sound and stiffened. He was naked, and his white skin was marked, but with dirt or blood and bruises, it was impossible to discern.

Renno squeezed Little Hawk's arm and pointed toward the nearest trees outside the village. Little Hawk pointed toward Beau, but Renno shook his head.

Hugues let out another bellow, and a voice answered. The entire settlement was coming to life. Renno, leading the way, slipped from shadow to shadow in the pale dawn until, using the bulk of one last hut as a shield, he and Little Hawk ran quickly into the shelter of the forest.

"Father," Little Hawk protested when they had put enough distance between them and the village, "my sister has already lost one husband to that animal."

"True," Renno agreed, then added in formal Seneca, "and would you have her lose a father and a brother along with a second husband?"

"You know best, of course," Little Hawk conceded.

"Thank you very much," Renno said in English, but

he softened the sarcasm with a quick pat on the back. "They will do Beau no irreparable harm during the day-light hours. He will be tormented by the women and children, but no serious injury will be inflicted until the evening comes again."

"I pray that you are right," Little Hawk said fervently.

Renno reverted to Seneca again. "I have seen, and I have felt shame for our own past, for the women of the Seneca were famed for their ability to keep a man alive while inflicting agony on him. You are too young, thank the manitous, to have witnessed this."

Little Hawk was silent, obviously trying to picture his grandmother, Aunt Ena, Ah-wa-o, We-yo, and other women of his tribe engaged in the torture of a helpless victim. Unsuccessful, he shook his head to dispel the thoughts as he followed his father to a little glen deep in the forest.

"We will sleep here," the sachem said.

"Sleep? By the manitous—"

"Sleep," Renno repeated. "We had no sleep this past night, and the coming night will find us among the en-emy. You sleep first, while I watch."

"Father, I just don't think I can," Little Hawk protested.

"Try," Renno said with a grim smile.

Little Hawk shrugged, then lay down on soft leaves, closed his eyes, said a little prayer to both his divinities— the Master of Life and the God of his mother—for the safety of his sister and her husband . . . and was awak-ened by his father's hand on his shoulder with the sun well past its zenith. A smokeless fire was burning under a roasting rabbit. They ate in silence, and then Renno lay down and was asleep immediately.

The change of light and temperature as the sun touched the trees to the west awoke Renno. He and Little Hawk ate the remains of the rabbit, drank at a small stream, and crept to a point of vantage overlooking the village. By day the place looked even more squalid, with its crude log-and-mud huts and pole lean-tos. A polyglot population of Negroes, Indians, and filthy-looking white men was begin-ning to gather at the commons where Beau stood straight and proud at the stake. He ignored the small pebbles that were being thrown by a group of Indian and black children to sting his naked body. Some of the women had also given Beau a bit of attention during the day, as evidenced by streaks of blood on his torso. As Renno had predicted, however, no serious harm had been done.

The white Indian whispered instructions to his son, and Little Hawk listened with a grave face. For the first time in his young life he was going knowingly into a situation where he could very easily be killed. It gave him great pride to know that his father trusted him to carry out instructions, that the greatest of warriors was treating him as an equal. He nodded and repeated the orders.

Then there was the waiting. They both tensed when the witch, dressed in white, emerged from the big hut. Her ebony hair was loose and hanging down her back. Her bizarre black teeth glistened in the last light of the sun. She walked to stand near Beau, then sprinkled something over his head. Beau stood with dignity and looked unblinkingly into her eyes. Little Hawk stirred uneasily as the witch lifted herself on tiptoe and passionately kissed the French nobleman.

"Even now she can bewitch him," he said in awe, "for he has made the mistake of looking into her eyes. Can you see, Father? She has made him forget his pain and the promise of imminent death."

Beau leaned forward against his bonds, his mouth reaching for the lips of the witch. As she walked away he called out to her. His voice drifted to Little Hawk and Renno faintly. The crowd laughed and taunted him, but he seemed not to notice.

"Indeed, she has the power of evil," Renno whispered.

"And yet," Little Hawk said, "my mother's heaven could have offered me no greater bliss." He cleared his throat. "At least for a time," he added sheepishly.

Renno nodded. As twilight closed over the village he began to move stealthily toward the nearest house. He felt impatient with the knowledge that Beau's trial would soon begin in earnest. Little Hawk was right behind him. Having reached the edge of the village, father and son walked

side by side toward the commons. As instructed, Little
Hawk gathered the material he would need as he passed
among the huts. Besoms. Brush brooms. He had three of
them, taken from the thresholds of huts.

With the coming of darkness the villagers fed the
smoldering fires that circled the stake where Beau was
tied. As Renno and Little Hawk approached, the witch
began to dance. Two gleamingly black, strong-muscled
men were beating out a slow rhythm on drums fashioned
of hollow logs and leather. Little Hawk watched the slow
and sensuous undulations of Melisande's bare arms, her
silk-encased torso, and the long legs that protruded from a
short, raggedly cut skirt. He felt a stirring deep within
and, swallowing, looked away.

"Now," Renno told him.

Little Hawk ignited the brooms by sticking them into
a fire at the rear of the crowd watching Melisande's dance.
Then he ran to the far-most huts and began to torch them
one by one from the inside, thrusting the burning brooms
against bedding, thatch roofs, anything that would catch
fire quickly.

Renno, meanwhile, was edging toward the big hut.
He kept one eye on the witch, who had bared her breasts.
As he neared his destination a gasp went up from the
crowd. The sachem looked back to see that the witch had
thrown aside her garment and was dancing naked, twisting
and bending sensuously, her lips moving with the words
of a song in a minor key.

Renno turned his head back toward the big hut.
Othon Hugues, perhaps at having heard Melisande begin
singing, emerged from the hut, wiping blood from his
cheek where more long slashes had been added. Renno's
hand tightened on the haft of his tomahawk, his every
fiber longing for the feel of the Frenchman's cracking skull
under his blade.

Chapter Fourteen

Renna had not slept for over twenty hours, and although she was on a bed, thoughts of sleep were far from her mind. She was spread-eagled, her wrists and ankles bound securely to the buried posts that formed the corners of the bed frame. She was not entirely nude, but her clothing was ripped and awry. Her hands had been loosened twice since she had been thrown roughly down onto the bed and tied.

She tossed her head angrily as she thought of those times, and her fingers curled as if she could feel the skin of the Frenchman's face under her fingernails. She had been helpless, her clothing ripped and opened to reveal her breasts and the creamy, pale hair of her sex. She had been struck in the face.

He had told her, "My little flower, you will come to love me. I want to feel the gentle touch of your hands. I want to know your deepest longings, your passions of fire."

Her deepest longing had been to slash at his eyes with her nails. When, for the second time, he tried to convince her to accept his vile touch willingly, she had moved with surprising swiftness to claw at his face. He had slapped her so hard that the world went dim. Other than that one blow, she had not been physically harmed.

The damage to her spirit was still to be assessed, for right now, unabating anger drove her. When that fury receded, then she would remember his hateful hands, his insensitive probings and squeezings while he spouted flowery language, as if she were some sort of demented fool who did not care that she had seen him torture a defenseless Choctaw girl. And later she would remember how the dark woman with the revolting black teeth had watched and crooned instructions to Othon, then laughed when his face was clawed and he cursed.

Now it was dark again. A full day had passed. She fought her bonds with hopeless but relentless persistence. She had to do something to keep from thinking about Beau, for she didn't know whether he was dead or alive. She had asked Hugues more than once, and each time her question had been met with silence.

She was struggling listlessly against the unbreakable leather straps when she heard a sudden shouting from outside. She distinguished one word in at least three languages—*fire*.

She lay still, listening. And then her father miraculously appeared at her side, as if he had materialized from the spirit world. His jeweled Spanish stiletto slashed at her bonds as his concerned eyes searched her face.

He quickly examined her swollen cheek, her half-closed eye. "I am here, my daughter."

"Is the evil Frenchman dead?" she asked.

"Not yet," Renno answered.

"Father," she said, the words grating from her throat, "I ask only that I be allowed to kill him."

Renno grinned in spite of himself. "Most women in your position would have been weeping and hysterical. But you, Daughter, have the blood of the white Indian and think only of revenge. I am proud of you, Renna!" He cut the last of her bonds and seized her arms to jerk her up off the bed. "Perhaps your revenge will come."

She brushed carelessly at her clothing. Renno motioned her behind him and moved to the door. Outside, fires were burning in huts along the western half of the village. Renno took Renna's hand and led her around to the back of the hut. Little Hawk was waiting for them. He grinned hugely to see she was all right.

"Beau—" Renna said.

"Go quickly," Renno told her.

"I will not leave without Beau," Renna insisted.

"You . . . will . . . obey," Renno ordered, and the tone of his voice, the sternness of his look, caused her to cease all objections as her brother grasped her hand and led her toward the river.

Renno's attentions had not been totally on his daughter while he had been inside Hugues's hut. He had noticed, in fact, that the hut also served as an arsenal. Against the walls were arrayed several small kegs of black powder, a supply of balls, the equipment for molding balls from lead, and several spare muskets. After his children were out of sight, he slipped back to the front of the hut. Most of the crowd had rushed to fight the fires, but a few had remained to watch a bizarre ceremony being played out in the center of the commons. The witch, still accompanied by the drums of the two large Negroes, was weaving a spell of sensual mystery for the comte de Beaujolais. It was embarrassingly obvious that he was extremely interested in the nude woman who writhed so enticingly in front of him. He strained to reach out to her, and when she paused before him, pressed her lower body to his, and then lifted to impale herself, Renno heard a gasp of ecstasy escape the enchanted man's lips.

More and more men were turning away from the fires to watch Melisande. Renno, taking advantage of their preoccupation, seized a burning brand and ran into Othon's hut, where he turned over one keg of black powder and spilled the contents around the other kegs. He made a little trail to act as a fuse, then he looked out the door. The crowd, fully interested now in the witch's exhibition of lust, was drifting back to the commons from the fires.

Renno placed the burning brand carefully so that quite soon—it was impossible to estimate exactly when—the fire would reach the little trail of powder. The white Indian knew that he would have to trust to the manitous for the timing of the explosion. Renno ran with all his swiftness toward the stake. He seized the panting, writhing witch by her long black hair and roughly pushed her away. She lost her balance and fell hard. Renno's blade flashed out and cut the leather thongs that held Beau's arms aloft.

"No, no," Beau was saying in a stunned voice as Renno bent to slash the leather binding his feet together.

"If you want to live, Beau, then run," he said.

Melisande had picked herself up. Her dark eyes were gleaming like burning coals, and her black teeth reflected the gleam of the flames. She lifted one clawed hand and pointed it at Renno.

He felt a sudden and excruciating pain in his chest. He tried to throw his tomahawk at this incarnation of evil, but his arm was leaden. He had made the mistake of looking into her eyes.

The witch laughed and, coming to her feet, swayed toward him to meet a fury that materialized between her glowing, enticing eyes and Renno. The white Indian recognized the form of his deceased Seneca wife, An-da—wife, lover, friend—making her first appearance as a manitou to protect him.

"Now we go!" Renno said, grabbing the recalcitrant Beau's arm and fighting the desire to drink in the image of his beloved Seneca wife.

The forces of good were pitted against the powers of evil, and flames shot out from the meeting. Streaks of light were accompanied by the smell of something scorched. There was no more evil a woman than Melisande, but the innocent An-da, mother of Renno's second son, Ta-na, had been a purely kind and gracious entity during her tragically brief time on earth.

"No, no," Beau was protesting, trying to move toward Melisande.

The villagers, awed by the pyrotechnic meeting of

witch and manitou, made no effort to intervene. Renno slapped the Frenchman hard across the face, then seized his arms. "Run!" he shouted, shaking Beau hard.

"Renno!" Beau's eyes flew open wide as if he were coming out of a deep sleep. He followed the sachem, stumbling for a moment, then finding his stride as a ragged fusillade of musket fire sent balls whistling past his ears.

Renno risked one last look just in time to see the witch reel backward, a hoarse scream coming from her mouth. The light that had been the manitou of An-da abruptly disappeared. He dared not slow to look further because the only avenue of escape led directly alongside the big hut, wherein sat several kegs of black powder about to explode. He pulled Beau along. The stench of burning powder came drifting from the hut, encouraging him to run for his life.

The kegs of black powder erupted in a series of thunderous blasts. The force of the explosion momentarily deadened Renno's hearing. A hot blast of wind picked up both men and flung them forward, onto the ground. Behind them a man was screaming in agony. Renno, grateful he could hear again, lifted Beau to his feet, and they ran for the river. Beau, running barefoot, wasted precious breath on a fine assortment of French profanity each time his tender soles encountered stone, stick, or sticker, and Renno was forced to slow his pace for Beau's benefit.

Over the residual ringing in his ears, Renno heard the shouts of Othon Hugues urging his men to pursuit. The sachem knew that it would take a few minutes for Hugues to organize his forces, but there was always the chance that one or two men, quick to react, had not waited for orders. He pulled Beau to a stop. "Silence," he whispered.

He heard running footsteps quite near behind them. He pulled Beau off the trail and waited until a man came almost even with them. Then the sachem stepped out to halt the Creek's headlong rush down the trail with a blade to the throat.

He cocked his head, listening. "Only one was brave,"

he said to Beau. The white Indian stripped the Creek of his deerskin tunic and trousers. Around the man's neck hung a leather pouch. Renno removed this also, and hefted it in his palm. The unmistakable jingle of coins caused the white Indian to flash a quick grin. Renno slipped the pouch's thong around his own neck then helped the French noble into the dead man's clothing. The moccasins of the Creek were a bit large but better than nothing. The two men continued toward the river at a slower pace.

"Renno," Beau said, "was I dreaming? Did the woman with black teeth actually . . ." He couldn't say the words.

"She did," Renno confirmed.

"My dear father-by-marriage," Beau said quite formally, "would it be possible to ask you to keep that, uh, rather unsavory information from your daughter?"

Renno laughed in spite of himself. It was, as Roy Johnson might have said, one hell of a time to worry about the small stuff. "I might keep the actions of the witch our secret," he said, "if I can persuade you to walk a bit more quietly."

"I'll try," Beau promised, relieved.

"It was *he*," Melisande said, her voice chilling the very air. "I saw him. He had the audacity to put his hand on me with force. His whiteface . . . his blue eyes. For the second time now, Othon, you have allowed him to enter our home and steal something from me."

"I don't know who he is," Othon said. "I know only that next time he will die, and very slowly."

"He touched me," the witch said angrily, "and you were not at my side to cut off the hand that offended me."

"I am wasting time," Othon told her. He was already disgusted with himself; he didn't need Melisande to admonish him.

"Go, then." Her voice became sarcastic. "If one man and a boy are too much for you, Chief Executioner, you may want to wait for me to come along so that I may protect you."

"Why do you insult me?" Othon asked plaintively. But he didn't wait for an answer. He jerked a musket out of the hands of a nearby man, took the powder horn and shot bag, and set off at a run, yelling at his men to follow him.

Melisande, still nude, walked regally to the stake, picked up her fallen garment, and pulled it around her shoulders. The two black drummers were squatted beside their instruments, looking blankly at her. She kicked one of them and said, "Fools! Why did I see fit to bring you?"

Her own house was a smoldering pile of rubble, so she chose an undamaged hut, entered, and sent a blast of hatred and terror at the woman occupant there, causing her to flee without question. All of Melisande's clothing, potions, powders, herbs, and paraphernalia were gone. Even Othon had failed her. She had only herself. She sat down on the bed and went into a deep trance.

Little Hawk and Renna were waiting anxiously beside the river. Contact was made by a series of soft dove calls, and then Renna was in Beau's arms. Renno heard her whispering euphemistic assurances to her husband that she had not been "harmed." He himself had not asked, fearful of the answer, for she had been a captive of the Frenchman for part of a night and an entire day. If she was telling Beau the truth, then he thanked the manitous for protecting his daughter. If not, then she was still Renna, and he would stand beside her. Whether or not she had been violated by the pockmarked man, Hugues would die. That death would have to be postponed, for his first responsibility was to deliver his son, daughter, and son-by-marriage to safety. The situation was not without challenge—they were days away from Natchez and on the wrong side of the Mississippi. Furthermore, Othon Hugues and a number of renegades would be intent on avenging the destruction of a large portion of their village.

The river was at its fall low, so for a time the going was fairly easy along the immediate bank. Then they began to encounter mud flats bordered by dense brush. Renno turned his steps toward the west. It was a difficult passage in the darkness. Each family member was thoroughly scratched by the riverside thickets by the time dawn came and Renno called a brief rest. Little Hawk doubled back along the obvious trail they'd created and returned at a run half an hour later.

"Two lead the way," he reported. "I do not recognize their paint."

"And the others?" Renno asked.

"They travel in a group, strung out through the thickets. I did not stay to count them all. I saw the big Frenchman with the marked face and at least fifteen others."

"Those who lead the way are moving rapidly?"

"We left such good sign that they can follow at speed," Little Hawk answered.

"We will curb their eagerness," Renno responded with grim determination. "Beau, Renna, you will go directly north, there." He pointed. The sun, an hour high, glowed on the treetops on a ridge that ran roughly north–south. "When you reach the top of the ridge, rest and wait for us. When you hear me call, thus"—he sent the harsh call of a hunting hawk reverberating through the trees— "answer with the call of the dove."

"Renno," Beau reminded, "I could stay here and help you and Little Hawk. I am not entirely inexperienced in battle."

"I am counting on that," Renno said, "to help assure the safety of my daughter."

Beau nodded, satisfied that he would be playing a part.

Father and son slipped into the trees, moving silently, making no more noise than the wind as they disappeared into the thickening underbrush.

In her trance Melisande saw the two Natchitoches brothers scouting ahead of Othon's main group. The brothers, tracking well, were forced to slow their pace to wait for the others. She chanted encouragement to Othon and sent mental pictures to him of the two tall, sturdy blond rescuers tied to stakes, suffering from a thousand cuts. She sent out telepathic warnings to the two Natchitoches warriors when her farseeing eyes sensed the presence of the blond and beautiful boy and his cold-eyed father. Her warning was in vain, for no channel of communication existed between her mind and the brothers'.

Renno positioned his son on one side of the trail that they had left, and he took the other side. Their weapons at such close quarters would be tomahawks. He heard the two young warriors before he saw them. They were trotting toward his place of concealment. Little Hawk tensed and readied his weapon, then watched Renno for a signal. The two warriors came closer, but Renno waited.

The object was to kill and, by killing the two who marked the way for the others, to slow the pursuit. There would be other times for bravado, for facing the enemy toe to toe and eye to eye in an equal fight; but this situation called for subterfuge, for the white Indian and his heir wanted to survive against overwhelming odds. Othon Hugues had, according to Little Hawk's quick survey, at least ten men with him. The odds needed reduction. The renegades with the Frenchman needed something more to think about as they followed their leader.

Now, now, now, Little Hawk was saying to himself, but still Renno waited. Then there was a nod, and together they stepped out into the open to halt the Natchitoches in their tracks with simultaneous and deadly blows of their blades.

With Little Hawk at his heels, Renno moved back toward the river until he heard the noisy progress of the main body. He picked a tree for himself, another for Little Hawk, and gave his son a boost to a high fork. "This time we use the bow," he whispered. "Wait until I have sent the first arrow."

The sachem had chosen his spot well. There was a relatively open area of tall grass and low brush lying before the thick wall of vegetation that grew in the rich, well-watered lowland near the river. To his disappointment, Hugues was not among the first few men who emerged from the thickets. He nocked an arrow to his English longbow and sent it winging death for a Creek warrior. As he reached for another arrow, he heard the *zing* of Little Hawk's bowstring releasing.

Renno fired three bolts to his son's two. Five men were down. The others, bellowing in rage, warning, and sudden fear, had rushed back into cover.

"Quickly, now," Renno said as he slid down the tree.

They ran side by side, making no effort to hide their trail. The time for concealment would come later.

Angry and frustrated, Othon Hugues screamed and lashed out at the nearest man, bloodying his nose and sending him sprawling. "Fools!" he yelled. "Are you children to let two men do this?" He knew full well as he looked at the five dead men lying in the tall grass that he'd find the corpses of the two Indian brothers farther along the trail.

"From now on," he said, "we will keep our eyes open. And if our enemies try to ambush us again, we will show them that we are not to be surprised a second time."

He ran his hand over his sweaty, filthy face. The scratches left by the pale-haired woman were scabbed over, but touching them reminded him of his loss. He had planned to begin his true enjoyment with her soon after the death of the blue blood at the stake, and he'd been robbed. Twice now the man with the steely blue eyes had challenged him.

"I want the older one alive," he ordered. "I myself will kill any man who kills him, for I want to hear that one beg for death as my knife speaks to him throughout a long, long day."

The slowed pursuit continued with a Choctaw in the lead—but not too far ahead, for he was not as brash and eager for death as were the young Natchitoches brothers . . . whose bodies had been found just past the area of tall grass.

Once more that day Renno took steps to lessen the eagerness of Hugues's adherents. This time he and Little Hawk struck from the rear. They let the cautious Choctaw tracker pass them, then waited for the main body to follow. To Renno's surprise he counted a full score of men. Either Little Hawk had not seen the entire force, or others had caught up with Hugues during the morning.

The trail left by Renna and Beau was leading away from the river and into woodlands, where movement was easier. The renegade posse—Spaniards, Indians, and a few Negroes watching the deep shadows with white, rolling eyes—were staying as close together as possible. Sometimes they walked three abreast when the distance between trees allowed it. Hugues was at the fore, and as he passed Renno's place of concealment, the Seneca sachem exerted great control not to put an arrow or a musket ball into the evil one's heart. The odds of twenty to two were too great. Alone, Renno might have risked it, for there was a good chance that if he killed Hugues, the renegades would gladly give up the pursuit. There were, however, Little Hawk and Renna and Beau to consider, for if he killed Hugues and, by some lucky stroke, the renegades killed Renno and Little Hawk, Beau and Renna would be easy prey.

So he watched the Frenchman move past, waited for the rest of the main body to follow, then nodded to Little Hawk. Their arrows flew once, twice, before musket balls began to crack in response through the leaves around them. The escape route had been planned in advance—a dry wash leading south. Renno let Little Hawk go first, then he followed his son at a dead run until the sounds of indiscriminate firing were far behind. Three more of Hugues's men were dead or dying on the forest floor.

Atop the ridge pointed out to him by Renno, Beau found a cozy, moss-covered nook under a rocky ledge. From the rocks he could monitor the steep approaches. Behind him, the ridge peaked in stone, with a few stunted trees growing in pockets of soil. In this refuge he had his first opportunity to look closely at his wife, to speak to her in gentle tones, to hold her close, and to tell her of his love and how thankful he was to God that she was safe.

Like Renno, he nearly exploded in fury and frustration when he looked at her poor, swollen face and the eye that was beginning to be tinged with purple under the blackness of the bruise. Her deerskin skirt had been ripped, so that she showed a lovely length of thigh as she reclined on the moss. The thoughts engendered by the display of smooth skin were contradictory. He berated himself for feeling a quick need for her but cringed inwardly as he thought of Othon Hugues's eyes falling on that same long, graceful thigh.

When Renna slept, Beau moved a few feet away to have a better view of the slope. He was armed with Little Hawk's musket. The day was advancing, and the noontime heat made him drowsy. He nodded, only to awaken in panic as Renna moaned and cried out. He scuttled to her side on his hands and knees. She was sitting up, breathing hard, her eyes wide, her mouth open.

"My darling, I am here," he said.

She clung desperately to him. He feared the worst— that Renna had been lying to him, that the abhorrent Hugues had violated her. The thought was bitter, but it served to strengthen his love for her. He held her closer even while he was condemning himself for having allowed it to happen.

"It was the old nightmare," she whispered.

"It's over," he soothed. "And this time I swear to you that Hugues will not live."

"By the manitous," she said between clenched teeth, "how I'd like to kill him myself."

The tone of her voice made him believe more than ever that the worst had happened.

"He touched me, Beau," she whispered with a deep shudder. "He ripped away my clothing, and he touched me. His filthy finger—" She wept piteously. "And he wanted me to—wanted me to touch him, wanted me to caress him." Her voice hardened. "I touched him all right. I tried to dig my fingernails into his eyes."

"I saw, darling," Beau said. "You left marks."

"I didn't know what had happened to you," she said. "It was so dark in the hut. For all I knew you were dead, and I found myself praying for death. If he had—"

"You don't have to talk about it," Beau said.

"Yes, I think I do," she said, "for if I don't clean the dirty thoughts of him from my mind, they will prey on me forever. As I lay there with my hands and feet tied, with my legs . . . spread . . . and my . . ." She swallowed. "I prayed that when he came into me, my heart would burst at that moment."

Beau's mouth was dry. He could only hold her and pat her back lightly.

"And the woman with the black teeth. She watched and laughed, and she insulted him for procrastinating. She kept asking him why he was delaying, and she used vile words and laughed. Once he tried to kiss me, and I almost caught his lip between my teeth. I swear I would have bitten it off. And twice he released my hands, and still he—he touched me, and I feel so very, very dirty."

"No, never!"

"I would have died if he had come into me."

Beau's heart pounded with joy. He knew that she had not lied to him. He said a quick prayer of thanks.

"I could hear the woman singing and the people urging her on. I didn't know that it was you out there, but I guessed that they had someone to torture. I supposed that he was waiting to take me until whoever it was had died. He likes death, likes to kill. And then I heard someone enter, and I prayed for death, thinking that it was he. But I looked up to see the face of my father."

"I am so greatly in your father's debt," Beau said, "that I can never repay him. First for your birth, and now for saving you."

"Beau," she whispered, "do you hate me? Do you think that I have been dirtied?"

In answer he kissed her, and to his utter amazement she pulled him down atop her, and within moments the youthful exchange of love blanked all else from their minds. . . .

Afterward, she slept. When she awoke, there was a smile on her face. Beau was sitting a few feet away, watching the approaches to the hideaway. When he heard her move, he turned and saw her smile.

"Ah," he said, "that is more like my Renna."

"I'm feeling more like myself," she concurred. "Again I feel as if I belong to myself and to you and my family."

*   *   *

The witch saw men fall, saw the ineffective, random
discharge of muskets in every direction but the one from
which death had come out of the trees. She screamed in
anger, rose, and ran from the hut. When she found her
two Negro attendants lounging in the shade, she roused
them with kicks and curses and was soon moving at a pace
that caused complaints from the two men.

"Don't lag behind, you animals," she scolded. "Keep
up with me, or I will improve your service to me by
making you walking dead."

The threat galvanized the two slaves, for they knew
that these were not idle words. Each of them had seen
enough of the witch's work to believe that she could do
exactly as she threatened. One man took the lead, moving
at a trot. To his surprise the witch kept pace with him.

Hugues himself took the fore. He put some of his
most reliable men, with orders to shoot first and investigate later, at the rear of the column. He could almost feel
the presence of Melisande, and it gave him confidence.
He knew the power of her sight, knew that she would not
allow him to stumble blindly into an ambush.

The Choctaw tracker told him that they were now
following two—a man and a woman.

"The blue blood," Othon muttered.

*It is not the blue blood about whom you should be
concerned,* a voice said in his mind, and he strongly felt
the warmth of Melisande.

"You are coming to me," he said aloud, just as hoarse
shouts erupted from the center of the extended column of
men.

Little Hawk was getting a seminar in death. First
Renno had struck from the front, then from the rear. This
caused Hugues to reorder his force and put his best men
at the fore and at the rear. This time father and son struck
at the center of the column, firing as one to drive arrows
to the hearts of two renegades. As usual, Renno was
faster. He killed twice more as Little Hawk sent a musket
ball into the right eye of a terrified Choctaw. The swift

and deadly strike had left five men dead. Within three hours of marching, Hugues's force had been reduced with alarming efficiency. First the Natchitoches brothers had died, and now the main force, which had consisted of twenty men including Hugues, had been cut to twelve.

Fool, came the witch's comment, and then a torrent of words that Othon did not understand.

"What would you have me do?" he bellowed to the inner voice, startling the men near him.

Wait, came the reply. *Wait.*

He pulled his eleven men together, forming a perimeter, giving unnecessary orders that each man stay alert. Then they waited.

Melisande, her ebony hair soaked with perspiration, her arms and legs gleaming with sweat, came trotting into the little clearing selected by Hugues. By this time the sun had been sliding down the western sky for just over two hours.

"We have given them more of a lead by waiting for you," Hugues complained.

"If you had not waited for me, my darling," she said with rich sarcasm, "you yourself might be dead by now, along with all these other fools. How many are left?"

"Twelve including myself."

"With these two"—she indicated her two attendants—"fourteen men. Against two men, a useless nobleman, and a girl. Perhaps we should send for reinforcements and wait for them."

Othon growled. She seemed to delight in hurting him. It had not always been that way. Suddenly he longed for the sweet, uncomplicated days with Melisande in her hut in the dark forests of his homeland.

"The Choctaw tracks well?" Melisande asked.

"Yes."

"I want two good men with him. Have them flank him, walking off the trail thirty or forty feet from him."

"Fine," Othon said. Instead of resenting her orders, he felt relief. As a man of direct action, he knew little of guile and trickery. He would leave the planning up to Melisande. Once the two men who were frustrating him had been captured, he would do what he knew best: the slow, mirthful killing.

Renna answered the cry of the hawk with the soft cooing of a dove. Little Hawk emerged from the trees down the slope, followed by Renno. The sachem had everyone on the move immediately. He set the pace at a warrior's trot but had to slow it within an hour out of deference to Beau, whose moccasins flopped on his feet, causing blisters. Moreover, the comte was not conditioned to run at the warrior's pace all day and into the night as were Renno and Little Hawk and, to only a slightly lesser extent, Renna.

"Father," said Little Hawk, "is it time for me to drop back and check on our enemies?"

"The bear who goes back to the bee tree too often gets stung," Renno said. "We will visit them tonight."

Only from the river had Renno seen the country through which they traveled. He knew that the village of the Choctaw Iron Legs was north of the conjunction of the Red River with the Father of Waters, but he could only guess at how many days of foot travel would be required to reach Natchez. At some point it would be necessary to cross the river, but before he attempted that, the pursuing posse would have to be further weakened and demoralized.

Toward evening he killed a yearling deer with the English longbow and, after posting Little Hawk well down their back trail, built a fire for cooking. He instructed Beau and Renna to cook much more meat than would be eaten; then when the roasting meat began to send out savory aromas, he cut a slice for himself and one for Little Hawk. The Seneca went to join his son on the back trail.

As they ate, Renno predicted, "There will be sentries. At least two, perhaps more. We will circle to the rear and come to their camp from the south. Make your actions small, silent ones. We will take the sentries thus." He made a throat-cutting motion with his stiletto. "When they are dead, our strategy will depend upon how well the enemy sleeps."

"Thus you and my uncle El-i-chi harried the Spanish

as they retreated from the Mountain of Gold in the Far West," Little Hawk recalled.

"So," Renno agreed.

There were three sentries. One proved very alert and heard Renno at the last moment. Renno's swift blade prevented an outcry, however, and he lowered the twitching body to the leaves of the forest's floor. Little Hawk had done his job well. Three more were dead.

The fires had been allowed to burn into embers. The only light was that of a half-moon. From the darkness the Seneca's arrows flew, driving deeply into sleeping forms. Unfortunately, Renno could not distinguish Othon Hugues from the others and could only hope that by choosing the largest of the sleeping forms, he might kill the Frenchman.

Five more men died in their sleep before, with a high-pitched scream of warning, Melisande awoke and illuminated the forest with supernatural light. Streams of fire darted from her hands, and although Renno and Little Hawk escaped being touched by the magic, Renno cooed out an order to his son to withdraw.

Behind him, Othon's force had been reduced to six men and the witch.

Chapter Fifteen

After the attack, Othon needed comfort. He got it from his Melisande in the early hours, and by dawn she had restored his courage and his determination.

Melisande's sporadic gift of sight often confused the immediate future with events so far removed that she could only guess at the significance of her visions. In times of great stress, her sight was intensified. Although Renno and Little Hawk had begun to bring the odds facing them into a more even balance, the witch was able to see the white Indian and his son almost at will. Now that she was with Othon, she was in a position to guide him, to enable him to reap the most benefit of her advance knowledge of Renno's movements.

After the attack on the camp had cut the number of Othon's men to six, the witch, furious, called on her master for both aid and explanation. In response she was given a vision that altered everything. She saw the broad, muddy river as if from midstream. She knew that she was

looking west at a point where the river made a sharp eastward turn. Since flowing water tends to take a straight-line
route, the main force of the current had scoured out a deep
channel near the concave western bank and had formed a
steep bank atop of which was a dense growth of trees.

She saw *him,* the one with the cold, blue eyes, lead his
little party to the bank and stand there for a minute
looking both ways on the river. When he pointed to a
more gentle slope in the bank, the vision faded. She called
Othon and told him to bring to her men who were familiar
with the country. One of the men brought by Othon was a
Choctaw, the other a Natchitoches. She described to them
the river point she'd seen with her sight.

"I know the place," said the Choctaw. "It is called
Point with High Bluffs."

"The Choctaw speaks true," agreed the Natchitoches,
"except for its name, which is Place Where the Breezes
Blow."

"How far?" Melisande asked.

"A half-day's march, no more," answered the Choctaw.

Othon did not question Melisande when she told him
that they would travel hard and fast as close as possible to
the river, to the Place Where the Breezes Blow. The
remaining men asked no questions. They were brought
one by one to the witch, who looked into their eyes for
long moments. They were transformed into a force that
was eager to pursue and hungry to kill. On the march they
were tireless.

Only the witch harbored doubts. She could never be
sure of the exact time frame for her visions. She knew that
the blue-eyed one would go down to the water at the
Place Where the Breezes Blow, but she was not certain
that she and Othon would beat their quarry to that
destination.

Since the trail led inland, away from the river, it
appeared that they might, by hard travel, be waiting when
the foursome arrived. Then the father and son would have
a taste of how it felt to be ambushed, although Melisande,
like Othon, wanted them taken alive. She remembered
the youthful vigor and enthusiasm of the boy. She would

savor more of that before she gave the boy to Othon for his bloody ministrations.

They reached their goal while the sun was still three hours high. No signs indicated that their prey had been there already. Othon had the men obliterate their tracks, then positioned them to cover the brink of the high bank with a clear field of fire. He ordered everyone to shoot to wound, to aim for the legs of the two bronzed men, and not to shoot the blue blood and the girl, for they would be easily recaptured.

Then it was only a matter of waiting. Surely, after all the recent setbacks, the master would be generous and deliver their quarry into their hands. The girl would be savored last, slowly, and in a way so complete that when he was finished with her, she would be carrion.

Renno had started to curve back toward the river early in the afternoon. His plan was to cross the stream by floating on logs, as he and Little Hawk had done before, letting the current carry them downstream as they kicked the logs toward the eastern shore.

During the afternoon he circled back once, running as fast as the terrain allowed, covering their back trail for a full three miles. It puzzled him when he found no sign of the pursuers. A ten-year-old boy could have followed the trail left by four people, and yet it was as if Othon Hugues and his men had disappeared. He ran to catch up with the others and suggested a brief rest while Little Hawk scouted ahead to find a high bank at the bend of the river. A good pile of drift was nearby, from which they could select logs to use as floats. He led the others to the spot.

Renno was still bothered by the question of what had happened to Hugues and his followers. Having experienced the strength and the evil of the man in the house in New Orleans, the sachem could not believe that Hugues had given up.

The white Indian led the way toward the river. His every sense was alert because he had a heavy feeling of dread, of something being very wrong. He approached the river carefully, left the others protected in cover, walked to the bank, and gazed up and down the stream. An eagle soared quite high over the water. Around him, however, an unnatural quiet prevailed. No bird song broke the silence. No squirrels scampered to hide at his approach. He saw nothing to warrant his unease, but with a quickness that surprised those who were watching from hiding, he turned and dashed back into the forest.

"With me," he said as he reached the spot where his family rested. No one waited to find out why Renno was moving so swiftly. Renna lifted her torn skirt and ran. Beau labored along just in front of Little Hawk, who halted, turned, and with a whoop dropped one of the enemy who had given chase when it became evident that the trap had been sprung without the quarry inside. Crashings through the brush told the foursome that the rest of Hugues's men were not far behind.

Renno did not want to risk a long chase, because Beau's feet were blistered and sore. He looked for a place to make a stand, saw a dry erosion ditch running toward the river, and halted. The ditch made a natural rifle pit. He positioned Beau and Renna in the ditch, with only their heads and muskets taken from the fallen enemy showing.

"Make your shots count," Renno told Beau and Renna as Little Hawk came on the run. The sachem selected a place behind a tree where he would be free to use his longbow to best effect. He had only four more arrows. Little Hawk jumped down to join Beau and Renna.

Renna sighted along the barrel of her musket, envisioned the face of Othon Hugues, and bared her teeth in an involuntary snarl. Beau checked the priming of his weapon. Around them the woods remained quiet, still, long after enough time had passed for an assault to be made. Nerves began to fray in Renna and Beau.

Renno motioned them to be patient, then he crept forward, gliding from tree to tree. As soon as he was out of sight of those in the erosion ditch, he had the sensation that he was not alone, that eyes were on him. He stopped and studied every shadow. Nothing stirred. He moved forward once more, and a thing of horror leaped from behind a tree, a thing half-beast, half-man.

It happened so suddenly that at first he tried to fight as if the monster were flesh and blood. His reward was fiery pain. He recognized his attacker then as a manifestation of evil, a thing from the same source as the imps in New Orleans and the spirit wolves of Hodano. He banished the freak with the power of his mind and backed away, eyes and ears open. It would be up to him to fight the imps and other incarnations of evil. Renna, Little Hawk, and Beau had no experience, no training, to face such monsters. The young ones would have to handle Hugues and his men.

Renno was only a few yards from the ditch when the witch unleashed her full menagerie of demons against him. She sent her fleshly followers to attack from the other side of Little Hawk's position. Renno used a combination of mental and physical power. He slashed and battled his way through gibbering, slavering miscreants of slime, scales, dense hair, and distorted flesh. He heard the bark of muskets and saw Little Hawk put his bow aside and drop a Spaniard with his musket before taking up his tomahawk.

Othon had believed that he had the advantage of numbers when he sent his men rushing against the three in the ditch; but now four were down, and the others were slowing. The blond boy rushed up from the ditch and with a swift and deadly blade met the charge of a Creek. The nobleman had reloaded his musket in an amazingly short time, and its blast blew a hole through another.

Across the ditch, in the woods, Othon could hear the demons' unearthly howls. He shivered in spite of himself and gave up any hope of seeing the man with the cold blue eyes suffer under his knife. Melisande's minions would leave nothing. In the meantime, his men were dead. He screamed angrily at the master, dared the evil one to strike him down, and cursed his name, his image, and his lying promises.

Melisande's attention was focused on the battle with Renno. Her eyes were wide as if in horror, her black hair rose up from her head and waved in the breeze. Her black teeth gleamed and seemed to narrow into sharp points. She screamed in frustration as Renno, with a blow from his mind, disintegrated an imp, then slashed a spirit animal with his tomahawk. Steel was not supposed to harm the spirit things, and yet this man's steel was as deadly as his will. She, too, cursed the master. The imps and spirit monsters faded, and an unnatural silence descended.

"Melisande?" Othon whispered from behind the trees. He was frightened. All his men lay dead, and the tall, slim boy was advancing toward him, tomahawk at the ready. The witch had assured him that this time they would be invincible, but no longer did he hear the unearthly howling of the demons. He saw the older warrior emerge, also poised for the fight, tomahawk in hand.

Othon lifted his musket and took aim at the chest of the man who had so continually foiled him. His finger tightened, but just as he fired, Little Hawk's tomahawk struck the musket with such force that the ball blasted harmlessly into the air.

With a snarl, Othon hefted his own ax and, enraged, ran to meet the unarmed blond boy. But the father moved even faster, coming between Othon and the boy.

"I have been waiting for this," the blue-eyed man said, and his voice, along with his cold eyes, caused a chill of apprehension to ripple down Othon's spine.

He is yours, the voice of the witch whispered into his mind. *Be not afraid.*

With a howl, Othon rushed forward and sought to end it all with one blow. Steel clashed on steel, then both men drew back, each surprised by the incredible force of the other's blow. Imps formed around the combatants and, unable to harm Renno, sought to impede him by flinging pine needles and dirt into his face. His vision impaired, Renno fell back, barely able to parry Othon's next strokes.

With a cry of alarm, Renna vaulted up from the ditch. Beau made a move to stop her, but she was too fast. She rushed into the midst of the imps bedeviling her father. She was her father's daughter; her faith made her invincible. She smashed imps with the butt of her musket and tossed them spinning and whimpering with the force of her anger.

Little Hawk, inspired by his sister's action and shamed that he was left behind, joined the fray. He suffered painful bites and scratches before he heard Renna cry out to him, "They are not real, Brother. They are spirits of evil and can be overcome by placing trust in the Master of Life, in goodness."

Little Hawk called upon the manitous, upon the spirit of his mother, who had protected him from Melisande in New Orleans. He felt the power of the manitous in his limbs. His tomahawk smashed the head of a half-serpent, half-lion beast and sent bloody fragments everywhere.

By now, Renno's eyes had cleared of grit, and he could face Hugues on equal terms.

Othon moved in, taking the role of aggressor. His face and stance looked confident, as if he believed himself to be the stronger. He was emboldened by the encouragement of the witch, but wherever he struck, his weapon was met by the parrying steel of the enemy, or his blade whistled through empty air.

Renno could see that Othon's arm was becoming heavy. His reflexes were slowed ever so slightly by his growing fatigue, while Renno felt fresh.

The white Indian saw his opportunity and struck low, cutting the hamstring in Hugues's left leg. Hugues roared, glanced down at the spurting of blood, and slammed a blow toward Renno's chest. But the stroke rang on steel as Renno parried and leaped away.

"Melisande," Othon moaned as he put weight on the damaged leg and felt himself falling. He rolled away just in time to prevent his skull from being crushed.

The momentum of Renno's blow drove his tomahawk into the earth. By the time the sachem jerked the blade free, Hugues was back on his feet, miraculously walking on his injured leg and moving in for the kill. Renno twisted aside and countered.

Othon, whispering "Melisande, help me," began to back away toward the river.

Renno sensed the kill and pressed forward, intensifying his efforts. His blade brought blood from Hugues's shoulder. He positioned himself for the final blow, but his arm struck something invisible.

Melisande, realizing that Othon's death was inevitable unless she took desperate measures, used her most potent spell. Only once before had she called upon that ultimate power to make herself totally invisible, and the price she had paid in physical depletion had convinced her that she would use that spell only to ward off total calamity. Unseen but burning already with the pain of invisibility, Melisande warded off the white Indian's otherwise fatal blow and seized Othon, dragging him toward the river and escape.

The contact caused Renno's arm to tingle and burn. He rubbed it, watching as Othon was half carried by something unseen. "Manitous," he said, "give me the sight. Let me see my enemy."

He was Seneca. He had always been a loyal Seneca warrior, and a brave Seneca never goes into battle alone—he is surrounded by all those who have gone before him to the Place across the River, the spirits of Seneca fighting men going back to the beginning of time.

A patch of mist with a vaguely human shape appeared off to one side of his vision, and suddenly he could see the witch. He marveled at her amazing strength, for she was half carrying the big Frenchman. Renno ran after them.

It was as if the witch had read his mind. Wolves more fierce than Hodano's spirit wolves, carnivores with eyes that burned like coals and fangs that slavered acid, barred his way. For a moment the white Indian was daunted. Then he pushed forward, slashing and cutting his way through.

Melisande had reached the brink of the bluff overlooking the river.

"Melisande . . ." Othon was moaning over and over. "Melisande . . ."

She set him down. "You will be safe. Trust me."

When he realized what she intended, he screamed like a gelded pig. He could not swim. Below the bluff the deep, muddy water swirled, forming eddies and ripples.

"Jump, you fool," Melisande ordered. "Jump for your life, for this fair-haired man has the forces of light on his side."

Othon screamed again as Melisande picked him up bodily and threw him into the river. He shrieked as he plunged through the air and landed with a huge splash. Water forced itself down his throat with a rush. He tried to call out, but there was a constriction in his throat. He couldn't breathe. He tried to gain his footing, but the deep, swirling water swept him along. His head went under, then came up. He tried to breathe, and water burned its way into his lungs.

Melisande, he thought. *Oh, Melisande*. He felt himself spinning, sinking. Then he began to feel quite warm and he fancied himself to be in Melisande's arms, with her soft, sweet, nourishing breasts bared to his hungry lips.

Renno prepared himself for the unaccustomed duty of doing battle with a woman. The witch turned to face him, and for a moment her eyes caught his, and his mind filled with images of sensuous pleasure. He saw her as being youthful and lithe and inviting, lying on a couch, her arms outstretched to him. His body could feel in advance the goodness she promised. He called on his manitous and shifted his gaze, looking only at her torso. She screamed curses at him and, with one last burst of invective, threw herself over the edge of the bluff.

He ran forward. Hugues was nowhere to be seen. The witch floated lightly atop the water, lying on her back, her black hair streaming behind her. She lifted her hand and sent one last spell at Renno. He felt the force of it, and his heart stopped for a beat, but then it resumed its strong natural rhythm. He turned as Little Hawk and Renna ran up beside him.

"Will she drown?" Little Hawk asked as the witch turned on the current like a bobbing, drifting log.

"I fear not," Renno said.

"And Hugues?" Renna asked.

Renno shrugged.

Renna did not want to attempt a crossing of the river in the same waters that had accepted Hugues and the witch.

Beau agreed with her. "I would imagine all the way across that she was down there, just under the surface, reaching up for me," he said.

The foursome used what was left of the day to travel upstream, glad to leave behind the scenes of battle. Little Hawk, scouting, fell back to remark to Renno, "Beau was afraid."

"Or was he brave," Renno proposed, "to voice his fears to others?"

Little Hawk laughed uneasily. "When he suggested that *she* might be down there reaching up for us, I will admit that I felt a little shiver."

At dusk they built a large fire and ate meat taken from a large land turtle. Tasty purple grapes were ripe on a jungle of grapevines near the river, so the turtle meat was topped off by sweet, juicy fruit.

When no one could eat another bite, Renna voiced a thought that, considering what the young woman had been through, surprised the others. "As wicked as the renegades were," she said, "as deluded as they were to follow Othon Hugues and the witch, it seems sad to leave them lying there where they fell, with no one to know, no one to care, no one to sing the songs of the dead for them."

"I, for one, don't intend to go back and bury them," Little Hawk said.

"She will take them," Renno said, spreading his arms to indicate the earth, nature. "Perhaps it is grisly to think of it, but small animals and birds and insects will feed, and the flesh will be consumed. In time the earth will take even the bones that remain."

They sat in moody silence until Beau spoke. "I have seen a battleground where thousands of corpses lay in the sun. The flesh darkened, then the bodies swelled and burst. Scavengers, sated, engorged, could eat no more. When I returned to the site a year later, wildflowers covered the land."

"Aren't we a cheerful lot?" Renna asked, shaking herself as if to dispel thoughts of death and decay. "How long will it take, Father, before we are home?"

The white Indian shrugged. "As long as it takes," he replied. A smile softened his face as he looked at Renna. He spoke softly, and in Seneca. "I would like to say, Daughter, that my pride for you is like the Father of Waters, deep, wide, and eternal." He turned to Little Hawk. "And you, my son, fought by my side in a way that would have made even old Ghonka say, 'Ah, there fights a Seneca warrior.'"

The praise caused Renna to smile, her face glowing. Little Hawk pretended to be impassive, but the corners of his mouth twitched, and then he, too, was smiling.

"Your strength, my son, and your courage, my daughter, honor the blood of our fathers that flows in our veins," Renno said. "You, Os-sweh-ga-da-ga-ah Ne-wa-ah, will be a great sachem. And you, Renna, may the manitous guard you as you pursue the life you have chosen."

Renna was silent as she and Little Hawk exchanged a look. Both of them seemed to sense the spirits themselves hovering over them, to second their father's praise.

The journey took a shorter time than Renno had expected. Since the Treaty of Fort Adams in 1801, the United States had been at work building a road from Natchez northeast across Choctaw country to Nashville. The gold taken by Renno from the dead Creek's pouch purchased six horses, four saddles, two packs, new weapons, supplies, and clothing.

The road known as the Natchez Trace took them to the old Choctaw agency and within a few miles of a place that Renno had long wanted to see—the sacred mound of the Choctaw, Nanih Waya. He did not allow himself to be lured into the side trip, however, for two reasons: the time for Little Hawk to have reported to Mr. Jefferson's military academy was past, and ahead were the Tennessee, and the Cherokee Nation . . . and Beth.

The foursome met travelers coming down from Nashville. They exchanged news, or the lack of it. War still threatened between England and France, but nothing much was happening in the so-called war against the pasha of Tripoli. The United States was now seventeen strong with the admission of Ohio, and Andy Jackson had been elected major general of the Tennessee Militia.

On a late September morning Renno looked up to see honking, southering geese in a V-formation, and he wondered if Beth, perhaps, had seen the same winging fowl, so close was he now to home.

And then the party was riding up the long, pecan-tree-lined approach to The House. Two wild Indians—Ta-na and Gao—rushed out to greet them with whoops and yells of joy.

The boys were happy to see the travelers, but they were also celebrating because they knew there'd be no more school that day while Beth and Renno went off alone to do that kissy-kissy stuff.

Chapter Sixteen

"It seems that we are never all together," Beth said. She and Renno sat with their Cherokee friend Se-quo-i on the front veranda of The House. Se-quo-i had paid a visit to ask if word had come of Little Hawk's arrival in the new capital of the United States on his way to New York and the military academy at West Point.

"Saying good-bye is never pleasant," Se-quo-i said.

"I pray that we won't have to say good-bye to Beau and Renna for a long time to come," Beth remarked.

Renno looked at Se-quo-i and grinned. Both men had become very fond of the comte de Beaujolais. He had been a good sport when El-i-chi and Little Hawk took him off snipe hunting, even if he hadn't been as quick as Philip Woods to see the joke. Beau seemed to be having the time of his life. He wore buckskins comfortably, was becoming a crack shot with a musket, and was more than adequate with a bow. He loved the hunt and was, in fact, off in the forest now. A warrior-maiden with pale hair walked at his side, carrying her own weapon.

* * *

Another year had spent several of its allocated months before four letters arrived all at once from faraway New York State. They were delivered by Beth's favorite postman, Roy Johnson, and were shared with the entire family on the veranda.

Renna, in her clear, strong voice, read aloud that Little Hawk had arrived in good time. He had not been among the first students of the academy at the old Revolutionary War fortress, but he voiced the same complaints that had been published in the eastern papers—that the academy was more an elementary school than a college, since many of the students arriving there could not read or write. Renna continued:

> "Mother Beth, I am honored to inform you that your patience with this hardheaded Seneca lad must have borne fruit, for I find myself well ahead of my fellow students. This is both good and bad. It is good because it gives me time for other activities while my fellows study. It is bad because I find classes to be not at all challenging. I am told by those who should know that other schools offer higher mathematics, philosophy, plus such sciences as chemistry and even astronomy. Here we cover only rudimentary arithmetic and the building of military fortifications."

"My, my," said Roy, "how erudite and arrogant our Little Hawk has become."

"Not arrogant at all," El-i-chi protested. "It does not take an arrogant man to feel superior to military thinkers."

Roy laughed. "This from the ex-lieutenant El-i-chi?"

"Little Hawk will be called an engineer," Renna said, reading on. "And he'll be commissioned a lieutenant in the United States Army."

"That is good, perhaps," said Toshabe, "but would it not be better to have him here, among his own people?"

"We cannot fight the changes that sweep over us," Renno said. The tone of his voice caused Beth to look at him with concern, but he smiled and seemed at ease.

Much later, with the family scattered to their various

homes and with Roy asleep in a guest room, Beth clung to
Renno, trying to dispel her fears.

"Something bothered you when your mother said that
it would be better for Little Hawk to be here with us," she
said.

"It was nothing."

"Nothing?"

He kissed her and smiled. "So. I can keep nothing
from you."

"As you have said many times, Indians do not lie well
to other Indians."

He laughed and tousled her flame-colored hair, then
kissed her peach-tinted cheek. "Well, my little Seneca
wife," he said, "it was truly nothing, just a momentary
twinge of—I don't know."

"Oh, God," she said. "That bad?"

"Not bad. Change, yes. But not necessarily bad."

"Hold me close. Whatever comes, I will not let you
leave me again. You will tell them no, no, a thousand
times no, that your wife forbids it."

"Yes," Renno agreed, but the ominous feeling of irre-
vocable change was still there, deeply embedded. Fortunately, the attentions of a splendidly mature fiery-haired
woman could submerge it entirely.

Robert Livingston strongly resented the arrival of James
Monroe in Paris. Livingston even offered to send his official
notes to Secretary of State Madison to prove that he had
not been negligent in his duties. He reported that Talleyrand,
the French minister, was using Monroe's appointment as
co-negotiator as an excuse to delay further talks.

But news from the Caribbean was changing everything. Napoleon had come to abhor the name St. Domingue.
Already the unruly island had absorbed one grand expedition—Leclerc's—which had originally been destined for
Louisiana, and now Rochambeau had surrendered to the
ex-slaves. Napoleon was in the midst of planning a new
war with England, but all his advisers wanted to talk about
was St. Domingue and sugar, and wheat, and coffee, and
colonies.

"Damn sugar," the great general had told them forcefully. "Damn coffee. Damn colonies."

For without a secure naval base at Port-au-Prince, Napoleon's grandiose plans for a new empire across the seas were useless.

On 10 April 1803, Napoleon told Barbe Marbois, his finance minister, that he was thinking of giving Louisiana to the United States.

"I can scarcely say that I cede it to them," he said, "for it is not in our possession. If I waste any time, however, our enemies will take full advantage, and I shall only transmit an empty title to those republicans whose friendship I seek. They ask of me only one town in Louisiana, but I already consider the colony as entirely lost; and it appears to me that in the hands of this growing power it will be more useful to the policy, and even the commerce, of France than if I should attempt to keep it."

To try to keep Louisiana, the general felt, would result in its being delivered part and parcel to England through the strength of the Royal Navy.

On the very next day Napoleon made it official: he told Finance Minister Marbois, "I renounce Louisiana. It is not only New Orleans that I cede; it is the whole colony, without reserve." He then directed Marbois to negotiate with Livingston.

Meanwhile, James Monroe had been stricken ill. Alone, Livingston bore the brunt of tough French demands, listening to offers and making counteroffers until, on 2 May 1803, the French-language treaty was signed, ceding Louisiana to the United States for the sum of fifteen million dollars to be paid partly in U.S. bonds.

"My dear Monroe," said Robert Livingston, "this is the noblest work of our whole lives. From this day the United States take their place among the powers of the first rank."

Coming in 1992
A special-edition volume in the best-selling
WHITE INDIAN Series . . . Book #22:

SENECA
PATRIOTS

For an exciting preview, turn the page . . . .

The American brig *Dora E.*, laden with naval stores, had all sails set before a fair breeze for Naples. Taking the air on the *Dora E.*'s deck was a man dressed in a drab suit just a bit too tight for his soft, slightly overweight body. His name was William Eaton. He was a Connecticut man who had made his permanent residence in Brimfield, Massachusetts, with a contentious woman almost old enough to be his mother.

Slightly before midday the wind became less favorable, and the brig wallowed in the troughs as she held to her course. Eaton was not the best of sailors, and the uncomfortable motion sent him to his cabin. He threw himself into his bunk after loosening his collar and waistcoat and prayed earnestly to be allowed to live long enough to feel solid land under his feet. He dozed and did not hear the commotion on deck that was caused by the sighting of a sail. The bellowed orders of the *Dora E.*'s captain did not wake him as the brig was slowly overtaken by a swift, low, black ship of war. It was the change in the ship's movement that revived him and sent him on deck to see that the *Dora E.* was lying dead in the water with a sinister-looking vessel closing on her.

"I'd advise you to go below, sir," a seaman said as he hurried past.

Eaton stood stiffly as the dark ship flying the flag of the pasha of Tripoli grappled the *Dora E.* Swarms of swarthy, bearded Arab seamen dressed in dingy, one-piece robes and sweat-soaked head windings scrambled aboard the brig and began to scream orders that were incomprehensible to everyone but William Eaton. Two of the pirates leaped toward him, their scimitars at the ready. One of them said in the patois—a mixture of Italian, Turkish, and Egyptian Arabic—that was the lingua franca of the North African pirate nations, "Your clothes. Take them off."

Eaton replied in the same language: "You fly the flag of Yusef Karamanli, Pasha of Tripoli. Before you act further, consider what he will say upon learning that you have insulted the United States consul to the Barbary nations."

"Your clothing, infidel," the pirate said, jerking at Eaton's coat.

Eaton made the same decision that had been made by the captain of the *Dora E.* The captain had known that for his unarmed ship to fight the Tripolitan man-of-war would mean death for his crew and him. Surrender meant slavery for the ordinary seamen, but at least there was hope of repatriation as long as the men were alive. Eaton could see murder in the eyes of the two pirates who demanded his clothing. To resist meant death. The captain of the Arab ship would have to account to the pasha for the captured ship and its cargo. The personal possessions of the crew and passengers were loot for the pirates. Clothing—shirts, vests, trousers, smallclothes—all were valuable commodities in the scruffy cities of the North African coast.

To be shamed, to be stripped naked before the crew of the *Dora E.* and the scabrous Arabs, was to remain alive to do the job to which he had been assigned by Thomas Jefferson. Eaton had no doubt that if he resisted, he would be killed in spite of his diplomatic credentials. After all, his captors were savages by ancient Greek definition. The Barbary Coast: coast of the barbarians, home to merciless pirates for centuries. And of the four Barbary states—Algiers, Morocco, Tunis, and Tripoli—the last was the most barbaric. Tripoli's ruler, Yusef Karamanli Pasha, had declared a unilateral war not only on American shipping but on the United States as a whole.

As he removed his clothing, being prodded more than once by the sharp tip of a Moorish scimitar, he vowed that he would not leave North Africa alive with his purpose unfulfilled. Within moments he stood naked on the deck. Gone along with his clothing were his watch, his purse, and a pair of gold-rimmed eyeglasses that he used for reading.

His cabin was thoroughly ransacked while the crew of the *Dora E.* was herded roughly onto the pirate vessel, to be imprisoned belowdecks. Arabs in their filthy, flapping robes leaped to the orders of an especially evil-looking brigand to set the captured ship sailing before the wind toward the African coast.

To the surprise of Eaton and the *Dora E.*'s officers, they were put ashore not in Tripoli but in Tunis. The officers were put under light guard in a vermin-infested mud building. Two days later Eaton was able to obtain an audience with the bey Ahmed Pasha, as much a pirate as his ally in Tripoli, but, perhaps, a bit more aware of the affairs of the world outside North Africa.

Eaton's anger did not move Ahmed, nor did a formal written protest receive an answer. "I have been appointed by President Thomas Jefferson as special consul to the Barbary nations," Eaton told the impassive pasha. "Moreover, I am attached to the United States Navy as a special adviser. You are going to find, sir, that the time when the Barbary nations can prey on unarmed American ships with impunity is past."

Ahmed Pasha made no reply. He could respect the power of the Royal Navy and the navy of the French, although even those great nations chose to buy peace with the pirate states rather than assure it by force of naval arms. Once, that obscure little nation across the Atlantic, the United States, had been under the wing of the Royal Navy. Now, however, with war looming between the two giants of Europe—Great Britain and France—the impotent United States was left to her own devices in the Mediterranean. Ahmed smiled benignly at the brash infidel. It was quite amusing to listen to his empty threats.

"It can be arranged that your ships will have safe passage through Tunisian waters for modest sums," Ahmed said. "One hundred fifty thousand dollars—"

Eaton snorted.

"—and certain quantities of ship's stores," the bey continued.

"And what of the waters of Tripoli, Morocco, and Algiers?" Eaton asked.

"I fear that you will have to discuss that question with my brothers in those countries," Ahmed said with a smile.

Ahmed, as had other men before him, underestimated William Eaton. On the surface the American looked weak, pudgy. In Ahmed's estimation he would not have been a match for the smallest man in the pasha's bodyguard. The ruler of Tunis did not think it worthwhile to inquire into William Eaton's background. The bey was not even curious as to why the president of the United States had sent such an unprepossessing man as Eaton to negotiate with the Barbary nations. He assumed that if President Thomas Jefferson had sent such a plump little dumpling to do his work, then Jefferson, too, was weak. The bey would have been surprised if he could have read the contents of William Eaton's letters to Jefferson, far away in Washington.

"I would use American arms to force these brigands to respect our flag. Only gunshot and powder will compel the deys and the beys of Barbary to treat us in a civilized manner, to honor the lives and property of American citizens. Their attitude is insulting not only to every American but to every man who considers himself to be more than a savage barbarian. Pray consider my urgent request that a fleet of American warships be sent to the Mediterranean along with five thousand trained, armed, and well-equipped American infantrymen and cavalrymen. With these troops at my disposal I can guarantee that the rulers of the Barbary Coast will sing a new song more to our liking.

Oddly enough, Eaton had long taken an interest in Islam. Before joining the American Legion and fighting with Anthony Wayne in the Ohio Valley Indian War, Eaton was reading the *Koran* and other volumes about the Mohammedan countries. In his journal he wrote at that time, "I wish to learn Arabic and to find out all I can about the Ottomans. Someday I shall visit that far-off part of the world, and if the Almighty wishes it for me, may even live there for a while."

Later, Eaton would call it kismet, the Arabic word for a predetermined fate willed by God, for there had been no evident reason for him to become interested in North Africa or the Middle East. There was to be no mention of Algiers, Tunis, Morocco, or Tripoli in American newspapers until sometime in 1797.

By the time William Eaton joined the consular staff in the Barbary states, the United States had paid over one million dollars in blackmail to the dey of Algiers. When Eaton walked the streets, Arabs spat at him and cursed him, not knowing that he understood their language. He restrained himself on those occasions, as he did when he was presented to the dey of Algiers, Hussein, whom Eaton described as "a great, shaggy beast, sitting on a low bench with his hind legs gathered up like a tailor or a bear."

He was compelled to kiss the dey's hand.

"The animal at that time seemed to be in a harmless mood," he confided to his diary. "He grinned but made little noise."

Eaton astounded the dey and other diplomats by speaking in flawless Arabic. Later he wrote in his journal, "I believe it is my kismet to treat these thieves with the contempt they deserve."

He had only to bide his time and to convince Thomas Jefferson to send him men, ships, and guns.

For an event of such great magnitude, it happened quickly. The French-language treaty to transfer the Louisiana Territory to the United States—thus doubling the size of that young country—was signed with Napoleon, and the Senate quickly ratified the document. The House passed the necessary acts of appropriation so the land could be purchased. A date for the formal ceremony of transfer, to be held in New Orleans, was set. Jefferson himself wanted to attend, but he knew that his place was in the drafty executive mansion. He named men to represent him. He penned a personal letter to a man to whom he had written once before, because he remembered the advice given to him by George Washington: Maintain communications and friendship with those Indians who were allied with and were friendly to the United States. It was to Renno, sachem of the southern Seneca, that the president addressed his personal request to represent the Indian nations at the ceremony of transfer of the Louisiana Territory in New Orleans on 20 December 1803.

Thomas Jefferson's letter reached Knoxville and was subsequently carried to the Seneca village in the

Cherokee Nation by Renno's ex-father-by-marriage, Roy Johnson. Renno's youngest offspring, Ta-na, and his cousin Gao, son of the shaman El-i-chi, greeted their "Grandfather Roy" with enough enthusiasm to make Roy stagger and almost go to the ground under the combined attack.

"By gum," Roy said, ruffling the thick, Indian black hair of the two boys, "if you two aren't big enough to cut up and fry for breakfast."

"The hunting has been good, Grandfather," twelve-year-old Ta-na said. "But we can't get our fathers to take us."

"Well, we'll see about that," Roy said, "if you two rapscallions will turn me loose long enough to see if Toshabe's cookpot is full or empty."

"Horsemeat stew," Gao said, licking his lips with satisfaction at the memory of the meal.

"Horsemeat?"

"A panther got one of Beth's colts," Ta-na said, referring to his stepmother.

"Well, waste not want not," Roy said.

Toshabe, mother of Renno, El-i-chi, and Ena, having heard the rumpus, came out of her longhouse and smiled to see Roy approaching, with two wild young warriors leaping and cavorting on either side.

"Welcome," Toshabe said. Her almost six decades of age rested lightly on her. She was not as slim as a maiden, but the fullness of her breasts and hips became her. Her French blood both lightened her skin and emphasized her Erie characteristics— high cheekbones, dark eyes, and thick, straight hair snow-sprinkled with gray.

"I thank thee that thou art well," Roy said in perfect Seneca.

"Will you take food?"

"With the greatest of pleasure," Roy said, grinning widely. He turned to the boys. "You two find Renno and tell him I've got a letter for him."

"Shall I take it to my father?" Ta-na asked.

"Nope." He winked at Toshabe. "We old ones get nosy, you see. I want him to open it here so Toshabe and I can hear what it says."

The boys went whooping off, and Toshabe ushered Roy into the longhouse that she had shared with two husbands, both of them victims of murder, the great Ghonkaba, grandson of the original white Indian, and the Seneca senior warrior Ha-ace, the Panther. Within minutes Roy was seated cross-legged on a mat and eating horsemeat stew from a delicate bone-china plate that had been a gift to Toshabe from her daughter-in-law Beth.

"One of Beth's good colts?" Roy asked around a mouthful of savory, tender meat.

"She was very upset. She herself demanded to be allowed to shoot the panther."

"And did she?"

Toshabe shrugged. "She is the chosen wife of Renno."

"Meaning she did?"

Toshabe nodded.

Roy laughed. "Might as well face it, Toshabe—she's quite a gal, that Beth."

"But she is not Seneca," Toshabe said.

Roy finished his plate and accepted seconds, soaking up thick potliker with cornbread. After a comfortable silence he said, "I'm not exactly Seneca, either, Toshabe."

"That is true," she said, looking at him questioningly.

"That's why I've been reluctant to speak what's been on my mind," Roy said.

"The grandfather of my grandchildren should feel free to speak."

"Well, that's it," Roy said. "We have a lot in common, you and I. We both love our grandchildren, Little Hawk and Renna, and those other scamps out there. You know that I still look on Renno as a son and . . ."

Toshabe was silent. She looked straight ahead, her face giving no hint of her thoughts.

"And well, Toshabe, I'm sick and tired of living alone in Knoxville. I'm tired of playing part-time soldier in the Tennessee Militia with Andy Jackson, 'cause most often when they talk about fighting, they want to fight the wrong people. I don't get a kick out of it anymore. I don't find anyone in Knoxville I want to talk to or be with. I keep thinking about how Renno and I covered a lot of ground up north with Anthony Wayne, or I remember being off and away over a ridge with El-i-chi or with Little Hawk, the way we used to hunt before he went off to become an officer and a gentleman at West Point."

He paused. Toshabe looked straight ahead impassively.

"You're not making it any easier," he said accusingly.

"I have always known that you were like my sons and my grandsons in many ways," she said.

"Well, there are other things I'm tired of, too, Toshabe. I'm tired of not having anyone to help me warm my bed." He flushed.

There was a long silence.

"There are widows," she suggested. "Young widows."

"I don't want a damned young widow," Roy said. "I want you."

She turned to face him and her expression softened. "I am old, and much of the warmth has gone from me."

"Fiddlesticks," Roy said. "You're more striking than most women half your age." He reached out and took her hand. "How about it, Toshabe? Think you could put up with an old codger like me?"

Toshabe spoke in English. "You will become a squaw man?"

"Now you hush that mess," Roy said. "If you'll have me, I want to live here in the village."

"And leave me at a whim to go off on a hunt or a ramble?"

He grinned. "Well, not for a while, Toshabe. Not for a while." He felt the need for her. He had been long without a woman. He pulled her into his arms and kissed her neck, her cheek.

"Old man," she said, "the boys will be back soon."

"Yep, and that's too bad," he said, for she was responding to him, pressing her body to his. "Do I take this unmaidenly behavior of yours to be agreement?"

"If you can put up with me, I think I just might be able to put up with you," she said.

"Good girl," Roy said, then muttered in frustration when he heard the noisy approach of Gao and Ta-na.

Renno entered the longhouse immediately after the two boys burst in. He exchanged greetings with Roy, shared the warrior's handclasp, then sat down cross-legged before he accepted the letter. He gave an un-Indian-like frown when he saw that it was from the president. The last letter he had received from Jefferson had taken him south to New Orleans and to encounters with evil of a force he had not experienced since his battles with the shaman Hodano, so long ago.

Now he was content and didn't want to go anywhere. He led his tribe with relaxed but steady discipline. He lived with a wife whom he loved deeply. Although Renna was far away in France and Little Hawk was in New York State, he had the pleasure of raising Ta-na, his full-blooded Seneca son. There had been no pressures against the Cherokee Nation, of which his Seneca had become a part.

"Well, are you going to open it or not?" Roy demanded.

Renno smiled and extended the letter toward Roy. "Here, you do it."

"Well, don't think I won't," Roy said, jerking the letter from Renno's hand.

"Might as well," Renno said. "Save me the time and trouble of telling you what it says."

"It's from President Thomas Jefferson," Roy said.

"That much I know," Renno said.

Roy wrinkled his brow with the effort of reading Jefferson's handwriting. "You hankering for a trip, Renno?"

"Do me the favor of throwing the letter into the fire," Renno said.

"No, wait. This one might be fun," Roy said. "Mr. Jefferson wants us all to go down to New Orleans to represent Indian interests at a fancy shindig."

"All?" Renno asked. "He mentions names other than mine?"

"Well, not exactly," Roy admitted. "But he says that you should take other representative members of the tribes."

"And of what tribe are you a member?" Renno teased.

"Well, if you want to be technical about it," Roy said, "Little Hawk made me a blood brother of the Seneca years ago." He chuckled. "Almost cut my finger off trying to draw blood."

"Well," Renno said, "since the president wants us all to go to New Orleans, you can go in my stead."

"Now, Renno," Roy said, "it's you he really wants, but he says to take along any other representatives who would do credit to the Indian. I reckon I meet that definition if I brush my hair and shave. It'll be fun, Renno. We can take El-i-chi—"

"And me," Gao and Ta-na said as one.

"And Beth. I'll bet she gets cabin fever, even if she does live in a house big enough to hold three barns and a goat farm."

"So," Renno said, reaching for the letter to read the words for himself. He left the longhouse, followed by Gao and Ta-na.

"You forgot rather quickly," Toshabe said to Roy.

"Nope, I didn't forget. I thought you'd enjoy a trip down to New Orleans."

"I am too old and tired for such nonsense."

"Fiddlesticks. I'll buy you a French gown, and we'll show those youngsters how to dance."

"I have no need of a French gown," she said. "And I was never good at the white man's dancing." She put her hand atop his. "I have said yes to you, Roy Johnson, but that is no reason why you can't go with Renno. I will be here when you return, the manitous willing. We have lived almost sixty years without being man and wife. Another few months won't matter."

"Well," Roy said.

**FROM THE PRODUCER OF WAGONS WEST
AND THE KENT FAMILY CHRONICLES—
A SWEEPING SAGA OF WAR AND HEROISM
AT THE BIRTH OF A NATION**

THE WHITE INDIAN SERIES

This thrilling series tells the compelling story of America's birth against
the equally exciting adventures of an English child raised as a Seneca.

☐	24650	White Indian #1	$4.50
☐	25020	The Renegade #2	$4.50
☐	24751	War Chief #3	$3.95
☐	24476	The Sachem #4	$3.95
☐	25154	Renno #5	$4.50
☐	25039	Tomahawk #6	$4.50
☐	25589	War Cry #7	$3.95
☐	25202	Ambush #8	$3.95
☐	23986	Seneca #9	$3.95
☐	24492	Cherokee #10	$3.95
☐	24950	Choctaw #11	$3.95
☐	25353	Seminole #12	$3.95
☐	25868	War Drums #13	$3.95
☐	26206	Apache #14	$3.95
☐	27161	Spirit Knife #15	$4.50
☐	27264	Manitou #16	$4.50
☐	27841	Seneca Warrior #17	$3.95
☐	28285	Father of Waters #18	$4.50
☐	28474	Fallen Timbers #19	$4.50
☐	28805	Sachem's Son #20	$4.50

Bantam Books, Dept. LE3, 414 East Golf Road, Des Plaines, IL 60016

Please send me the items I have checked above. I am enclosing $_____
(please add $2.50 to cover postage and handling). Send check or money
order, no cash or C.O.D.s please.

Mr/Ms _____

Address _____

City/State _____ Zip _____

LE3 -3/91

Please allow four to six weeks for delivery.
Prices and availability subject to change without notice.

★ WAGONS WEST ★

This continuing, magnificent saga recounts the adventures of a brave
band of settlers, all of different backgrounds, all sharing one dream—
to find a new and better life.

☐	26822-8	**INDEPENDENCE! #1**	$4.95
☐	26162-2	**NEBRASKA! #2**	$4.50
☐	26242-4	**WYOMING! #3**	$4.50
☐	26072-3	**OREGON! #4**	$4.50
☐	26070-7	**TEXAS! #5**	$4.99
☐	26377-3	**CALIFORNIA! #6**	$4.99
☐	26546-6	**COLORADO! #7**	$4.95
☐	26069-3	**NEVADA! #8**	$4.99
☐	26163-0	**WASHINGTON! #9**	$4.50
☐	26073-1	**MONTANA! #10**	$4.50
☐	26184-3	**DAKOTA! #11**	$4.50
☐	26521-0	**UTAH! #12**	$4.50
☐	26071-5	**IDAHO! #13**	$4.50
☐	26367-6	**MISSOURI! #14**	$4.50
☐	27141-5	**MISSISSIPPI! #15**	$4.95
☐	25247-X	**LOUISIANA! #16**	$4.50
☐	25622-X	**TENNESSEE! #17**	$4.50
☐	26022-7	**ILLINOIS! #18**	$4.95
☐	26533-4	**WISCONSIN! #19**	$4.95
☐	26849-X	**KENTUCKY! #20**	$4.95
☐	27065-6	**ARIZONA! #21**	$4.50
☐	27458-9	**NEW MEXICO! #22**	$4.95
☐	27703-0	**OKLAHOMA! #23**	$4.95
☐	28180-1	**CELEBRATION! #24**	$4.50

Bantam Books, Dept. LE, 414 East Golf Road, Des Plaines, IL 60016

Please send me the items I have checked above. I am enclosing $_____
(please add $2.50 to cover postage and handling). Send check or money
order, no cash or C.O.D.s please.

Mr/Ms _____

Address _____

City/State _____ Zip _____

Please allow four to six weeks for delivery.
Prices and availability subject to change without notice.   LE-6/91

The New Frontier Series Of The Texas Rangers

CODY'S LAW
Book 1
GUNMETAL JUSTICE
by Matthew S. Hart

He rides alone for a breed that stands apart. He wears the badge of the Texas Rangers and a pair of silver spurs. He is the master of every weapon of the West -- white man's or Indian's -- and the servant of a fiercely held code of right and wrong. His name is Cody. The Rangers made Texas a land of law. Men like Cody made the Rangers a legend.

In Twin Creeks outlaws sport the lawman's star. No man, woman, or child in town is safe from the tyranny of Reb Turner and his gang -- and Comanche renegades are on a rampage against the outlying ranches. But behind the marauders stands an even more ruthless power: a land baron named Bigelow, dammed by greed to want more than any man can ever have. His aim is to terrorize the populace until everything of value lies in his iron grip.

But Ranger justice has finally caught up with Bigelow and his henchmen. A showdown's coming, and no man is more eager than Cody. Now he'll have to ride into hell at its hottest -- without revealing the mighty force for law and order that set him on Bigelow's crooked trail.

A new series about a special breed of men starting this month from Bantam Domain Books.